TALKING TO THE DEAD

Please return on or before the latest date abo
You can renew online at *www.kent.gov.uk/lib*
or by telephone 08458 247 200

CUSTOMER SERVICE EXCELLENCE

Libraries & Archives

Kent
County
Council

00884\DTP\RN\07.07

TALKING TO THE DEAD

HARRY BINGHAM

ISIS
LARGE PRINT
Oxford

First published in Great Britain 2012
by
Orion Books
An imprint of The Orion Publishing Group Ltd.

Published in Large Print 2013 by ISIS Publishing Ltd.,
7 Centremead, Osney Mead, Oxford OX2 0ES
by arrangement with
The Orion Publishing Group Ltd.
An Hachette UK Company

British Library Cataloguing in Publication Data
Bingham, Harry, 1967–
    Talking to the dead.
    1. Detective and mystery stories.
    2. Large type books.
    I. Title
    823.9'2–dc23

ISBN 978–0–7531–9156–9 (hb)
ISBN 978–0–7531–9157–6 (pb)

Printed and bound in Great Britain by
T. J. International Ltd., Padstow, Cornwall

To N., as always

CHAPTER
ONE

Interview, October 2006

Beyond the window, I can see three kites hanging in the air over Bute Park. One blue, one yellow, one pink. Their shapes are precise, as though stencilled. From this distance, I can't see the lines that tether them, so when the kites move, it's as though they're doing so of their own accord. An all-encompassing sunlight has swallowed depth and shadow.

I observe all this as I wait for DCI Matthews to finish rearranging the documents on his desk. He shuffles the last file from the stack before him to a chair in front of the window. The office is still messy, but at least we can see each other now.

"There," he says.

I smile.

He holds up a sheet of paper. The printed side is facing him, but against the light from the window I see the shape of my name at the top. I smile again, not because I feel like smiling but because I can't think of anything sensible to say. This is an interview. My interviewer has my CV. What does he want me to do? Applaud?

He puts the CV down on the desk in the only empty patch available. He starts to read it through line by line, marking off each section with his forefinger as he does so. Education. A levels. University. Interests. Referees.

His finger moves back to the centre of the page. University.

"Philosophy."

I nod.

"Why are we here? What's it all about? That sort of thing?"

"Not exactly. More like, what exists? What doesn't exist? How do we know whether it exists or not? Things like that."

"Useful for police work."

"Not really. I don't think it's useful for anything much, except maybe teaching us to think."

Matthews is a big man. Not gym-big, but Welsh-big, with the sort of comfortable muscularity that suggests a past involving farm work, rugby and beer. He has remarkably pale eyes and thick dark hair. Even his fingers have little dark hairs running all the way to the final joint. He is the opposite of me.

"Do you think you have a realistic idea of what police work involves?"

I shrug. I don't know. How are you meant to know if you haven't done it? I say the sort of thing that I think I'm meant to say. I'm interested in law enforcement. I appreciate the value of a disciplined, methodical approach. Blah, blah. Yadda, yadda. Good little girl in her dark grey interview outfit saying all the things she's meant to say.

2

"You don't think you might get bored?"

"Bored?" I laugh with relief. That's what he was probing at. "Maybe. I hope so. I quite like a little boredom." Then, worried he might feel I am being arrogant — prize-winning Cambridge philosopher sneers at stupid policeman — I back-track. "I mean, I like things orderly. *I*s dotted, *t*s crossed. If that involves some routine work, then fine. I like it."

His finger is still on the CV, but it's tracked up an inch or so. A levels. He leaves his finger there, fixes those pale eyes on me and says, "Do you have any questions for me?"

I know that's what he's meant to say at some stage, but we've got forty-five minutes allocated for this interview and we've only used ten at the outside, most of which I've spent watching him shift stationery around his office. Because I'm taken by surprise — and because I'm still a bit rubbish at these things — I say the wrong thing.

"Questions? No." There's a short gap in which he registers surprise and I feel like an idiot. "I mean, I want the job. I don't have any questions about that."

His turn to smile. A real one, not fake ones like mine.

"You do. You really do." He makes that a statement not a question. For a DCI, he's not very good at asking questions. I nod anyway.

"And you'd probably quite like it if I didn't ask you about a two-year gap in your CV, around the time of your A levels."

I nod again, more slowly. Yes, I would quite like it if you didn't ask about that.

"Human resources know what's going on there, do they?"

"Yes. I've already been into that with them. I was ill. Then I got better."

"Who in human resources?"

"Katie. Katie Andrews."

"And the illness?"

I shrug. "I'm fine now."

A non-answer. I hope he doesn't push further, and he doesn't. He checks with me who's interviewed me so far. The answer is, pretty much everyone. This session with Matthews is the final hurdle.

"OK. Your father knows you're applying for this job?"

"Yes."

"He must be pleased."

Another statement in place of a question. I don't answer it.

Matthews examines my face intently. Maybe that's his interview technique. Maybe he doesn't ask his suspects any questions, he just makes statements and scrutinises their faces in the wide open light from the big Cardiff sky.

"We're going to offer you a job, you know that?"

"You are?"

"Of course we are. Coppers aren't thick, but you've got more brains than anyone else in this building. You're fit. You don't have a record. You were ill for a time as a teenager, but you're fine now. You want to work for us. Why wouldn't we hire you?"

I could think of a couple of possible answers to that, but I don't volunteer them. I'm suddenly aware of being intensely relieved, which scares me a bit, because I wasn't aware of having been anxious. I'm standing up. Matthews has stood up too and comes towards me, shaking my hand and saying something. His big shoulders block my view of Bute Park and I lose sight of the kites. Matthews is talking about formalities and I'm blathering answers back at him, but my attention isn't with any of that stuff. I'm going to be a policewoman. And just five years ago, I was dead.

CHAPTER
TWO

May 2010

It's true — I do like routine work — but you can have too much of a good thing.

A copper with the Met in London — twenty-two unblemished years on the force — was obliged to retire following an injury received in the line of duty. He took a job as bursar of a Roman Catholic boys' school in Monmouthshire. He started nicking bits of money. Didn't get caught. Nicked more. Didn't get caught. Went crazy: bought himself an upright piano, a golf-club membership, two holidays, a conservatory, a share in a racehorse.

The school authorities were dopey but not actually brain dead. They came to us with evidence of wrongdoing. We investigated and found a whole lot more evidence, then arrested the suspect, Brian Penry, and took him in for interview. Penry denied everything, then stopped talking and saw out the session staring at the wall and looking like crap. On the tape, you can just about hear his slightly asthmatic breathing, a thin nasal whine sounding like a note of complaint between our questions. We charged him on eleven counts of theft, but the correct number is probably somewhere closer to fifty.

He's still denying everything, which means that we have to prepare the case for court. Five minutes before the trial starts, Penry will change his plea, because he's completely stuffed and he knows it and it won't make much difference to his sentence whether he pleads guilty now or on the day itself. In the meantime, I've got to go through every single detail of his bank records over the last six years, every single card payment, every single withdrawal from the school's bank account and identify each and every rogue transaction. I've got to do all that and document it so meticulously that a defence lawyer won't be able to pick trivial little holes in our case when it comes to court, which, as I say, it never will, because Penry is stuffed and he knows it.

My desk is covered with paper. I loathe all banks and card companies. I hate every digit between zero and nine. I despise every dopily run Catholic boys' school in South Wales. If Brian Penry were in front of me now, I would try to force-feed him my calculator, which is as large and chewable as a Bakelite phone.

"Having fun?"

I look up. David Brydon, a detective sergeant, sandy-haired, thirty-two, a moderate case of freckles and a disposition so friendly and open that I sometimes find myself saying something obnoxious because too much of a good thing can be disconcerting.

"Sod off."

I don't count that. That's just my version of friendly.

"Still on Penry, is it?"

I look up properly. "His correct title is Bastard, Thieving, Wish-He'd-Go-and-Drown-Himself Penry."

Brydon nods sagely, as though I said something sensible. "I thought you had sophisticated views on moral responsibility." He holds up two mugs. Tea for him, peppermint for me. Sugar in his, none in mine.

I stand up. "I do, just not when I have to do this." I gesture at the desk, already hating it a bit less. We go over to a little seating area in the window. There are two chairs there and a sofa, the sort you get in offices and airport lounges and nowhere else, with tubular chrome legs and stain-resistant grey upholstery. There's a lot of natural light here, though, and a view of the park. Plus I do actually like Brydon. My bad mood is increasingly just for show.

"He'll plead guilty."

"I know he'll plead guilty."

"Got to be done, though."

"Ah, yes, forgot it was State the Obvious Day. Sorry."

"Thought you might be interested in this."

He passes me a clear plastic evidence bag that contains a Visa debit card. Lloyds Bank. Platinum account. Expiry date October last year. Name of Mr Brendan T. Rattigan. Card neither shinily new nor badly marked. It is a dead card, that's all.

I shake my head. "Nope. Don't think so. Not interested at all."

"Rattigan. Brendan Rattigan."

The name means nothing to me. Either my face says it or I do. I sip the tea — still too hot — rub my eyes and smile an apology at Brydon for being a cow.

He wrinkles his face at me. "Brendan Rattigan. Newport's finest. Scrap-metal man, moves into steel. Mini-mills, whatever they are. Then shipping. Worth some ridiculous amount of money. A hundred million pounds or something."

I nod. I remember now, but it's not his wealth that I remember or care about. Brydon is still talking. There's something in his voice that I haven't yet identified.

"He died nine months back. Light-aircraft accident in the estuary." He jerks his thumb in the general direction of Roath Dock in case I don't know where the Severn Estuary is. "No cause established. Co-pilot's body recovered. Rattigan's body never was."

"But here's his card." I stretch out the clear plastic around the card, as though getting a clearer look at it will unlock its secrets.

"Here's his card all right."

"Which hasn't spent nine months in salt water."

"No."

"And you found it where exactly?"

Brydon's face hangs for a moment. He's stuck between two alternatives. Part of him wants to enjoy his little triumph over me. The other part of him is sombre, a fifty-year-old head on younger shoulders, gazing inward at the dark.

The sombre part wins.

"Not me, thank God. Neath police station gets a call. Anonymous caller. Female. Probably not elderly, probably not a kid. She gives the address of a house here in Cardiff, Butetown, says we need to get over there. A couple of uniforms do that. Locked door.

Curtains over the windows. Neighbours either out or unhelpful. Uniforms go round the back. Back garden is" — Brydon turns his hands palm upward and I know immediately what he means — "rubble. Bin bags that the dogs have been at. Rubbish everywhere. Weeds. And shit. Human shit . . . The drains inside are blocked and you can imagine the rest. The uniforms had been hesitating about going inside, but not any more. They break down a door. The house is worse than the garden."

Another short pause. No theatre this time. Just the awful feeling that decent human beings have when they encounter horror. I nod, to say that I know what he feels, which isn't true but is what he needs to hear.

"Two bodies. A woman, maybe twenties. Red-haired, dead. Evidence of class-A drug usage, but no cause of death established. Not yet. And a little girl. A cutie, apparently. Five, maybe six. Thin as a matchstick. And . . . Christ, Fi, somebody had dropped a fucking sink on her head. A big Belfast jobbie. The sink didn't break, it just crushed her. They hadn't even bothered to fucking move it afterwards."

Brydon has emotion in his eyes, and his voice is crushed too, lying under that heavy stoneware sink in a house that stinks of death, even from here.

I'm not that good at feelings. Not yet. Not the really ordinary human ones that arise from instinct like water bubbling up from a hillside spring, irrepressible and clear and as natural as singing. I can picture that house of death, because the last few years have taken me to some pretty bad places and I know what they look like,

10

but I don't have Brydon's reaction. I envy it but can't share it. But Brydon is my friend and he's in front of me, wanting something. I reach for his forearm with my hand. He's not wearing a jacket and the exchange of warmth between his skin and mine is immediate. He breathes out through his mouth. Noiselessly. Releasing something. I let him do it, whatever it is.

After a moment, he throws grateful eyes at me, pulls away and drains his tea. His face is still sombre, but he's one of those elastic sorts who'll be fine. It might have been different if he'd been one of the ones finding the bodies.

Brydon indicates the Platinum account card. "In amongst the crap, they find that."

I can imagine it. Dirty plates. Furniture too large for the room. Brown velour and old food stains. Clothes. Broken toys. A TV. Drug stuff: tobacco, needles, lighters. Plastic bags filled with useless things: car mats, clothes hangers, CD cases, nappies. I've been to those places. The poorer the house, the more the stuff. And somewhere in among it, on a dresser under a pile of enforcement notices from utility companies, a single Platinum debit card. A single Platinum card and a little girl, a cutie, with her head smashed to nothing on the floor.

"I can imagine."

"Yeah." Brydon nods, bringing himself back. He's a DS. This is a job. We're not in that house, we're in an office with low-energy ceiling lights and ergonomic desk chairs and high-output photocopiers and views out over Cathays Park. "Major hoo-ha."

"Yes."

"Jackson is running the inquiry, but it's an all-hands-on-deck affair."

"And he wants my hand on his deck."

"He does indeed."

"This card. Why it was there."

"Yep. It's probably just some druggy card-theft type thing, but we need to follow the lead anyway. Any connections. I know it's a long shot."

He starts telling me things about the investigation. It's being called Operation Lohan. Daily briefing at eighty thirty sharp. Sharp means sharp. Everyone expected to show, that includes non-core team members like me. The press has a very brief statement, but all further details to be kept quiet for now. Brydon tells me all this and I only half hear him. It's called Lohan because there's an actress called Lindsay Lohan who's a redhead and has had drink and drugs issues. I only know this because Brydon tells me, and he only tells me because he knows I'd have no idea otherwise. Famous for my ignorance, me.

"You got all that?"

I nod. "You OK?"

He nods. Attempts a grin. Not a brilliant attempt, but more than passable.

I take the card back to my desk, pulling the plastic bag tight round my finger and tracing the outline of the card with the thumb and forefinger of my free hand.

Somebody killed a young woman. Somebody dropped a heavy sink onto a little girl's head. And this card — belonging to a dead millionaire — was there as it happened.

Routine is fine. Secrets are better.

CHAPTER
THREE

The briefing room next morning, where sharp means sharp.

One side of the incident room is taken up with noticeboards in pale buff, which are already starting to swarm with names, roles, assignments, questions and lists. The bureaucracy of murder. The star of the show is a set of photos. Crime-scene images, which are all about documentary accuracy, not careful lighting, but there's something about their bluntness that gives them an almost shocking truthfulness.

The woman lies on a mattress on the floor. She could be sleeping, or in some drug-induced coma. She doesn't look either happy or unhappy, peaceful or unpeaceful. She just looks like the dead look, or as anyone at all looks when they're sleeping.

The child is another matter. You can't see the top half of her head, because it isn't there. The kitchen sink stretches right across the photo, out of focus on its upper edge, because the photographer was focusing on the face, not the sink. Beneath it peep the child's nose, her mouth and chin. The force of the sink has ejected blood through her nose and sprayed it downwards, like some joke-shop trick gone wrong. Her mouth is stretched back. I imagine that the weight of the sink caused the skin or muscle to pull backwards. What I'm looking at is simple mechanics, not an expression of feeling. Yet humans are humans and what looks like a smile is interpreted as a smile, even if it's no such thing, and this girl with the top of her head missing is smiling at me. Smiling out of death, at me.

"Poor little bleeder."

The coffee-breathed speaker behind me is Jim Davis, a veteran copper, in uniform for most of his time on the force and now a sturdily reliable DS.

"Yes, poor little girl."

The room is full now. Fourteen of us, including just three women. At this stage of an investigation, these briefings have an odd, jumpy energy. There's anger and grittiness on the one hand, a kind of remorseless male heartiness on the other. And everywhere, people wanting to *do* something.

Eight twenty-eight. DCI Dennis Jackson motors out of his office, jacket already off, sleeves already rolled up. A DI Hughes, Ken Hughes, whom I don't know very well, follows him, looking important.

Jackson gets up front. The room falls silent. I'm standing by the photo wall and feel the presence of that little girl on the side of my face as intensely as I would if it were a real person. More intensely, maybe.

The case is less than twenty-four hours old, but routine enquiries have already thrown up a good pile of facts and suppositions. Jackson goes through them all, speaking without notes. He is possessed by the same jumpy energy that fills the room, snapping off his phrases and throwing them out at us. Iron pellets of information.

No one on the electoral roll registered at that address.

Social Services appear to know the woman and child, however. Final identification is hoped for later in the day, but the woman is almost certain to turn out to be Janet Mancini. Her daughter is April.

Assuming those identifications are confirmed, then the backstory is this. Mancini was twenty-six at the time of her death. The child just six. Mancini's home background was lousy. Given up for adoption. Taken into care. A few foster families, some of which worked better than others. Started at adult education college. Not bright, but trying to do her best.

Drugs. Pregnancy. The child moving in and out of care, according to whether Mancini or her demons were on top at the time. "Social Services pretty sure that Mancini was chaotic but not a lunatic." A grin that was more of a grimace. "Not a sink-dropper anyway."

The last contact with Social Services was six weeks back. Mancini had been apparently drug-free. Her flat — not the address where she'd been found, but one in one of the nicer bits of Llanrumney — was reasonably tidy and clean. The child was properly dressed and fed, and was attending school. "So. Last contact, no problems."

The next time Social Services come round to visit, Mancini is a no-show. Maybe at her mam's. Maybe somewhere else. Social Services are concerned but not hitting alarm buttons.

"The house where they're found is a squat, obviously. No record of Mancini having any previous connection with it. We've got a statement from the neighbour on one side. Nothing helpful." Jackson stabbed at the noticeboards. "It's all there and on Groove. If you haven't got up to speed already, then you should have." Groove is our project-management and document-sharing system. It works well, but it wouldn't feel like an incident room unless there were noticeboards fluttering with paper.

Jackson then stands back to let Hughes rattle on through other known facts. The evidence from utility bills, police records, phone use. The things that a modern force can acquire almost instantly. He mentions Rattigan's debit card, without making a big thing of it. Then he finishes and Jackson takes over.

"Initial autopsy findings later today, maybe, but we won't have anything definitive for a while. I suggest, however, we proceed on the assumption that the girl was killed by a kitchen sink." His first attempt at humour, if you can call it that. "The mother, OD, possibly. Asphyxiation? Heart attack? Don't yet know.

"Focus of the investigation at this stage is, continue to gather all possible information about the victims. Past. Background. Known associates. Query drug dealing. Query prostitution. House-to-house enquiries. I want to know about anyone who entered that house. I want to know about anyone Mancini met, saw, talked to, anything in those six weeks since Social Services last saw her. Key question: why did Mancini move to that squat? She was drug-free, looking after her kid, doing well. Why did she throw all that away? What made her move?

"Individual assignments here" — meaning the noticeboards — "and Groove. Any questions, to me. If you can't get hold of me, then to Ken. If you uncover anything important or anything that might be important, let me know straight away, no excuses."

He nods, checking he hasn't left anything out. He hasn't. Briefings like this, early on in any serious crime investigation, are partly theatre. Any group of coppers will always treat murder as the most serious thing they ever have to deal with, but team dynamics demand a ritual. The Haka of the All Blacks. Celtic woad. Battle music. Jackson puts his weary-but-determined look to one side and puts on his grim-and-resolute one instead.

"We don't yet know if Janet Mancini's death was murder, but we're treating it that way for now. But the girl. She was six years old. Six. Just started at school. Friends. At their Llanrumney flat, the one she left six weeks ago, there were paintings of hers hanging up on the fridge. Clean clothes hanging up in her bedroom. Then this." He points to the photo of her on the noticeboard, but none of us look at it, because it's already inside our heads. Around the room, the men are clamping their jaws and looking tough. DC Rowland, Bev Rowland, a good friend of mine, is crying openly.

"Six years old, then this. April Mancini. We're going to find the man who dropped that sink, and we're going to send him to jail for the rest of his life. That's our job. What we're here to do. Now let's get on with it."

The meeting breaks up. Chatter. A charge for the coffee machine. Too much noise. I grab Bev.

"Are you all right?"

"Yes, I'm fine really. I knew today wasn't going to be a mascara-ey kind of day."

I laugh. "What have they got you doing?"

"Door to door mostly. The woman's touch. How about you?"

There's a funny kind of assumption in her answer and her question. The assumption is that I don't quite count as a woman, so I don't quite get the jobs that female DCs are usually assigned. I don't resent that assumption. Bev is the sort to cry when Jackson puts on his gravel-voiced tear-jerker finale. I'm not. Bev is the sort of comfortable soul that people will happily open up to over a cup of tea. I'm not. I mean, I can do the door-to-door stuff. I've done it before and asked the right questions and sometimes obtained valuable information. But Bev is a natural and we both know I'm not.

"I'm mostly on the Brian Penry case. Bank statements and all that. In my spare time, if I stay sane, I'm meant to track down that debit-card thing. Rattigan's card. Funny place for it to show up."

"Stolen?"

I shake my head. I called the bank yesterday after talking with Brydon and — once I'd managed to clamber through all the bureaucracy to someone who actually had the information — got answers fairly easily. "Nope. The card was reported lost. It was duly cancelled and a replacement issued. Life goes on. It could literally be just that. He dropped it. Mancini or whoever picked it up. Kept it as a souvenir."

"Brendan Rattigan's Platinum card? I would have done."

"You wouldn't. You'd have handed it in."

"Well, I know, but if I wasn't the handing-in type."

I laugh at her. Trying to use the inner workings of Bev Rowland's mind as a model for guessing at the inner workings of Janet Mancini's mind doesn't feel to me like an obvious recipe for success. Bev makes a face at me for laughing, but wants to rush off to the Ladies' so she can sort her face out before hitting the road. I tell her to have a good day, and she says, "You too."

As she leaves, I realise that what I said to her wasn't true. Janet Mancini *couldn't* have picked up Rattigan's debit card from the pavement. It wasn't possible. Mancini and Rattigan didn't walk the same streets, didn't go to the same pubs, didn't inhabit the same worlds. The places where Rattigan might have dropped his card were all places that would, explicitly or otherwise, have forbidden Mancini entry.

And as soon as this thought occurs to me, I understand its implication. The two of them knew each other. Not casually. Not by chance. But meaningfully, in some real way. If you asked me to take a bet on it right now, I'd bet that the millionaire killed the drug addict. Not directly, I assume — it's hard to kill someone when you're dead — but indirect killing is still killing.

"I'm going to get you, you fucker," I say out loud. A secretary looks at me, startled, as she walks past. "Not you," I tell her. "You're not the fucker."

20

She gives me a little smile. The sort that you slip the schizo type muttering swearwords in the street, the sort you offer park-bench drunks quarrelling over cider. I don't mind. I'm used to that kind of smile by now. Water. Duck's back. Paddle on.

I head back upstairs.

My desk stares balefully at me, flaunting its cargo of numbers and sheets of paper. I go over to the kitchenette and make myself a peppermint tea. Me and one of the secretaries drink it, no one else. Back to my desk. Another sunny day. Big windows full of air and sunshine. I lower my face over my mug of tea and let my face warm up in the perfumed steam. A thousand boring things to do and one interesting one. I'm reaching for the phone, even as I pull my face away from its steam bath. It takes me a couple of calls to get Charlotte Rattigan's number — widows of the super-wealthy are ex-directory, inevitably — but I get it anyway and make the call.

A woman's voice answers, giving the name of the house, Cefn Mawr House. She sounds every inch the servant, the expensive sort, titanium-plated.

"Hello. My name's Detective Constable Griffiths, calling from the South Wales Police. May I speak with Mrs Rattigan, please?"

Mention of the police causes a moment's hesitation, as it almost always does. Then the training kicks in.

"Detective Constable Griffiths, did you say? May I ask what it's regarding?"

"It's a police matter. I'd prefer to speak to Mrs Rattigan directly."

"She isn't available right now. Perhaps if I could let her know the issue . . . ?"

I don't really need to see Rattigan's widow in person. Talking to her on the phone would be just fine, but I don't respond well to titanium-plated obstructiveness. It makes me come over all police-forcish.

"That's quite all right. Will she be available for an interview later on today?"

"Look, if you could just let me know the matter at hand . . ."

"I'm calling in connection with a murder inquiry. A routine matter, but it needs to be dealt with. If it's not convenient for me to come to the house, then perhaps we could arrange for Mrs Rattigan to come down to Cardiff and we can talk to her here."

I enjoy these little power struggles, stupid as they are. I like them because I win. Within two minutes Titanium Voice has given me an eleven-thirty appointment and directions to the house. I put the phone down, laughing at myself. The return journey will take me an hour and a half, and what could have been a three-minute phone call will end up wasting half my morning.

I spend the next hour and a bit working through Penry's hateful bank statements, lose track of time a bit, then find myself bolting downstairs for my car. It's a white Peugeot Coupé Cabriolet. Two seats. Soft top. High-pressure turbocharger that gets you from nought to sixty in a shade over eight seconds. Soft leather seats in pale fawn. Alloys. My dad gave me my first car when I got my job three years ago, then insisted on replacing it with the new model this year. It's a totally inappropriate car for a junior detective constable and I love it.

I throw my bag — notebook, pen, purse, phone, dark glasses, make-up, evidence bag — onto the passenger seat and nose out of the car park. Cardiff traffic. Classic FM inside the car, pneumatic drills ripping up the A4161 Newport Road. Carpet stores and discount bed places. Clearer on the A48, the music turned up for the motorway and its views out over Newport — just possibly the ugliest town in the world — before snaking up past Cwmbran towards Penperllini.

Because of the traffic and the roadworks, and because I set off late in the first place, and because I got myself lost in the lanes beyond Penperllini, I'm about twenty-five minutes late when I do manage to find the entrance to Cefn Mawr House. Big stone pillars and fierce yew topiary. Posh and English-feeling. Out of place.

I make the turn and, shades on against the sunlight, I speed up the drive in a stupid attempt to minimise my lateness. A last twist in the way catches me out and I emerge into the large gravelled parking area in front of the house doing about thirty miles an hour, when under ten would have been more appropriate. I brake hard and go for a long, curving slide on the gravel until my speed falls away. I only just manage to stop the engine stalling. A wide spray of ochre dust hangs in the air to mark the manoeuvre. Silent applause. Fi Griffiths, rally driver.

I give myself a few seconds to get my head together. Breathing in, breathing out, concentrating on each breath. My heart's going too fast, but at least I can feel it. These things shouldn't worry me so much, but they do. There shouldn't be such a thing as poverty and starvation, but there is. I wait till I think it's OK, then give it another twenty seconds.

Out of the car. I slam the door closed, but don't blip it locked. On the front steps of the house, there's a woman — Miss Titanium, I presume — watching me. She doesn't look like she likes me.

"DC Griffiths?"

It's DC now, I notice. Miss Titanium doesn't strike me as altogether au fait with CID ranks, so I suspect her of doing some quick research on the Internet. In which case she knows how junior I am.

"Sorry I'm late. Traffic." I don't know if she witnessed my rally-driving arrival, so I don't apologise for it and she doesn't mention it.

The house is a modest affair. Ten or twelve bedrooms. Immaculate grounds. A leylandii hedge screening what I presume is a tennis court. Further away, a couple of cottages and what I guess is a stable or gym complex. The river Usk flows picturesquely over rocks at the end of a long sweep of lawn. We're only a few miles away from Cwmbran and the old coal mines that injure the hillsides above. Crumlin, Abercarn, Cwmcarn, Pontywaun. Standing here, with the river Usk parading its party tricks in the sunlight, you'd think you were a million miles away from all that. That's the point, I suppose. What the money is for.

Titanium takes me on through the front door. Inside, everything is as you'd expect. Interior-designed so completely that any trace of human personality vanished along with the Victorian subfloors. Our heels click across limestone in the hall, past vases of fresh flowers and photos of racehorses, through into the kitchen. A huge room, an add-on to the main body of the house. Handmade kitchen furniture in ivory. A range cooker in Wedgwood blue. More flowers. Venetian blinds, sofas and sunlight.

"Mrs Rattigan has been called away on something else, just temporarily. We were expecting you at eleven thirty."

"Sorry, my fault. I'm happy to wait."

I say this sincerely. Genuinely sorry. Genuinely happy to wait. Mature of me. Nice person. Trouble is that I'm only being nice because I scared myself a few moments back and can't take any hassle now. For the time being, just sitting in this kitchen listening to my heart beat is enough for me.

Titanium — who gave me her name, along with a limp but elegant hand, at the front of the house — is doing things with the kettle. I try to remember her name and nothing comes to me. I sit at the table and get out my notebook. For a moment I can't even remember why I'm here. Titanium puts coffee down in front of me, as though it's some art object the family has just invested in.

I can't think of anything to say, so say nothing. I blink instead.

"I'll go and see if Mrs Rattigan is ready for you."

I nod. She goes. Clicks out of the kitchen, through the hall, to somewhere else. I'm calming down now. I can hear a clock ticking somewhere. The range cooker emits a kind of gentle rushing sound from its flue, like a stream heard a long way away. A few minutes go by, lovely empty minutes, then a woman comes into the kitchen, Titanium in position on her wing.

I stand up.

"Mrs Rattigan, I'm sorry to have been late."

"Oh, don't worry."

The Internet has already told me that Mrs Charlotte Frances Rattigan is forty-four. She has two kids, both teenagers. She is a former model. Only the last part of that is obvious from her appearance. A pale grey shirt worn above pale linen trousers and sandals. Shoulder-length blonde hair. Nice skin, not much make-up. Tall, maybe five foot ten, and then an inch or so more from her heels.

She is pretty, of course, but it's not the prettiness that strikes me. There's something ethereal about her. As though it's not just the house missing its Victorian subfloors. I'm immediately interested. I ask Titanium if she would mind giving us a few moments of privacy and, on a look from the boss, she leaves us.

I fix Mrs Rattigan with my firm, DC-ish, professional-quality smile.

"Thank you so much for agreeing to see me, madam. I've just got a few questions. A routine matter, but an important one."

"That's all right. I understand."

"I'm afraid that I shall have to ask you some questions about your late husband. I do apologise in advance for any distress that may cause. It's all perfectly routine and —"

She interrupts. "That's all right. I understand."

Her voice is soft, a peach without a stone. I hesitate. Nothing whatsoever in this situation calls for me to come over all hard-edged, but I can't quite resist and I can feel my voice harden.

"Did your husband know a woman called Janet Mancini?"

"My husband . . .?" She tapers off and shrugs.

"Is that a no or an I don't know?"

Another shrug. "I mean, not that I know of. Mancini? Janet Mancini?"

"Do either of these addresses mean anything to you?"

I show her my notebook. The first address is where Mancini was found. The second is where she had been living previously.

"No, sorry."

"This second address here is in Butetown. Were you ever aware of your husband having any business in that area? Visiting people?"

A headshake.

Quantum physics tells you that the act of observation alters reality. The same is true of police interviews. Mrs Rattigan knows that I'm a detective constable assigned to a murder inquiry. There's some absence in her answers that teases me, but that could just be an effect of my job function and my assignment. Titanium's cafetiere of coffee is steaming beside us. Mrs Rattigan hasn't offered it, so I do.

"Would you like coffee? Shall I pour?"

"Oh, yes, please. Sorry."

I pour out one coffee, not two.

"Won't you have any?" That's the first positive action of any sort she's taken since I've met her, and it hardly rates high on the positivity scale.

"I don't drink caffeine."

She pulls her cup towards her but doesn't drink from it. "Good for you. I know I shouldn't."

"I have a few further questions to ask, madam. Please understand that we want the truth. If your husband did things in the past that he might not want us to have known about, well, that's all in the past now. It's no longer our concern."

She nods. Light hazel eyes. Fair eyebrows. I realise that I was wrong about the house. I'm sure it has been interior-designed to within an inch of its life, but the designers caught something real about the person commissioning the work. Pale linen, light hazel, a stoneless peach. That was this house and its owner.

"Did your husband ever take drugs?"

The question jolts her. She shakes her head, looking down and to the left. Her coffee cup is in her right hand. If she's right-handed, then the down-and-to-the-left look suggests some element of construction in her answer.

"Cocaine, maybe? A few lines with business associates?"

She looks at me with relief. "You know, sometimes. I didn't . . . What he got up to when he was away . . ."

28

I reassure her. "No, no, I'm sure you didn't. But loads of business types do, of course. You didn't want it in the house, though, I can see that."

"You know, there are the children."

That sounds to me like the comment she made to him when he was still around. Oh, don't do that. It's not me. It's the children. I'm only thinking of you.

I get out the debit card and show it to her.

"This is your husband's, I presume?"

She looks at it, then at me. She doesn't get quite as decisive as a nod, but she gets halfway there.

"The card was reported lost. Do you recall when or where he lost it?"

"No, sorry."

"Did he ever mention losing it?"

"I don't think so. I mean . . ." She shrugs. When millionaires lose cards, they have people who sort it out. That's what the shrug means, or what it means to me anyway.

"The card was found at a crime scene in Butetown. Does that make sense to you?"

"No. No, I'm sorry."

"You're not aware how this card could have come into the possession of Janet Mancini?"

"Sorry. I'm really not."

"Does the name April Mancini mean anything to you?"

"No."

"You are aware that Butetown is a poor part of town? Quite run-down. Rough. Can you think of any reason why your husband might have had business there?"

"No."

I've come to the end of all the questions I could possibly ask, all the ones I'd have got through on a phone call. I'm repeating myself, even. Yet there's that absence in the air, teasing me with its scent. It's not that Mrs Rattigan is lying to me. I know she isn't. But there's something there.

I go for it.

"Just a few more questions," I say.

"Certainly."

"Your sex life with your husband. Was it completely normal?"

CHAPTER
FOUR

The traffic is slow as I come back past Cwmbran. I fiddle with the radio to try and find a channel I want to listen to, but end up settling for silence. To the left of me, green hills and lambs. To the right, the intricate folds of the old mineworks. Long, black tunnels leading down into the dark. I prefer the lambs.

Into Cardiff. I can't quite face going back to the office immediately, so I don't. Instead of keeping straight ahead on the Newport Road, I pull off left.

Fitzalan Place. Adam Street. Bute Terrace.

People say they like the new Cardiff. The redeveloped centre. The Assembly Building. Fancy hotels, regional offices, coffees at £2.50 a cup. This is the new Wales. A Wales taking charge of its future. Proud, confident, independent.

Me, I can't get my head round any of that. It feels like a con trick with me as the patsy. Everything about it is wrong. The look. The style. The prices.

The names too. The city centre has a Churchill Way, a Queen Street, a Windsor Place. Where's the sodding independence there? If it were up to me, I'd name every damn street after one of those thirteenth-century Welsh princes who spent their life fighting the English and getting massacred in the process. Llewelyn ap Gruffydd — Llewelyn the Last. He'd get the biggest street named after him. The last king of Wales. A heroic, ambitious, quarrelsome failure. Tricked, attacked, murdered. His head ended up on a spike over the Tower of London. I'd name every major landmark in Cardiff after him. If the English didn't like it, they could give us his head back. The Queen's probably got it in a boot room somewhere. I expect Wills and Harry use it to practise their keepie-uppie.

I relax only as I get away from the centre — the part where I work — and out into Butetown. In Butetown, people drink tea more than coffee, and neither ever at £2.50 a cup. In Butetown, it's true that the odd drug addict gets murdered, and every now and then you find a little girl whose head has been splattered under a large piece of upscale kitchenware, but I prefer it that way. Crimes you can see. Victims you can touch.

My car pulls to a halt just up the road from 86 Allison Street.

I get that creepy feeling I get when I'm close to the dead. Tingly.

I step out. Allison Street isn't much of a place. Cheap 1960s council houses that look like they've been made of cardboard boxes. Same colour. Same blocky construction. Same thin walls. Same resistance to damp. There's no one around except a kid repetitively slamming a red ball against a windowless wall. He looks at me briefly, then continues.

Number 86 still has a few ribbons of black-and-yellow crime-scene tape round it, but the forensics boys will be mostly done by now. I pick my way through the tape and ring the doorbell.

First silence, then footsteps. I'm in luck. A solid-looking SOCO, with short gingery hair and pink ears, comes to the door.

I show him my card. "I was just passing," I explain. "I thought I'd look in."

The SOCO shrugs. "Five minutes, love. I'm just resampling fibres, then I'm done."

He goes upstairs, leaving me alone downstairs. I step into the living room, where April and Janet died. Red curtains hang over the front window — just as they were hanging on the day of the killing — but yellow halogen lamps of the type that builders use have been strung up here and in the kitchen. Their glare is too strong to be real. I feel like I'm in a film set, not a house.

Some of the stuff that was here in the house has been removed as evidence. Other items have been sifted, inventoried, then destroyed. Still other items have been left in place, tagged as appropriate. I don't know enough about how these big forensic investigations work to recognise the logic behind what has or has not been done.

I walk around, not doing anything, just trying to see if I feel anything being here. I don't. Or rather, I feel a dislike for the place, its red swirly carpet, its ugly sofa, the dirt marks on the wall, its smell of discount store and blocked drains. I feel strange and disconnected.

From the crime-scene photos on Groove, I recognise where the two corpses were lying when they were found. Where April was lying, a pool of dried blood has caked into the carpet. It doesn't look like blood, though. A curry stain, more like.

I bend down and feel the floor where April breathed her last, then move round till I'm in the spot where Janet died.

You want to feel things at times like this. Some sense of the dead. A lingering presence. But I don't get anything. Just nylon carpet and a faint smell. The halogen lamps make everything unreal. Under the front window, there's a wooden storage unit, which has been given a back and arms, so that it can double up as a window seat.

The SOCO comes downstairs, two steps at a time, crashing his way into the living room.

"All right?" he says.

I indicate the window seat. "That thing. Did it have seat cushions?"

The SOCO points to a place, four feet away, where a dirty black checked cushion leans up against the wall. The cushion clearly fits the seat.

"And were there drawings on the property? Kids' drawings, the sort of thing that April would have done."

"Big stash of them there." The SOCO points down the back of the window seat. "Flowers mostly."

"Yes."

I lift the red curtain and stare out onto the street. You get a good view from this window. Half of Allison Street and a parking area beyond. I sit on the window seat, imagining that I'm April.

34

The SOCO stands close, breathing audibly through his nose. He wants me gone and I have no reason to be here, so I oblige him by leaving.

I step from the too-bright living room out into the too-dark hall, then out onto the hot, sunshiny street. Everything feels odder now. The boy has taken his red ball somewhere else. The house and street look as normal as anything, but inside number 86, April Mancini was definitely murdered and her mother quite likely was. All the difference in the world. I've had my mobile phone off ever since Cefn Mawr. I turn it back on now and there's a short blizzard of incoming texts, none of which are interesting enough to respond to.

I think about going back in, but I haven't yet had lunch, and besides, my visit to Allison Street has left me feeling unsatisfied. Itchy.

I wander around hunting for a corner shop. I was sure I saw one on my way over here, but typically, I make a hash out of tracking it down. I'm not always good at locating large, static, well-advertised objects in brightly lit locations. But I find it at last and go inside.

Newspapers. Chocolates. A chiller cabinet with milk and yoghurt and the sort of cooked meats that will block your arteries in about the same time as it'll take an intensively farmed piglet to bulk up, squeal and die. Some tinned foods, sliced bread, biscuits. Some sad-looking fruit.

I help myself to orange juice and a cheese and tomato sandwich. The girl on the till is called Farideh. She has a plastic badge that says so anyway.

"Hi." My opening gambit.

She ducks that one and reaches for my goods to put them through the till. A CCTV monitor above her head flicks between pictures of different viewpoints in store. It's scrutinising an OAP bending over the chiller cabinet right now.

"I'm on the police inquiry," I say. "You know, the mother and daughter who were murdered up the road."

Farideh nods and says something bland and pacifying, the sort of thing that people say when they're trying to indicate a general willingness to be helpful but without the crucial ingredient of such an attitude — namely, actually being helpful.

"You must have known them, I suppose?"

"She came in here, I think. The mother."

"The redhead? Janet?"

Farideh nods. "You people were here already. I already told them."

I don't quite catch whether she says "you people" or "your people". The former sounds a bit edgy, a bit them and us. "Your people" sounds rather flattering, like everyone in the police is part of my tribe, worker bees buzzing around their queen. Then again, Farideh's English is heavily accented, so maybe I'm reading too much into her word choice.

Farideh rings up my purchases and puts on her pay-and-get-out-of-here face.

"You never saw the girl? Not even to buy, I don't know, choc ices?"

"No."

"Girls don't really buy choc ices, do they? What do they like?" I think out loud, not feigning my uncertainty. I know I used to be a six-year-old girl once, equipped with pocket money enough to buy sweeties at the corner shop, but those days seem unbelievably distant. I'm always bewildered at other people's memories of their own pasts. But still, I thrash around trying to guess at April's confectionery habits. "Rolos? KitKat? Gummi Bears? Smarties?"

I don't know if I'm even vaguely close, but Farideh is insistent. She hasn't seen the girl. The OAP who came in behind me has finished foraging in the chiller cabinet and is waiting to pay. I find some money and hand it over.

The front of the shop is adorned with handwritten adverts. People selling off their mountain bikes or offering garden clearance and handyman services. "No job too small." There's a police notice already up in the window too. Smartly laid out by one of the people on our communications team. Printed out on glossy card in four-colour reprographics, with a freephone number in red at the bottom. And it's useless. An alien intruder. The sort of thing that people around here will simply blank from view. The same kind of disappearing act that is performed on utility bills, planning notices, Social Services forms, tax requests.

I let the OAP pay, then ask Farideh if I can put up a notice.

"A5 or card?" she asks.

"Card," I say. I like card.

She gives me a card and I write on it in ballpoint pen, *Janet and April Mancini. Lived at 86 Allison Street. Killed on 21 May. Information wanted. Please contact DC Fiona Griffiths.*

I add not the 0800 freephone number but my own mobile one. I don't know why, but it looks right once I've done it, so I don't go back and change it.

"One week, two weeks or four weeks?" asks Farideh. It's 50p a week or £1.50 for four weeks. I go for four weeks.

Farideh sticks the card up in the window as I leave.

Sunshine, secrets and silence.

Outside, I sit on a bollard in the sun, eat my sandwich and call Bev Rowland on her mobile. She's in the middle of something, but we chat for a minute or so anyway. Then a text comes in from David Brydon inviting me for a drink that evening. I stare at the screen and don't know what to do. I do nothing, just finish the sandwich.

Back in the office, I don't get the "Where the hell have you been?" question I was more or less expecting. I don't think anyone's even noticed that I've been on walkabout. I email Dennis Jackson with a quick report on Cefn Mawr. Then type up my notes properly and get them on Groove.

Then it's back to Penry's damn bank statements, which don't add up, or don't when it's me operating the calculator anyway. I call the school to check there wasn't some other bank account that he could have been nicking money from and am a bit peeved when they say no, definitely not. No let-off there.

My mood is just beginning to take a turn for the worse when I get a call from Jackson, summoning me downstairs.

He wants to know more about Cefn Mawr. I give him the gist. I try to keep my language bland and professional, the way we're trained, but Jackson isn't fooled.

"You said *what?*"

"I asked if Mr and Mrs Rattigan had enjoyed normal sexual relations, sir. I apologised for the intrusive nature of the enquiry, but —"

"Cut the bullshit. What did she say?"

"Nothing directly. But I touched a nerve. She could hardly speak." And her ears burned. And her eyes were full of injury. And the absence that had been drowning me before was suddenly very, very full of matter.

"And you left it there. Please tell me you left it there."

"Yes. Almost. I mean, she'd already half told me that —"

"She hadn't *told* you anything. You said she could hardly speak."

There's a long beat. Jackson uses it to glare at me.

"I did ask if her husband might have enjoyed rough sex with prostitutes," I admit finally.

"That's what you said? You used those words?"

"Yes, sir."

"And?"

"I interpreted her look as confirming my suspicion."

"A *look?* You interpreted a *look.*"

"It was a legitimate question to ask. His bank card *was* found there."

"It might have been a legitimate question coming from an experienced member of the team, after appropriate consultation with the operation commander. It was not an appropriate question asked by a lone detective constable operating without permission, with no supervising officer present and addressed to the grieving wife of a dead man."

"No, sir."

Jackson glares at me again, but his heart's not in it and he rocks forward again, all businesslike. He riffles through some papers on his desk till he finds the sheet he was after.

"Vice Unit records. A few contacts with Mancini. Never on the game full time, as far as we know, but she was certainly open to it when she needed cash." His eyes move rapidly down the printout. "We let her know the risks she was running. Helplines, that kind of thing. Probably didn't make a difference — well, it didn't, did it? Look where she ended up."

"You never know. It might have helped a bit. Seems like she mostly tried to look after her kid."

"Mostly."

Jackson puts a lot of emphasis on the word. He's right, of course. It's not much use being *mostly* good enough when your occasional lapses include heroin, prostitution, your child being taken into care and ultimately murdered. Whoops, April dear, sorry about that.

40

I shrug to acknowledge his point, but add, "For what it's worth, I am pretty certain that she wasn't selling plain vanilla, at least not where Brendan Rattigan was involved. Charlotte Rattigan's reaction wasn't just the reaction of someone whose husband has cheated on her. It was more than that."

"Go on." Jackson's voice is still grim, but he wants to hear what I have to say. A victory of sorts, I suppose.

"Rattigan had his pretty model wife for social and domestic use. She ticked all the right boxes. But I think Rattigan liked women he could abuse. I don't know in what way. Slapping them around, maybe. Roughing them up. If you want me to speculate wildly, then I'd guess that Allison Street would have been part of the fun. The squat, I mean. The squalor."

"Wild speculation is exactly what we expect from our officers."

Jackson is already moving on. From his point of view, he's got what he needs. Vice Unit's records place Mancini as an occasional prostitute servicing an on-off drug habit. My jaunt down to Penperllini added nothing. Maybe Mancini sold her services to clients who liked it rough, but then most prostitutes will cater for most tastes. No big deal. Jackson is about to let me go with a senior officer-type caution not to let myself get carried away when interviewing multimillionaire widows when his phone goes. I'm about to make a move, but he raises a hand, stopping me.

I'm alert for the first few seconds of the call. I'm worried that it is someone from Cefn Mawr House ringing to complain about me. Then it's clear it's not that kind of call and I dim my attention accordingly. It's coming up to five o'clock in the afternoon. There's not much point in going home before meeting up with Brydon, so it's probably more of Penry's paperwork instead.

Jackson clatters the phone down.

"That was the pathologist. They're not done, but they're mostly done and they're ready to brief us. You can come over and take notes. A reward for your enterprise at Cefn Mawr."

Because neither of us is planning to come back to the office afterwards, we drive up to the hospital separately. The North Road is its normal bad-tempered rush-hour crush. Stop-start all the way. I can see Jackson's shirtsleeved arm hanging out of the window, thumping the side of his car to the beat of some unheard music. When we get up to the hospital, we park in the big 1,300-capacity car park. I take a POLICE BUSINESS notice out of the glovebox and stick it in the windscreen. It saves the pay-and-display charge. Jackson's ahead of me, hurrying over to the entrance, out of the wind, lighting up.

"Want one?" he says as I catch up.

"No, thanks. I don't smoke."

"Are you the one who doesn't drink?" Jackson tries to remember me from beery police piss-ups. I'm usually the one holding the orange juice and leaving early. But he doesn't really care and carries on without waiting for my answer. "Only time *I* smoke, pretty much. Bloody corpses."

Three or four puffs, a grimace and he's done. A shoe heel does the rest. We go on in.

I'm not good with hospitals. The endless buildings, trees dotted around like apologies, and inside, it's job functions you can't understand and that air of incomprehensible busyness. Curtained-off beds and death settling like falling snow.

But it's not the hospital itself that concerns us. We head over to the least signed building in the entire complex. Aidan Price, the senior pathologist, meets us at the mortuary door. He's tall and thin, with the fussy pedantry you need to do what he does. Right now, he's fussing over the time, shooing out support staff and checking keys.

Hospital mortuaries have two or three functions. Number one, they're storage units. Larders. Any big hospital generates plenty of corpses. Folk get antsy if the corpses are left on the wards too long. So the dead are whisked away, to be replaced with clean sheets and a smell of detergent. The bodies have to go somewhere, so they come here to the mortuary, like aircraft in a holding pattern, before being sent onwards to the undertakers or the crematorium.

Number two follows on from one. If grieving relatives want to grieve over something, they need a bit more than clean sheets and a smell of detergent to get their tears flowing. And in any case, hospital PR wants the relatives off the public wards almost as badly as they want the corpses gone. So hospital mortuaries all have a place where next of kin can come to view the corpse. It's a functional space, snipped away at by architectural practicalities and budget restrictions. The University Hospital facility has a framed print of birch trees in spring and a view out over the roof of a catering facility downstairs.

Then there's number three, the one that brings us here. The University Hospital of Wales runs the largest forensic and high-risk post-mortem autopsy service in the country. Two bodies a day are sliced and diced. Most of the work is routine. A drug addict dies. The coroner needs a cause of death. The public health authorities need to know whether the corpse had HIV, hep B, hep C, so toxicology panels are run, organs removed and weighed, the brain examined. The pathologist reports to the coroner. The coroner delivers a verdict. A report is filed. A life ends.

We get changed and Price waits for us at the door of the autopsy suite. He's in a long-sleeved white coverall with a plastic apron, worn over surgical scrubs. Rubber boots, face mask, a white cotton hat. We have to put on similar gear ourselves before moving further.

When we're done, we enter the suite. Price closes the door behind us. There are two gurneys, both in use, both covered with a pale blue cloth. Strong overhead lighting and the hum of ventilation. The air in these rooms sucks from clean areas to dirty, changing the air at least once an hour, passing it through a HEPA filter before releasing it. Filtering out germs, filtering out the dead.

Price pulls the cloth away from the larger body. Janet Mancini.

She's pretty. That was clear from the photos, but she's more delicate in real life, fine-boned and sensitive. I want to trace the line of her eyebrow with my finger, lay my hand against her coppery hair.

Price doesn't like dead people and he doesn't like drug-addicted prostitutes with their high-risk infectious corpses. He doesn't like policemen. I get out my notebook and clear a space down by Mancini's feet so I can write as he talks. She has small feet and slim ankles. I find myself arranging the gown around her feet as though wanting to show them to best advantage. I stop as soon as I notice Jackson staring at me.

Price starts to speak with fussy precision.

"Let's start with the easy bits. We've tested urine and blood for drug use. Urine tests were negative for marijuana, cocaine, opiates, amphetamines, PCP and various other substances. We detected low levels of alcohol and methamphetamine, but her bladder was relatively full, so we can't be sure of the extent or recency of her drug use. A clearer positive result for heroin. I'd guess a more recent use there."

"That'd be consistent with what we found lying around the house," says Jackson.

"Yes. Quite." Price isn't interested in crime-scene details and it takes him a moment or two to restart. "Blood tests offer a more reliable guide, because they're less affected by fluid intake. Immunoassays confirm heroin use. Either very heavy use some time before death or moderate-to-heavy use closer to death. It's not possible to distinguish the two. Moderate blood alcohol levels. She'd have been below the drink-driving limit, for example. Some methamphetamine use, but not heavy *and* recent."

He talks a bit more about drugs and general health and the size of her liver and the absence of various conditions. I take notes, but Jackson is impatient for Price to get to the point, which finally he does.

"Cause of death? Uncertain. There are only two ways a person can die. Their heart or their lungs. Drowning, fire, gunshot. It all comes down to whether the heart or the lung stops working first. In this case, it could be either. Her heart is in the state of health consistent with her age and lifestyle. You wouldn't expect a twenty-something heart to stop beating, but if you bombard it with drugs, then of course you can't rule out an attack, even a lethal one. Methamphetamines are a known risk factor. Plus as soon as you start mixing drugs, the interactions can become highly unpredictable."

I'm writing as fast as I can and my handwriting starts to space out and get messy as I speed up.

"All the same, I'd say that the lungs would be a likelier cause. Fatal respiratory depression. Slow breathing. Disorientation. The problem is the build-up of carbon dioxide. Acidosis. Taken too far, that'll kill you." Jackson nods and looks at me to make sure I've got it, which I have. But Price is still going. "Do I understand that the user may have been in an unfamiliar environment?"

It takes Jackson a moment to respond.

"Unfamiliar? We don't know. It wasn't her home environment. We don't know how long she'd been there."

46

"Or with unfamiliar people? Or in some other way in a new situation?"

"Yes, definitely possible. Probable, in fact."

Price nods. "A lot of heroin overdose isn't overdose at all. It's the same dose as normal, but taken in an unfamiliar setting, it overrides the body's homeostatic mechanisms."

This is a new one on me and on Jackson. Price explains at excessive length. The gist is this. When somebody starts taking heroin, the body does all it can to counteract the effect of the drug. When the drug is taken in a familiar environment, the body is prepared for the toxic assault and is already doing its best to counteract it. The result is that users come to tolerate very high levels of the drug. If you pull them away from their home environment, the body's defence mechanisms haven't been primed to respond. Result: even an ordinary dose of the drug — the same dose as the user was tolerating in their home environment — can become lethal.

"So," Jackson says, "she leaves home. She's having a bad time. We don't yet know why. She takes heroin. Same dose as normal, but it's a big mistake. Her body's not ready for the drug. Next thing, bang! She's dead."

Price fusses over this summary. It's all too clear and sharp for him. He starts qualifying every statement and then adds riders to his qualifications. He prefers the fog of precision to the clarity of a decent hunch. On a look from Jackson, I stop taking notes while Price's pedantry burns itself out. Jackson looks like an idiot in his white overalls and rubber boots, but then so do I. We exchange smiles. When either one of us moves, we rustle like taffeta. Price is wearing more or less the same kit, but it suits him for some reason. Also, he doesn't rustle.

When Price is done with his pedantic overdrive, he goes back to his briefing. Routine, necessary, boring. I take notes. Jackson prowls. Price lectures. I think he enjoys boring us. They haven't found HIV or anything like that, but the tests aren't yet complete. No obvious sexual assault. No recent semen found in or by the body.

Then we're done with Janet. I wrap up her feet again and cover her head, only this time I can't resist and I move one of her coppery locks with my hand as I bring the gown down over her face. Her hair feels recently washed, clean and silky. I want to put my head down to smell it.

The second gurney holds April Mancini. Someone has taped a dressing over the top of her head so that the splatter of her skull and brains is hidden, but the dressing sags where it should be smooth, a gap where there should be a head.

"Cause of death," says Price, coming dangerously close to a joke, "is fairly evident. No drug use. We haven't been able to find any evidence of sexual abuse. No semen. I think we can say there was no *major* violence — aside from the sink, I mean — but there's plenty of stuff that can happen without leaving marks. We haven't yet found any infection, though blood analysis is still ongoing. I'm not sure what else you want."

He stands at April's head and tweaks the dressing, trying to stop it sagging. I don't know if he's fidgeting, if he wants to preserve the little girl's dignity or if he's just a neatness freak. I'm guessing it's the last of those.

Jackson isn't looking at either body. He's over in the corner where an anglepoise lamp hangs over a workbench. He's swinging the lamp around, working the springs.

"Any sign of struggle? Blood under the fingernails, that kind of thing?"

"We've taken a look, of course. Haven't yet completed DNA testing and we might find something there, but if there is anything, then certainly not a lot. No obvious signs of struggle anyway."

Jackson is frustrated, but Price is just a pathologist, a reader of evidence. He can't look into the past any more than we can. I've filled out thirteen pages of my notebook in the loopy handwriting that I dislike. My first job tomorrow will be to type it up and get it on Groove. But there's one big question still to be asked. If Jackson doesn't ask it, I will, but Jackson is an old pro. He bends the anglepoise down until its springs groan.

"Fatal respiratory depression," he says.

Price nods. He knows where this is going.

"What about respiratory depression that isn't enough to be fatal? Presumably the symptoms are still there. Slow breathing. Weakness. Disorientation?"

"Correct. There's not enough air coming into the lungs to permit the necessary gas exchange. Taken too far, and it'll prove fatal. But even if it doesn't go that far, you've still got a person who's badly disoriented.

Maybe conscious, maybe not. Weak and uncoordinated. Quite possibly not able to stand. Perhaps temporary problems with vision."

"A near-overdose, in other words," says Jackson. "If she's left alone, she'll live. Lucky to be alive, maybe, but she'll recover."

Price nods again. "And if she's not left alone . . ."

"Whoever it is has got themselves the perfect victim. If anyone wanted to kill her, they could just put their fingers over her nose, close her mouth and wait."

"A minute or two," said Price. "Easy."

CHAPTER
FIVE

Job done.

We're standing outside the autopsy suite in a little reception area that boasts an empty desk, a row of empty chairs and one of those office plants that look as though they're made of plastic and never seem to grow, flower, form seed, die or do any of the other things that ordinary plants do.

Jackson and Price are standing outside the men's changing area, talking about when the autopsy report will be finalised, how long DNA identification will take and the like. Man-talk. I'm not included. I'm standing next to them in my long, white gown and ridiculous boots, feeling like an extra from some low-budget horror movie, when I notice that my heart is fluttering. Not a bad flutter, like when I had my moment at Cefn Mawr, but something definite all the same. I pay attention to these signals, because I often need physiology to show me the way to my emotions. A jumpy heart means something, but I don't know what. I let my awareness expand and go where it wants.

Almost instantly it finds the answer.

I haven't finished in the autopsy suite. I need to go back there.

The answer, when I find it, clicks into place. It makes sense. *Why* it makes sense, I have no idea, but I don't always bother with the whys. I just do what I have to do.

"Oh, just a minute — I think I left my spare pen in there," I mumble.

The two men don't break their talk. Jackson just looks down at me and nods. He's about six foot two, I guess, which makes him about a foot taller than me, and Price isn't much less. It's worse than I'd thought. I'm not just in a horror movie, I'm a dwarf in a horror movie. I taffeta-rustle back through to the autopsy suite, letting the door swing shut behind me.

The peace of the room welcomes me. I relax almost instantly. I can feel my heart rate slow and lose its jitteriness.

I reach for the light switch, but realise that I like the violet twilight that's starting to possess the room, so I leave the switch well alone.

I take my only pen and shove it under the cloth shrouding Janet Mancini, so that I have something to "find" if need be.

Apart from that, I don't *do* anything. I have one hand on Janet's enviably slim calf, the other on the gurney. The peace of the room sinks into my bones. It's the most peaceful place in the world. I bend my face down, so it's touching the blue hospital cloth over Janet's feet. There's a faint medical smell, but the human smells are long gone.

I'd like to stay there for ages, quite still, just breathing the empty, medical air. But I don't have long, so I force myself to move. I uncover the two bodies, just so I can see their faces again. Janet's expressionless one and April's smiling half of one. April's head bandage has fallen in again, so I smooth it out for her.

Here, without anyone to bother them, they look like mother and daughter. I can't tell anything about the eyes, of course — April doesn't have any — but her mouth is a miniature version of her mam's. Her little dimpled chin too. I stroke April's cheek, then Janet's as well. They're each as dead as the other. No reason to make distinctions now.

I stare at them.

Janet stares back at me. She's not saying anything just yet. Still getting used to being dead. April can't look, but she does smile at me. I don't think being dead is going to be too hard for her. Life was tough. Death should be a cinch in comparison.

We smile at each other for a while, just enjoying each other's company. I bend down to Janet's hair. Smell it, touch it, comb it through with my fingers. The combing releases both a smell of antiseptic and of shampoo. Apple, or something like it.

I stand there with my fingers in Janet's hair, trying to trace the root of the impulse that brought me here. Janet's scalp feels surprisingly delicate under my fingertips. I can feel little April smiling beside me.

Something in our interaction seems incomplete, but I don't know what's needed to complete it.

"Goodnight, little April," I say. "Goodnight, Janet."

It's the right thing to say, but the incompleteness remains. I pause a few seconds more, but to no avail.

The thing that was left hanging a few moments before is still hanging now, and I don't think I'm going to find it by waiting.

I don't want Jackson and Price to think I'm a freak, so I "find" my pen, cover the girls and go rustling out of the suite, brandishing it with a dumb look of triumph. The guys don't care. They're moving through to their changing area anyway.

I get changed slowly. Rubber boots in one bin. Oversized gown in another. The door to the cleaning cupboard stands next to the entrance of the women's changing room. Nice touch that. Don't frighten the men by letting them see mops and buckets. I swing open the door and stare inside. It's a big, roomy cupboard — a small room, really — with cleaning equipment. I don't know why I'm staring, so go out into the lobby beyond.

The men still aren't done. I don't see why I should wait for them, so I yell, "Thank you, Dr Price. See you tomorrow, sir." I push the door to leave and can't budge it. It doesn't pull open either. I'm trying to work out if these are unusually heavy doors and I'm just being weedy when Price comes out to help.

"I've got to buzz you out," he explains. "It's a secure area."

"Oh."

Everything's a secure area these days. What do they think? That the corpses will escape? We say goodnight — him automatically, me woodenly — and he buzzes me out.

Because I'm feeling a bit odd, I manage to get lost and end up tramping up and down some of those endless hospital corridors, looking for the way out. Pale yellow vinyl tiles that squeak underfoot and reflect too much fluorescent light. My head is full of hospital words. Paediatrics. Orthopaedics. Radiotherapy. Phlebotomy. I don't do well with the light or the words and I end up walking around at random. Taking lifts, up or down according to which way they were going at the time. Getting on and off when anyone else does.

Haematology. Diagnostic Imaging. Gastroenterology.

At one point, a nurse stops me and asks me if I'm all right. I say, "Yes. Quite all right," but I say it too loudly, and I go squeaking off down the yellow vinyl to show how all right I am.

Eventually, I realise it is the hospital itself that is making me feel weird. I need to get out. I find myself at a T-junction in the corridor, wondering how to find the exit, then realise I'm staring directly at a large black-on-metal sign, which says, WAY OUT→. I treat this as a clue and pursue it all the way to the main exit, where I find fresh air and a swell of wind. Cardiff air smells of grass or salt, depending on which way the wind blows. Or so they say. Mostly it smells of car fumes, the same as anywhere.

I stand in the entrance for a while, letting people push past me, feeling myself return.

I'm trying to remember where I parked my car when my phone chirps the arrival of a text. Brydon nudging me about the drink. The drink I'd forgotten about. I should go. I'm already late.

On my way to the car, I salute the mortuary.
"Goodnight, April. Goodnight, Janet."
I don't get an answer, but I bet April is still smiling.

CHAPTER
SIX

Sharp means sharp, and today no one is sharper, smarter or more bushy-tailed than me.

Not long into Jackson's morning briefing, I get my moment of glory.

He summarises the result of the meeting at the mortuary yesterday, then adds, "Fiona Griffiths will be getting her notes onto Groove as soon as she can. Right, Fiona?"

"Already done, sir," I say.

"You've done it?"

He doesn't believe me.

"All done. I didn't want to waste time."

He raises his eyebrows, which have turned shaggy before their time, so the gesture is a bit of a signature look for him. He's either impressed or (more likely) doesn't believe that I've done a decent job. But I have. I came in early and whizzed through it. I learned to type at Cambridge and I'm blitzkrieg fast.

"OK. Good. That means you lot can read all about it."

Jackson delivers a few other nuggets — the most important of which is that we've now got the full case files from Social Services up on the system — then hands over to Ken Hughes. Hughes summarises the first batch of findings from the door-to-door work. Number 86 Allison Street had accrued a good bit of hostility from its neighbours, being variously described as a drug den, a squat, a place taken over by the homeless and much more.

"Putting aside more fanciful ideas," says Hughes in his depressive, and ever so slightly hostile, monotone, "the general picture seems to be this."

He tells us that the house had been let out for some years, then fell vacant around two years ago. Landlord not yet traced. For some time it just stood there, getting quietly damper and older. Then the back door was forced, possibly by kids out to cause trouble, possibly by a drug dealer wanting a place to operate from, possibly by a homeless person wanting a roof for the night. In any case, once the back door was gone, the house began to attract trouble.

From the visual evidence, the house had certainly been used as a squat for a period longer than the Mancinis' few weeks of residence. It was highly likely that drugs had been taken in the house for some considerable period. If drugs were used there, they were probably dealt there too. If drugs had been bought and sold there, then it was likely enough that there were women selling themselves for drugs, although the place wasn't remotely nice enough to have prospered as even the most basic of brothels. (At this point, there's a muttered comment from one of the lads nearest Hughes and there's a burst of hard male laughter. Hughes catches the comment and glowers at the culprit, but we girls, standing at the back and edge of the room, are excluded from what will most certainly have been an extremely hilarious observation. Ah well.)

So much for the background. Specifics. Janet Mancini had definitely been seen around the place for the past several weeks. Farideh, the girl I'd talked to at the convenience shop, had reported seeing Janet several times. She remembered her hair — which meant nothing, because Janet's hair colour had been widely mentioned in the press — but she also correctly described some clothing and an item of jewellery that had been found at the house. She also, and this was the clincher, remembered selling Janet a frozen Hawaiian pizza, whose wrapper featured in the long inventory of the rubbish that had been found at the house.

"Hawaiian, sir?"

This question from Mervyn Rogers, who has been taking notes. His pen is poised and his face is serious.

Hughes is suspicious, because he thinks Rogers is taking the piss (which he is), but he's not sure enough to make a thing out of it, so he just confirms the pizza identification and moves on. A little ripple of amusement runs round the room and includes us girls this time. We're thrilled, I can tell you.

"Yes, Hawaiian. Mancini clearly had April with her in the house, because the same source confirms purchases of such typically childish foods as Cocoa Pops and Nesquik banana milk."

He knows he sounds idiotic saying this, so he glares angrily at us as he says it. He can't tear himself away from his written notes, though, and on he ploughs.

59

"Sources whom we take to be reliable and have confirmed Janet Mancini's presence in the neighbourhood all agree that they did *not* see April Mancini with her at the time. We are for the moment presuming that April was present in the house but not inclined or not permitted to go out."

He's got another few pages of notes to get through, but none of us can bear much more of it and Jackson steps in to rescue things.

"Anything else is up on Groove. Familiarise yourself with it all. Short summary: we have no reports of anyone other than the two Mancinis at the house. No reports of April Mancini being seen outside at any time. No reliable reports of any regular visitors, or irregular ones for that matter. Curtains always closed, lights off — no electricity, remember. No music. The place was quiet.

"So we have to shift resources to other lines of enquiry. CCTV. The nearest cameras — the nearest working cameras — were five hundred and seven hundred yards away. It's fairly likely that one of these picked up Janet Mancini at some point over the last few weeks. We need to see if she was with anyone at the time. Jon Breakell — where are you, Jon? There — you'll take the lead on that."

Because I feel on the fringe of the inquiry and want to make myself more central, I lift my hand. Jackson doesn't notice me, so I butt in.

"There's CCTV at the convenience shop too, sir. Maybe they'll have recordings."

There's a short exchange of conversation up at the front. Apparently someone's already noticed the shop's CCTV and getting access to their recordings is already on an action list somewhere.

"OK. Meanwhile, Janet. We need to dig into her past. There's a good chance she knew her killer, so we need to locate the people she knew and how she knew them. If she was working as a prostitute and was killed by one of her punters, then it's a fair bet that this wasn't the first time they'd had sex together.

"And let's not forget our anonymous female caller, the one who tipped us off about the house. That caller is still out there. There's been plenty of media, she knows we want to talk to her, but she hasn't come in yet. Anything that can lead us to her is also valuable.

"So. Tasks for today . . ."

Jackson starts listing tasks and responsibilities, and the briefing room starts to break up. No breakthroughs, no easy victory. No one's concerned yet, and there's a general assumption that the killer will be found and jailed. All the same, it's hard not to notice that we remain completely in the dark about who might have killed the Mancinis. Sooner or later, this optimism will demand fuel to keep it burning.

I head downstairs for the print room, but am interrupted by a knot of officers round the coffee machine, where Merv Rogers is being honoured for his wit.

"*Pineapple*," he is saying. "Adding fruit to a dish that is basically savoury. That's not right, is it?"

I squeeze round them. They don't make way for me or seek to include me in their banter. That's partly because I'm physically small. Partly because I'm junior. Partly because I'm a girl. And partly because people think I'm odd.

I continue down to the print room, where the ever-so-slightly Polish print manager, Tomasz Kowalczyk, is bustling around in charge of his papery domain.

"*Dzień dobry*, Tomasz," I tell him.

"*Dzień dobry*, Fiona. How can I help you today?"

"You shouldn't say that. It makes you sound like you're about to offer me fries."

At least Tomasz likes me. I'm here for some photos and I show him the ones I want from the system, which now boasts not only the crime-scene images but also some of those found among the Mancinis' possessions. Not so many of Janet, because I suppose she never had a regular person to take photos of her, but plenty of April. April in party dresses, April on a beach in Barry, April holding a huge toffee apple and laughing. She had wide blue eyes, like her mam, and when she laughed, everything in her face was laughing too. April Mancini, the toffee-apple kid.

I pick out about a dozen pictures in total. Some of Janet. Some of April. Obviously we've got printers upstairs, but only regular black-and-white ones. Tomasz's empire is responsible for all bulk runs, all colour printing, all fancy print jobs — and I'm after photo-quality reproduction. Tomasz makes me fill out some forms, which annoys me because I don't like forms, which means I make a mess of them, which means that Tomasz ends up doing them for me. I polish up one of my nicest smiles and give it to him when he's ready. He tells me to come back in forty-five minutes.

Back at my desk. Aside from my work on the Penry case, I've been tasked with two jobs for today. One is answering any Lohan-related phone calls from the general public that come in as a result of our media appeals for information. The other is to get stuck into Janet's Social Services records and see if there's anything useful there. A grandly named executive summary is what Jackson is after. I take three calls — one nuts, two sane but probably useless — and get stuck into the paperwork. I'm good at this kind of thing. That's what Cambridge training does for you: reading mounds of stuff fast and extracting the useful part quickly and clearly. All the same, I'd prefer to be on the inquiry proper, so I work fast, accumulating brownie points.

I'm hard at work when my phone goes. It's Jackson, using the speaker phone on his desk, to tell me to come over. No reason offered.

I enter his office, but hover by the door. Jackson does door-open meetings and door-closed ones. The former sort are usually better, but I've had more than my share of the latter. I wait for a signal as to what kind of meeting this is and, from the way he looks at me, guess it's a door-shut one. I close it.

"Yes, sir?"

"Good work on the autopsy. Fast, accurate. Good stuff."

"Thank you."

"You're doing the same on the Social Security files, I expect?"

"That's the plan."

I sit down. Jackson is being nice to me, which is a bad sign. I wonder what I've done wrong.

"A sudden burst of hyperactivity on the Fiona Griffiths front usually means you want something. So why don't you tell me what that is?"

This throws me a bit, because I didn't know I was so obvious.

"If possible, sir, I'd love to be full time on Lohan. I think I could contribute."

"Of course you could. Every officer in the department *could* contribute."

"Yes, but at the moment, I think there are only two women on the team: DC Rowland and DS Alexander. Obviously, they're both brilliant officers, but I just thought that they might be stretched a bit thin. I mean, I know you can get men to do some of the interviews, but it's not quite the same, is it? I mean, if prostitution is involved."

I've hardly explained myself brilliantly, but Jackson knows what I mean. It's all very well getting men to interview prostitutes, but there's a certain kind of interviewing they just can't do. There's always a shortage of women for those interviews, and uniformed officers are often brought in to try and address the shortfall. Which is fine, except that having a female officer in full uniform, baton, handcuffs, radio, protective jacket and boots doesn't exactly get the girly juices flowing. Jackson is a grizzled old sod, which means that he remembers the old days, when prostitutes were just bundled off down to the interview rooms to be shouted at by a whole bunch of blokey officers who exuded dislike, lust and distaste from every masculine pore. But he's also an intelligent officer who recognises that the old days weren't exactly bathed in an eternal glow of success, and that other approaches have their merits too. Merits like actually working, for example.

"No," he says, "it's not the same."

I'm not sure if he's saying that I'm on the team or not, so I stay in my chair, trying to read the runes.

"What else are you on? You're getting Penry ready for court, aren't you?"

I tell him that I should be done with that by the end of the week, which seems implausibly early, even to me.

"And our friends and colleagues at the CPS think so too? Gethin Matthews thinks so?"

CPS: Crown Prosecution Service. And no, they don't think so, nor does DCI Matthews, but I tell Jackson that they will think so by the end of the week.

He does the shaggy-eyebrowed thing at me. "And if you join Lohan full time, which DC Griffiths am I going to be getting?"

I open and close my mouth. I don't know what to say.

"Look, Fiona. Lohan would benefit from additional female staff. Of course it would. Gethin asked me if I wanted you transferred over when the case broke. And I thought about it. I wanted to say yes."

I mouth the words "Thank you" again, but the thank you isn't the point just now. It's the thing that's hovering over the horizon, about to sock me between the eyes.

"The good DC Griffiths I'd have like a shot. But the other one . . .? The one I ask to do something and that something never seems to get done. Of if it gets done, it's done wrong. Or done slowly. Or done after fifteen reminders. Or done in a way that breaks the rules, causes complaints or pisses off your fellow officers. The Griffiths who decides that if something is boring her, she's going to make a mess of it until she's moved to something else."

I make a face. I can't say I don't know what he's talking about. I do.

"Am I, for example, going to get the officer who makes Brendan Rattigan's widow break down over some bit of total speculation about her dead husband's sex life?"

I bite my lip.

Jackson nods.

"I got a call from Cefn Mawr this morning. Now, I handled it. No official complaint. Nothing that's going any further. But I didn't want to have to take that call. I don't want to have to wonder all the time if you're going to use your mature, intelligent judgement or if you're going to say and do the very first thing that comes into your head."

"Sorry, sir."

Jackson doesn't mention it — he doesn't have to — but he and I are both well aware of another incident last year. I was still in my first year in CID, meaning that I was still a training detective constable, effectively on probation. There was a missing persons case, and we were going through the long process of interviewing friends and family. I'd been paired up for most of the interviews, so I could learn from my elders and betters. Then I was given my first solo gig out in Trecenydd — basically a person we were sure had nothing to tell us, just so I could practise my skills and develop my confidence. Unfortunately, the interviewee thought it would be a clever idea to put his hand on my breast. I didn't react with dignity and maturity, and a few minutes later I was calling an ambulance, so that my interviewee could receive treatment for a dislocated kneecap.

The whole incident was a bit hard to get into any kind of perspective. On the one hand, no one doubted that he had sexually assaulted me and that I had a right to defend myself. On the other hand, there were questions raised about the appropriate and proportionate use of force. A disciplinary inquiry cleared me of wrongdoing, but these things do leave a smell.

Jackson was in charge of that case too. He handled it well, I guess. He yelled at me the regulation amount, then did a "Help us to help you" bit, which I think he meant. We had a long discussion, in which he said all the right things and I said all the right things — or most of them, at any rate — and the right forms were filed and the right procedures followed. Five weeks later, I found myself on a course in Hendon with officers from all over the country on managing dangerous and ambiguous situations, the gist of which was that you were meant to talk firmly to people before dislocating their kneecaps. There were eighteen officers present on the course. I was one of just three women and the only one who didn't look like a lesbian. The course must have worked since I haven't disabled anyone since.

"It's not really about sorry, is it now, Fiona?"

"No, sir."

There's a long pause. I'm normally OK with pauses. I can pause with the best of them, but this one is weirding me out because I don't know what Jackson is doing with it.

"If I may," I say, "I think it's significant, the reports we've had about April Mancini at Allison Street."

"We haven't *had* any reports of her there. Not a dicky bird."

"Exactly. There's this window seat in the front window there. One of the SOCOs told me that they found piles of April's pictures dropped down behind the back. She must have sat there for hours, drawing. Hours and hours. In the front window."

"Yes, but there are curtains across the windows. Doesn't look like they were ever opened."

"That's what I mean. What kid wouldn't open up those curtains when Mam went out? You get a good view from the front of the house. I mean, good for Butetown. You see everything that's going on. Most kids, even if they weren't allowed out, would be sitting in that window staring out. April didn't. I think she was terrified, and I think she was because her mother was. It was fear that took them to that house, and whatever it was they were frightened of caught up with them and killed them. I mean, I know we can't be positive, but it seems like a theory for now."

Jackson nodded. "Yes. Yes, it does."

We seem to have tumbled into another pause, but I decide that it's Jackson's turn to get us out of this one, so I just stay sitting with my mouth shut, trying to look like a good, professional detective constable, a little half-smile on my face by way of defence.

"Fiona, I don't want you on Lohan. Not properly. Not while I'm in charge. If you want to continue working on Lohan in a support capacity, then that's fine with me, as long as I don't get any more calls like the one I had this morning —"

"No, sir —"

"And as long as you don't injure anyone, piss off DCI Matthews, make a mess of any work you don't enjoy doing, get on well with your colleagues and in general act like a good, capable and professional detective constable."

"Yes, sir."

"Any fucking around and you're off the case altogether. You're this far from being a phenomenal officer." He opens the finger and thumb of his right hand a couple of inches. "And you're this far from being a right pain in the arse." He holds up his left hand, and his finger's resting on his thumb and not going anywhere.

"Yes, sir."

Another pause kicks off, but I'm all out of exciting pause strategies and I just sit there waiting for it to end.

"I think you could be right about April. Why nobody saw her. Poor little bleeder."

Yes, poor little bleeder.

Little April, drawing flower pictures in a stinking room. Little April, told never, ever to open those curtains. Little April, whom Farideh never saw. Little April, invisible to everyone except her killer.

Jackson nods to say I can leave, so I go downstairs and pick up my photos from Tomasz.

CHAPTER
SEVEN

Back at my desk, I run into Brydon. Our drink together last night confused me. When I'd got his text yesterday, I'd assumed that the drink was a coppers'-night-out sort of affair. The kind of thing that happens at least once a week, a bunch of people ending up in Adamstown, drinking in the sort of bars that will be making work for our uniformed colleagues a little later in the evening. I'm not always invited to those things, but I've been to a few. Me and my orange juice. Only later did I realise that Brydon had maybe meant his invitation as a date. Not a big flowers-'n'-candles date maybe, but as a sort of toe in the water, a deniable date, a drink ready to morph either into a flowers-'n'-candles jobbie or a simple drink between work buddies. I'm rubbish at decoding these things. I don't even realise that there are codes involved until it's all too late.

Last night was a case in point. Because I hadn't given the drink any great weight, I turned up late and without letting Brydon know that I was on my way. Result: when I finally arrived Brydon had indeed joined up with a couple of office colleagues, and we all had a faintly tedious but good-hearted coppers' night out. With hindsight, I think maybe that's not what he'd originally intended — and now maybe I've sent him a signal indicating that I'm not interested in a flowers-'n'-candles evening with him. I never meant to send any kind of signal, and I'm not sure that I'd have sent that one if I had meant to.

"Hey, Fi," he says.

"Hey." I grimace at him. An attempted smile really, except I've got my head full of Jackson's bollocking and my hands full of photos of dead people.

"All right?"

"Yes. You? Sorry about yesterday."

"That's OK."

"I was in a muddle last night. I didn't mean to. I wasn't trying to —"

"That's OK. Don't worry."

"Maybe we could do it again sometime. A drink. I'll try my honest best not to make a complete pig's ear of it."

He grins. "Good. Half a pig's ear would do fine. Definitely. Sometime soon."

"OK. Good. Thanks."

I don't want Brydon poking around my photo pile, so I put them face down on the desk and sit on them.

"You're OK? You're not looking your normal relaxed and untroubled self."

"Jackson just gave me a bollocking. About, um, seven out of ten. No. Six out of ten." I try to calibrate the bollocking, benchmarking myself on the assumption that the whole kneecap thing was worth a ten.

"Oh, who's in hospital this time?"

"Very funny. No, listen, could you do me a favour?" I shove some papers at him, the ones I've been working on for Penry. "If I get some teas, will you add up this list of figures and tell me what you get?"

I set him to work with a pencil and calculator, shove the photos in a drawer and go to get tea. When I come back, Brydon has an answer, the same as the one I had, and about £40,000 higher than it ought to be.

"Problem?" he asks.

"No. Not really. Just too much of a good thing."

"You know, if you get stuck with this, you should get the accountants in. No reason for you to do all the number-crunching."

I nod, too lost in my own world to tell him that we've already got some accountants involved, and they're coming in for a meeting tomorrow morning. A shortage of accountants is not my problem.

"Who the fuck steals from their employer to buy one-sixth of a racehorse?" I say out loud.

Brydon probably answers me, but if he does, I don't hear him. I'm already reaching for the phone.

CHAPTER
EIGHT

I work like a bluebottle all that day. At half past twelve, Bev Rowland passes my desk on her way down to lunch and invites me to join her. I'd like to, but I've got a mountain of work to climb if I'm to have half a chance with Jackson, so I tell her that I'm going to eat a sandwich at my desk, and I do. Feta cheese and grilled vegetables. Bottled water. Consumed in a nice little hum of busyness. I don't even let any chargrilled aubergine slip from the sandwich down into the keyboard, a faultless exhibition of desk lunching technique.

I find out lots of things I never knew. Things about thoroughbred registers. How racing syndicates work. Where the money gets paid. I find out things I didn't want to know. Things that disturb me when I find them. Things that I wouldn't have bothered to look for if Jackson hadn't given me a kicking. By the end of the day, I've done nothing at all on Mancini's damn Social Services reports and my desk is awash with printouts from Companies House and Weatherbys, the thoroughbred breed register.

The phone rings and I answer it, absently.

It's a Lohan caller, one of only five that day. The case has had plenty of publicity, but it's a sad fact that, despite April's death, the public aren't much moved by the killing. The death of a mother and child would normally generate upwards of a hundred calls in a day. Because of Janet's murky past, however, this case has generated almost nothing.

The caller introduces herself: Amanda, knew Janet slightly, only calling up because her daughter had been friends with April — same age, same school.

"I didn't know whether to phone or not, then thought I might as well. Hope that's all right."

"It is. Any information can make the difference." I run through the questions I'm meant to ask. Known associates, stuff like that. Amanda's as helpful as she can be, but she doesn't know much. The only "known associates" she knows are other school mams, none of whom sound like obvious sink-droppers.

"Did she have a reputation?" I ask. "You know — did other mothers talk about her as being a bad sort or a bit wild?"

Amanda pauses. That's usually a good sign and it is now. Her answer is reflective and considered.

"No, I wouldn't say so. I mean, the school was quite mixed. I don't mean race-wise, though that too. I mean, there were the yummy mummies, the dolled-up chavs, the ordinary mums, everyone. Janet, well, she wasn't well-off, was she? She was never going to get invited along to the next yummy-mummy coffee morning or whatever. But she was OK. She used to worry over things. Like she asked me how Tilly — that's my

75

six-year-old — got on with her reading. I think she felt she should be doing more to help April, but didn't quite know how. But a couple of times Tilly went over to April's for tea, and there's no way I'd have let her go if I'd had any worries."

"Amanda, do you know how they died?"

"Pardon?"

"How and where. They were in a squat. It was filthy. There was just one mattress upstairs, which they must have shared. No sheet. One not very clean duvet."

Another long pause. I worry that I've cocked up again. Said too much. Been untactful. Upset someone who's now going to go and call Jackson. I think maybe Amanda is crying on the other end of the line. I try to put things right.

"Sorry, Amanda, I didn't want to —"

"No, it's OK. I mean, what happened happened."

"I was only telling you because —"

"I know why. You wanted to see if I said, 'Well, that just proves that Janet Mancini was a waster after all.'"

"And?"

"And she wasn't. She *wasn't*. You know, I didn't *like* her particularly. I'm not saying I disliked her, we just didn't have much in common. But she lived for April. I know she did. If she took April to a place like that, well, she must have been terrified of something. That or her whole life just fell apart for some reason. Even so, *I'd* have looked after April. Course I would. I can't believe it. Sorry."

By the end of this, Amanda is crying outright, apologising, then crying some more. I listen to her and say the things that I'm meant to say. I might even say the words "All right, all right" at some point, which sounds naff to me, but Amanda seems OK with anything.

I've never cried once during my time on the force. Indeed, that hardly says it. I haven't cried since I was six or seven, ages ago anyway, and hardly ever even then. Last year, I attended a car accident, a nasty smash on Eastern Avenue, where the only serious casualty was a little boy who lost both his legs and suffered significant facial injuries. All the time we were getting him out of the car and into the ambulance, he was crying and holding his little tiger toy against his neck. Not only did I not cry, it wasn't until a few days afterwards that I realised I was meant to have cried, or at least felt something.

I reflect on all this as Amanda cries and I say, "It's all right," like a mechanical toy, wishing one day to find some tears of my own.

Eventually, she's done.

"Amanda, would you like to come to the funeral? We don't yet know when it'll be, but I could let you know."

That sets off another round of crying, but Amanda comes good with a "Yes, yes, please. Someone ought to be there."

"I'll be there," I say. "I'm going to be there."

The call ends, leaving me faintly dazed. I'm going to the funeral, am I? That's the first I know of it, but I realise that I do really want to go. I've also got DCI Jackson's comments buzzing in my ears from earlier. Was that the good DC Griffiths, the one with the great interview technique? Or was that an example of the bad one, a fingernail's breadth away from triggering another complaining phone call to the boss? I don't know and right now I don't care.

I've got too many things in my head and don't know where to put them all. The racehorse that Penry co-owned had five other owners. Four of those five were individuals. One was an offshore, privately held company, with no publicly available information about its ultimate ownership. But it had two directors and a company secretary — D. G. Mindell, T. B. Ferrers and a Mrs Elizabeth Wilkins, respectively — who were also directors and company secretary at one of Brendan Rattigan's shipping companies. One of the individual co-owners of the racehorse was also a senior executive at Rattigan's steel company. A second man was godfather to one of Rattigan's children, something I learned from a Google search that took me to various gossip magazines. I couldn't trace any links between the other two owners and Rattigan, but that doesn't mean they didn't exist.

And besides, even the links I knew about seemed to imply something. A company, almost certainly belonging to Rattigan, owned a chunk of a racehorse, as did one of his company executives and one of his oldest friends.

As did Brian Penry.

Maybe that was just coincidence. Maybe he had nothing to do with Rattigan and he was just there to make up the numbers.

Or maybe not. Penry had spent about forty grand more on his bullshit purchases than he had stolen from the school or than could be accounted for from his salary. It was, I reckoned, just about possible that Penry had found some way to cash in his police pension in order to fund his purchases, but who on earth would do that? And why?

Why, why, why?

Isn't it more likely that Penry had a source of cash from elsewhere, and if he did, then isn't it also possible that Rattigan was in some way the origin of that cash? And if so, and if Rattigan did have some connection to Mancini, then doesn't that imply that Penry is in some way involved with the Mancini murders?

If, if, if.

It's five o'clock.

Because I haven't made any progress on the Mancinis' Social Services records, I decide to take them home. Little Miss Perfect has a minor issue of conscience there. The records are confidential and we're not meant to take confidential data out of the office on a laptop, but that's the kind of rule which is broken all the time and I feel the need to get home reasonably early. Tonight is meant to be a gym and ironing and tidying-up sort of night, but I have a feeling that it's going to be nothing of the kind.

Before I leave, though, I decide I need a bit of human contact. I go on the prowl and come across Jane Alexander, who's just back from house-to-housing. I find Jane a bit scary, if truth be told. The sort of person who always manages to find outfits that are seasonal and fashionable, but also affordable and sensible, simultaneously professional and CID-ish yet at the same time gently calling attention to her gym-bunny physique. Plus her hair is always immaculately blow-dried. Plus she never gets food stains on things. Plus she doesn't make perfectly helpful witnesses cry for no reason, and I bet she can go years at a time without kneecapping perverts. She doesn't disapprove of me exactly, but I can't believe that she approves of me, and I'm always five per cent scared when I'm with her.

On the other hand, right now Jane seems genuinely pleased to see me. She complains about the day she's had and how she still has to get her interview notes up on Groove. I'm a much faster typist, so I offer to help in exchange for some tea. It's a done deal. She gets us tea. I sit and type. She sits on the desk and interprets her writing whenever it's hard to read, and in the gaps we gossip and fall silent or drop our voices whenever a male colleague strolls by. It's a nice way to spend time.

At the end of the type-fest, I say, "It's pretty skinny stuff, isn't it?"

For a second Jane thinks I'm criticising her notes and I fall over myself trying to set her straight. It's not her notes I've got an issue with, it's the lack of leads that seem to be coming from all our work.

"Oh, but the forensic stuff will give us a few names. Maybe CCTV. A few interviews. Something will start to come out. That's the way these things go."

Jane's attention is wandering away from me now. Jacket on. Hair flicked in one blonde shampoo-ad movement out from the collar. A quick inspection to make sure that every fold of fabric is obeying orders. Handbag, mobile, purse? Check. Perfect lifestyle all present and correct. Spaceship Alexander is ready for blast-off.

"See you tomorrow," I say, already scared of her again.

She gives me a nice big smile, bigger than regulations require, although also one that shows very orderly white teeth, nicely arranged against exactly the right shade of lipsticked lips.

"Yes, see you tomorrow. Thanks, Fi. I'd have been stuck here for ages otherwise."

"You're welcome."

And she is welcome, truly. She blasts off to wherever it is she berths for the night. She has a husband and a young son. I have neither and go back to my desk to pick up my stuff. My computer is still on. Brendan Rattigan's Platinum card is catching a last ray of evening light.

Janet Mancini was so scared of something that she took her daughter to that house of death.

Brendan Rattigan liked rough sex with street prostitutes. His wife didn't tell me with words, but she said it every other way she possibly could.

Brendan Rattigan died in a plane wreck, but his body was never found.

His card was reported lost, but Janet Mancini had it.

Brian Penry bought a horse with stolen money, and Brendan Rattigan, it seems, was one of its co-owners.

Five thoughts buzzing round my head like flies in a glass jar. No one but me appears to care about these things, but that doesn't make the flies go away.

I Google around and come up with the names of some racecourse photographers who do a lot of work at Chepstow. Also one who works at Ffos Llas in Carmarthenshire, and another couple who work at Bath. I make some calls, get through to four voicemails and leave messages. Get through to one real person — Al Bettinson, one of the Chepstow boys — and make an arrangement for tomorrow.

I don't have a good feeling about any of this, but there's at least one fly I reckon I can squash, so I do my best to squash it. The Air Accidents Investigation Branch reports on every plane accident in the UK, no matter how small the plane or how minor the incident. All AAIB reports are available online, so I call it up, print it off and shove it into my bag, along with my laptop, the photos and a bundle of papers.

It's been a long day.

And it isn't over yet.

CHAPTER
NINE

Home. Blue sky and golden light.

I live in a newbuild house in Pentwyn. A modern semi built on an estate of modern semis. Every house has its own bit of paved driveway, its own garage, its own tiny patch of close-board-fenced garden behind. Human rabbit hutches.

I let myself in.

The garden faces west and light fills the back of the house. I wander outside and have a smoke, a slow one, sitting on a metal garden chair with the sun full in my face. When was the last time it rained? I can't remember.

Why was I so sure that I was going to go to the Mancinis' funeral? Don't know.

I sit outside until the sun leaves my face, then go to the shed to check my plants, before locking up and going inside. There's not a lot in the fridge and I feel tempted to nip over to my mam and dad's, just ten minutes and half a world away. When I first moved in here, I did that all the time, so much so that I realised I hadn't properly left home. These days, I work hard to be more independent, so the fridge is all I've got to work with. Some lettuce. Some sushi, which is a day past its sell-by date, and a bean salad, which is turning fizzy three days after its. I decide that fizzy beans won't kill me, plonk everything onto a plate and eat it.

After a few minutes of vegetating, doing nothing, I stir myself. Upstairs, I have some Blu-Tack somewhere and retrieve it, rubbing it around in my hands to warm it up. There's a mirror over the mantelpiece in the living room. I don't know what the point of mirrors is. They tell you what you already know.

I take it down and lean it up against the fireplace, which — talking of useless — has never been used. I get the Mancini photos out of my bag and spread them out across the floor and sofa. A dozen faces staring out at me. Faces I last saw in the mortuary.

I arrange and rearrange the pictures, trying to make sense of them.

The ones of Janet are good. There's one that we found inside a bundle of photos at the squat. One of her alive. Face to the camera. Decent lighting. Nice, clear, useful. It'll be a perfect picture to use when asking people to identify her. But it's dull. It doesn't hold my interest. I don't like it.

I much prefer a shot of her taken at the crime scene. All expression gone. The contingencies of life wiped away. The person herself remaining. That photo I could look at for hours, and might well do except that it's April who fascinates me. April Mancini, the sweet little dead girl. I've got six pictures, all eight by tens.

In a sudden burst of decisiveness, I thrust the pictures of Janet back into my bag and Blu-Tack the pictures of April up over my mantelpiece, in two rows of three. She's a peaceful presence. No wonder she was a popular child. I like having her in the house. The toffee-apple kid.

"What do you have to tell me, little April?" I ask her.

She smiles at me, but tells me nothing.

I work hard for the rest of the evening. Social-work case files, the AAIB report. My Penry case notes, ready for the accountants tomorrow. Names. Numbers. Dates. Questions. Connections. At a quarter to one in the morning, I stop, feeling done in and surprised at the time.

April's face is staring down at me in sextuple. She's still not telling me anything, so I tell her goodnight and go to bed.

CHAPTER
TEN

Accountants come in pairs these days. A middle-aged man in a dark suit and a film of perspiration, plus his younger accomplice, a woman who looks like her hobbies are arranging things in rows and making right angles.

I don't know if I'll be able to persuade Jackson to let me on to Lohan. He said not, but he also bothered to call me over to his office to say so. I can't help feeling that our session was three-quarters bollocking, one-quarter encouragement, or something like that. In any case, it's clear I won't be allowed to work on Lohan properly until I've got the Penry case tidied away. I can't do that until the lads and lasses of the Crown Prosecution Service tell DCI Matthews that they're as happy as pigs in muck, and that won't happen until the accountants have produced a report that will give the CPS what they need.

"We're missing about forty grand, yes? Known expenditures about forty grand greater than incomings, even taking into account the money we know he stole."

"Yes, £43,754," says the more senior accountant, giving me the precise number, as though I were unable to read it. "Of course, that's only an estimate. We don't have receipts for most of the expenditures."

I stare at him. *Don't have receipts?* The man's an embezzler, for fuck's sake. You expect him to keep *receipts?* But I don't say so. Instead I say, "The question is, when can you get us your report?"

"I believe we're scheduled to deliver in the second week in June. Karen . . .?"

The younger accomplice has a name, apparently. She also has a goal now. Find a precise date. Eliminate numerical uncertainty. She dives into her papers to give me the exact date.

I interrupt.

"Sorry. That won't work. We've got a gap of forty thousand pounds to make sense of. We'll need your report right away, even if it's only in draft form."

We squabble for a bit, but I hang tough. I make it sound as though the forty-k gap is their fault, which it isn't. As though DCI Matthews is pissed off, which he isn't. Just to make my arguments even more effective — and to annoy the female accomplice — I seize the moment to make a mess of the papers in front of me. No right angles anywhere now. No rows of anything. She's feeling twitchy.

Eventually, I win. They'll deliver a draft report to the CPS by the end of the week, and a final version later in June. I'm delighted, but do my best not to show it. To celebrate, as I'm showing the accountants out of the building, I shake hands with the female accomplice very earnestly and for three seconds longer than she is comfortable with. "Thank you *so* much for your help,"

I say, looking into her eyes. "Thank you *so* much." As she's retrieving her hand, I give her upper arm a quick squeeze and fire off a for-your-eyes-only smile at her. She almost runs for the door.

Upstairs again, I arrange things for the day. DCs are meant to show initiative, but my experience has been that no one likes it if you show too much and I've got a feeling that DCI Jackson would like it if I showed a whole lot less. On the other hand, DCI Jackson has spent less time than I have with the Weatherbys breed register, and a lead is a lead is a lead.

So I arrange a meeting with the Crown Prosecution Service. I say I'll come over to their place. I let Matthews know that's what I'm doing and tell Ken Hughes (because Jackson is out of the office) that he's going to have to put someone else on Lohan telephone duties.

When I'm done, I take my papers, get into my car, drive out of the car park and call the CPS people. I tell them that something's come up and is it possible to postpone things? We make a new appointment for four that afternoon. Six clear hours to use as I please.

I drive as fast as speed cameras permit over to Chepstow. A Welsh town, but one that smells English. One of Edward's castles plonked high above the river to remind us all of how it is. There are invaders and the invaded. The English fuckers and the Welsh fucked.

Bettinson's house is a redbrick 1970s thing, all sliding doors and brown carpets. I don't get to see it, though. His office is in his garage. No natural light, just halogens overhead and on the desks. Two desktops and

88

a laptop. A printer. Camera gear and lighting equipment stashed in a corner.

Bettinson has got that look photographers have. Like a teenage boy has been given stubble, a hangover and freedom from female interference. He's wearing a black T-shirt, cargo pants, and a much-pocketed canvas waistcoat hangs over the back of a chair. He is brown-haired and doesn't use deodorant.

"Coffee?"

"I'm fine, thanks. If you don't mind, I'd rather just get cracking."

Bettinson is surprisingly solicitous. He's going out on a job, but he's happy to let me browse. He sets me down at one of the two desktops and shows me how things are arranged. Photos from each day are filed in their own folder. The photos have numbers for filenames, and the folders are arranged by date, but nothing else. A spreadsheet logs which assignments were done on which days, plus some cost and billing information. He shows me how to toggle between viewing the photos as thumbnails and full images.

"They're arranged by date, so if you don't have a date . . ."

"I know. And I don't."

"Do you want to say what you're looking for?"

I hesitate. "I'm trying to find a connection between two individuals. They both had an interest in racing, both lived locally. A photo of them together at the track could establish a connection." I don't want to say more. I'm paranoid about Jackson finding out that I'm here.

"Well, you've got some dates, then."

Bettinson gives me a couple of old racecourse calendars with race dates marked, asks me again if I want coffee, then swings off with his camera gear.

To judge by his accumulated images, Bettinson does all sorts. Weddings. Schools. The races. A bit of news photography. But his biggest gig by far is the racetrack and maybe forty per cent of his images are shot there. Most of those, inevitably, are of horses, but twenty per cent of Bettinson's racing images — so getting on for ten per cent of the entire archive — deal with shots of owners and punters, social scenes down at the track.

I can't think of any better way of doing it, so I start the week before Rattigan's death and work backwards. After forty minutes of solid work, I've covered one month of the archive. Coloured shapes move behind my eyelids when I close them. Endless photos of men in tweed jackets, horses' noses, rosettes, silver trophies, award ceremonies with low stages and country-themed adverts, horsey women in padded gilets and fashionable babes with big smiles and low tops. Nothing of Penry. A few of Rattigan when one of his horses won something, but nothing that seems to help much.

I wonder if I've missed something.

I check my voicemail, worried that there's a message from Hughes or Jackson. There isn't.

I carry on working. More horses. More tweed. More rosettes. The more photos I look at that aren't the photos I'm after, the less optimistic I become. By the time Bettinson gets back, I haven't found what I'm looking for and I'm very unsure if there's any such thing to be found. I need to leave.

He asks if I've got what I was after, and I tell him no.

"They're, like, specific individuals you're searching for?"

"Yes."

"Are you allowed to say who?"

"Well, don't shout it around, but yes, Brendan Rattigan is one of the two. I've —"

"Rattigan? You should have said. Fuck, I've got about a million Rattigans."

Bettinson taps the other machine. The one I wasn't working on. He starts to jiggle it out of hibernation.

"I thought I was looking at the complete archive? I thought I was running through your archive?"

"The *archive*, yeah, that's the archive. Actual *projects* and stuff are here. I'd never find the stuff otherwise." He clicks around on the other desktop and brings up a whole list of files. He clicks the first one and gets up a shot of Brendan Rattigan grinning with a bay racehorse leaning over his shoulder. "I did loads of stuff for the Rattster. Lost my best client when that plane went down."

He asks me if I have a laptop, which I do, and he attaches a cable to it from the desktop, then copies across the entire collection. Five hundred and sixty-three megabytes of it.

I arrive forty minutes early for my meeting with the CPS.

CHAPTER
ELEVEN

The CPS meeting goes OK. I accomplish less than I wanted but more than I expected. There's some sort of plan in place anyway, and they're happy with the stuff that the accountants are preparing.

It's not strictly required, but I go back into the office afterwards to finish up a few things. Inevitably, I can't resist looking at my laptop. And within five simple minutes I have what I'm after. Penry and Rattigan together at the racetrack. Champagne glasses in hand. Laughing hard at something off camera. Celebrating a winner, from the look of it. Friends, not just casual acquaintances. I flick on through the entire collection. Perhaps I'm missing some shots — I'll need to do this more thoroughly at some point — but I can log at least seven dates when Bettinson snapped Rattigan and Penry together at Chepstow. Fifteen months. Seven dates. The millionaire and the embezzler.

One of the dates is in March 2008. That fact resonates for some reason, but I can't work out why. I stare at the list until I decide that staring isn't a useful investigative technique. I also realise that I haven't done any of the things I came into the office to do, so I hurry up and finish them quickly now.

I work till eight, then go over to Mam and Dad's for dinner. It's been my first time this week, so I don't feel like I'm breaking my own rules. They live over in Roath Park. A place of big houses, mature trees and geese flying overhead, heading for the lake, commuters late home from work. I only have to turn up Lake Road to feel easier in my spirit. This place calms me. Always has, always will.

Dad's not at home, his huge mock-Tudor home, because he's off at work, but Mam's there, and Ant-short-for-Antonia, my youngest sister, who's turning thirteen now and is already nearly my height. I'm the runt of the family, it is clear.

We eat ham, carrots and boiled potatoes, and watch a TV chef telling us how to bake sea bream in the Spanish fashion.

Ant has homework that she wants help with, so I go upstairs with her. The homework in question takes about fifteen minutes. Ant waits for me to give her the answers, then writes what I tell her to. She plays music, fiddles with her hair and tells me some involved story about her friend's dog who damaged its forelegs and now has a kind of trolley it pushes itself around on. She lies on her belly on the bed, kicking her calves in the air. She's at that age when she's almost exactly half girl, half young woman. I wonder if I did that at her age. Lie on my belly, kicking my calves behind me. Feeling ordinary, feeling safe. Three years before my life exploded.

"It hurt its legs?"

Ant looks at me as though I'm an idiot and continues talking to me in that way which makes every sentence a question. "*Yes*, the front legs? She didn't lose them exactly, but there was some problem with the joints? So she couldn't walk on them any more?" She continues with her tale. I don't bother to listen and she doesn't expect me to. She wants a TV in her room and is trying to enlist my support in lobbying Mam.

"Don't ask Mam, Ant. Ask Dad."

"He says, 'Ask your mam.'"

"I know. And she's never going to say yes, is she? It's Dad you need to work on."

"Kay has one."

Kay's my other sister. Eighteen. Smokily sexy with random teenage sulks. Trails broken hearts behind her, I'd imagine.

"She didn't get one till she was sixteen. But you need to forget about Mam anyway. Work on Dad."

"But tell her, though, will you? She listens to you."

I don't know that Mam does listen to me, but I'm flattered that Ant thinks she does. In any case, I doubt if Ant's life would be made better by a TV in her room.

"You can get everything on iPlayer anyway."

Ant makes a face at me. I think betrayal of the sisterhood, teenage alienation and a certain existential suffering are the major themes of the look in question.

I spend a bit more time with Ant. Then go down and have a cup of herbal tea with Mam, who's on to a box set of some Trollope costume drama by now and switches it off with reluctance.

"Have you seen it yet? It's good."

"Not yet."

"I'll lend you the set when I'm done, if you like."

I smile at Mam in a way that allows her to believe that a box set of Trollope would make my life complete. Slipping my shoes off, I poke my feet onto her lap for a foot cuddle, an old tradition of ours.

"Ant seems to want a TV a lot."

"Only because her friends do. She doesn't really like the telly that much."

"It'd keep her off the computer, though, I suppose. God knows what kids find on there these days."

Mam makes a face. Everything was better when people wore corsets, that sort of face.

"You can get limiters, you know. Things that stop the kids watching TV after a certain point in the evening or whatever."

Mam pulls my toes for that. "You're as bad as your father, you are."

I smile at her. Ant is halfway to her telly, I reckon.

"I should go, Mam. Thanks for supper."

"Don't be silly, love." She hesitates momentarily, but doesn't invite me to stay the night, which she used to do reflexively for the first nine months I was living away from home. She still does it sometimes. "You coming over at the weekend? Your dad would love to see you."

"Maybe."

"Oh, don't be like that, love. You know he would."

I laugh and explain as I put my shoes back on. My "maybe" meant *maybe* I might come over at the weekend, not *maybe* my dad would love to see me. But Mam's misinterpretation was instructive. When I'd got my job as a copper, Dad went through a bit of a thing with me. Me choosing to do that with my life, given the things he had chosen to do with his — it wasn't treachery, exactly, but he couldn't quite get his head around it either. All that created an atmosphere, but it only got actively difficult when I transferred into the CID. Dad thought that was uncalled for, and said so. I thought it wasn't his business what I did with my life, and said so too. Forcefully. We had our first ever proper row, in fact, a row I believed now lay far behind us. Perhaps Mam's reaction indicates not.

"I'd love to come over if he's around," I say. "He's off all weekend, is he?"

"No, he'll probably go in on the Saturday. They've been busy this year."

I laugh. "That's good. It's good to be busy."

I get a face from Mam for saying that. She's a good Methodist girl married to a man who's never been a very good Methodist boy and Mam's liked none of the businesses that have claimed her husband's attention.

Or so she says. She could have married a bank manager.

I tell Mam to enjoy her Trollope, and she promises again to lend me the DVDs when she's done. I say goodbye and not to get up, but she does get up and sees me to the front door. It's a big house, without Dad in it.

I head home.

I'd forgotten the photos of April, so they take me by surprise. I don't turn the living-room light on and instead stare at the photos in the half-light of the streetlamps outside and the ceiling lamp through the half-open hall door.

Six little Aprils. No answers.

There's one answer I can find, though. I boot up my laptop and check the notes I made on all those racing websites. March 2008, Penry's horse had some veterinary problem that kept it from racing for eight weeks. A problem with its leg. It was Ant's story about the trolley-dog that jogged my memory. Yet Penry and Rattigan were still there, down at the track, all buddy-buddy over champagne and horse dung. Horseracing friends without the horse.

I'm tired. I close down the laptop and grin up at April. I get six little smiles back again.

"It's been a long day," I tell her.

No answer to that, but it wasn't a clever thing to say. She's only got night and it stretches for ever.

"I know where you did your drawing," I say, changing tack.

No comment.

"I used to draw a lot as a kid. I probably did flowers like you."

No comment again six times over, which makes for a lot of silence in one small living room.

I don't know if I did draw a lot as a child. Because of the illness in my teens, my childhood seems like something viewed over the other side of a hill. Little snippets come back to me, but I don't know where they've come from or if they're true. I've got a story about my past more than actual functional memories of it, but for all I know, everyone is in the same position.

Maybe childhoods are things we live through once, then reconstruct in fantasy. Maybe no one has the childhood they think they've had.

"You think too much," says April, or at least, that's what she'd probably say if she didn't have this *omertà* thing going.

"Goodnight, sweetheart. I'll see you tomorrow."

I sleep well and dream of Ant endlessly combing her hair in front of a mirror. In the dream, I want my hair to look like hers, but I know it never will.

CHAPTER
TWELVE

Five the next morning.

Phoebus and a rosy-fingered dawn are already busy, lighting up the sky over Llanrumney, Wentlodge and all points east. I know within a minute or two of waking that that's it for my night.

I sit up in bed for a few minutes. It's strange. I live on a modern housing estate crammed with humans and I can hear almost no human noise. There is a strange feeling in my body, a kind of prickle, but I can't put words to it and I don't know why it's there. When I was coming out of my illness, my doctors gave me exercises to practise. They were mostly bullshit and had very little to do with my recovery, but they're still a fallback for me and I practise them now. Try naming the feeling. Fear. Anger. Jealousy. Love. Happiness. Disgust. Yearning. Curiosity.

My doctors had imaginations as narrow as their educations and never came up with more than six or eight emotions in total. I've got more imagination than is good for me and I have far too many words. A sense of excess. That's a feeling, isn't it? Desire for simplicity. Envy of my sister's hair. I've got a hundred names for a hundred feelings and they all seem clumsy and inappropriate, like wooden coins. Clothes fitted for a different body shape.

My failure to get to grips with whatever I'm feeling freaks me out a bit. I practise my breathing, the way I've been taught. *In*, two, three, four, five. *Out*, two, three, four, five. Long, slow breaths, bringing my pulse rate down. A good exercise. When my breathing and my heart rate are both in good shape, I give it another two minutes, then pull a dressing gown on over my pyjamas and go out into the garden. I smoke, drink tea and eventually eat a bowl of muesli and half a grapefruit.

The morning becomes gradually noisier. More traffic. The sound of breakfast TV from next door. Kids kicking balls around outside. A delivery van. I like it. I want to go on sitting around in my dressing gown, looking at my stupid shred of lawn, smoking and thinking of nothing, but duty calls. The last couple of days have been good ones for me, and I don't want to lose their momentum. I don't want to lose the security of doing something in a way that earns the respect of my peers. In an ideal world, I'd earn the respect of my bosses too, but you can't have everything.

I shower and get dressed — reasonably hurriedly, because inevitably I've let things get late and I'm in danger of missing the sharp-means-sharp morning briefing. As I leave the house, I notice my clothes. Beige trousers. Brown boots. White shirt. Khaki jacket. The office version of combat wear. Ah well. I don't have time to change and probably wouldn't even if I did. I compromise by applying a neutral, almost self-coloured, lipstick using the car's rear-view mirror. It doesn't make much difference, but I bet Ant and Kay would approve.

Up and at 'em. I drive, too fast, into the office and am in the briefing room by eight eighteen, and only the fourth officer present. The prickle is still there, albeit fainter, and I'm deciding to treat it as a good thing, a positive energy. An energy I intend to put to work.

When I log into the Weatherbys website, I know what I'm looking for and I'm not surprised when I find it. Brian Penry only owns a share in one racehorse, the one I already know about, the one whose existence I've already cross-checked. But Brian Penry has an alter ego, a Welsh one, Brian ap Penri, who owns shares in a further four horses. Two of those have Rattigan as a co-owner. One more has at least two close Rattigan associates as co-owners. The last has no obvious connection to Rattigan, but I bet there is one all the same. One of Brian ap Penri's horses was a winner at Chepstow the day that Brian Penry's horse was laid up and unable to race.

Five horses, not one.

The two men were friends, not acquaintances.

And yesterday's £40,000 hole has just grown into something a whole lot deeper, and ten shades darker. I wonder whose bodies may be lying at the bottom.

I'm standing up and reaching for my car keys before I've even logged out of the site.

CHAPTER
THIRTEEN

Rhayader Crescent, off the Llandaff Road.

The ordinariness of the place is almost overwhelming. The street is modern, but nice modern, semis mostly. The architectural touches are gently reassuring — dark hardwood details, those expensive bricks mottled by the firing process to give an old-fashioned look, paving slabs that are made of concrete but have been made to look like they're stone or clay. This is the kind of street that politicians seek to conjure when they talk about the hard-working families of Middle Britain. A street for teachers married to nurses. Middle managers and youngish solicitors. Also, it turns out, a street for bent ex-coppers.

I ring the doorbell of number 27. There's a car — an old Toyota Yaris — in the parking area. No area set aside for lawn or flowers. No pots. The neighbours have at least made an attempt at planting. The weather's warm again today, but with a kind of pressing closeness. Distances blur into haze, while objects that are close at hand seem preternaturally distinct. The whole world wants a good hard rainstorm to wake it up. Or I do.

I'm about to ring again when I catch noises from within — a shape glimpsed behind frosted glass — then the sound of the catch and the door swinging open.

"Mr Penry, I'm DC Griffiths. We met six weeks ago, down at Cathays Park."

I say this to jog his memory. We met when he was being interviewed, but I wasn't, by a long shot, the main entertainment of the day, and I don't expect him to recognise me. I use the term Cathays Park, not police headquarters, because first of all Cathays Park is the term any copper would use, and second of all, I'm not here to set neighbours gossiping.

Penry's a tough-looking fifty. Hair still dark, worn longish and untidy. His face is mostly unlined, but the lines that are present are deeply marked. He's the sort of cop that would have fit straight into a 1970s TV drama, all leather jackets and free-flying fists. Right now, he's wearing jeans, with no shoes or socks, and a ropy old T-shirt that advertises some sailing club. His feet are tough and brown, with nails like slices of old horn.

He doesn't answer immediately, or open the door any further, or indeed do anything else, other than look at me and smirk to himself.

"Well, it must be important if they've sent you."

"May I come in?"

It's a real question, that, as Penry well knows. If he says no, he means no, and the English law of "My home is my castle", the law made sacred by Magna Carta and everything since, means that his "no" has the strength of iron bars. He pauses a long time before answering.

Then, "Do you want coffee?"

His question sounds invitational, but his posture is anything but. He's still hanging on the door, scratching his chest inside his T-shirt, showing me his abs and pecs and body hair as he does so. Oh, here we go.

I don't normally respond well to macho stuff, but I'm being very professional here, and in any case, Penry knows every police trick in the book, so I stay calm.

"I don't drink coffee, but if you've got herbal tea, then I'd like that."

"You'll need to wash up first. The mugs are in the sink."

Ah, it's the washing-up now, is it? But I stay professional. "Well, if you sort out the tea things, I'll wash the mugs."

That response gets another second or two of posturing, then Penry swings the door open and walks through to the kitchen. I follow.

The house is messy, but not slum messy, just single-man messy. Or perhaps more accurately, single-man-who's-not-expecting-to-pull messy. He's not kidding about the mugs either. His kitchen sink is piled with dirty crockery, with a fatty scum on the surface of the water. The lid of his kitchen bin is missing, and the bin bag is full of beer cans, juice cartons and ready-meal wrappers.

Penry ostentatiously flicks the switch of the kettle from the off to the on position. That's his share of things done, he's telling me. He stands behind me, too close, deliberately crowding my space. I don't want to touch his mugs or his crockery, let alone put my hand in the orangey oil slick of the sink. I compromise by picking the two least repulsive mugs, running the tap into the sink and doing a quick, crude decontamination job. I present Penry with the mugs, wash my hands in the still running water, then turn off, just as the orangey slick threatens to spill out over the draining board. There's an overflow pipe in there somewhere, but it's not draining anything fast, if at all.

Penry puts coffee granules in his cup and pours hot water on. No milk. No sugar.

"I don't have any herbal tea, no."

He grins at me, challenging me to respond.

"Good. Then I won't need this." I take the unused mug and toss it into the open bin. "Shall we talk?"

Penry leaves the mug where I threw it. He seems genuinely pleased by this interaction and barefoots his way into the living room, which is untidy but not squalid. There's a view through to the back of the house, where Penry's Georgian-style conservatory juts out into suburban Cardiff like a schooner nosing into Cowes Week. I pause for just long enough to take it in. The conservatory is empty, except for some plastic wrapping and some builder's debris, swept into a corner but not cleared. A pair of keys hang on a nail banged into the frame next to the door. The piano is there, but dusty from the building work and I can't see any music for it.

Penry sits in what is obviously his armchair — unobstructed view of the TV — and I take a seat on a sofa, where I get a slightly angled view of his face.

"I thought you might like to know where our case stands. I also have one or two further questions. And of course the more you cooperate, the more your cooperation will be taken into account when it comes to sentencing."

Penry stares at me some more, then sips his coffee. He says nothing. It was a back injury that forced retirement, and I notice that his chair is one of those ugly orthopaedic numbers. There's a packet of paracetamol on the table. You always suspect that when a cop retires with a back injury, it's mostly a question of the job having taken its toll over the years. Too many years of hassle and retirement the easy option. The paracetamol suggest otherwise, however.

I quickly summarise where we are in preparing the prosecution case, which is pretty much all systems go, following my meetings with the CPS and the accountants yesterday. I advance a guesstimated timeline for the prosecution.

He answers with a question.

"How old are you?"

I pause for long enough to demonstrate that I'm answering because I choose to, not because I'm stuck in one of his stupid games.

"Twenty-six."

"You look younger. You look like a baby."

"Good skincare."

"Who are you working with?" I don't immediately answer, so he prods away. "Gethin Matthews probably. Him or Cerys Howells, I should think."

"Matthews."

106

He acknowledges the answer with a slight grunt, but he's already sacrificed a little of his authority. He's managed to establish that I have answers that he wants, and he's reminded himself that baby-faced DC Griffiths here is representing grizzled old DCI Matthews. It's the first tiny victory I've won. He must know that somewhere, because he reverts to silence. For the first time, I hear the slightly asthmatic whine in his breath, the only thing you could hear on the interview tapes.

I let the pause continue. It's my pause now. I own it and I ride that fact for all it's worth. When I do speak, I say this: "The thing is, we're both coppers, so we both know the deal. You stole money. We found out. You're going to jail. The only question is, how long for? That's the only factor you can influence.

"And we both know that the less cooperative you are, the longer you go down for. In a way, your life is fucked up whatever, but you can choose just how fucked up to make it. Anywhere on a range from quite a bit to quite a lot.

"With ordinary crooks, I don't expect too much. They don't cooperate, because they're not being rational, or they can't bear to help us out, or whatever else it is. You're not like that. You're a pro, so you'll be hard-headed about these things. And the fact that you're telling us nothing makes me curious about a few things. And if you care to know what I'm curious about, then I'll tell you."

The silence in the room now has a frozen quality to it, as though it might crack like ice if you tried to move against it. Penry can't tell me that he's hungry for information, because that would offend against his crappy little power games. On the other hand, he can't say anything else, because he wants to hear what I have to say. Once again, I let the silence do its work.

"Number one, where did your money come from? Some of it came from the school all right, but you spent more money than you stole, or your friend Mr ap Penri did anyway.

"Now, I'm going to take a wild guess and say I know the answer to that. I think the money came from Brendan Rattigan. But that brings us to question number two: what services were rendered in exchange for that money? As far as I know, multimillionaires aren't in the habit of giving something for nothing.

"And number three, just how much precisely do you know about this?"

From my case I extract the evidence bag with Rattigan's Platinum card inside it. Penry reaches for it, stares at it and hands it back. He's not even pretending to be uninterested now. His brown eyes have a complexity in them that was missing before.

"You might also like to know where we found it. We found it at number 86 Allison Street. An address where we found a woman dead and her daughter murdered. The mother may have been murdered too. We can't yet say for definite.

"So you see why I'm curious. If it were only the debit card and the fact that you happened to share an interest in racing with its owner, then I'd say it was all a coincidence. Something worth investigating maybe, but not the sort of thing that Gethin Matthews would start throwing resources at. As it is, though, your silence kind of connects you to that house, doesn't it? Any reasonable ex-policeman in your position would be cooperating with us to bring his sentence down. And you haven't cooperated at all. And the more you don't tell us, the more you're telling us that we have to investigate as closely as we possibly can. Which turns an ordinary little bit of embezzlement into something altogether more interesting. Something that's maybe just a step or two away from murder."

I finish.

I say nothing. Penry says nothing. As a way of gathering information, this trip has not precisely yielded a rich harvest, but not all harvests look the same or ripen quickly.

I stand up. From my case I dig out the INFORMATION WANTED notice that was up in Farideh's shop window and elsewhere in Butetown. I drop it onto the coffee table, but it slithers from there to the floor. Neither Penry nor I stir to pick it up.

"That's the murdered woman. That's her murdered child. That's the number you'd need to call with information."

I snap my case shut and go to the front door to let myself out. Penry doesn't move. "By the way, this house is a shit-hole," I call through to the living room. "And you should see someone about that asthma."

Outside on the too-bright street, I take stock. Penry is probably watching from the living room, but if he is, I don't care.

His Yaris is dark blue. There's a rust spot above the offside wheel arch and the whole car could use a wash. Who owns shares in a clutch of expensive racehorses and drives a car that, if not quite rubbish, isn't exactly a thing of beauty? The only CDs I could see in Penry's house were modern rock music and a couple of Classic FM compilations. Those musical tastes might impel you to buy a piano, or then again they might not. But Penry bought one. An upright piano, a Georgian conservatory and a sink full of orange scum.

I look back into the living room. Penry is at the window scrutinising me. I smile, give him a twinkling wave and return to my car.

On my way back into the office, my mobile bleeps the arrival of a text.

Because I'm an extremely skilled police-trained driver, I have the resources to check my texts while driving without compromising the safety and security of other road users. Either that or I'm a selfish idiot. And this text is an interesting one. It reads, JANS NOT DEAD YOU LIARS IF SHE IS SHES LUCKYER THAN SOME. My first thought is that this is a wind-up from a colleague, my second that this is an answer to the notice I'd put in the shop window.

I pull over and jam the car into an available space on the Cowbridge Road. I text back, WHAT HAPPENED TO HER THEN?

And wait. I'm parked up by a chip shop. A young mum, overweight, leads two overweight kids of her own outside. One of the two, a boy with a taut red face, starts eating from a bag of chips, holding them away from his brother, jamming them successively into his mouth with a savage intensity.

Obesity. Violence. Drugs. Prostitution. A million different ways to screw up your life. Brian Penry chose embezzlement, his own sweet route to self-destruction. What made him take that turning? What accounts for the beat-up Yaris and the expensive empty conservatory?

Then, just as I think I'm not going to hear back, a text comes in. It reads, RICH PEPLE DONT HAVE POLICE SHIT ITS PEPLE LIKE JAN THAT GET IT.

There are two ways to read these texts. The obvious one is the way my colleagues will read them. They're deranged. They have zero evidential value. Maybe even subzero, given that the accusation made in the first text is obviously false. My colleagues might also gently note that there is a reason why requests for information are channelled through official 0800 numbers, not to officers' personal mobiles.

But that's not the only way to read these messages. For one thing, anyone who knows what happened to Janet Mancini is quite likely a poorly educated, drug-addicted prostitute, so bad spellings and non-existent grammar may actually be a sign that the texter is in a position to know something. And that second text is odd. It's making a connection — albeit a kind of crazy one — between Janet's death and "rich peple". That would mean nothing, except that Brendan Rattigan's card was found in Janet's squat. And that in itself would mean nothing, except that Charlotte Rattigan implied that her husband liked it rough and nasty. And all of that might still mean nothing, except that the frozen silence I experienced with Brian Penry told me that there were big things hovering close by, unsaid.

No other text comes through, so I send one back. I say I won't make any further attempt to make contact, but that whoever it is should feel free to call or text me at any time. I WANT TO HELP JAN AS MUCH AS YOU DO, I write, then press send.

Nothing makes sense.

It's why I became a policewoman, this ambition to make sense of things. As though the various mysteries and challenges of my life could be made better through the repetitive solution of other people's puzzles. I'm on a hiding to nothing, you might say, but even that phrase intrigues me. An act of concealment in one half. Nothing at all in the other. The phrase itself is a mystery wanting solution.

My brain is too busy. I figure that there's one way to lower the pressure and that's to make sure that Rattigan is well and truly dead. I root around in the back of the car for the AAIB report. I find a number and dial it.

With an extraordinary lack of bureaucracy, I am put through swiftly to the person I need to speak to.

"Robin Keighley." English voice. The sort of voice that Americans love to mock. The sort they associate with effete, end-of-empire aristocracy. But it's friendly and competent. Good enough for me.

I introduce myself and tell him why I'm calling. I ask him about the plane crash. He's open and easy with his answers, which roughly speaking follow the gist of the report. The plane had taken off from Birmingham and was heading for Rattigan's holiday home in southern Spain. They ran into bad weather, and the pilot reported an unidentified problem with the right-hand engine. He asked Bristol airport for permission to make an emergency landing. Permission was given. His course duly altered, then silence, then a short radio burst that basically consisted of two short expletives from the pilot, then nothing.

I speak to Keighley for about twenty minutes. The plane was a Learjet, a good plane, properly maintained. Until the very end of the flight, proper procedures had been followed. I notice, though, a slight hesitation in Keighley's voice when he mentions the pilot. When I ask, he says, "Well, nothing really. The pilot was experienced enough, but had no background in either the RAF or any of the big commercial airlines."

"Any significance in that?"

"Not really. RAF pilots are obviously trained to operate in extreme conditions. Equally, any pilot for a big commercial airline like BA will be put into a flight simulator every six months and have every kind of disaster thrown at them. Those guys have to take it all and pass their tests or they're grounded till they do."

"So maybe a pilot a bit less experienced than you'd like?"

"Less experienced than *I'd* like, yes. But then flight safety is my business. Rattigan's pilot was fully qualified to be flying the plane he was flying."

"Any evidence of foul play at all in the wreckage? Anything at all? Even a whisper of a hint that you

113

couldn't put in your report because there wasn't enough to go on?"

"No, nothing, but most of the plane is at the bottom of the sea. I couldn't rule out foul play, but have no reason to suspect it."

"Was this an aircraft type known to have problems? Does the accident fit any kind of known pattern?"

"Yes and no, I suppose you'd say. No in the sense that this was a perfectly decent plane and all the rest of it . . ."

"But?"

"But then again, if you do get human or maintenance error, you're most likely to get it with smaller aircraft owned by outfits that don't have the depth of technical and safety culture that you're going to find at BA, say, or any one of its peers. That's why most accidents are, and have always been, in the general aviation sector."

"So putting aside any official report, your gut feeling would be that someone cocked up. If the plane weren't sitting somewhere out in Cardiff Bay, you might have a chance of identifying the culprit. As it is, you're obliged to shrug your shoulders and chalk it up as one of those things."

"Putting any official report a *long* way to one side, then yes."

"Can I ask one last question? Off the record, non-official, wild speculation."

"Fire away."

"OK. Do you attach any significance to the fact that Rattigan's body was never found?"

I can hear an intake of breath down the line. Keighley is taken aback by the sudden turn in the conversation and he answers cautiously. "Significance, such as what, for example?"

"Let's just suppose there were a theory that Rattigan in some way arranged the plane crash. That he escaped, his pilot died. Or perhaps the accident was perfectly genuine, but Rattigan seized the opportunity to disappear because he happened to want to for some reason. Is there anything at all in the circumstances of the crash that would make better sense in the light of such a theory?"

Keighley is silent for a long ten seconds. Then he says, "Sorry, got to think about that," and is silent for another fifteen.

"OK, then I've got to say probably no. Nothing comes to mind, except maybe . . . well, Rattigan's body was never recovered. The pilot wore a lifejacket and was quickly identified and his body retrieved. If Rattigan had been wearing a lifejacket, then his body should certainly have been recovered too. And there was no sign of it at all. That *is* odd. Contrary to the rulebook, if you like. Yet even for that, there are a million innocent explanations, all of which might be more likely than your theory. If, for example, he panicked and simply failed to release his seat belt, then he'd have been dragged under by the wreckage. Or if he refused to put his lifejacket on, even if the pilot told him to, then that would account for it too. Stranger things have happened."

We talk on, and Keighley remains helpful, but I get nothing definite. I'm further ahead than I was. Further ahead into nowhere.

I hang up.

The prickle of energy that woke me this morning is still here and it occurs to me seriously for the first time that it might be fear. I try the word against the feeling. *This is fear. This is fear.* But I'm not sure. There's not that clicking-into-place sense when the word really matches the feeling. I'm not sure what it is. I don't yet have enough clues.

I drive slowly back to the office, breathing properly as I go.

CHAPTER
FOURTEEN

At four that afternoon, there's a briefing. All hands on deck. The DNA results are back from the lab and word is that some of the DNA comes with names.

You wouldn't quite say there was a hubbub, but there's a stirring in the waters, a frisson, a raised energy level that comes from people assuming that the investigation is about to start coming up with real results. It'll be the first time we can actually place named individuals in the house of death. All the report-filing, statement-taking, pavement-pounding and phone-answering that we've done so far hasn't, in truth, yielded a single clue of solid, undeniable weight.

At ten to four, the incident room is already busy. I've come down armed with my peppermint tea and one of those wholegrain energy bars. Jim Davis is at the coffee machine, driven as a piglet at a teat.

"Hey, Jim," I say, a little warily. Davis is not my greatest fan, but then the Fiona Griffiths Fan Club is a fairly select body in the CID. I got on better when I was in uniform, probably because I had less opportunity to express myself.

Davis acknowledges me with a nod, but he's in the midst of a moan-in with some of his buddies. The scuttlebutt is that recessionary budgets mean no promotions. Not from DS to DI. Not from DC to DS.

"More work, less pay. Always the bloody way, isn't it?"

That's Jim Davis's verdict. Personally, I can't see that a lack of DI slots is going to affect Davis's life chances all that much, but I don't say so. He has his coffee now and is about to plunge his yellow teeth in for another caffeine bath. I don't want to watch that and squeeze by him. One of his buddies whispers something — possibly about me — and I do catch Davis's response: a cynical laugh, hur-hur, hur-hur, accompanied by lots of savage head-nodding.

My lovely colleagues.

By this point the room is full. Hughes and Jackson do their processional thing to the front of the room and everyone falls silent.

Jackson runs through the DNA findings. The lab has examined over a hundred samples taken from the house. Of those, DNA was successfully extracted from a total of thirty-two samples, yielding seven different profiles. Of those seven, two were Janet and April.

Jackson pauses a moment, enjoying the moment of suspense, then releases his news.

"Of the five remaining profiles, we've got names on the database for four. That means we can place those four people at the house. We don't know *when* they were there. We don't know *why* they were there. But at least we're in a position to go and ask."

118

The briefing continues. The four names are Tony Leonard. Thirty-eight. Drug user. Small-time drug dealer — that's how he got his record. No known involvement in prostitution. The DNA sample in question came from a single hair, found on the dirty velour sofa in the living room.

Karol Sikorsky. Forty-four. Prosecuted three years ago for a replica-firearms offence, but the prosecution failed because of a screw-up in our chain of evidence-handling procedures. He was prosecuted and convicted instead for a minor charge of affray. Born Russian, but possesses a Polish passport, otherwise he'd have been deported. Sikorsky is suspected by the Vice Unit of having involvement in drugs, prostitution and perhaps extortion too. A poor-quality saliva sample was found on a glass in the kitchen. A much better sample — courtroom quality, no less — was found on the tip of a nail that projected from the living-room doorframe. Sikorsky must have pricked himself on it as he leaned against the door, and enough tissue remained to leave a high-quality trace of his presence. "A brilliant bit of forensic investigation, that," comments Jackson. "To notice the nail, to investigate it, to successfully extract a sample. Brilliant." We all give the absent SOCO a round of applause.

Conway Lloyd. Thirty-one. Arrested for a public-order offence in his early twenties. Never prosecuted, but his DNA has stayed on our database ever since. Thank you, Big Brother. Who needs civil liberties anyway? Big splatter of semen on the mattress upstairs. And hairs found. And saliva. And further semen stains found on the carpet downstairs. Not a tidy boy, our Conway. Bet his mam loves him, though.

Rhys Vaughan. Twenty-one. Might have been Lloyd's twin. Semen found in four different locations, including — get this — a knotted condom that sat in a little china ashtray by the upstairs mattress. Nice touch, that. Also saliva. Also hair.

"And," says Jackson, holding up his hand to shush us, "we've got one extra name from fingerprints too. We had preliminary results there last night, but I wanted to wait until we had the DNAs in as well, so we could plan our strategy better."

The extra name is Stacey Edwards. Thirty-three. Convicted of a couple of soliciting offences in her twenties. Five contacts with our vice officers in total over the years. Assumed to be still on the game now. Her fingerprints were scattered all over the downstairs of the house. "Including," says Jackson, "the one place we didn't expect to find anything." Dramatic pause for effect. "The washing-up brush." Laughter and a spatter of sycophantic applause.

"Now," he goes on, "strategy."

Jackson is a smart cookie. The bullheaded approach would be to go in all hot and heavy on the names identified. Try and force a confession. Trouble is, there's a good likelihood that anyone who came to the house to commit murder would have taken basic precautions. Even if the murder wasn't premeditated — and the choice of a sink as a murder weapon suggests that the level of planning was rather minimal, to put it mildly — any vaguely competent killer these days

120

attempts to defend themselves against crime-scene investigation. Indeed, our killer took at least basic precautions, since there were no prints at all found on the sink, which would have collected them perfectly.

Vaughan and Lloyd, on the other hand, took no precautions at all. Ditto Stacey Edwards. Maybe Leonard might have tried to clean up after himself, but I'd guess that Jackson doesn't believe he is likely to be our killer. Of all the names, Sikorsky is the only one who feels like either a possible killer or a man with connections to the killer. The prime suspect.

Jackson's conclusion — which is the same as mine would be — is that we need to treat at least four of the five names with a little delicacy. Treat them not as killers but as witnesses. People who can provide information. That may involve a little bullying, but not the kind of thing that Brian Penry was probably best at in his prime. Jackson starts to hand out assignments, as Hughes writes a new list of actions up on the whiteboard.

The briefing breaks up. I charge across the room to grab Jackson. I'm not the first there, but I'm persistent. As he ploughs his way back to his office, I tag alongside and enter his office in his wake.

I have a banter-rich intro all lined up, but the boss's face is tired and the way he says, "Yes?" isn't precisely designed to encourage. I decide to alter my approach.

"Stacey Edwards, sir. If I can be of help there —"

"Fiona. We've got Jane Alexander on that. She's working with" — he checks his notes — "Davis. Between them, those two have a million years doing this kind of thing. And Jane Alexander is a woman — I don't know if you've noticed — so we've got all the feminine tact we need on this."

I don't have a counter-argument. I just have an urgency of desire that I don't wholly understand. I use what I've got. "Sir, if you were a prostitute. Maybe a friend of Mancini's. Probably scared of the police. Maybe in possession of crucial evidence. Would you rather talk to Jane and me or Jane and Jim Davis? These girls are —"

"Women. They're not girls."

"I don't know why, sir, but this case really matters to me. I think I can contribute. I really want to contribute."

"You *are* contributing. You contribute by doing what you're told to do. That's your job."

"I know. I —"

I don't know what to say, so I don't say anything. Just stand there.

That seems to have the desired effect, though. "Where have you got to on the Penry thing?"

I brief him quickly. He half listens to me and uses the rest of his attention to check out my notes on Groove. I've got much further with the Social Security stuff than he has any right to expect and I can see he's impressed. I don't say anything about Penry's extra horses, those strange texts or about my conversation with Keighley. I just keep it clean and simple. The way the good DC Griffiths would do it, or the way I imagine she would.

122

He pulls his attention away from the computer and shoves the keyboard from him with an annoyed flip of his fingers. Going to the door, he yells for Davis and Alexander. They're not there, but minions scurry to do his bidding.

Returning to his seat, he tells me, "You fuck up, you fuck up at all, and you're never working on a delicate assignment for me again."

"Yes, sir."

"I'm going to ask Jane Alexander to give me detailed feedback on how you comport yourself in your dealings with Stacey Edwards. Alexander makes the running. You make the notes. She makes the decisions. You make the tea."

"Yes, sir."

He gives me a few seconds of shaggy-eyebrowed scrutiny.

"You must have worked late to do this lot." He gestures at the computer.

I nod. The repeated "Yes, sirs" are beginning to strain my subordination muscles and I let them pause for rest.

Our conversation is brought to a close by Davis and Alexander appearing at the door.

"Come in. Jim, I've decided we need an all-female team interviewing Edwards. Jane, I want you to lead. You'll have Fiona for support. Jim, go to Ken Hughes, get an alternative assignment off him. Is that all clear? OK, then get on with it. Out of here."

As we leave, Davis throws me one of the blackest looks I've ever witnessed. As he tramps off to find

123

Hughes, he's saying something under his breath and the only distinguishable word is "fucking". No question this time. He's talking about me. I wonder if Jackson deliberately put me in a position where Davis would see that I'd successfully bumped him from one of the crucial assignments.

Jane looks at Davis's retreating back. It's pretty clear that she's taken aback by the strength of his reaction. As she turns to me, she adjusts her face until it shows nothing but friendly competence. The perfect CID superior. But in between looking shocked at Davis' hostility and reframing itself for me, her face betrayed something else. A micro-expression that didn't last long enough for me to capture and understand it. But if I were having to guess, I'd say she's less than thrilled by having me as her interview buddy. Which is great. Just the effect I aim for.

"Let's go and . . ."

She indicates that we should go and have a pow-wow at her desk. No offices for the likes of us.

"Yes, ma'am." I try to make the "ma'am" light and jokey, but also respectful and genuine. I don't know how well I succeed. She doesn't award points.

When we're at her desk — her in her regular chair, me in a seat pulled up opposite — I say, "I suppose you'll want me to prepare an interview briefing? See what we can rustle up on Edwards before we go to see her?"

That's clearly a new thought for her. It wasn't the way Jim Davis had been going to go at things.

"Briefing? You think there's enough material for that?"

"She's had five contacts with our Vice Unit over the years. We've almost certainly got people who have a reasonable idea of what she's like. She's probably had contact with the StreetSafe people — you know, the prostitution outreach charity. I'm sure they'd be willing to chat with us, as long as we made it clear that Edwards isn't a suspect."

"OK, but, look, it's Friday afternoon now. We need to get on with it. Jackson is going to —"

"I'll get straight on to our vice records now. Then go and talk to the StreetSafe people this evening — they work nights, obviously. I can get some notes typed up overnight. Then I'll run those past whichever one of the vice boys I can lay my hands on tomorrow morning. We should be prepped to see Edwards by midday. It doesn't make any sense to call on her before that anyway."

Alexander raises her eyebrows at me in a "Why?"

"Because she's a prozzie. She works nights. Midday might even be a bit early."

Alexander listens to all this with a combination of surprise and amusement.

"Are you always like this?" she says.

"Like what?" I wonder if I've fucked up already. If so, that's just about my fastest ever fuck-up. I have my humble, anxious face on, and mean it.

"Like a one-woman work monster. If you think you can do all that, brilliant. But if not — you know, it would be OK just to go and talk to her."

She's being kind, not something I'm used to, so I blurt it out. "I'm not usually like this. It's just this case has really got to me."

"Is this your first child murder?"

"I suppose. I don't think it's that, though. Maybe it is."

"It is." Jane gives me a supportive grin. She's still blonde and blow-dried and perfect, but I think I've just located Jane Alexander the human being. "Why don't you give yourself a break? Jim and I were just going to go and call on Edwards. Play it by ear. That's what everyone else will be doing."

"Will it bother you if I do what I suggested? I honestly think I'd prefer to do it that way."

"OK. But careful, Fi. If you get overinvolved, there'll be a crash. There always is."

I want to ask her if she's speaking from personal experience, but I'm not brave enough, so I just nod.

"Yes, Sarge."

"OK, Fiona. Take care."

Back at my desk, there's a voicemail from Robin Keighley. An addendum to our earlier conversation. On reflection, there was something odd about the crash. The double expletive from the pilot, then silence. "Even in a serious crash, that kind of pattern is highly unusual. We'd normally expect continuing radio contact, even in cases where the pilot isn't sure himself what's going on. I wouldn't make too much of it. There could be a dozen different explanations. But there you go. You asked if there was anything

126

untoward, and on that basis I have to say yes. Not much. But something."

I listen to the message three times over, then log on to the *Financial Times* website and search for Rattigan Industrial & Transport Ltd. You can never read too much or too widely, I reckon. I research solidly for three-quarters of an hour.

CHAPTER
FIFTEEN

Bryony Williams wears a padded canvas jacket over a sweat top and jeans. Shortish hair with a bit of curl. She's tough, but in the right way. The kind of tough that doesn't rule out tender. She's rolling herself a ciggy and sitting on a low wall that marks the front garden of a boarded-up house.

"Want one?" She offers me her roll-up.

"No, thanks. I don't smoke."

I sit next to her on the wall.

"Busy evening?" I ask.

"Not yet."

She lights up and tosses the match away on the street. The Taff Embankment. About nine in the evening. Twilight. The orange sodium lamps are producing more light than the embers of sunset over the Irish Sea, invisible behind us. Blaenclydach Place comes down to meet the river here. Behind us, a row of Edwardian houses. In front, a strip of grass. Then the river. The grass has been recently mown and the air smells of cut grass and river mud.

A nice scene. Quiet. Pleasant. Except that we're in the heart of Cardiff's red-light district and, like the stars in the sky above us, the first prostitutes are

128

beginning to appear. I see one — leather jacket, pierced nose, short skirt, three-inch heels — strolling up and down the strip of grass opposite us. It was only on her third pass that I realised what she was. A couple of lads emerge from the Red Lion pub up the road from us, walk past the girl, then turn round and whistle at her. She flicks a V-sign at them and they walk on.

"You know why I'm here, right?"

"Yeah. Gill said you'd be coming."

Gill Parker: StreetSafe's project coordinator. Been running the show since 2004. Saint, hero, angel, nutcase. Take your pick. Bryony's hewn from the same stock.

"Stacey Edwards. Gill tells me you know her."

"Yep. We know Stace very well. Unfortunately."

"And you know why we want to talk to her?"

"Not really."

Williams's tone isn't exactly hostile, but it's not welcoming either. StreetSafe is a charity that hands out soup, condoms and health advice to prostitutes. When they can, they help prozzies off the game, off drugs, off the whole self-destructive merry-go-round. They've got good relations with the police, but what we do and what they do aim in different directions. Enforcing the law is one kind of challenge. Handing out friendship and sympathy is quite another.

I tell her, "Janet Mancini, drug user and part-time prostitute, died, probably killed. Her six-year-old daughter was killed too. There's evidence that the Mancinis were afraid, possibly in hiding, before their death. Stacey Edwards wasn't the killer." I tell her

129

about the state of the house and Edwards's prints on the washing-up brush. "It looks likely that Edwards was a friend, trying to help."

"Probably. The women usually stick together."

Williams doesn't seem keen to help much, so I apply a little force. "Bryony, you need to respect confidences, I know that. But my colleagues want to go in, kick down her door and give her a 'Where were you at the time of her death?' type interview. That kind of thing isn't going to help her. It probably isn't going to help us either, or the two dead Mancinis."

"So what do you want?"

There's another prozzie working the beat opposite us now. The two girls spend a few moments saying hi, then break the street into halves, each working her patch. Their heels don't make walking easy, so they mostly lean up against a lamppost, looking out at potential punters with vacant eyes. I realise that they're here because Williams is. She makes their world safer.

"I want to know ... everything. About Janet Mancini. About Stacey Edwards. About who Mancini might have worked with. About who controls these girls. Who makes money off them. Who might have a reason to kill Mancini."

Williams looks sideways at me, with half a grin. "That sounds like a two-ciggy question to me."

"I'd budget three, if I were you."

Williams's grin widens into a proper laugh. "Okie-doke." She makes herself another cigarette and starts opening up.

130

The "who makes money?" question turns out to be the easiest one. In the end, everything comes down to drugs. Ninety-eight per cent of all Cardiff's prostitutes are on class-A drugs. Any money they make from punters goes straight to their dealers.

"What about their pimps? They take a cut, presumably."

"Kind of. Most of the pimps are basically drug dealers. That's how they get the girls to stay on the game. It's a toss-up whether you want to call them pimps or pushers."

"And these people — pimps cum pushers — are local, or they're . . . ?"

"Mixture. Used to be mostly local girls and local pimps. Then there are more and more from Eastern Europe. South Eastern. Romania, Bulgaria, Albania. I'd say probably the majority of girls are foreigners now."

"Trafficked?"

"Don't know. What's trafficking? If you get some Albanian girl hooked on heroin and tell her she can earn better money in Cardiff, she'll probably choose to come. No one's putting a gun to her head. Is she trafficked or not? You tell me."

All the time she's talking to me, she's got her eyes on the street. Without a word, she suddenly gets up and walks a hundred yards, up along the angle of the river. Williams is talking to a third girl, one I hadn't even seen. She's away for five or ten minutes before returning. While she's gone, a couple of blokes walk past me, on their way back from the pub.

They stare at me as they pass. Their stare probably means nothing, but I feel like I'm being priced up. I also realise that the street is worse lit than I'd first thought. Scary. I nod at the lads as they pass, and they nod back. Probably not punters. Not everyone is.

Williams returns.

"The girls wanted to know who you were. I said you were police liaison."

"Near enough."

"Yep. You'll need to bugger off in a bit, though. You're making the girls nervous."

"*I* am!"

"Yeah, I know, I know. There used to be benches here, then the council took them away because they thought they encouraged prostitution. Like, what kind of analysis is that? Excessive street furniture. Yeah, that's the problem all right."

"Janet Mancini?" I ask.

"Never met her. Never heard of her — I mean, until reading it in the papers. She wasn't a full-timer. If she had been, we'd have come across her. Not me necessarily, but Gill or one of the others."

"A kind of amateur prostitute?"

"Yeah, if you like. She was on drugs, you say?"

"Yes, but she was a battler. It was up and down."

"She should have come to us."

"She had Social Services. They thought she was a trier. That's what makes it worse."

Williams nods. "Domestic abuse?"

"She was single."

"There'll be abuse in the background somewhere. There always is."

I hesitate for a second. Jackson's "Don't fuck up" message is playing loudly in my head, but I don't think I'm about to say anything wrong.

"Bryony, we've got a hunch — nothing more than that — that Mancini might have specialised in what you could call rough sex. Filthy squat. Maybe a bit of slapping around, that kind of thing."

"Slapping around? You're talking about violence against women."

"I know, I know. I'm on your side here, Bryony."

"Yeah. Could be. Kinky stuff pays more. Dangerous pays more. If she had a child, then in a weird way maybe she thought she was protecting her by working with fewer clients for more pay."

"Would you know which punters enjoy that kind of thing?"

Bryony laughs at that. "Fuck, no. Most of them, I should think."

"Do you recognise either of these men?"

I show her photos of Brendan Rattigan and Brian Penry. The longest of long shots.

Williams studies them before handing them back. "Nope. He looks like a piece of work, though" — meaning Penry.

"He is, yes."

"Don't recognise them. But it's the women we work with, not the men. Why? Who are they?"

I give her the names. Brian Penry, a former police officer. Brendan Rattigan, former rich guy.

She shakes her head. "Sorry."

"Nothing at all? Even hearsay is useful at this stage."

"Not necessarily — oh, sod it, I've forgotten your name."

"Fiona. Friends call me Fi."

"Fi. Fi, Fi, Fi. I'm crap with names. Sorry. But look, rumours are everywhere in this game. Girls who disappear from view have never just moved on. Something dark has always happened to them. There was one woman — I won't say her name — who everyone said had been killed by a couple of your colleagues in the Vice Unit. Then they'd disposed of her body in a warehouse fire, apparently."

"Huh?"

"She'd moved to Birmingham to live with her sister. I got a Christmas card from her."

I laugh at that, but there's not much mirth in my laughter. What must it be like to work in a profession like that? Where violence does happen and when fear of violence haunts everything you do or say or know? Janet Mancini may have lived with all that, but she'd wanted better for April.

Williams's eyes are back on the street. Up the river, one of the girls is talking to a guy. Then the two of them walk off, away from us. In the dying light, all I can see is her long, white legs walking away upriver.

"I'm going to make a move soon. Check on my flock."

"Sure thing."

"What's next?"

134

"Stacey Edwards. I'm seeing her tomorrow. Anything at all you can tell me about her?"

"Stacey. She's all right, actually. Heroin issue, of course. She's been working with us and really wants to get off the game. She's been helpful. Spreading the word for us. Her problem is getting over her addiction. It's not just a chemical thing for these women, it's an everything thing. Childhood abuse. Domestic violence by partners and drug pushers. 'Slapping around' by punters. A hostile approach from the police, often as not."

"But she was an evangelist for you. You reckon she'd have been there trying to help Mancini escape?"

"Yes, I do. From what you say, Mancini wasn't as far gone. She stood a better chance. Also . . ." She trails off, wondering whether to complete the thought.

"Yes?"

"Well, I don't know if it helps, but Edwards has a big anti-immigrant thing. I don't think it's racist, particularly. Her best friend is a West Indian woman. It's the business end of things she doesn't like. She reckons all these women coming in from the Balkans have made the game more dangerous. The drugs are worse, she says. More heroin coming in from Russia. Afghanistan originally, but it comes via Russia. And meantime, the women are made to work harder. Violence has become more common."

"From punters?"

"No, from the pimps and pushers. It's all got more organised, nastier. Anyway, if Mancini had had anything to do with the Albanian crowd, Stacey would have been doing her best to warn her off."

"We're looking for people who might have known Mancini. Obviously, Stacey Edwards would be one. If you know any others who might have done? Maybe friends of Stacey's?"

Williams considers that request, then shakes her head. "No. Can't help you there. I mean, I know who Stacey hangs out with, but I've got a duty of confidentiality."

"Janet Mancini is dead. That's why I'm asking."

"And Stacey Edwards is alive. That's why I'm shutting up."

I accept that.

I say, "I'm going to show you a phone number. I don't need you to give me a name or an address, but can you just tell me if you recognise the number?"

I show her the phone number that texted me outside the chip shop this morning.

Williams gets out her own phone and scrolls through her address book, searching.

"Yes."

"Would I be right in thinking that the owner of that phone number would be a prostitute who might well have known Janet Mancini?"

"I don't know if they knew each other, but yes to the first part of that question, and quite possibly to the second."

"And it's not Stacey Edwards?"

"You're not allowed that question, but the answer's no. Not Stacey."

The night is black now. The bushes on the riverbank are clotted with shadows. Williams in her canvas jacket is fine, but I'm feeling the cold now. The night and the danger. I don't like being here and I want to go.

"Good luck, Bryony. Thanks for talking."

"Sorry I couldn't help more."

"You don't know how much you've helped. *I* don't. Sometimes the little things turn out to be the most helpful."

"Hope so." Williams is doing her eagle-eyed thing, examining some interaction upriver that my eyes aren't practised enough to see. She gets up as well, ready to plunge into the fray.

"One last thing," I say. "When Mancini died, we were alerted by an anonymous phone call to a police station. But not here in Cardiff. In Neath. We've got no explanation for why it was Neath. Female caller."

Williams grimaces. "Stacey's sister lives in Neath. That's where she goes to get away. If she was shaken up by something . . . she'd have gone to Neath."

"*Thank* you. Fantastic. *Thank* you."

"You're welcome."

Williams reaches a hand out to me and I shake it. We like each other.

"You catch the fucker who did it," she tells me.

"I will. And you get your girls away from all this." I wave my hand at the riverbank and the darkness.

"Women, Fiona. They're women." But she's grinning as she says this, and I watch her white teeth and her ciggy pass away into the night. Saint, hero, angel, nutcase.

I make it back to my car and click the doors locked. I don't usually lock the car doors when I'm inside, but I do now. I didn't like that riverbank and its fluvial stink is with me still. Its smell is violence.

The plan — so brightly hatched next to Jane Alexander's desk — was to go on to talk to a couple more of the StreetSafe volunteers, but right now I'm not sure if I can face it. I think about calling home, but it's Dad I want to speak to more than Mam, and he'll be at work and calling him at work is always a nightmare. He shouts all the time and I never have his attention.

Then I think about calling Brydon. We haven't yet rescheduled that drink, but I don't read anything sinister into that. Lohan is eating a lot of energy from the department and Brydon will be feeling that just as much as me. But I can't bring myself to call him. He's a creature of sunlight, and I don't feel in a sunshiny place myself right now. Not since this case started to get a hold on me. I don't know what I'd say to Brydon.

I jiggle the phone up and down, needing something, but I'm not sure what.

Then I send a text. HEY, LEV. ARE YOU AROUND? JUST WONDERED. FI.

I press send. From where I'm parked I can just see the house on Blaenclydach Place where Bryony and I sat, but what lies beyond is hidden from me. I start the engine and am pulling out when I get a text back.

CAN BE IF YOU NEED. WHY? ARE YOU IN TROUBLE?

Don't know what to say to that. Yes, Lev mate. I'm a fuck-up and I worry that I'm on the brink of something horrible. So instead I calm things down.

NO. DON'T THINK SO. JUST CHECKING. FI.

I feel better knowing that he's around if needed. The thought fires me up enough that I call on another two StreetSafe volunteers. The information they give me fills out Bryony's picture a bit, but doesn't fundamentally change anything. The thing about Neath seems like a huge piece of information. Even Jackson is going to love me if I've found his anonymous caller.

At ten forty-five, I'm done interviewing. I zoom home. My car has a sat nav that alerts me to speed cameras, which is just as well, really. There's nothing much to eat when I get back. Forgotten to eat, forgotten to shop. I pile fruit and muesli into a bowl, then add an energy bar all crumbled up. That's a meal, isn't it? I scoff it. Then, as I'm tidying up — my version of tidying, I mean — I find an old packet of salami and eat that too, along with an only slightly suspect tomato. Feast.

Type up my notes, fast and furious. By a quarter past midnight, I'm all done. I close up. April's sextuple face shines out at me.

"We're getting closer, lamb," I tell her.

She shows no sign of caring. I've been awake since five and I'm knackered.

CHAPTER
SIXTEEN

The next day, what is there to say? I wake up far too early again. The kind of waking that prohibits any thought of further sleep. Same weird prickling in my body, made a bit better by knowing that Lev was on call if required. Another smoke in the garden, taking me well over my self-imposed weekly limit. Then another breakfast. Another drive into the office. Another briefing. It's Saturday, but you'd hardly know it. Lohan is the beast that eats weekends and munches overtime. Everyone's tired. Everyone's working hard.

Ted Floyd, a uniformed sergeant and a good friend of Jim Davis's, is having a quick cigarette outside Cathays Park when I turn up. Floyd was one of my early training partners on the force, but he cuts me now, in a way I think is almost certainly deliberate. Great.

And now this.

Jane Alexander and I arrive at Stacey Edwards's flat just a fraction before eleven thirty. She lives on a rough-looking estate in Llanrumney. Blocks of flats on the left, houses on the right. The kind of houses with builder's rubble in the front garden, rubble that's been there so long there are weeds growing in it. Broken fridges and decaying mattresses. And those are the houses. The flats will be worse.

I've dressed casually on purpose, but Jane Alexander is in a pale green linen suit over a creamy scoop-neck top, and her shoes have been chosen to match her suit. No one here looks like that, not even the social workers.

Edwards lives in a ground-floor flat in one of the blocks. Her doorbell isn't working. I try it a couple of times, and the flat's small enough and crap enough that we'd hear the doorbell if it were ringing.

Someone inside clatters down the stairs from the flats higher up and lets us into the entrance area. Stacey Edwards's front door is a flimsy thing with a polished plywood front. I knock on it. Then Jane knocks.

Still nothing.

I'd managed to persuade Gill Parker from StreetSafe to give me Edwards's mobile number. I call it. The phone rings inside the flat, but it's not answered. Jane and I look at each other. At the front of the block, there's a parking area with room for six cars. Just two spaces are taken. There's a silver Skoda and a dark blue Fiat.

I call Bryony Williams and ask her if she knows if Edwards has a car and if so what. She says she thinks it's a dark blue Fiat. I thank her, hang up and tell Jane.

"Maybe she's just popped round to a friend," she says.

Maybe. The estate doesn't look like the popping-round sort of place to me. I doubt if Stacey Edwards has Jane Alexander's popping-round sort of life. Further on down the road, a footpath out to the fields is enclosed between spiked railings that have been looped with barbed wire. It's that sort of place.

"We wait half an hour, then try again?" I say, making it a question.

Jane nods and we go back to our car — Jane's, not mine. If it were me, I'd want to drive a little distance away, so we didn't look like we were watching the house, but I'm trying hard not to boss things too much. For the time being, I'm trying to be the sort of officer that DCI Jackson wants me to be.

We wait half an hour, mostly in silence. Jane has a couple of hairs on the shoulder of her jacket and I pick them off for her, absent-mindedly, then stroke the fabric flat. She turns to me and smiles. I wonder what it would be like to kiss her. Quite nice probably. When I was at Cambridge, still trying to get my head together, I wasn't sure whether I was straight and had a short lesbian phase. Experimenting. I liked kissing women, but that was about it. Lesbian sex never quite worked for me. I don't miss it.

I don't share these thoughts with Jane. I'm not sure it would be a winning development for our friendship.

After twenty-six minutes, we're both twitchy and I try Edwards's mobile again. Still no answer. There's been nothing happening at the front of the flat and when we knock at the door again, there's still no answer.

Decision time.

We inspect the flat outside, peering in where we can, but there are heavy nets down over grimy windows and it's not possible to see very much. At the back, we get a

142

clear view into a small kitchen — cleaner than Penry's but hardly a model of its kind — and nothing else. There's a small frosted window — the toilet, presumably — which has been left ajar for ventilation. The window's at head height and offers a gap of about six or seven inches if opened to the max.

The gap's too small for a normal adult to climb through, but Jane has the same thought that I do. She looks appraisingly between me and the window.

Entering premises without permission and without a warrant is a big deal. Obviously, rules need to exist around these things, but that doesn't stop them being a nuisance. They make our life harder, which is precisely what they're designed to do. Anyway, we can't enter the property unless we're there to make an arrest, or unless we have reasonable grounds to suppose that entering is necessary to save a life or prevent serious injury to person or property.

"I'll call one of the StreetSafe people," I say.

I ring Bryony Williams on her mobile, basically fishing for her to tell me that she's worried about Stacey Edwards. She *is* worried, but doesn't quite come out and say it.

"Bryony, I need you to tell me that you fear for Stacey Edwards's safety and that you need us to enter her property. I need you to say that in so many words."

She thinks a moment, then says it. I hold the phone between Jane and me so that we can both hear her saying it. Then I thank Bryony and hang up.

Jane nods. "I'll just run it past Jackson first." She does. He's OK with it, even asks us if we want support.

Jane raises her eyebrows at me. Support means that if we want a couple of burly uniforms to bash a door down, then we can have them.

"I'll be OK," I say.

Jane hangs up.

"I think," I add.

There's a horrible rickety picnic table, one of those all-in-one things incorporating the benches as part of the structure, on a paved area at the back. We drag it under the window. I catch Jane looking at her hands afterwards, wondering where she can clean them. She's not the one who's about to slide through a toilet window.

I climb up on the table, which wobbles a bit but not too much. My version of "casual" for this visit involves a loose grey cotton skirt, flat shoes and a long-sleeved top. I can't see how me and the skirt are going to negotiate the window simultaneously, so I remove it. Jane takes it from me and tells me again that we can get support in. Too late really. By the time a girl is half naked on a wobbly garden table under a toilet window, she doesn't have much more dignity to lose.

I open the window as far as it'll go and stick my head and shoulders through. Inside, there's a toilet, a small basin with a mirror over, some clutter. I guess there's probably a correct technique for managing these things, but I don't know what it is. I thrash with my legs and squeeze with my arms and soon I'm balanced on my belly in the window aperture. I can see my own face red in the mirror and Jane's shape through the frosting on the other side of the window.

144

I kick on. My thighs scrape painfully as they come through the window and I'm suddenly scared that I'm going to lose my grip on the inside windowsill and come crashing down on my head. But I don't. I'm not quite sure how I manage it, but I slither through without calamity. I'm inside. The front of my thighs are scraped red and angry. Jane pokes my skirt through the window after me and I put it on. I've got dust and black mould marks all over my top, and my hair is full of crap as well. Jane definitely won't want to kiss me now.

I wash my hands and open the toilet door, then release the back door so Jane can come in as well.

We try the living room first. Nothing. Or rather, some needles, bits of foil, candle and matches. An old half lemon too. Some of the foil is blackened with candle smoke. Jane and I exchange glances, but we're not here to hunt for drugs.

Then the bedroom. White walls and tarty red drapes. A big purple duvet. Mirror. And Stacey Edwards. Her hands have been cable-tied behind her back. There's duct tape over her mouth. No pulse. No breath. Her skin is at room temperature. The only expression in her eyes is no expression at all. Not fear. Not rage. Not anguish. Not love. Not hope.

Jane steps to the doorway and dials out. We want support now. We want all the support we can get.

While Jane makes the call, I sit down on the bed and put my hand on Edwards's belly. She's fully clothed and her clothes don't look disordered in any way. I don't know what that means, but perhaps it means she wasn't raped before she was murdered.

In my head, a hundred thoughts, but one stands out. Jane Alexander and Jim Davis would have gone to interview Stacey Edwards right after the briefing yesterday afternoon. They wouldn't have had my lovely briefing notes. Jim Davis would have been a crap interviewer. I doubt if Edwards would have said anything to either of them. But she'd have been visited by police officers before her death. She'd have been given a chance, a warning, an escape hatch. Most likely, she wouldn't have taken it. Drug-addicted prostitutes with zero self-esteem usually don't. But the hatch would have been there all the same. That's all we can ever offer.

And I was too clever for that. Got Davis out and me in. Persuaded Jane to let us prepare for the interview beforehand. Arrived, oh so cleverly, at just the right time to catch Edwards having her morning cornflakes. And found her dead. No escape hatch. Just duct tape, cable ties and — I'll bet my car on it — a skinful of heroin and a murderer who closed up her nose. The lightest of pressure with finger and thumb. A minute. Two minutes. Five at the outside. Then he'd have been on his way, job done, as Stacey Edwards's thwarted little soul flew out of the window beyond him.

CHAPTER
SEVENTEEN

Seven thirty that evening and the incident room breaks up. Lohan is now in overdrive. When Janet Mancini died, most officers on the force would say, correctly, that these things happen when you mix drugs and prostitution. They don't mean that they should happen, that it's remotely OK for them to happen, just that they do. True, April's murder made the whole thing worse, but she seemed like collateral damage. Don't take drugs. Don't be a prostitute. Bad stuff happens when you break those rules. If your daughter happens to get killed, well, treat that as a memo to self on the importance of sticking to the straight and narrow.

But Stacey Edwards's death was no coincidence. Jackson's assumption — which I and everybody else share — is that the manner of Edwards's death was intended to send a signal. That Mancini's death was murder, not accidental overdose. That her death wasn't just a one-off. That there could well be others under threat right now. Edwards's murder was presumably intended as a warning. Keep your mouth shut or else.

As officers disperse, Jackson jabs a finger at me, then at his office. His face is craggy and inexpressive. I can't read anything there, but assume that there's going to be

147

some kind of bollocking, since Jackson seems to have a taste for it at the moment.

"Sit down," he says. "I want some tea. Do you want anything?"

The coffee machine dispenses teas and coffees. For my herbal stuff, you have to go to one of the kitchenettes and make it yourself. I can't ask a DCI to make herbal tea for me, so I just say, "No. I try to avoid caffeine."

"No fags. No booze. No *caffeine?*"

I shrug. A sorry-without-being-sorry shrug.

"You vegetarian?"

"No, no, I eat meat."

"That's something." Jackson makes a shaggy-eyebrowed look that would probably speak volumes if I had the code-book. But I don't. "You want herbal or anything?"

My face must show my indecision, as I try to figure out the right response. Jackson solves the problem by opening his door and yelling at someone to bring him tea "and something that tastes like wet hay for DC Griffiths here". He bangs the door shut.

"That the first time you've found a corpse?"

"Yes."

"Pretty grim, isn't it? I've found four in my time. No bloody fun at all."

"I had DS Alexander there. I'd have found it worse without her."

"You did the right thing. I shouldn't have assigned Jim Davis to that interview. You were right to prepare. I

148

think we can take it as read that Stacey Edwards was our anonymous caller."

"We'd have got to her alive if we'd gone straight out."

"Maybe. You don't know that. You might not have found her. You don't know where she was last night. We had no reason to think she was under threat. And even if you had gone out last night, she might still have been killed this morning."

"I know."

"You need counselling?"

"No. At least, I don't think so."

"It's there if you need it. Just say."

The teas arrive. Mine's camomile with the bag removed, so it's probably had about ten seconds to steep, not five minutes. It tastes like hot water with a very slight edge of hay, so Jackson's orders were obeyed to the letter.

"Go on, then," says Jackson, snouting up some tea. "Shoot. I know you've got a headful of theories and I'm dying to hear them."

"Not theories. Nothing as advanced as that."

"Right. Well, my theory and everyone else's theory pretty much fell apart today. That theory held that some punter killed Janet Mancini — deliberately or on purpose, who knows? — then killed the kid to shut her up. No forethought. No planning. No point. No follow-up. I'd say that theory is pretty much fucked."

"I don't have a theory. I really don't."

"But . . .?"

149

"But here are the bits and pieces as I see them. One, Brendan Rattigan's card was in that house. That's a hell of a strange place for a rich man's card to be. Two, his wife pretty much told me that he liked rough sex. She obviously didn't share that taste, she wasn't cool with it at all, but he did."

"That's still speculation."

"This is all speculation really. None of this is courtroom evidence."

"OK, but let's go with it. Let's say that Rattigan knew Mancini and used to visit her. Somehow or other she got hold of his card."

"Right. Number three, Brian Penry. Wild speculation, remember."

"Go on."

"OK, the thing that was making my head explode with that case was that he seemed to have stolen more money from the school than the school knew about. I just couldn't figure out how he'd bought all the stuff he had."

"That's hardly the point."

"No, I know. We have evidence enough to convict him on a dozen counts of embezzlement, so it was curiosity more than anything that kept me scratching. That, plus a feeling that I'd been doing my sums wrong."

"But you hadn't."

"No. Or rather I had, because I'd managed to miss the fact that Penry owned shares in more racehorses than we knew about. He'd taken some very basic steps to disguise his name, that's all. His horses all seem to be co-owned with Brendan Rattigan or his chums. Logical deduction: Rattigan was paying a bent ex-policeman for something. Must have been something big because the payments were big."

"Why didn't you report this earlier?"

"Um, a few reasons for that. One, I've only just found out the full picture. Two, I *have* reported it. It's in my most recent batch of notes and it'll be in my report for DCI Matthews when I present it. But three, it's hard to investigate a crime when you don't know if there's even been a crime, and when we've already got easily enough evidence to bang Penry up for embezzlement. I thought if I'd come out with it straight, you and DCI Matthews would have told me to forget about it."

"Maybe. And you don't *know* that it was Rattigan making those payments. Could have been anyone."

"Could have been. Except for the coincidence of shared ownership of those horses. And the money. I haven't yet had time to chase up the value of those extra horses, but Penry's share must have been worth tens of thousands, minimum. You've got to be rich to toss out that kind of money."

"But Rattigan is dead, which rather removes him from the list of suspects."

"*Presumed* dead. I spoke to the AAIB — the Air Accidents Investigations outfit — and asked if there was anything funny about the crash."

"You have been busy."

"And the answer was no, not really, only maybe yes, a bit."

Jackson considers that for a moment, then says, "No. People don't vanish like that. Especially not people worth a hundred mill or whatever. Unless you've got anything else you want to tell me."

Those chip-shop texts don't really count. The look on Penry's face won't count. The fact that his Yaris has rust above its wheel arch or that there's no sheet music for his piano.

"No. No, I don't think so."

Two other things actually, but so small they almost don't count for anything. Number one, Penry's last extravagant purchase — the conservatory — came fifteen weeks after Rattigan's reported death. That was well after his last illegal withdrawal from school funds. Number two, although Rattigan was wealthy by almost any standards, his business had been having a rough old time of it. His highest ranking on a sterling rich list came in 2006, when he notched up an estimated value of £91 million. But his businesses were steel and shipping, among the industries worst hit by recession. At the time of his death, in December 2009, both halves of his company were loss-making and he was seeking to reschedule some of the debt associated with the steel business. Given the credit markets at the time, that was like asking to be beaten over the head by his creditors, then robbed. After the hurricane had passed, the *FT* estimated the value of the remaining business at just £22 to £27 million. I'm not sure how you think about those things if you're a Rattigan type. Are you sad because you've just lost £65 million? Or happy because you've got £25 mill and you're still in the game? And would any of that make you fake a plane crash? And how does any of that connect with murdering Janet Mancini, and her child, and Stacey Edwards? I don't know.

Then another thought bubbles up, and this one I do volunteer.

"The StreetSafe people say that Stacey Edwards had a particular hatred for the Balkan types who have been taking over the city's prostitution racket. Her death has an organised-crime feel to it, I guess, so maybe there's a connection there. And Rattigan's shipping interests were mostly in the Baltic trades, whatever that means. From Russia to the UK anyway. Maybe some kind of drugs connection. Who knows? If you did want to smuggle drugs, then owning a shipping line would be a nifty way to do it."

"Seems rather cumbersome, though, doesn't it?" Jackson laughs at me, but it's a friendly laugh. "Go to all the trouble of making yourself a shipping millionaire just so you can run drugs into the country."

"I know. None of it makes sense."

"OK. Thank you. That's all helpful. Very speculative, but you did warn me. We might yet get something helpful from forensics on Stacey Edwards. Meantime, we need to talk to every prostitute we can find. You getting on all right with Alexander?"

"Yes, sir."

"OK. Then the two of you can stay working as a team. I'll see if we can drag some other female officers in to help as well. Brian Penry. What do you think we

153

should do with him? We could drag him back here and give him the third degree."

"Won't do any good. He told us sod all last time. And it's not as though we can connect him to this inquiry in any meaningful way."

"No."

That's a big, round, Welsh senior officer *no*. An end-of-the-conversation *no*. A go-home-and-get-some-sleep *no*. A *no* that doesn't bother to wonder why a certain DC Griffiths wakes at five every morning with a prickling feeling running through her body, like a premonition of murder.

Jackson checks his mug for the third time, only to find it still empty. He bangs it down on the desk.

"We forget Rattigan. He's dead. He's not a part of this. We forget Penry. We've got nothing to connect him to it and he'll be a tough sod anyway. As you say, this looks like an organised-crime thing. Somewhere out there, there'll be people, probably prostitutes, who know what's going on. We find them. We hit the forensics hard. We get our killer. OK?"

"Yes, sir."

"Yes as in 'I hear what you say but I propose to ignore it', or yes as in 'yes'? You know. The old-fashioned sort."

I smile. My mug's still full. I don't like watery hay. "I'll make it the old-fashioned sort, shall I?"

"Good. Good. What day is it tomorrow? Christ, Sunday already? You had any time off this week yet?"

"No."

154

"OK. Take tomorrow off. Go home. Do whatever you do to relax. Sleep in. If you feel up to coming in on Monday, then it'd be helpful. But look after yourself. You need to pace things. Big cases like this, you've got to look after yourself."

"Yes, sir."

I stand up and say goodnight. Because that's the thing about life. There's nowhere to go but forwards.

CHAPTER
EIGHTEEN

I get my things, head downstairs, blip open my car and climb in. Just sit there, door open, mind and body vacant. *Do whatever you do to relax.* What do I do to relax? Illicit smoking in my garden is the obvious answer, but that seems too solitary. It leaves my head too much room to cause havoc. I need people.

It's not as hot as it has been. Sometime this afternoon, there was a breeze from the west and a few sudden, dense showers of rain. Big raindrops hitting the street like a rattle of hail. The clouds have cleared now and the car park has steamed off, but you can tell the change in the atmosphere. The evening seems sharper and brighter than the last few we've had.

I can't help but remember that night on the Taff Embankment, watching prostitutes disappearing into the darkness. I can't imagine living that life. I can't imagine dying that death.

People come and go. Some of them — those who know me and don't dislike me — raise a hand to say hi. I raise a hand back.

I don't want to go home. I don't want to pop over to my mam and dad's. I don't want an evening out with a colleague. I've got more family — aunts and cousins —

out in the farms beyond the city. The real Wales. The old Wales. The one that looks at this crazy, crowded coastal strip with incomprehension. I'd like that. A day or two of getting up at milking time. Hill walks, with buzzards curling overhead and plovers strutting pompously through the bilberries. Mending fences and feeding chickens.

Another day. I wouldn't have time to unwind there. Instead, I swing the car door shut and get the car into gear. I drive out of town just as far as Penarth. St Vincent Road.

Commuterville. Victorian houses, tidy gardens. Seaside shrubs that I don't like: viburnum, euonymus and, my least favourite, escallonia. The damn things all seem to be about survival, not beauty. I'd rather have something that lived fast and died beautiful. A scented jasmine that dropped dead in the blast of the first December gale. At least it'd have tried, not just held out.

I park up and make a call.

"Hello?"

"Hey, Ed. It's me, Fi."

"Hi, Fi. Good to hear from you. How are you?" His voice is enthusiastic. Energetic.

"Yeah, not bad. What are you up to?"

"This minute, this evening, or in my life generally?"

"The first two of those."

"Pouring whisky, settling down to watch a *Morse* repeat on the box."

"Which episode, and have you seen it before?"

He tells me which episode and no, he hasn't. I tell him the name of the murderer, the critical clue and how Colin Dexter handles the misdirection. I hear the TV snap angrily off in the background.

"Thanks, Fi. Well, you've really freed up my evening." He doesn't sound completely thrilled.

"Good. I was hoping I could drop by, maybe. But I didn't want to watch *Morse*."

"Whereabouts are you?"

"Peering in through your front window. Is that a new sofa?"

He whips round, sees me looking in and his expression is mixed, but at least two-thirds welcoming. Good enough. He chucks his phone down on the possibly new sofa and goes round to the front door to let me in. We kiss, cheek to cheek, but warmly.

"It's not the best *Morse* anyway. Saggy middle."

He rubs my back, the way you're allowed to do with someone you once slept with. "Come on in. You're looking tired. Drink?"

"I'm knackered, but I'm not sleeping. A big case that I'm finding a bit freaky."

"Is that a cry for whisky?" His hands are hovering over a collection of bottles and glasses.

I hesitate. I used to avoid drink completely. My head was fragile enough that I didn't take anything that might unbalance it. These days, I'm a tiny bit more adventurous, but only a tiny bit and my head doesn't feel too solid at the moment.

"Um. Too alcoholic. I want something that tastes alcoholic but isn't."

"Gin and tonic, with lots of tonic and just a smell of gin?"

"And ice and lemon. Sounds perfect."

Good old Ed. He mixes me the perfect drink, knows to ask me if I've eaten, isn't surprised that I haven't and digs out some spinach and ricotta tortellini for me, serves them warm with a splash of olive oil and a bowl of green salad.

"Homemade," he says, indicating the tortellini. "I've been playing with my new pasta-maker."

"God, I like the English middle classes," I say with my mouth full. "Who else has homemade tortellini waiting for drop-by waifs and strays?"

"The Italians?"

"Don't quibble. Their homes would be full of grandmothers and screaming babies. Give me the divorced English middle classes any day."

Ed has moved from whisky to red wine, presumably in accordance with some bit of English etiquette that he knows and I don't.

We have an odd relationship, him and me. We first met when I was a heavily medicated teenage nutcase in the hands of shrinks who thought their job was to pour more pills down my throat if I showed any sign of independent thought, movement, emotion or argument. Especially argument. Ed — Mr Edward Saunders — was a clinical psychologist who thought that maybe independent reasoning was a positive sign in a patient, even if that reasoning tended to suggest that all mental health professionals, and psychiatrists in particular, should be towed out to sea in a big boat,

159

which would then be surrounded by sharks and scuttled. And then depth-charged.

As for Ed, well, he just spent time with me. I don't know how many weeks or hours were involved, because time was so unclear for me back then. But he treated me like a human being and eventually I became one again. It wasn't only his help that brought me round. It wasn't even mostly him. I owe more to my family and my own bollocky stubbornness. But of the entire mental health crew, Ed was the only one I'd have airlifted to safety from that boat. He kept the faith. Faith in me. That was precious to me then, and still is now.

Then we lost touch. I went to Cambridge. Ed went on being a solid-gold nugget in the heap of ordure that is the South Wales Mental Health Service. He's a Home Counties boy — solicitor father, brother who's something tedious and lucrative in the City — but he wound up in South Wales and seems to have stuck. We met again, because he had some temporary research gig in Cambridge for a couple of terms. We bumped into each other on the street. One thing led to another. His marriage had essentially died, but was still in the process of completing its funeral rites. We began a friendship, then thought since that was going well, we ought to go to bed together. We did, off and on for a few months. It was nice. Ed was a good lover, as a matter of fact. I didn't know they bred them that passionate in Hertfordshire. But we were never really meant to be lovers. The sex got in the way of the friendship, so we eased back to where we were and have been there pretty much ever since. We see less of each other than we ought to, because he's busy and I'm busy, but also maybe because he's got some funny feelings about having had a sexual relationship with an ex-patient of his.

I eat up like a good girl. It turns out that I'm famished — when was the last time I ate a hot meal? — and I wipe out his entire stock of tortellini, make a serious dent in his salad reserves and do considerable damage to an apple crumble that I find in the fridge. Ed has this idea of me as someone who eats all the time. That just shows what a bad scientist he is. If he made the experiment of having no food in his house, other than some old salami and tomatoes decorated with two different types of mould, he'd get a more balanced view of my eating habits.

Ed puts some cheese on a plate — Cheddar, Welsh goat and a squishy French one — and we go back through to the living room. Ed has two kids from his marriage, a boy of ten and a girl of eight. He's got photos of them both at different ages around the place, and I'm fascinated by them for some reason. There are a few of the girl — Maya — at about the age that April was when she died. These in particular catch my attention. There's a vital difference between these ones of Maya and the ones I have of April. There's some tantalisingly important discrepancy between the two, but I can't seem to reach it.

"What's up?"

"Nothing. Just trying to figure something out, that's all. How are the kids?"

161

Ed starts to tell me. They're fine. Doing well at school. Having problems with their stepfather, a property developer in Barry. Blah, blah.

We pick away at the cheese, chat a bit, cuddle on the sofa and end up watching the last half-hour of *Morse*. I announce all of the essential plot points before they arise and Ed rumples my hair or, if I'm being particularly annoying, pulls my ears till I say, "Ow." When *Morse* runs out, we segue into *Newsnight*.

Terrorism. Cuts. An argument over education reform. We talk about whether Jeremy Paxman has had his teeth whitened.

When *Newsnight* gets too boring even for us, I roll over and lie on Ed's chest.

"If I wanted to go out with you again, would you?"

He kisses me softly on the forehead.

"Probably."

I sit up on him. I can feel him getting hard underneath me. I bounce up and down a bit, to get him back for pulling my ears. He holds me so that I can't do too much damage, but mostly just lets me bounce.

"I don't think we should," I say, "but I like knowing that you wouldn't necessarily say no."

"Not necessarily, no."

"Why don't you ever come round to see me?"

"I don't know. Busy, I suppose."

That's no sort of answer and I escape his grip to give a more vigorous bounce, hard enough to make him wince.

"Proper answer," I demand.

"OK, then. I think if I came round to see you, we would end up going to bed. We would end up back together."

"And you don't want that?"

"No, it isn't that. I'm not sure if it's what *you* want. I don't want to be hanging around waiting for you to make your mind up. Waiting for you to find out who you are."

"You think I don't know?"

"I'm damn sure you don't. You're a work in progress."

I think about bouncing up and down some more, but decide that he's right on all counts and that being right doesn't necessarily require punishment. I give him an affectionate squeeze and slide off him, groping around on the floor for my shoes. "That's what I like most about you, Mr Edward Saunders. You're not a work in progress at all. You're the finished article. Shrink-wrapped and ready to ship."

He smiles mildly, watching me get ready to leave. "I'll take that as a compliment."

"It is. From me, it is."

I go into the kitchen to find a plastic bag so that I can steal his cheese.

"What are you doing?"

"Stealing your cheese."

He lets me take it. We kiss each other on the cheek, the way we did when I arrived, but we also say that we'll see each other again soon, and I think we both mean it. On my way out, I look again at those photos of

163

Maya, and this time I get it. I get what's been puzzling me about them. I laugh at myself for being an idiot.

I drive home, staying within the speed limit for a change, and with another wash of rain painting the road black in front of me. I've got the Bach cello suites in my CD changer and I play them loudly enough that the swish of the wipers doesn't get in the way. I wish I had further to drive. The day we went to Paradise by way of Kensal Green.

I get home. No escallonias, but not much to cheer the heart either. It's very magnolia, my house. Magnolia, white and stainless steel, and I don't like any of those things.

The sextuple April grins down at me as I remember to put the cheese in the fridge. I get a glass of water and sit down opposite her.

Looking at the pictures of Maya, I eventually figured out what was funny about my photos of April. All the ones I had printed off were of her at the crime scene. April with the top of her head missing. April with a smile but no eyes. Six little dead Aprils, and not a single little live one. It took me this long to notice that all my photos were of April dead.

I grin at myself and feel her grinning with me. Seven grins. I plod upstairs, run a bath and allow myself a long soak, wondering vaguely whether to take the pictures down or leave them up and add some of the party-dress/beach/toffee-apple ones.

Questions for another time, but I'll probably stick with the photos I've got. I've never minded the dead. It's not them who cause the trouble.

CHAPTER
NINETEEN

I wake the wrong side of 6 a.m., still far too early, but at least I'm expecting it now. I sneak downstairs in my dressing gown, get some tea and cereal, and come back up to eat it in bed. Then, because the house seems too quiet, I go out to the car, still in my dressing gown, to get the Bach cello CD. I whack it on loud enough to hear upstairs and continue my breakfast in bed. Sunday-morning bliss, just three hours out of place.

I play the conversation with Jackson over in my head. He's right, of course. My suspects are one, a dead man, and two, a man who is going to jail anyway. Also, of course, I don't think that either of them actually killed the Mancinis or Edwards. They're just involved. That means that as well as having a dead suspect and an about-to-be-jailed suspect, I'm also missing a crime to connect them to. I don't remember every word of my CID training, but I'm pretty sure that you need a crime before you can start arresting people, alive or dead.

The trouble is that intuitions like mine are wholly at odds with the way police investigations work. There's an old joke about an Irish attempt on Everest. It failed because they ran out of scaffolding. Ho, ho. But that's precisely how we coppers would climb the damn thing.

The only difference is that we wouldn't run out. We'd just keep going, pole after pole, clamp after clamp. Interviews. Statements. DNA tests. Prints. A million bits of data. Thousands of hours of patient, grinding analysis. Remorseless, methodical, inevitable. And one day, as your frozen fingers are hauling up yet another scaffolding board into position, you notice that you've run out of mountain. The sunlight is coming at you horizontally. You've reached the top.

That's how Jackson plans this particular mountain climb and he's right enough. He'll get his killer.

But will I get mine? I didn't make any promises to Jackson. When he asked me for an old-fashioned "yes", the sort that actually betokens obedience, I answered him with a question. The way I see it, that allows me a little enterprise on the side. And he's a shrewd old sod. Perhaps he was even happy to leave it that way. In any case, there's no time like the present.

No time except for the present, if it comes to that. A frightening thought, if you dwell on it.

I get dressed fast. My regular casual wear involves a base coat of jeans and T-shirt, plus whatever else the weather or occasion demands. But it's too hot for jeans today. Mid-twenties and rising. So I go for something more summery. A floaty pinky-beige skirt and a pistachio-and-coffee striped top. Summer wear. Good-mood wear.

Downstairs, I take the Bach CD off and va-va voom across town. Eastern Avenue is almost completely empty, so I get to my destination fast, even without speeding.

166

Rhyader Crescent. The teachers, nurses, middle managers and youngish solicitors are still in bed, or maybe yawning their way through toast, or getting ready for a day of marshalling hyperactive kids. The bent policeman at number 27 shows no sign of doing anything at all. The Yaris is there. Its bonnet is cold. No lights in the house. No sign of life.

The bent policeman at number 27 is almost certainly snoring away upstairs. A late riser.

I don't have a plan, which I see as a positive. Nothing to go wrong. A side passage leads to the back garden and I go through, if only to feel less conspicuous. A lady in a garden diagonally opposite is putting her washing out. She clocks me but doesn't say or do anything. No reason why she should. I don't look much like a burglar and it's hardly burglar o'clock. Gulls are circling over Victoria Park, looking for something to do.

I sit on the back step and wait for the lady to go inside.

Penry's keys have been bothering me. His house is L-shaped, with the kitchen extension forming the arm of the L. In the crook of the L is the conservatory. The keys to the conservatory door were visible enough in the house — no reason why not — but they're equally visible from the garden. A burglar armed with a brick could quite easily knock out a pane of glass, take the keys, let himself in. It's security 1.01 and Penry used to be a copper.

That's what got me thinking in the first place.

Now, I'm not about to smash any windows, but I'd bet that Penry doesn't have friends on this street.

167

People to say hi to, perhaps, but not go-down-to-the-pub-with mates. The street is too suburban for that, a bit too wife and 2.4 children. So no neighbours who hold a key.

Then there's his kitchen sink. He's not slovenly, but he's not organised, not house-proud. He's a man's man. Beer cans in the kitchen bin. More beers down the pub. That sort of man either needs a wife or a spare key. And he doesn't have a wife.

The lady opposite goes inside, so I can turn my attention to the back door. The one belonging to the kitchen, not the conservatory.

I turn the handle, super gently. It's locked.

No flowerpots. A couple of bricks and a few rotted lengths of garden timber, but nothing under those. The doorframe's set into the wall, so nothing concealed on top of it or at the sides. *Nada*.

Damn. I feel a brief surge of frustration, but it's quickly replaced by a sense of confidence. I'm not wrong. I know I'm not. My reading of Penry is correct. There must be a spare key here somewhere. There *must*.

Then I realise. The conservatory was the last thing, not the first. Those keys on the doorframe breach security 1.01, but he hung them at a point when he'd already embezzled so much money he must have known he'd be caught. It was a "What the fuck?" kind of thing, and Penry hadn't always been that way.

I turn round and survey the garden. I'm Penry. I've just retired from the force. Honourable career, ended by injury. Police pension. Single man. I need a set of keys handy, but I'm not going to be stupid about it. I haven't even completed the thought experiment before I'm walking over to an old brick-paved area at the back, complete with bench, tottering gazebo and barbecue. I check the bench, then the barbecue, then the paving area itself. At the side nearest the garden fence, a brick is loose. I tease it out in a crumble of old mortar and a key winks brassily out at me from its nest.

CHAPTER
TWENTY

Front door, or back door?

The key looks like it could fit the back door, so I try it and it works first time. I'm into the kitchen. Still squalid. The mug that I threw into the bin has been taken out and left on a corner of the sideboard. I drop it back in the bin. Remind him to be tidier.

Shoes off and dangling from my hand, I go further into the house. It's still early, not yet seven fifteen. No way is Penry an early riser, but I don't know how lightly he sleeps. I would seriously not enjoy him waking up and finding me here. I'm not feeling frightened exactly, because my head's a bit too spacey to feel anything as specific as that, but I recognise the symptoms. Heartbeat. Rapid breathing. An over-alert jitteriness. Not good.

I want to be here, though.

The conservatory is still empty. I've got an impulse to lift the piano lid and thrash out a tune, bring some noise into this place. I don't, of course. I still can't see any music and I've got a sneaky feeling that Penry can't even play the piano. A music room with no music. A conservatory with nothing to conserve.

170

The living room looks much the same as it did last time. The INFORMATION WANTED notice has been folded up and left on the table. I spread it out again to make it easier for him to read and circle the telephone number that people are meant to call if they have information.

In the corner of the room by the hi-fi, there's a mobile phone charging. Ah! Thank you kindly, I don't mind if I do. I drop the phone in my pocket and look around to see if there's anything else worth taking. There isn't. No papers. No diary or Filofax or address book. The only desk has nothing much on the top of it — some computer cables, a note dispenser, a mug of pens, some phone directories — and the only drawer is locked.

There's probably a key to the drawer somewhere, there are probably more things to find, but I've lost my nerve. My fear has caught up with me properly and I don't like being here. I don't want to make a noise and risk waking the beast.

So I leave again. As fast and quietly as I can. I lock up and leave the key back where I found it. I don't feel safe again until I'm in my car, and even then I have to drive for ten minutes before I begin playing with my new toy. It's got twenty-six numbers in its address book, which I copy into my notebook. No messages in inbox or sent items. I try to check voicemails, but it asks me for a password. I try 0000, then 1234, then 9999 and then find myself locked out. Silly me. His date of birth, 4 May, 0405, was probably a better bet.

And I forgot to take his charger. Never mind. Twenty-six phone numbers is a good haul.

I drive back home and get myself some peppermint tea. Bach feels too dull for a moment like this, so I replace it with Dido's *No Angels*. Not the coolest music choice in the world, but if it's cool you're after, then you're knock-knock-knocking at the wrong door. My maximum ambition is to make it to normal. I jump back into bed, fully clothed except that I take my skirt off first, with Dido hollering away underneath me. You go, girl.

Twenty-six phone numbers and a whole day to play with them.

I go for the landlines first. I decide that I'm a flower delivery company sorting out our Monday delivery schedule. I call the first number — a Cardiff one — and get an answering machine. No names. Just "The person you are calling is not available" in a pre-recorded voice. Not helpful. I hang up. The second number is just entered as "Jane" in Penry's phone, but the answering machine message refers to "Jane and Terry". I make a note, but don't leave a message.

Then the third number, a woman picks up. I go through my spiel. Missing address for the delivery tomorrow. I've got 22 Richards Court, but there must be a muddle because I've got three deliveries booked for that address. The woman buys it and gives me her address, which is in Pontprennau, up by the golf club. I say, "Oh, yes, up by the golf club," and she says, "That's right, just by the golf club."

Then I ask her just to confirm her name "because we just need to know we're delivering to the right person".

There's no logic there at all that I can see, but the woman says, "Yes, of course," then gives her name as Laura Hargreaves.

"Thanks, Laura," I say. "That's fine. I'll probably see you tomorrow, if you're in."

"Oh, thanks so much. I love flowers. I wonder who they're from."

"Well, I'm not allowed to tell you that, but it's a lovely bouquet that they've ordered. What's your favourite colour?"

"Oh, I don't know. Cream probably, in flowers. I love roses, but I love all flowers really."

I promise her a huge bouquet of cream roses and hang up. I'm enjoying myself now. It's nice to be able to spread a little joy. I make a further twenty-three calls, get through to fourteen people, collect twelve addresses and ten names. I make another round of calls to the numbers where I only got through to voicemails and this time collect another name and address. I think I'd make a good flower delivery person. I've got a lovely telephone manner, even if I do say so myself.

Underneath me, Dido has run out of song and in any case I need to go out. I send a batch of texts to the people I didn't get through to, then tootle over to Sainsbury's and stock up for the week. I've got a theory that if I buy lots of easy-to-cook, healthy food, then I'm going to start eating properly. Not quite the homemade-tortellini version of proper, but then I'm only a flower delivery girl. We're not posh. I get a few extras, including one of those little potted begonias that come with their own wickerwork Red Riding Hood basket. It's a bit twee for what I want, but it'll have to do.

I pay up. Tootle home. Put the shopping away. Make some more calls. Prepare a meal for two. It's a bit hard knowing what to prepare, because I'm not sure when my guest will be arriving and how hungry he'll be, so I settle for a brunchy spread of bagels, cream cheese, smoked salmon and OJ. Easy to top up with scrambled eggs if needed. Good for any time of day or night if you ask me.

I sling Paloma Faith on the stereo, think about hoovering, but decide to tough it out for another week. I have no musical taste at all. I never know who I am, so I buy randomly and try different things wondering if one day I'll find the real me. Will I know when it happens?

While I'm waiting for enlightenment, I take Penry's SIM card out of his phone and drop it into a kettle full of boiling water, then drain the water and pop the SIM card back in the phone. Penry will want to make good any damage I'm causing, but nobody backs up their phone contacts properly. If I destroy his SIM card, I've probably bought myself a little extra room for manoeuvre.

With regret, I take my pictures of April off the wall and am annoyed to find that the Blu-Tack has left marks wherever it's been. I pick at the Blu-Tack scabs with my fingernail but already know that I'm going to take no further action.

174

CHAPTER
TWENTY-ONE

Penry arrives at four.

My name and address are in the phonebook, but I'm hardly the only Griffiths in Cardiff and not even the only F. Griffiths. When Penry's ugly old Yaris pulls up, it's pretty clear that he isn't sure that he's got the right address. He probably thinks this bland little estate is too upmarket for a humble DC. I twinkle a wave at him through the window and throw him a reassuring smile.

At the front door, I tell him to come on in, but he shoulders past me, smouldering with aggression.

I've put his phone out on the living-room floor, along with the Red Riding Hood begonia and a little bit of Christmas ribbon. My way of saying thank you. He takes the phone but leaves the pot plant.

By this stage, I'm in the kitchen putting the kettle on.

"What the fuck is this?" he says at the door.

"I'm not sure. I think you'd call it brunch, but I suppose it's more of a brinner now. I wasn't sure what time you'd be coming. There's scrambled egg, if you're hungry."

He doesn't say anything about egg, or whether he'd prefer tea or coffee. I'm guessing coffee, so I make him a brew. I never drink it myself, but I always keep some for visitors — only instant, mind you. I put in four teaspoons of coffee and stir it round. Peppermint tea for me.

"You know how people who don't drink coffee always say they love the smell of coffee?" Penry doesn't reply. He still hasn't moved from the doorway. "Well, I don't. I don't like the smell or the taste."

I sit down. The kitchen is the nicest room in my house. Not because I've done anything to make it nice, but because it's reasonably clean and has big French doors onto the garden. If it's even a half-nice day outside, then the kitchen feels bright and airy.

"Help yourself. Tuck in. This is Sainsbury's Taste the Difference smoked salmon, but I think they just charge you more and you can't actually taste the difference. Or can you?"

Penry seems a rather passive conversationalist, but he does come over to the table, yank out a chair and sit.

"You are a fucking tit," he says.

"Oh, these are nicer toasted, aren't they?" I busy myself in toasting the bagels. "It is a murder inquiry, you know. Janet and April Mancini. Stacey Edwards too now, as well."

He doesn't react to Edwards's name. I hadn't expected him to, but it was worth a try.

"I found her, actually. Climbed in through a window and there she was. Do you want to know how she died?" Penry doesn't respond, so I tell him anyway, right down to the cable ties and duct tape. "Obviously, no autopsy results yet, but she died the same way as Janet did. High as a kite. Airways blocked. Dr Price, who did the autopsy work on the Mancinis, reckoned it could just take a minute or two. Finger and thumb. Just like that."

I drop a bagel on his plate and one on mine. I haven't eaten since breakfast, so I'm genuinely hungry and I tuck in straight away. Penry must be hungry too because he drops a bit of salmon onto the bagel and starts eating. He hasn't pulled his chair into the table. He's not eating with a plate, knife or fork. And he's not trying the cream cheese, which is a shame.

"Did you call anyone?"

"Yes. Everyone. I thought your mam was nice. She called me love and said 'bless you' twice. I told her that she'd be getting a bunch of tulips tomorrow, so you might want to arrange that if poss."

Penry opens his mouth. Not to eat, but to say something. It's not just a "fucking tit" type comment either, because there's a depth of calculation in his eyes. I silently urge him to say whatever it is that he's contemplating, but he decides against. He doesn't even come up with another insult. He just slaps a chunk more salmon onto a bagel and stands up. Ready to leave.

I stand up too, in order to see him out. We're standing in the space between the living room and the hall when Penry turns to me. Half of me thinks he's going to say something useful. Half of me thinks he's going to swear at me. But both halves are wrong. *Nul points* all round. With almost no warning or back lift, he hits me open-handed across the face. I'm stunned — literally and metaphorically — by the force of it. The

177

blow knocks me across the hall and I think I strike my head on the wall opposite. At all events, by the time I've recovered my wits, I'm lying crumpled up on the floor at the foot of the stairs. Penry is towering over me.

He's two miles high and he's going to kill me.

I don't say or do anything. I can't. My vision is shot through with bolts of black and red. There's blood inside my mouth. My head feels as though it's been detonated by professionals, then reassembled with sticky tape. I honestly didn't know that one blow could do this. I've never lacked physical confidence, but I've also never been hit like this. It feels like a brick wall just reached out and whacked me. My skirt is thrown up above my knees and I find my right hand tweaking it down. That is the extent of my resistance. Even my hand feels weak.

This is what it is like. Total surrender. I never knew what that meant before. Never knew how total it could be.

Penry towers over me for another few seconds, then turns on his heel and goes. Only when the front door closes — and even then not straight away — do I attempt movement.

I kick my legs out in front of me and arrange myself so that I'm sitting on the bottom step. I review the damage. The right side of my face, where Penry struck me, is moving from numb and shocked to hurting and furious. I poke it gently with my fingertips. Everything is bruised, but neither cut nor broken. I think the blood inside my mouth comes from my cheek being slammed against my teeth. There's also a cut on the other side of my head, where I hit the wall. My teeth seem loose, but I think that's down to shock. My neck also feels painful everywhere, but I think that's just the combined effect of shock and whiplash. There's a taste in my mouth that I identify as vomit.

I'm not angry with Penry. Hitting me seems like a fair enough response to my stealing his phone. He could have injured me far worse than he did. Part of my shock comes from seeing how unbelievably simple it was for him. I'm angry at my own feebleness. Why the fuck do we live in a world where women are at such a physical disadvantage to men? Why do my genes yield me five feet two inches of height when my sister Kay is five feet eight and Ant is rapidly heading the same way? Not that either of them would have stood much chance with Penry. Abs, pecs and body hair.

I stand up.

The experiment goes pretty well. My balance feels strange — like when you get out of a swimming pool after swimming for a long time — but everything works pretty much as it ought to. I go into the kitchen, spit some blood into the sink and freshen my tea with hot water.

Do I call Lev?

Do I call Dad?

Do I call Jackson?

Do I call Brydon?

I don't do any of those things. I pick my way upstairs, almost welcoming the headache that is beginning to crash in on me because it's a sign of normal function. In the bathroom mirror, the right side of my face looks puffy, but amazingly ordinary given the way it feels. I can see the dazed look in my eyes, but only because I know it's there anyway. The world still feels tilted and out of kilter.

I run myself a hot bath and go crazy with the soothing bath salts. My neck hurts like hell.

I can only feel three things. Numbness, pain and fear. As the numbness starts to lessen, the other two things take their place.

And downstairs, on my phone, I can hear the first texts coming in.

CHAPTER
TWENTY-TWO

The rest of that evening seems to go OK to begin with. After my bath — a long one — I chew up some more aspirin. I'm two over the limit already, but I don't care. The hammering in my head is now just a background thudding. Doping myself back into numbness.

I lie down on my bed, intending to air-dry before dressing, but end up snoozing for a couple of hours. Dreamless deep sleep. The kind I've been missing. I'm short of kip and those two hours feel like a gift.

It's half past seven when I eventually get up and there's a strange kind of summer-evening normality in the air. A few lawnmowers still buzzing. Kids being ordered off their bikes into dinner. A couple of fat blokes with white legs and unflattering shorts talking rubbish over a garden fence. A granny going home after a day with the family. If someone were making an infomercial about the delights of bourgeois living in Pentwyn, then they might well want to splice scenes like these into their piece. It's not glitzy, but it's real. Loving, in a low-key sort of way. Safe.

Then I go downstairs. Down past the bottom step. Past the bit of wall where I cracked my head. Through the doorway where Penry drew his arm back to hit me.

Into the living room, where he formulated his move and began to execute it.

I feel sick. Physically sick. I actually have to rush through to the kitchen to hang over the kitchen sink, dry-retching to see if anything will come out. It doesn't, but the feeling doesn't go.

Safe? The idea is ludicrous. Nothing to do with the real world. Penry walked in here, ate smoked salmon, then hit me. I let him in. I know that. Practically invited him round, but what on earth is there to stop anyone entering whenever they want? Yes. My door is locked — and as soon as I'm done dry-heaving over the kitchen sink, I check every door and window lock in the house. But the house itself seems flimsy. I've seen these damn things being put up. Everyone has. A few low-density breezeblocks. A bit of yellow fluff for insulation. A skin of bricks. That's it. Someone could be through the wall with a few hard blows of a sledgehammer. And that's the wall, for God's sake. What the hell am I doing with windows? The window looking over my strip of lawn at the front, my stupid bit of paved parking area, is just an invitation to come on in. Hello, Mr Burglar. You can't get me. I've locked my doors. I've locked my windows. I'm like the Three Little Piggies, pink, smug, chuckling to themselves at the Big Bad Wolf outside. And then, good heavens above, the Big Bad Wolf remembers that he might have flunked his maths GCSE. He might not be able to read a book without moving his lips. But he doesn't need to! There's a window! One short, sharp tap and it's not a window any more, it's a PLEASE COME IN sign. Please come in, start spit-roasting those piggies, start slapping around that foolish little DC Griffiths. Do whatever the hell you want, because no one inside is going to be able to stop you. Fuck her. Beat her up. Cable-tie her hands together and put duct tape over her mouth. Experiment. Have fun. Help yourself.

And that's not all. It gets better. Because there's not just one window in this house, there are loads of them. Every room has at least one. Take your pick of entry methods, because not a single room in this entire house is safe from assault.

This is crazy thinking, I know, but it's got me in its grip. I don't know which room to be in. I get a sharp knife from the kitchen and a hammer that my dad gave me when I moved in. I draw every curtain tight shut and put lights on in every room. I put Paloma Faith on again, not because I want to listen to a single word of whatever she has to tell me about life, but just to make a noise. I put the TV on as well. There are people in this house, Mr Wolf, and you don't know how many, or how big, or how fierce.

I'm shaking. I don't think the shaking is visible on the outside, but the inside counts for more. A vibration that runs through me and that I can't control or stop.

Three times I almost call Lev, before holding back. What can he do anyway? He's not a bodyguard. He can't protect me from this.

My head tells me that Penry is not a risk. And he's not. I know that. Slapping me this afternoon was a tit-for-tat thing. In some awful pre-feminist way, according to some black-as-pitch medieval reckoning, I

183

had it coming to me. I invited it. Literally. I'd *wanted* Penry to know I'd been in his house, wanted him to know that it was me who took his phone. I wanted to stir things up. See what happened if the pot was shaken. And so he gave me a slap. I don't blame him. He's a thief and a self-destructive fool, but he's not a killer. Not even close. He didn't kick me when I was down.

Yet what about the dark shapes that move out of sight behind Penry? Someone killed Janet Mancini. Someone dropped a sink on April Mancini. Someone taped Stacey Edwards's mouth shut, tied her hands behind her back, then closed off her nose until she was dead. Stacey Edwards was killed, presumably, because she knew too much about the Mancini case and someone thought she was dangerously likely to talk about it. But if she was a threat, then isn't DC Griffiths even more of one? You can't take out a whole police inquiry, of course, but DC Griffiths has gone rogue. Only a bit, but just enough. She's lifted a corner of carpet in a bit of the room that her colleagues aren't much interested in looking at. She hasn't found much, but she's still poking around. Who knows what she might find next?

These thoughts aren't comfortable. I take the path of least resistance. The inevitable one. The one I knew I'd end up taking.

I call Dad. Ask him to come round and pick me up. He does a short double-take, then says, "Right you are, love. I'm coming over." I sit by the front door, with my knife and my hammer, listening to Paloma Faith fight

184

with the TV and trying to hear every squeak of noise from outside. My headache is terrible now. My jaw feels dislocated. Shudders run through me every twenty seconds or so. I can't help them. Nor am I able to turn my head, because turning my head would reveal the bottom of the stairs, and I half expect to see myself still lying there in a crumpled heap, skirt above my knee. Unable to avert whatever is going to happen next.

My one positive action is to call a twenty-four-hour flower delivery outfit and order some tulips for Mrs P. I send them "With love from Brian." Making peace. My voice is wooden, and when I hang up, there's blood in my mouth again.

My dad, bless his cotton socks, is here in under fifteen minutes. He's not the sort to delay, my pa. Best thing about him. I hear his car despite the ongoing Paloma-TV warfare. Still holding my knife and my hammer, I turn off the TV, then the music, then some lights. Dad knocks at the door. Because he is the way he is, a knock alone is never enough. "Fi girl, it's your pa." Shouted, not spoken. Everything with Dad is shouted, not spoken. Another good thing about him in the present context. I shove my hammer and knife away under a sofa cushion and go to let him in.

Even then, my mind is untrustworthy. Scenarios play out in my head that couldn't possibly exist. My dad being held at knifepoint. Made to shout, "Fi girl," at my front door. Watched by men in black, who are holding my mother and two sisters in a four by four with tinted windows. All bollocks. Even so, it takes an effort of will to unlock the door and throw it open.

Dad's there. No knife. No gunmen. No four by four. Or at least, no four by four other than his own silver Range Rover.

The normal crushing kiss. Pounding on into my house, because Dad is the ultimate *mi casa es su casa* man, but these things cut both ways.

"Smoked salmon! And bagels, love. You do do things nice." A wodge of salmon and bagel disappears into his gob. "Lawn OK, is it? Looks all right. Not growing quite so fast now. Course, a bit more sun and it'll shoot up again." He talks as much to himself as to me and part of the *su casa es mi casa* deal is that he gets to inspect my lawn, roll my kitchen drawers in and out, and throw my fridge door open wide as though to inventory my food stocks. "Smashing," he says at the conclusion of his inspection, which means nothing at all in his mouth, more a punctuation mark than anything.

"Do you need your things, love? I'll pop this up, shall I?" He swings the living-room mirror up onto its hook, but not before scratching at the Blu-Tack marks on the wall behind.

It would be easy to see my dad as bossy and intrusive, but he's not those things. There's not that kind of edge to him. If I told him that I preferred the mirror just where it was, standing in front of the faux fireplace, slightly tilted so all you could see in it was your leg from the ankle to the knee, he'd just say, "Right you are, love," and swing the mirror back down and try to make sure that he sat it back in the indentation it's made in the carpet, not an inch out of its original position.

186

I get my things — nightdress, toothbrush, change of clothes, a few other bits, my phone. I'm still shaking now, but the shakes have gone back inside. They're internal, not external. In the bathroom, I put on some extra make-up. Blusher. Something on my eyes and lips. It doesn't fool me, but it doesn't have to.

When I go down, Dad is in the hall, ready and waiting.

"Your face OK, is it? It looks puffy."

He puts his hand to my chin. Not holding it exactly, more steadying it.

"I went to the dentist yesterday. Had to have some injections. It felt fine at the time, but it's all sore today."

He doesn't immediately drop his hand. As though he's an antiques expert appraising some slightly unexpected find. And then he does. "Bloody dentists," he says, and he's off again. Turning off lights. Watching me lock up. Sweeping me over to his car. Telling me about the state of play at home. Ant and Kay both there, but Kay wanting an early night after a big party the night before. Mam's already cooked and everyone's already eaten, "but we've still got a lovely bit of beef left over from lunch, love, and I had your mam stick a potato in the oven for you. My favourite, that is. Just with a bit of butter and salt. Lovely!"

A gift, that. To have as your favourite thing whatever it is you're about to consume. Dad has a new favourite thing every day, often more.

We Range Rover our way through quiet streets. His car is bigger, quieter, higher, plusher than mine. My fear is locked up in the house behind me. It can't follow me here. It seems to me that I've never been afraid of anything when I'm with my dad.

We get home. Mam's got two plates out. One for me, one for Dad. Meat and baked potatoes on both. And horseradish. And mustard. And a big blob of coleslaw. "Marvellous!" Dad's amazed delight is genuine, even though it was inconceivable that Mam would have sorted out a plate of dinner for me and left him potato-less. We drink water.

There's an hour or two of family stuff. Ant likes it when the whole family are together, so just enjoys being around. There have been developments on the TV-in-bedroom front, but I can't quite make out what they are because everyone is talking and I've only got two ears.

Kay hangs around for a bit too. Badgering Dad to allow her half a glass of wine, which Mam disapproves of — "on Sunday!" — but which she gets anyway, quickly poured when Mam isn't looking. Kay's dressed casually for her. Leggings. A black sequinned tank top. Bare feet. A long silver necklace but no earrings. She looks gorgeous, as she always does. Long-limbed, silk-skinned and photogenic. She likes being part of things as well, though the teenager in her has to fight shy of looking too involved, so she sits side on to the table and listens more than she talks, running her finger round the rim of her glass, making it sing.

I love being part of things too. Families are strange affairs. Somehow Dad's genes and Mam's genes got sloshed together to create the over-intellectual, fish-out-of-water oddity that is me, and yet we all get along together. We love each other. We *belong*. That's been a rare feeling for me. The most precious one there is.

Eventually, though, things break up. Ant to bed. Kay to her room. Mam to the living room for some TV before bed.

"We'll go through, shall we?"

"Through" means to Dad's lair. Not even in the house, but a separate studio room built on top of what used to be the pool house in the garden, a pool house that was once Dad's most prize *grand projet* but that Mam persuaded him to abandon after an entire year went by with no one using it.

"Through" also means to Dad's world. Out of Mam's much ornamented, endlessly hoovered, precision-arranged utopia. Into Dad's world. A place of giant plasma-screen TVs. Huge leather furniture. Photos of his clubs. Not just the glitzy bars, the flashily expensive interiors, but the girls too: the pole-dancing, drink-bringing, short-skirted or no-skirted bikini-babes who bring the punters flocking in. Babes, many of whom will be around Kay's age or mine — though Dad manages to avoid having that thought, or at least manages to stow it somewhere safe, where it can't cause any damage. And in any case, the babe photos aren't a form of soft porn as far as my dad's concerned. They're as much and as little to be lusted over as all the other stuff in the room.

The *stuff*. Hard even to name it, because it's an endlessly shifting, endlessly varied collection. Right now, Dad is unable to contain his joy about his latest

189

acquisition. He shows me a giant bundle, wrapped in a green felt bag, standing on the snooker table.

"What do you think that is, love? Bet you can't guess. It's for your mam. It's bloody amazing, it is. Can't guess? You haven't tried. But you'll never guess anyway. Here, look, I'll show you."

He unwraps it. It's a giant silver trophy. Smaller than rugby's Heineken Cup, but not much. Dad's had it engraved to "World's Best Mam, Kathleen Griffiths." He's just waiting for a shelf to arrive. The plan is to install the shelf over the door into the kitchen and put the cup there one day as a surprise. It won't be a birthday gift or anything like that. It'll just happen. Mam will like the thought but hate the actual object. It'll sit there for a few months, until Dad has well and truly forgotten it. Then Mam will find some inconvenience with it. Or she'll acquire a neat little Victorian hunting print and wonder out loud where it could go — "Maybe over the kitchen door. Only, no, silly me, my lovely cup's there and that's got to stay really, hasn't it?" Anyway, she'll figure it out. Before too long, the cup will arrive back in Dad's lair, the house will have acquired another neat little Victorian hunting print, and Dad's attention will have moved on to something else entirely.

And "through" also means to the place where Dad decompresses. Where his huge, booming energy finds its settling place. In his long journey from Cardiff ne'er-do-well to successful entrepreneur, then I'd say that this pool house-turned-studio retreat has played a

190

part almost as central as Mam's eternally patient hand nudging at his tiller.

For about half an hour, Dad rattles around being my dad. He doesn't drink much, but he likes the whole cut-glass, lead-crystal, heavy-decanter type thing, so persuades me into having a whisky, which he knows I won't drink, and pouring himself one too, which he'll sip from then forget about. I swallow another couple of aspirin while he's not looking, just crunch them up in my mouth and swallow them without water. My headache is still there and my face is still sore, but they'll mend.

Meantime, Dad's conversation slowly calms. He talks about his clubs. Two in Cardiff. One in Swansea. Plans for a big one in Bristol, the biggest yet, but the plans have been pushed back a bit by recession. Strange thing is, he's become a really good businessman. Both bold and cautious. Meticulous in planning, swift and intuitive in execution. I wonder if he ever met Brendan Rattigan, if they'd have got on. I'm guessing yes.

I'm also, however, thinking about me. I fled home today because I couldn't stay there, but my windows will be just as fragile tomorrow. The dark shapes beyond Penry will be just as dark, just as dangerous.

I sometimes wonder if I've got an exaggerated sense of danger. Sometimes, not often, but at least once a month, I wake up in the night utterly terrified. No reason at all that I know of. Just something that happens. Maybe other people have this too and don't talk about it, but I don't think so. I think it's just me.

Dad is talking about the security issues that his clubs have faced recently. Nothing out of the ordinary. The occasional idiot with a knife. The odd binge-drinker who gets violent.

I don't premeditate the thought, just blurt out, "I know. I sometimes think I should get myself a gun. You never know what might happen."

That's all I say. A stupid thought that wouldn't have lasted out the minute. But Dad's on to it straight away.

"What do you mean, love? You want to become an armed officer, is that it? Are detectives even allowed to carry guns?"

I backtrack straight away. No, I don't want to join some armed response unit. No, I can't see the South Wales force thinking that DC Griffiths would be the right person to wave the heavy weaponry. No, it's probably a stupid idea.

"You mean have a gun at home? A licensed thing? But you know, these days, you can get a shotgun or whatever for going out hunting. Air rifles, that sort of thing. But they won't let people carry handguns. Not off a shooting range. And quite right too. The number of crazy people there are. If I could ban the whole damn lot of them, I would."

"Yes, me too. I'm not really saying anything. Just, like you say, there are some idiots out there."

"You worried about something, Fi girl? If you are, you need to say. Maybe the police isn't the right job for you. I mean, don't get me wrong, you're fabulous. CID bloody lucky to have you, never mind what I might have said. But you mustn't take risks you shouldn't, you know."

He pauses, the shadows of our old arguments crossing our lamplit present.

His suspicion of anything to do with the police. His fear. My determination to pursue the career of my choice. Two obstinate people, digging in.

And to be fair to Dad — and I didn't perhaps understand this as well as I should have done — he was worried about me too. He's always been protective of me, doubly or trebly so during my illness and afterwards. He didn't want me to go to Cambridge. For the first few weeks of my first term there, he was dropping by every second or third day, pretending he had business in East Anglia — which he most certainly did not — until I ordered him not to come again until the end of term. Then, even when my life was all put back together again — no recurrence of the illness, excellent degree, some friends — he felt that a career in the police force was absolutely the wrong one for me. Too much danger. Too much stress. Risks physical and mental. He'd have loved me to stay living at home. To work for him as office manager or something like that. Not front of house, but a back-office fixer. In his imaginings, he saw us as a possible dream team — which, I have to say, we might well have been.

But it didn't happen. Helping to run Dad's pole-dancing clubs was hardly my idea of a career, and after my first year or so in uniform, Dad gradually stopped expecting to me to crack up. That was when he put the deposit down so I could buy my house. He didn't want me to move out, but he accepted it, even if his version of accepting it meant that for the first few months he was always popping round, because he "was just driving past".

Anyway. The present pause compresses that whole debate into a few seconds of silence. It's Dad's way of saying that I can always quit the police, come home, take a job with him. My silence is my way of saying, "Thanks, Pa, but no way." Our argument unfolds in a few beats of nothing at all.

Then it finishes. Finishes with a truce.

"You look after yourself, love. If you need anything, you just say."

"I will, Dad. Thanks."

It's bedtime. I feel oceanically tired. Tonight, I know it already, I'm going to sleep well. I'm home.

CHAPTER
TWENTY-THREE

Late to work, but I've slept well, I've got one of Mam's cooked breakfasts inside me, and Kay has worked something close to magic on my bruises with an array of concealers and foundation. I stick to my dentist story, and she seems to buy it. As she works, she tells me that she's thinking about training as a beauty therapist. I've no idea what that means — she gives you therapy if you're beautiful? — but she'd get my vote. There's still puffiness, but at least it's not orangey-purple puffiness. Good enough.

Ken Hughes, who has taken to noting down the names of officers not present at the morning briefing, sees me coming two hours late to my desk. He starts to give me a bollocking, but I whip out my dental emergency card and play it before he's really got rolling. He lays off me at once.

Other people are being unnaturally nice to me too. It's not my grievous dental injuries that are affecting them so, more that I found my first corpse two days ago, an event that apparently entitles me to special treatment. It seems there's no quicker route to sympathy from your workmates than stumbling across a dead body. People are so positive and kind to me, you'd think I'd killed her myself.

Anyway. Catch-up time. The first twenty-four or forty-eight hours of an inquiry tend to move fast, and the Stacey Edwards arm of Lohan is beginning to crank out data, no matter that yesterday was Sunday. Meantime, most of the people whose DNA placed them at the Mancini house have been interviewed, and transcripts and summaries are now available on Groove.

Rhys Vaughan and Conway Lloyd have both been picked up and interviewed separately. Ken Hughes led the interview with Vaughan. Lloyd had the pleasure of Jackson's beetle-browed attentions. But neither Vaughan nor Lloyd had much to offer us. They both paid Janet Mancini for sex. Both swore that they weren't up to anything kinky. Neither of them had seen April Mancini, though there was enough space upstairs for April to have been in one room while Janet was busy in the other. Rhys Vaughan swore that he took no drugs at all. Conway Lloyd admitted to occasional marijuana and cocaine use. Both men were adamant that they'd taken no drugs with Mancini. Vaughan admitted to four visits, Lloyd to two. Both men were in full-time employment. Vaughan had paid between £60 and £80 for his pleasures. Lloyd had paid £120 on both occasions. They'd both found Mancini on the Taff Embankment — not far from where I'd sat with Bryony Williams — and had either walked or driven back to Allison Street from there. Mancini hadn't been all that talkative. In Vaughan's sweetly loving words on the transcript, "I mean, you're not paying to listen to her, are you?"

According to Brydon, who was in the office yesterday and was present for part of the Hughes-Vaughan interview, the youngster was almost peeing himself with fear. A stupid kid, paying for sex, not wanting to accept that he was funding an industry that routinely kills or injures its practitioners. Lloyd, from the sound of it, was pretty much the same.

So much for those two.

The next person to leave DNA at the house, Tony Leonard, was brought in this morning and is being interviewed now.

Karol Sikorsky, whose DNA was also found at the house, has not yet been located, but enquiries are proceeding actively. I notice that Brydon is on the team hunting Sikorsky.

"Any leads?" I ask him.

He shrugs. "We don't have an address, but we've got some idea who he hangs out with. Not a very nice man, we're guessing."

"Our killer, do you reckon?"

"Could be. Got to be possible. Organised-crime links. He's possessed weapons. And he *was* in the house."

"How about Stacey Edwards? Do we have much on her?"

"Nothing much. Not that they talked about at the briefing anyway. I think they've got you down for digging into her records. Social Services stuff."

"Oh great. Paperwork." I can predict the whole thing in advance. Alcoholic and abusive father. Mentally ill mother. Taken into care. Foster homes. Behavioural problems. Difficulties at school. An abortion somewhere along the way. Class-A drugs. Prostitution. And after a suitable length of time, death. Another car crash of a life, brutally ended. "I don't know why Jackson always throws the crap at me."

"He doesn't. You're interviewing with Jane Alexander as well. You're the only DC who's on the interviews list."

If it comes to that, then the hunt for Sikorsky is definitely the most urgent element of Lohan at the moment, and the fact that Brydon's been roped into it is a pretty strong clue about the way he's regarded by Jackson and Hughes. If there is a promotion to DI around, then Brydon must be in the frame for it.

We both pause, then both start to speak, then I do.

"We should sort out that drink," I say.

"Wednesday, maybe? Subject to operational requirements." That last bit said in Brydon's mock-serious voice, a bit deeper and slower than his normal one. He means that if Lohan jumps up a gear — perhaps because Sikorsky is reeled in — then anything could happen.

"Wednesday," I agree. "Assuming you're not beating the crap out of Sikorsky in a cellar somewhere."

"Or breaking his fingers, anyway."

"Ha, ha. Very funny."

"Or sticking a table through his cheek."

"Oh, ho, ho, ho. Don't you have to bugger off to polish your knuckledusters or something?"

Brydon smirks at me and lopes off. When I had my little contretemps with the breast-fondler, I managed to break three of his fingers, and followed up by kicking out at his kneecap with the toe of my boot, which was how I managed to dislocate it. Unfortunately, he rolled slightly sideways as he fell, gashing his cheek on the corner of the table. The table corner was sharp and went right through the flesh of his cheek, stopping only when it hit teeth. My dear colleagues love any excuse to remind me of all this, though I imagine that the joke will run dry after a few hundred further repetitions. In the meantime, I've got the sweet balm of endless work to keep me cheered and comforted.

Work such as catching up with everything that's been going on over the last thirty-six hours.

Work such as digging into Stacey Edwards's past and getting summaries and reports up on Groove.

Work such as checking in with Jane Alexander, because she and I are listed to interview prostitutes. Bev Rowland and a female DI from Neath are pairing up to interview others. Another female DI is said to be coming over from Swansea as well. I don't know who she'll be paired with.

And work such as checking my phone numbers. I've got eleven names and addresses from my flower-girl calls. Four of those turn out to be family numbers, one way or another. Three of them I don't know a whole lot about, but there was a straightforward blokeiness about the men answering, and the names don't flash up red on our criminal records system. At some stage, I suppose, I'll need to research them further, but they don't take priority now.

That leaves four remaining ones. All female, but no vice records on any of them, and at least three of the addresses are in good parts of town where I wouldn't particularly expect to find prostitutes living or working. The fourth address was more marginal, but when I phone it again, I get a brisk, no-nonsense voice and the sound of family clamour in the background. I can't be certain, but it doesn't look to me as though Penry's phone buddies have much to do with prostitution, so one of the easiest possible avenues of research seems to be a dud. Room for further thought, however.

Of the numbers on Penry's phone, there were eight where I couldn't get through to a human being. To those eight I sent a text — MUST MEET ASAP. THIS PHONE CD BE COMPROMISED. TEXT ME ON NEW NUMBER. BRIAN. I gave out my phone number and so far I've received five texts back. Of those, four come over as simply baffled. IS THIS A WIND-UP? said one fairly typical message. SEE YOU DOWN THE PUB. MIKE.

But the last of the five is my prize specimen. DON'T EVER CONTACT ME AGAIN. JUST FUCK OFF. FUCK RIGHT OFF. FLETCH.

I love everything about that message. I like the fact that it's properly spelled and punctuated. I like the repetition of "fuck off". Not elegant, but pithy, and you can give me pith over elegance any day of the week. Best of all, though, I love the "Fletch". A nickname that's no more than a sawn-off surname. I don't know who Mr or Ms Fletcher may be, or how he or she fits into this puzzle. I don't even know if this is one puzzle or two puzzles or maybe even more, but I do know that right now I'd rather lay my hands on the enigmatic Fletcher than on the darkly menacing Karol Sikorsky.

Just as I'm marvelling over Fletcher's text, Jane Alexander comes over to me.

"You OK?"

"Yes. Emergency dentist thing over the weekend. Feels like someone's run over the side of my face."

"God, yes, sorry. That does look sore."

"Oh, you meant —"

"Yes. After Saturday. It was brave of you to go in through the window."

I shrug. May as well give myself a reputation for toughness, even if it's not quite deserved. "I'm glad you were there."

"Still. You're OK to go out again this afternoon?"

"Prozzie patrol?"

"Yes." She gives me a slightly stern *yes*. "Start after lunch? Two o'clock?"

I agree. The timing's good. When Jane goes, I give Bryony Williams a call. She answers, but there's a din in the background as though about two hundred children are being asked to see how much noise they can make.

"Are you OK to talk?" I say, once I've succeeded in letting her know who I am.

"Sure, just give me a sec." A door closes somewhere and the sound level drops. "Sorry. My day job is teaching art. They'll be OK for a bit anyway."

I ask her if we can meet for lunch. It turns out that she's working quite close by and we agree to meet in Cathays Park at one. That's helpful. I'm interviewing all afternoon with Jane and I want to be as prepped as possible before I go.

I poke around on our records system for any interesting-looking Fletchers, but don't find anyone who takes my fancy. I check my Penry case files. I don't recall any Fletchers there and my memory for such things is normally good, but it seems an obvious place to look. No joy there, though.

Ten fifty. I'll need to leave in two hours. Two hours to find a Fletcher. A maker of arrows. That's what a fletcher was. A missile man. A weapons guy.

I do everything I can to trace him. Our databases. Newspapers. Google. I do everything a good copper should do and come up with nothing that seems to make any sense. I'm either not seeing a connection or I'm missing something obvious.

Then my time's up. It's one o'clock, near as dammit. I run to the park and get there just as Bryony Williams arrives.

CHAPTER
TWENTY-FOUR

Butetown.

The morning started out fine, but the clouds have run in from over Cardiff Bay and now lie damply gathered over the warm streets, as though anxious to cut off an escape. The city feels like what it is. A smear of brick and concrete slotted into the narrow gap between earth and sky, more beautiful than neither. This is the layer where the violence starts. We're only three hundred yards from 86 Allison Street and the ghosts of that place are pressing close.

Jane Alexander is her normal brisk, bright, efficient self. Me, I'm nothing of the sort, still disturbed by yesterday. My neck feels jolted, as though something was knocked out of line by Penry's blow and hasn't yet slipped back into place. But it's not so much a physical thing. More a mental one. As though some of my equanimity, my confidence, was dislodged. I keep remembering, not the actual blow as such, more the state of myself in the instant following. A rag doll useless on the bottom step.

Not a good state to be in.

Not a good state to be in when our third interview of the day — the first two having been bland and unhelpful — starts with a dark doorway swinging open and a pale face looming towards us from the darkness beyond. A pale, frightened face.

Ioana Balcescu. A prostitute.

No known link to Janet Mancini or to Stacey Edwards. No known link to organised crime. We've only got her data from the records kept as a routine matter by the Vice Unit. She's dressed in leggings and a loose cotton top. Long, dark hair, not styled or even, from the look of it, combed. A thin face, not unattractive. But it's not the shape of Balcescu's nose that catches the attention, or whether her lips are full enough. What catches the attention are the dark, purpling bruises around her eyes. The gashed lip and swollen jaw. The way one arm holds the other, providing a sling. The caution in every painful step.

I find myself staring at her in shock, as though into a mirror. I feel exposed, half expecting Jane to swing round, look me up and down, and say, "I *knew* it wasn't the dentist."

She does no such thing and the moment passes. Balcescu doesn't want to talk to us, but we're here on her doorstep and she can't summon the strength to tell us to get lost. We go through to her front room, which is halfway between somebody's grotty living room and a tart's boudoir. There's a red light and a large unframed poster of a topless girl with her lips open and her eyes half closed, pulling down on her bikini bottoms as though they're chafing. There are a few other pictures, not as big but more explicit. Also dirty wine glasses, a TV listings magazine, a gas bill, a portable telly.

Jane Alexander sits on the edge of the couch, as though to sit back in it will transform her into a drug-addled prostitute. She's dressed the way she's always dressed. Far too classy for her present surroundings. And though she's too professional to show it to Balcescu, I can tell straight away that she's not comfortable. She feels out of her depth. When she explains why we're here, her voice is excessively formal. Tight and unrelaxed.

I step in.

"Would you mind, Ioana? We've been on the go all afternoon, and if you had a cup of tea, it would be just brilliant." I've noticed before when working with these Balkan women that they're all scared of the police. They don't expect us to protect them. They assume we're here to jail them or beat them up or extort money. Those feelings can be helpful or harmful in an interview situation, depending on how you play them. My instinct is that we need to go softly, softly. "Here, if you show me where the tea things are, we can make it together."

Ioana takes me through to the kitchen. Jane remains where she is. If it were me, I'd be poking round the room. Since it's Jane, she won't be.

Ioana stops at the kitchen door. I go in, fill the kettle — an old-fashioned metal one — and pop it on. I find three cups, clean them, locate tea bags and make tea. No herbal, but this is about relaxing Ioana, not drinking tea.

I put my hand up to her eye and touch it very gently. "Poor you. That looks horrible."

She pulls her head away, but I gently persist. I move my hand to her side, which flinches from the touch.

"They gave you a really good going-over, didn't they?"

No response.

I lift her top very gently. There are bruises all down her side, front and back. "My God. You poor love." She's got prominent ribs and small breasts, like those of a girl. I wonder if she's got an eating disorder. When I touch one of her ribs where the bruising is at its worst, she winces. A possible fracture.

I put her top down. There is nothing premeditated in my look of sympathy. It's as real as the walls and air. "Have you been to a hospital?"

Stupid question that, because the answer is inevitably a "no".

"How do you take your tea, Ioana? How many sugars?"

"One sugar, please."

"Do you know what? I'll give you two today. You've had a big shock and a big cup of sweet tea will do wonders. It was yesterday they hurt you, was it? Those bruises look horrible."

Ioana doesn't answer directly, but adjusts her head in a way that makes me think that yesterday was correct. The teas are made and Ioana tries to pick up one of the cups.

"Here, no, don't take that, you just look after yourself. I'll follow you."

She moves back through. I follow with the cups.

206

"Now, Ioana, where would you be most comfortable? The big sofa maybe? Jane — this is Jane, by the way. You don't need to call her DS Alexander, and you can just call me Fiona, or just plain Fi if you prefer — Jane, I wonder if you could make space." Jane gets up, looking awkward, but also relieved that someone else is running things for the moment. "Ioana, why don't you sit here? Or lie, if that's more comfortable. Where does it hurt most? I can fetch you a pillow from upstairs if you'd like. I'll put the tea just there so you can reach it easily. There, that's better."

After a bit, Jane gets the idea as well and turns from a vaguely scary blonde detective into something a bit more maternal and mumsy. She does mumsy better than me, in fact, when she gets in the groove. I lift Ioana's top again so Jane can see her injuries. Jane looks on in silence, and her face is grim.

"Now, Ioana," I say, exchanging glances with Jane and getting her permission to continue, "we're going to ask you a few questions. You don't have to say anything to us at all. You're not under suspicion from us. We're not from immigration, so we're not about to ask to see your visa or your passport or anything like that. Do you understand all that?"

She nods.

"Now, if you'd like us to call you ma'am or Miss Balcescu, then we'll do that, but if you don't mind, I'd prefer to call you Ioana. Such a lovely name. It's the same as Joanna, is it?"

Another micro-nod.

"Now, then, we're here because we understand that you may have known Janet Mancini. Is that right?"

A leading question. Bad police practice, but Jane allows me to get away with it.

Ioana nods.

"Horrible what happened there. I don't know if you knew Stacey Edwards as well, did you?"

No nod at all this time. A stiffening. Fear.

"Well, you know what, let's not go into that now. I mean, after what happened last night, there's only so much you want to be reminded of. You're probably scared that if you say too much to us, they'll come back again. Is that what you're scared of?"

"Yes." A firm nod. Still the fear, but at least there's something else in the room now.

I exchange glances with Jane. She's meant to be leading this interview. She led the last two while I took notes. That's the way DCI Jackson said to do it. As I recall, his precise words were, "You fuck up, you fuck up at all, and you're never working on a delicate assignment for me again." But there's more than one way to fuck up, and though I'm not absolutely sure what Jane's glance meant, it didn't mean "Shut up right now", so I'm going to continue.

"OK, Ioana, we don't want to get you into trouble, so we're going to make it really easy for you. And I want you to know that we came here in an unmarked car. Do you know what that means? Not a police car with a siren and everything, just a perfectly ordinary car. And we look like two perfectly ordinary people. No one knows that we're police officers and we're not going to tell anyone either. Do you understand that?

"Good. And I think you're going to need some help. I think you need to see a doctor." Ioana instantly starts to protest and I raise my hand to stop her. "I know you won't go to hospital. That's OK. But if we send someone to the house, that'll be all right. We'll do it the same way. An unmarked car. Not a police car. And a doctor just in ordinary clothes. Looking like anyone else. All right?

"And then I know you know Bryony Williams. You know who I mean? The StreetSafe lady. Short curly hair." Ioana nods. The name relaxes her a little. "Now, I saw her this lunchtime. She said to me that she has a programme you can go on to help you deal with the drugs. We know you take heroin — smack — and that's OK. You're not going to get into trouble with us. We just want to help, don't we, Jane?" Jane is quick to nod and again we exchange glances. This time I'm pretty sure that she is telling me to go on, so I do.

"And, Ioana love, what we're really like to do is take you away from all this. I know that's scary, but it's what we want and what Bryony wants. You don't have to say yes now, but just don't say no. We'll take things one tiny step at a time. Do you understand what I mean? One tiny step at a time."

"Yes."

Ioana's yes is half saying that she understands, half saying that she's signing up for the deal. If I were a double-glazing salesman, I'd know this was the moment of maximum reward, maximum vulnerability. I shift over to the sofa where Ioana is lying and put my hand on her arm. Leave it there. Human contact, without threat, without money, without drugs, without demand. When was the last time Ioana felt that?

We fall silent for a bit. I trust Jane to keep her mouth shut. There's something precious in this silence.

Finally, "Ioana, you know we need to ask you some questions. I'm sorry, but we do. I don't want you to say anything at all out loud. Just nod or shake your head. If you don't know, raise your eyebrows. Yes, just like that. It'll only take a few minutes. We won't write anything down. We just want to know. Then we'll go again. The next person you'll see will be the doctor. Then maybe Bryony. Are you all right with that? Do you understand what I've said?"

Nod.

"Good. Then let's start." Jane shifts in her seat. If I'm interviewing, she's meant to be note-taking and I've just ruled that out. I'm outside procedure here, not in a bad way, but in a way that makes her uncomfortable. She's rolling with it, though. Good for her. Her notebook is on her lap, but it's lying idle for now.

Time for my first question.

"Did you know Janet Mancini?"

Nod.

"And little April perhaps?"

Nod. Sideways nod, with a hint of no.

"All right. You didn't particularly know April, but you knew her by sight. Were you there on the night of her murder?"

Shake.

"No, didn't think you were, but it's one of those things we have to ask. My boss would go nuts if I didn't ask it."

Smile.

My hand is still on her arm. I'm not going to move it if she doesn't.

"Now, I'm going to ask you if you know various other people. Some of them you will have heard of. Others you won't. Others maybe or maybe not. We'll see. OK?"

I get started.

I begin with names that I've got partly from Bryony Williams and partly from police records. East European girls with an involvement in prostitution. I'm betting that Ioana knows a good half of them, and she does. More than. More than half. She's getting comfortable with the nod/shake thing, which is my main reason for asking.

"OK. We're doing brilliantly. Now some other names. You won't know so many of these. Conway Lloyd."

Puzzlement. Shake.

"Rhys Vaughan."

Shake.

"Brian Penry."

Shake.

"Tony Leonard."

Shake, but not a very confident one.

"He sells drugs. About Jane's height maybe. Dark hair. Receding hairline. You know, bald."

I mime bald, to help with Ioana's comprehension. She smiles — crookedly, because the right-hand side of her face isn't doing anything much but causing her pain, but a smile's still a smile. It's accompanied by a mini-nod, indicating "sort of".

"He's not the one we need to worry about, though, is he?"

Shake. A very definite one. Tony Leonard owes Ioana Balcescu a box of chocolates, I'd say.

"How about Karol Sikorsky?"

Fear. No nod. No shake.

"Was it him who did all this?" I indicate her damaged body.

A very slow shake.

"OK. It was one of his friends. Part of his group anyway. That's right, isn't it? Just shake your head if I'm wrong."

No nod.

No shake.

But her eyes are telling me yes. One of Sikorsky's accomplices. Again, I exchange glances with Jane. She's reading it the same way.

I say, really carefully, "Ioana, we think that Karol Sikorsky may be a very bad man. We want to catch him and lock him up. But we do need you to help us. I think Karol Sikorsky is part of a group of men who brings girls like you over from Romania and countries around there to Cardiff and South Wales generally. They probably tell you how lovely your life is going to be here, then you find it isn't, but you can't get away. Am I right so far?"

212

A nod. A good-quality, courtroom-ready nod.

"Good. Thank you. Now, I think that same group of men get violent. Those men need to be in prison and we want to put them there. So will you do this for me? If you know that Sikorsky is responsible for killing Stacey Edwards, then please say, 'Yes.' I don't mean that he necessarily killed her himself, but that he had something to do with it. That he was closely involved. If those things are true, please say, 'Yes.'"

No nod.

No shake.

A frozen silence, bigger than the sky, emptier than the ocean.

I let the silence expand for as long as I can keep it going, before nudging one last time. Now or never.

"If you help us, we can catch him. We can stop him hurting you. We can stop him hurting anyone. Ioana Balcescu, was Karol Sikorsky responsible for the murder of Stacey Edwards?"

"Yes."

"And also for the murders of Janet and April Mancini?"

"Yes."

"And also for injuring you?"

"Yes."

"Maybe because you knew about him and what he did? Maybe they beat you this badly as a way to warn you to keep silent?"

"Yes."

It's hardly even correct to describe her answers as words. She moved her lips. Her eyes said yes. I didn't even know at the time — and I don't think Jane did either — whether any actual sound crept out into the room. It didn't matter. A loud yes works as well as a silent one. I notice that Jane has made notes of my last four questions and Ioana's answers. She wants evidence that can be produced in court. Notes made "contemporaneously" with the interview. The kind of evidence from which a prosecution is formed. But I'm also conscious of my undertaking to Ioana.

"Now, my colleague Jane here has just made notes. Not of the whole interview, just this very last bit. We need that because we want to arrest Sikorsky and put him in prison. For the rest of his life, I hope. Certainly until he's a very old man. But I promised you we wouldn't take notes. If you want us to tear up these notes, we will. You just need to ask us to. You need to say it out loud."

A second goes by. Two seconds. Five seconds.

Good enough for me. Good enough for Jane. On our side of things, the police side, the side that is always thinking about how something will play in court, there's a huge sense of relief, but I know that Ioana is feeling the exact opposite. She's worried that she's just signed her own death warrant, and maybe she has. In the country she was born in, the police are not to be trusted. The same is true here. Ioana doesn't have to worry that we're in the pay of the mob. She doesn't have to worry about corruption and criminality and violence. But she has to rely on our discretion, and a clumsy public statement or a snippet of gossip overheard in a pub could be enough to bring the

214

retribution Ioana fears. If we were seen entering her house, that might be enough to kill her too.

For a few seconds, I have the feeling that by answering as she has done, Ioana was choosing to end her own life. To end it bravely, selflessly, but still to end it, to quit the eternal battle.

Feeling uncomfortable, I complete my questions the way Jane is silently urging me to.

"Good. Thank you. Now I'll ask one last big question before we finish. Can you give me any other names? Friends of Sikorsky? The ones he gets to do his dirty work? Maybe the men who came here yesterday? If you can give me any names at all, then we can arrest them. We'll arrest them, then send them to jail for a very long time. That's what we want to do. We want to look after you and people like you. Do you understand?"

A nod, but a frightened one. She doesn't want to tell us. She's not going to do so anyway. Ioana's cooperation is pretty much at an end, I'd say. From her face, Jane thinks the same way.

"Can you excuse us a moment, Ioana? I just need to chat with my colleague quickly. You stay lying there. Just say if you want anything."

Jane and I go out into the hall, where we talk in a rapid-fire hum. I tell Jane about the extent of Ioana's injuries, which Jane hadn't seen as fully as I had. Jane is worried about whether the evidence we've just collected will survive in a courtroom. It's marginal, that's for sure. Any defence lawyer would rip into it, potentially accusing us of applying unfair pressure to the witness, breaching procedure in not noting down every transaction that took place. That's fair enough. If I were a defence lawyer, I'd do the same.

On the other hand, as I point out to Jane and as she knows full well, our choices were to act as we did or collect no serviceable evidence at all. We agree that as soon as we step outside the house, we'll independently make our own notes of the interview, sign them, then compare them. Hopefully, our two accounts will be identical, near enough.

The other big issue is how much more we can expect to achieve from continuing. The rulebook says we should be asking a whole slew of further questions. Ms Balcescu, will you please tell us when you last saw Janet Mancini? Describe for us your contacts with Karol Sikorsky. Are you aware, Ms Balcescu, that this is a murder inquiry and the withholding of evidence may constitute an offence? That, pretty much, was how we conducted the last couple of interviews and they came up with a big fat rosy nothing.

"Shall I step in there, one on one, and see if she tells me anything?" I ask. "If we catch the bastards, then we can probably coax her into making a statement. If I were her, I wouldn't say a thing as long as they're still out there. For now, I'm guessing that we'll do better by going softly, softly."

Jane thinks. She's stressed by this situation, I realise. It bothers her that she's flying out of radio contact with the rulebook. I'm not stressed. I feel more comfortable here. It's the radio contact that stresses me.

Jane nods. "OK. I'll see if we can get a doctor over, though really she needs to go to hospital."

I'm relieved. I wanted time alone with Ioana, but didn't want to force the issue.

Back inside the room, I sit down again by Ioana. She looks at me — wide, dark, East European eyes, her best feature — and I gaze back at her. Neither of us say anything. She doesn't need a doctor or a couple of intrusive coppers. She needs a time machine. She needs to go back to the age of eight or nine, or earlier. Back to being a newborn. She needs different parents, a different upbringing, a different past. She needs to be on a completely different planet in a completely different life. No matter which way you read the signs on this one, she's riding hard for an unhappy ending.

Through the wall, we can hear Jane on the phone to the office, sorting out a doctor to pay a visit. That's how we do things on Planet Normal. It's not how things have ever happened in Ioana's world.

"You've done well," I tell her. "That's Jane sorting out a doctor for you. He'll be here soon."

"Thanks you."

"You can trust him. It's safe to let him in."

"OK."

"Is there anything more you can tell me about Karol Sikorsky? Where he lives? Who his friends are? Anything at all?"

She shakes her head and looks away from me. I decide not to push it any further. Instead, I show her my card and write my mobile number on the back.

"This is me. My name's Fiona. You can call me anytime at all. If you feel up to telling me more —

maybe about the men who beat you up — then call me. OK? I'll put it here."

I thrust the card under the sofa cushion, so she knows where it is, but out of sight of any prying eyes. I don't want Sikorsky's thugs to find it, for Ioana's sake and mine.

"I'd better go now," I tell her. "Do you want anything from the kitchen before I go?"

"No, thanks you. I'm OK."

"Do you want to see the telly? Here. I'll put it here." I sort out the TV and remote control, then squat down beside her and hold her hand. "You've done really well. You've been very brave. You've helped a lot of people." Even to my ears, it sounds as though I'm not expecting her to survive, and maybe I'm not. But she grips my hand and smiles. Her life probably hasn't been full of people telling her she's done well.

Then, I don't know what possesses me, but I ask, "Ioana, can I ask you one last question? Have you ever heard of a man called Brendan Rattigan?"

I'm not sure what I was expecting when I asked that question. I haven't really believed that Rattigan was alive. I'm pretty darn sure that Penry and Rattigan were up to something, and something with a connection to the Lohan murders. But I think I asked the question because I wanted to know how that damn debit card ended up in Janet Mancini's squat. Idle curiosity. Something to say.

But that just shows why you have to ask.

Ioana tries to pull herself upright from her lying position. Those cracked ribs stop her and she cries out

218

in pain. Jane's done with her phone call and pops the door open to see what's going on. The door swinging open interrupts anything that Ioana might have been about to say. So she says nothing. Her forte throughout this interview. But her face is shock and fear and distress.

Jane and I gape at each other.

"Can you tell me anything about him, Ioana? Anything at all?"

Bad interview technique. Too non-specific. Too open-ended. All I get is Ioana's staring eyes and a long swinging headshake. I don't know if that's no, she won't say or no, he isn't dead. It seems like both to me. In any case, the moment passes and Ioana's back in her own world, remote and uncommunicative.

We say our goodbyes and leave.

The Butetown street seems like a different planet. A bit grubby, but normal. A place where women aren't beaten into a pulp and terrified into silence. The clouds that had bothered me before are still there, but they feel ordinary and comforting.

"What on earth happened in there?"

I don't tell her. Or rather I lie. Ioana sat up. She hurt herself. She's upset. She's frightened.

Jane makes no comment. Just says that we'd better write up our interview notes as soon as we get back to the car. A return to the rulebook. A nondescript Cardiff street. Planet Normal.

CHAPTER
TWENTY-FIVE

We'd planned two more interviews that day, but postpone them. It seems more important to deal with the Balcescu one. We drive a couple of blocks away, down to the railway station, just to be out of sight of Balcescu's house, then write up our notes sitting side by side in Jane's car, where the loudest sound is of our pens moving over the paper. Jane has another hair loose on her shoulder and I want to pick it off for her, but I only want to do that because I want her to turn to me with a smile, and I only want that because what I saw in Balcescu's house frightened me and made me anxious for comfort. Probably best not to try and get that by soliciting a cuddle from a superior officer, however. I've got good intuitions about these things. It wouldn't work out.

I finish my notes before Jane. She looks sideways at me, and I realise that she finds me intimidating too. Not my dress sense, obviously, or my social skills. But I'm very comfortable with words. I can zoom through things like writing notes or summarising documents in half the time it takes most of my colleagues. I feel slightly weird that I'm intimidated by Jane while she's intimidated by me. These things should cancel each other out, no?

Because I'm feeling weird, I tell Jane that I'm going to step outside and get some air. And as soon as I swing the car door open, in between pulling the handle and it swinging out to the maximum-open position, I realise where I'll find Fletcher. Sometimes the best thing to do is also the most obvious.

I call directory enquiries and ask for a number for Rattigan Industrial & Transport. I get put through to a corporate switchboard. I ask for a Mr Fletcher. I'm told there's no one at corporate HQ with that name, but which division was he in? I'm prepared for that question. Scrap metal doesn't seem to have a whole bundle to do with the case. Shipping just might. All those ships coming in from the Baltic could be loaded up with nice Afghan heroin, enough to keep any number of prostitutes hooked. Drugs and sex. One business, not two.

I ask for the shipping division and am put through to a separate switchboard in Newport.

"Mr Fletcher, please."

"Just putting you through now . . . Oh, hold on, would you?" Muffled whispering in the background, then the receptionist's voice clearer again. "I'm sorry, it was Huw Fletcher you wanted, was it?"

Eeny, meeny, miny, moe. I say, "Yes."

"I'm sorry, Huw Fletcher isn't with us any more. Is there someone else who can help you at all?"

"He's not with you? I had a meeting arranged for this coming week. I was just calling to confirm arrangements." I make my voice a little affronted. A "What kind of company are you?" sort of voice.

"Honestly, I'm afraid we have no idea where he is. He's been away a couple of weeks. But if you want to speak with one of his colleagues in the scheduling department, I'm sure someone there can help."

There's probably something clever to say at that point, but if there is, I don't find it. I mutter apologies and hang up.

Bingo! Big bingo! I don't yet know what I have, except that it's something special, something that DCI Jackson really and truly ought to know about, except that I can't think of a way to tell him. I don't think the bright-eyed, bushy-tailed DC Griffiths would thank me for fessing up to her evil twin, the house-breaking, phone-stealing bad DC Griffiths.

I get quietly back into the car and let Jane finish. When she's done, we drive back to Cathays Park, mostly in silence.

For a while, routine takes over. Typing up notes, briefing Ken Hughes because Jackson is out of the office, getting the info up on Groove. All this is of the utmost priority, because we now have grounds for arresting Karol Sikorsky for the murders of Stacey Edwards and April Mancini. A huge deal, that is. Now, for the first time, the case feels on the brink of something. We can't arrest anyone without reasonable grounds for suspicion. A DNA sample and criminal record alone don't provide those grounds. Those two things plus Balcescu's evidence do. Once we have an arrest warrant, a search warrant will ensue. With luck and a following wind, that'll be all we need to crack the case wide open. The office has a buzz again, with Jane and me as the heroes of the hour.

It's almost 7p.m. before I'm done. I want to search out Brydon just to share a few moments with his more-than-friendly face, but can't find him. These big investigations, everyone is always somewhere else, or too busy to stop and talk.

In the end, I pack up and go home, only to find I can't stay there. The prickling feeling that I had for all those days last week is here again, a permanent guest now. I ask it to reveal its identity. *This is fear. This is fear.* I try the phrase out in my head, but I can't tell if it fits or if it doesn't. What's worse, I notice that when I stamp my feet, I can only dimly feel my toes and heels striking the floor. When I rap my hand against a kitchen worktop, or press it up against the point of a knife, the physical sensations of hardness or sharpness seem to be coming from a long way away, like old news reports, conveyed in jumpy black and white, or down a crackling phone line. I'm becoming numb to myself, physically and emotionally, and that's no good at all. It's how it starts, the bad stuff. This is how it always starts.

I don't muck about in these situations. I've learned not to. I call Mam and tell her I'll stay over another night, if that's OK. She says, of course, come right away. I put some bits in a bag and get ready to go.

Last thing before leaving, I pull out those photos of April. Little April, blind and dead. Little April with a sink where her brains should be. A sextuple smile and a secret I'm too dim to see. I don't spend long with her, though. All I need is sleep and sanity. Right now, both things seem precarious.

CHAPTER
TWENTY-SIX

For two blessed days, life goes on. Ordinary life. Lots of work. Canteen lunches, office grumbles. It's intense, but it's what I know. I like it.

There's a strong sense that Lohan is making progress. Known associates of Karol Sikorsky have been found and interviewed. According to Dave Brydon, who did two of these interviews, and who's heard the gossip from those who have done the others, Karol Sikorsky's buddies aren't the kind of crew you'd be thrilled to see at your daughter's birthday party. The first of Brydon's two interviews was with a Wojciech Kapuscinski. "He was a piece of work, he was. A real dangerous sod, if you ask me. Got a couple of ABHs on his record" — that's actual bodily harm, a fairly mild offence — "but that won't be the half of it."

I believe him. Kapuscinski's photo and details are up on Groove. Not only does he have a firearms conviction to go with those ABHs, he looks every inch like the dutiful foot soldier of organised crime: tough face, narrow eyes, shaven head, leather jacket. The kind of physique you get from lifting weights and avoiding vegetables: the fat-but-strong bouncer look.

Brydon and Ken Hughes did that interview and got nothing from it. "The bugger wouldn't tell us a thing. Didn't expect him to really, except he didn't come up with an alibi and doesn't deny knowing Sikorsky." Brydon doesn't say it, but nor does he need to. These things don't work because a thug breaks down and confesses something. They work because you apply pressure. A non-denial here. A piece of CCTV evidence there. A phone call there. Perhaps something new from forensics. Before too long, you hope to scrape together enough for a charge of some sort, and then the odds start to rebalance in your favour. You get little extra disclosures, scraps of information released in return for minor favours. You get search warrants to enter places that had been closed to you before. You ratchet up the pressure and before too long you get a leak proper, the crack in the dam that will bring the whole thing tumbling down.

And meantime, unexpectedly, another breakthrough. The Serious Organised Crime Agency have — on the third time of asking — provided an address in London where they believe Sikorsky has holed up from time to time. Bev Rowland tells me that Jim Davis (still not speaking to me and, I'm certain, dripping poison about me into the office gossip stream) has been putting it about that SOCA want to take over the Lohan inquiry. I'd say they're not likely to get it if they do. We all suspect organised crime involvement, but there's not enough at this stage for SOCA to make a move on us. Besides, Jackson is a respected DCI. His inquiry has been well run. We have some names. We need to get

226

some more tangible evidence soon, but things aren't stuck, they're progressing. For the time being, Jackson is arranging for Sikorsky's London address to be watched in the hope that the guy is dumb enough to turn up there. If that fails, he'll apply for a search warrant and raid the place anyway.

Jackson is pleased with all this because, just after lunch on Tuesday, he comes to find me and Jane Alexander at her desk. "That Balcescu interview," he says, "Well done. Good job."

We do our "Thank you, sir's", and Jane glows like someone's told her she can be form captain.

"Is this one behaving herself?" That's Jackson asking Jane about me.

"Yes, sir. More than that, actually. I thought she was first class with Balcescu. It was Fiona who —"

Jane is about to say something nice, but Jackson's "Alexander makes the running" slogan is knocking around in my head, and I don't want him to know that I went off piste, even if it was in a good cause.

"It was me that made the teas, sir. She's milk-no-sugar," I volunteer, indicating Jane. "Balcescu was one sugar, only I gave her two, given the circs."

"Her tea was OK, was it?" That to Jane.

"It was fine."

"Good."

Jackson says, "Good," again and goes muttering off. Jane swings back to me in surprise. I tell her that I want Jackson to think I know how to follow orders. "It's not always my strong suit," I add.

"You don't say."

Jane looks for a moment as though she might say something further, but she doesn't, and we go back to doing what we were doing.

Lovely work. Tedious, necessary, safe.

On Tuesday night, I go back home, but once again find my house scarily empty and vulnerable, so I bail out and spend a happy evening with my family. Dad and I haven't had any further conversation about guns, but he asks me if I've had my burglar alarm checked recently. I say no. Who checks a burglar alarm? I didn't know you had to check them. He says he'll send someone round and because nothing I say is likely to stop him from doing just that, I say nothing.

Wednesday itself is mostly a paperwork day — I'm not unhappy about that — and the one interview that Jane and I manage is by the book and uninformative. Which is good. I could use a little boredom in my life at the moment.

Apart from Balcescu, Jane and I have found out nothing useful from our interviews, but I've enjoyed working with her. Except for that one time, she asks the questions, I take the notes. She does everything by the book. So do I. The comfort of routine. Three of the girls we've talked to have been reluctant to say more than the bare minimum. One, Tania, a Welsh girl from the Valleys, talked incessantly, mostly about what punters were and were not into, but conveyed nothing much of value. She seemed ditzy to me and muddled, but not a stereotypical victim. She talked endlessly about sex and I realised that she really liked it. Enjoyed having lots of it. Some prostitutes, presumably, do.

228

All told, there have been worse ways to spend time. The write-ups are a pleasant way to spend the morning.

Huw Fletcher bothers me. He matters. I *know* he matters, but I've got no way of roping him into our inquiry. He left work abruptly enough that his colleagues are puzzled, but not puzzled enough to call the police. He sent a possibly suspicious text, which I only know about because I broke into a suspect's house and stole his phone. And even that text is only significant if you think Penry is significant, and you only think he is if Rattigan is. And Rattigan is dead, which means that — in the eyes of my colleagues — he can't possibly matter. *I* don't see it that way, of course. I think the dead matter just as much as anyone else, but then what else could I think, of all people?

About halfway through the afternoon, these ruminations bother me enough that I call Bryony Williams.

She answers after the third ring. I tell her who I am, then come straight out with it.

"Bryony, I need to ask a favour."

"Sure, no problem."

"First off, can I ask if you've ever heard of a guy called Huw Fletcher? Some connection with prostitution and/or drugs, but I can't tell you more than that."

"Huw Fletcher? No. Never heard of him."

"OK, that's fine. But look, I think this man Fletcher is involved in something nasty. Something nasty to do with the women you try to protect. I can't tell you why, but I've serious reason to think so. Trouble is, I can't reveal the witness who gave me Fletcher's name and I can't introduce Fletcher into the inquiry proper unless

I can supply evidence that connects him to it. I want you to be that evidence."

"What do you want me to do?"

"Just say that you've heard rumours from the girls you work with that Huw Fletcher has been involved in sex trafficking and prostitution. You heard the rumours and wanted to pass them on to me."

"OK. Yes, I'm happy to say all that."

"You may one day be asked to say the same thing in court."

"I understand. That's fine."

"You may find yourself being asked the same questions in the course of a missing persons investigation."

"*OK.*" A drawn-out OK, that one. "Who's the missing person? Fletcher?"

"Yes."

"All right. Go on, then. In for a penny, in for a pound."

"Bryony, you're a star. Whatever's one step up from a star. A quasar? Something like that."

"That's all right. It's not every day I'm asked to fabricate evidence by a police officer."

We ring off. I don't yet do anything, but I feel better for knowing that the possibilities have just widened. Fletcher, Fletcher, missile man.

That evening, operational requirements are such that Brydon and I are in a position to go out together. We agree to meet in a wine bar at seven thirty.

"Gives me a chance to go to the gym and gives you time to get ready. Get changed or whatever."

Get changed? I hadn't been intending to. I don't even know if Brydon was nudging me that I ought to, or whether he was just being male-clumsy. But the awkwardness affects both of us. Are we friends? Colleagues? Potential romantic partners? We're both unsure but, I suppose, keen to find out.

In any case, I like it that I've been told what to do. I leave the office punctually at five and go home. It feels odd to be back. Still not safe, but not as radically threatening as it had been after Penry's visit. I open my fridge and am surprised to find it full of food. I forgot that I'd restocked it on Sunday. I think about having a smoke and decide against. I go upstairs to try and work out what a girl is meant to wear to a date that might not be a date. Then I hear a van pull up outside.

I'm flooded with fear.

My knife and hammer are downstairs. I should have brought them up. My curtains are open and I should have closed them.

A man gets out of the van, walks to the front door and knocks. He looks like an ordinary guy. Could be a plumber. A meter reader. A delivery guy.

But what do killers look like? What did the man who killed Stacey Edwards look like?

I don't move. I don't know what to do. The man knocks again and I let the sound echo around in the silence.

Then the man walks back to his van. Gets out a phone and dials. I can see him, but am careful to step back far enough from my upstairs window that he'll have a job seeing me.

Luckily, my bedroom window is open a tad. Just four inches to let air in, and there's a window lock preventing it from going any further. But the gap is sufficient that I can hear the man's conversation. Not all of it, but enough. He's got a loud voice and he's asking for Mr Griffiths. My dad.

Fear rushes out again. I'm shaky, but I'm moving again. My brain, which was completely stuck, can now operate. I go downstairs, holding both walls as I go, and throw open the door.

"Fiona Griffiths, is it? Your dad sent me. Wanted me to have a look at the alarm and a few bits and pieces."

South Wales is full of people that my dad knows. I guess he must pay a lot of them one way or another, but the relationship never seems to be about employment, or even much about pay. It's just that if Tom Griffiths asks a favour of you, then you do it, knowing that one way or another that favour will be repaid. I've never really thought much about how all this works. It's just the way it is. "Your dad sent me." Four words meaning that your problem is fixed.

"Come on in. Sorry. Did you knock? I was upstairs and wasn't sure . . ."

It's a feeble excuse, but doesn't need to be any better. The man (Aled someone or other — Dad's people work by first names only as a rule) doesn't care. He's inside, taking the front off my burglar alarm, getting me to punch in my access code as he ostentatiously looks away, then he's off doing tests and checking connections. And all the time he's talking. A big alarm installation job he worked on at a canning factory in Newport. The silly things some people do with their access codes. The importance of maintenance.

To begin with, I'm irritated, because I don't want to have to stand around and make chit-chat when I'm about to go out. Then I realise that he doesn't give a damn whether he has anyone to talk to or not. I tell him I'm going upstairs, and do. It's even, strange to say, easier to get myself ready with him downstairs. I get less lost in my own head. I make simpler, better decisions. This dress. (Midnight blue, Monsoon, nice but not fussy.) This necklace. (Silver and jet beads, an old standby.) These shoes. (Dark blue satin-trimmed kitten heels, comfortable enough to walk in.) I put the things out on the bed, then wash and blow-dry my hair. It looks much the same after as before, but I like knowing that I've made the effort.

I don't want to get dressed up while Aled Whatnot is still in the house, so I go downstairs to hurry him up. He's done with the burglar alarm and is busy polishing away the Blu-Tack scabs with fine wire wool and white spirit.

"I'll touch these up after. It's going to show otherwise."

"Do you want a cup of tea?" I offer, because it's what you say to workmen, and Dad's cronies like tea just as much as anyone.

"White, no sugar, please, if you're making it. I've got a cupboard door off there." And indeed, on going into the kitchen, I find what had been a perfectly serviceable cupboard door lying on the floor. "Hinge needed adjusting, you probably noticed. It wasn't opening right. It'll be back on in a tick, though. I expect you're wanting to get off, are you?"

"Yes, in a bit."

I'm not in any rush — it's still only six fifteen — so I make the tea and try to remember if I'd noticed any problem with the cupboard before. A little clicky thing, maybe, on opening. No big deal. Aled Doodah is busy with paint pots now, and whistling.

I prefer chat to the whistling, so I hand him his tea but hang around, inviting conversation.

It's like inviting a lecture from a Mormon, a rant from a jihadist. Aled Thingummy is a whirlwind of chat, he's the Muhammad Ali of white noise. Gossip, unconnected little snippets, political comment, questions that are asked but invite no answer pass his lips in an unending torrent. I say almost nothing and marvel at his ability to blather.

As he's putting the cupboard door back on, one thing he says does catch my attention. He's been moaning about youth gangs in the city centre, then talking about guns and knives, then — with the sweet inconsistency of his kind — switches the focus of his monologue to the over-regulation of gun clubs.

"People don't want that, see. That's why you get these places springing up. Unregulated, like, not that I should tell you that, seeing that you are who you are. There's one place, farmer's turned a barn into a firing range. Nothing dodgy, if you get me, it's just for people who want to have a bit of fun. Handguns, that sort of thing, nothing dodgy, like I say. Up above Llangattock, it is. If you take the Llangynidr Road from the Heads of the Valleys, then take the Llangattock turn when it comes. It's the barn on the turn of the hill. Big white thing. They probably need ear defenders for the sheep, eh? Health and safety."

With that thought his chat streams off again in a different direction. He's on health and safety fascism now. Bad things about the government. Bad things about the city council. But not for long. The Blu-Tack scabs are gone. The cupboard door is back. The burglar alarm is as happy as it's ever going to be. Aled Thingummy opens and closes all the remaining cupboard doors to check that they're swinging right.

"Sound as a pound," he tells me, banging them shut.

He scoops up his stuff and whizzes off. The house feels weirdly quiet without him. It does also feel a bit safer, though I hadn't actually thought to worry about the burglar alarm in the first place.

I go up, get dressed and put on some make-up. I don't often make the effort, but if I put my mind to it, I can look all right. Not Kay-like gorgeous. That'll always be well beyond me. But nice. An attractive girl. That's all I've ever hoped to achieve, and I feel a kind of satisfied relief at being able to achieve it. More than relief. Pleasure. I like it. I like the way I look tonight.

At seven ten, I skitter out of the house. I've still got an undercurrent of anxiety about my physical safety, so I carry a kitchen knife in my clutch bag, but the knife is quite a small one, and the clutch bag matches my dress, has silver trimmings and boasts an extravagant silk bow, so as far as I'm concerned, I'm still in girly heaven. I get to the wine bar at almost exactly the same time as Brydon does.

"Bloody hell, Fi, you look absolutely smashing."

He'd have said that whatever I looked like, because Brydon is a proper gent, but the look on his face and the way he keeps looking at me tell me that he means it.

"You too, Mr B," I tell him, and allow him to take me inside.

The first forty minutes we're together are pretty toe-curling, in all honesty. Neither of us had quite decided the date/non-date thing in our heads before arriving. Or rather, I think we'd decided that it must be a date, but didn't quite know how to get from comradely professional banter through to dating intimacies.

After forty arduous minutes, Brydon rather abruptly calls for the bill and says, "Let's eat."

The restaurant he's chosen is only a few minutes away — we're off the Cathedral Road, the other side of the river from Bute Park and our offices — but he walks half a step ahead of me, moving a bit faster than I can manage, and he has his chest thrown out and his shoulders pulled back as though he's a soldier bracing himself for combat. I realise that this is his way of preparing for an all-out assault on Fortress Fi, and I'm touched, though I would slightly prefer it if potential suitors didn't regard a date with me as akin to entering combat. It's possible that I was prickly with him in the wine bar. I sometimes am without knowing it, my habitual default position. Not good when it comes to flaunting those feminine charms.

236

I determine to do better.

When we get to the restaurant — a nice place, "modern Welsh cuisine", £15 a main course, no less — I tell him that the place looks lovely. When we get to the table, we have a comedy moment around my chair. I was about to tug it out and sit on it when I realise Brydon is wanting to do the gentlemanly thing and pull it out for me, so I can sit down in a gracefully ladylike way. I'm a bit slow to realise this, so we have a short tug-of-war with the chair back before I figure out that I'm doing something wrong and transition as quickly as I can into graceful ladylike mode. Then, because I'm not good at these things, I start to sit before he's ready, and he only just has time to get the chair under me in time to avoid disaster.

Brydon freezes for a moment — he's awkward too — then he starts laughing, and I do, and everything feels more relaxed. His air of grimness visibly dissipates. I smile at him when we're sitting and tell him again that this is lovely. I even go as far as being coaxed into ordering a glass of white wine. I realise that I'm operating as though following instructions from some kind of dating manual, but I've found out that that's usually OK with people. It's only me who feels weird.

From that point on, things go much better.

The manual says that I ask my date about himself, so I do. I can't ask about work without sounding all copper-ish, and I don't know much about his personal life, so I ask about his time in the army. It feels like a clunky question to me. "So, Dave, how come you've never told me about your time in the army? What made you join up?" As I say it, I feel like a bad chat-show host. Spray tan and an idiot smile. But it works. The manual works. Brydon tells me about his time in the army. In 1998, he'd applied for the paras, been accepted and found himself flung into conflict in Kosovo the following year. He's characteristically modest in how he says what he says, though for all I know he has a drawer full of medals for gallantry. A better friend than me would already have known some of these details, and I feel a bit ashamed of myself for not having found out before.

From then on, I stick close to the textbook. When the starter comes, I tell him it's delicious. When the main course comes, I tell him it's wonderful. We eat from each other's plates. Brydon tells me again that I look absolutely beautiful. I remember to smile a lot.

I also try to reciprocate Brydon's candour. A big ask for me. The one thing that everyone would want to know more about — those two years of illness — is off limits, as far as I'm concerned. The less said about that, the better. But I do what I can. I tell him bits and bobs about Cambridge. I talk about my family. When Brydon says with a grin, "Your dad's settled down now, has he?" I deflect the question and tell him about the club my dad is wanting to get started in Bristol. He asks if I want another glass of wine, and I say no.

"Alcohol and me didn't use to mix at all. It's not so bad now, but I don't like to push it."

We don't talk about work much, but we do talk about why we do what we do. For Brydon, it was a fairly natural step. He wanted to get out of soldiering.

"It wasn't the danger so much, more I got cynical about the way politicians used us. I didn't know if I was making a difference and thought that in the police I could use my skills, day in, day out, to make a difference." On other lips, it would sound like self-righteous bullshit, but not on his. When he says it, it's just the truth. I love that it's so simple for him. Admire it.

Then he says, "Go on, then. What about you? Why did you join up?"

I laugh.

"If I tell you, you'll think I'm nuts."

He expects me to go ahead and tell him anyway, but I don't. When you're proper nuts, as I am — or as I've been — then you're careful about what you do and don't reveal. But here it is.

Fi. That's "if" backwards.

Griffiths. Nice ordinary name, but two more "if"s lurking at the heart of it. My name, literally, is as iffy as you can get. The only solid sound, the only one you can actually hang on to, is that opening G, and it's not to be trusted.

I first noticed these things when I was nine or ten, and the feeling of giddiness it induced has never left me. My entire name feels precarious, a conjecture balanced on a riddle. That's partly why it felt right to become a detective. I've finally become what my name implies: a practitioner of "if"s. If Rattigan. If Mancini. If Fletcher. If Penry. If poor old Stacey Edwards. A million "if"s, all looking for me to solve them.

Brydon looks at me with his big serious eyes.

"But I already think you're nuts," he says.

I still don't tell him, but he's earned another smile.

When we leave the restaurant, it's only a quarter to eleven. Brydon is doing that male thing of making the space contain any possibility at all. Back to his place for eight hours of rowdy sex. Chaste kiss on the cheek and a meaningless promise to do the same again sometime. He's letting me decide. Bad idea on the whole. I tend to make these decisions by playing safe.

I try to figure out what the manual says to do. As far as I know, Standard Date Girl Operating Procedure is: bad date — polite goodbyes; good date — modest kiss.

As far as I can tell, this has been a good date. The start was rough, but everyone's allowed a ropey opening. After that, I think I had a good time. I think Brydon did. I'm in the doorway of the restaurant ludicrously hesitating.

"Shall I walk you back to your car?" Brydon says. He's smiling at me. I mean, I think he's laughing at me, but in a nice way.

He walks me back. Warm air and quiet streets. Daylight, or the memory of it, still alive in the sky. I'm feeling a bit spacey, but not necessarily bad spacey. I'm pretty sure I can feel my feet when they hit the ground, and my heart seems OK, if a little distant. Still, the point is, I'm feeling spacey. When we get to the corner with Cathedral Road, I start to step straight out into the traffic, where a series of fast-moving metal vehicles prepare to flatten me. Brydon, with surprising deftness, grabs me and swivels me, so I stay on the pavement and avoid being splatted. With equal deftness, he keeps his

240

arm on my shoulder as we walk on down the road. I'm not the wrong sort of spacey, because I can feel his hand on my bare arm.

Date Girl is taken aback by this. She's been outmanoeuvred, but she quite likes the result. I like his hand on me. I like the weight of his arm on my shoulder. I can't quite believe this has happened, but I like it.

We walk about two hundred yards past my car, because I didn't tell Brydon when we walked straight past it, then he asks me where it is, and we walk all the way back again. All I can think about is his arm on my shoulder and the fading violet sky.

When we get to the car, there *is* a decision I can't avoid, but that's OK. I have decided. I turn my back to the car so I can lean against it, and start to look up at Brydon. He's on the case, is the good detective sergeant. His mastery of Standard Date Guy Operating Procedure is frighteningly complete. He has a hand behind my back and kind of scoops me towards him for a kiss. A very good one too. Just for a moment, my head shuts down and my feelings take over. Something in my stomach flips.

Steady on now, Griffiths. Take it easy.

This situation feels risky now. My mental health workers all used to be delighted if I had natural, uncomplicated, ordinary human feelings. Big fat tick on their clinical interview sheets. Something to boast about as they sip their Styrofoam coffees at the Eighteenth Annual Psychiatric Conference of Whatever.

I'm pleased to have these feelings too. Really am. But these things aren't simple for me. I know that too much all at once can flip my fragile little boat and leave me much worse off than before. The whole Lohan stuff doesn't help. It's a risk factor. The anxieties I've had ever since Penry walloped me are the same, only more so. My little boat is in high seas already.

We kiss once more and I feel myself urgent with lust. Tugged by it. Eight hours of rowdy sex feels like a good option right now. But I'm in control of myself again and I know what I need to do. After our second kiss, I pull away, albeit gently.

"Thank you for dinner, Detective Sergeant," I say.

He gives me a little salute. "DC Griffiths."

"My treat next time," I tell him.

"There's going to be a next time?"

I nod. That's an easy one. "Yes. Yes, there will."

CHAPTER
TWENTY-SEVEN

Home.

Anxiety at the front door. There's a security light at the front of the house, so I'm not worried about possible lurkers outside. It's the possible lurkers within that freak me out. I know the burglar alarm is now working properly, just as I was perfectly sure it was working properly before, but this is a fear that goes beyond reason.

Fuck feelings, trust reason, I tell myself. An old slogan. Not much needed now.

I insert my key in the lock. Turn it. Let myself in. The alarm starts blipping at me, as it always does, and I put in my access code to silence it.

House empty. Lights on, as I'd left them. No noise. Nothing untoward.

My brain is running through the checks, but my heart is racing as though it's not too much interested in words from the boss upstairs. I go to close the front door. As I get there to swing it shut, my toe brushes against something on the floor.

Instant fear.

Instant, unreasonable fear. I fight down the unreason and make myself look down at my feet. It's just a sheet of paper. An advertising flyer or something like it. I close the door, lock it, check the lock twice, then bend to pick the paper up.

Not a flyer.

It says this: WE KNOW WHERE YOU LIVE. No name. Regular office paper. Ordinary household printer. No need for forensics, because I know already that there'll be nothing to find.

My panic is instant and convulsive. I'm down on my knees by the door, attempting the same dry-retching that I had after Penry left. My clutch bag is well named for once, because I'm clutching it obsessively in my right hand, so that I can feel the haft of the knife. I'm ready to stab straight through the end of the bag if needed, extravagant silk bow and all.

For ten minutes, fear is two tries and a penalty kick to the good. Griffiths, F. has yet to get out of her own half. I want to call Dad, have him come and rescue me. Call Brydon, have him come and rescue me. I'll give him the best night of his life if he does. Or call Lev and get his menacing effectiveness working for me once again.

But those old slogans have their uses. Fuck feelings, trust reason. Dad, Brydon and Lev are all stopgaps. Good for the night. Useless for a lifetime. If I'm in the grip of fear, I need to deal with it myself. And besides, I've a funny feeling that my dad's already helped me.

Checking the door locks again, I go through to the living room and my phone. I call Brian Penry. His landline, because I put his SIM card in the kettle. It rings four times and then he answers it.

"Penry."

"Brian? It's Fiona Griffiths."

There's a short pause. I'd pause if I were him. But maybe he just needs the time to find the right attitude to me. 1970s cop-movie attitude? Fucking-tit attitude? Slap-your-head-off attitude? He opts for none of the above and just says, "Well, and how can I help you today?"

"Did your mam get those tulips? I sent them. I felt bad."

"Yes, she did. Thank you for that."

"OK . . ." Don't know how to answer that. I stole his phone. He hit me. I bought his mam tulips. It's hard to work out who owes whom what exactly. "I got a note this evening. Through my letterbox. It said, WE KNOW WHERE YOU LIVE."

"That's a bit of a cliché, isn't it?"

"I wasn't asking for literary criticism. I know it's a cliché."

"Any case, I *do* know where you live. You gave me bagels and smoked salmon, remember?"

"It wasn't from you. I know that."

"But you're ringing me up."

"Did you know Huw Fletcher went missing from Rattigan's Newport offices two weeks ago? It's just you had his number on your SIM card."

A long silence. I let it run.

"Listen. None of this has to be your problem. You've got DCI Jackson on the murder inquiry, right? Let him run things. He'll get his guy. Forensics. CCTV. All that stuff."

"I know."

"You don't need to do any more."

"Only I already have done, haven't I? Apart from anything else, I've got people sticking threatening notes through my letterbox."

There's a sigh, or not a sigh, maybe — an intake of breath, down the other end of the phone.

"Huw Fletcher is an idiot. He's not a dangerous idiot, not dangerous to you, I mean. If you ask me, he's going to be a dead idiot before too long. I didn't give him your address. I *did* give him your name. Part of explaining that that text you sent didn't come from me. I *did* use your surname. I did *not* use your first name. I *did* say you were a cop."

I do the same calculation he's just done. There are plenty of Griffiths in Cardiff, but not that many F. Griffiths. If Fletcher knew I was a cop, he could probably have found out my first name simply by ringing the Cathays Park switchboard. They certainly wouldn't have given out a home address, but maybe every F. Griffiths in Cardiff got that message through their letterbox this evening.

"It's the sort of thing that idiots do," says Penry. "Doesn't mean you need to worry about it."

"I saw a prostitute on Monday. I doubt if you know her. Ioana Balcescu. Someone had beaten her up quite badly. Not a punter having a go. A punishment beating of some sort. She didn't tell us anything at all" — not true, but I want to protect her — "but she showed a lot of alarm when it came to a couple of names."

"Oh, yes?"

246

"Not your name, though I did ask."

"Nice of you."

"*De nada*. No, the two names that bothered her were Karol Sikorsky . . ." I leave a pause in case Penry wants to make a comment, but he doesn't ". . . and Brendan Rattigan."

"Brendan Rattigan is dead. Didn't you know that? Plane crash in the Severn Estuary."

"I know. Seems surprising that he's still terrifying prostitutes in Butetown."

"Yes, isn't it?"

A long pause. It would be the end of the call, except that neither of us is hanging up.

"Do you want a word of advice from somebody who once used to be a half-decent policeman?" says Penry finally.

"I'll take anything going."

"Then stay out of this. There's nothing you can do, and as you've already noticed, Brendan Rattigan is perfectly well able to injure people from beyond the grave. Ready and willing. Just stay out of it."

"Have you stayed out of it?"

He laughs. "I *used* to be a half-decent policeman. Doesn't mean I am now."

"And maybe I'm already in it, whatever it is."

"Maybe."

Another beat, then him to me: "Are you all right? After I hit you?"

"Fine. Yes. Don't worry about it."

"I haven't been worrying."

"No. Thanks anyway, Brian. You've been helpful."

"And Huw Fletcher's an idiot. Trust me."

"I do, weirdly. Can I ask just one more question? Brendan Rattigan, just how dead exactly would you say he was?"

Penry laughs. A proper laugh. No disguise or fakery in it. "Well, I wasn't watching at the time, but I'd say he was pretty damn dead. That'd be my guess anyway."

We wish each other goodnight, and I hang up. Oddly, I find myself trusting Penry more than not. I don't know if that's because he was a copper once, and in the end coppers stick together through thick and thin. Or if it's something to do with him hitting me. If that's exorcised something in our dealings with each other.

If the note came from Huw Fletcher, and if Fletcher is a non-dangerous idiot who might be dead soon, then I don't have more to worry about now than I did before I went out this evening. On the other hand, I honestly don't know if I'm "out of it" or "in it", whatever the "it" might be. And if the real danger comes from the possibly dead Brendan Rattigan, then the Penry-Fletcher axis is by no means the only way in which I might have been stirring up trouble for myself. There were all those calls and texts I made to the numbers in Penry's phonebook. There was my amazing ability to upset Ioana Balcescu by mentioning Rattigan's name. Who knows by what routes word of my activities might not have travelled back to people who might consider me a candidate for a punishment beating or worse?

Not a good thought, that. If those people ever do to me what they did to Ioana, then I wouldn't survive it. I'd be back where I was as a teenager. As good as dead.

The terrors that have so often assailed my nights seem to be creeping into my waking hours. Against some threats, a paring knife concealed in a blue silk clutch bag is not weaponry enough.

And without considering my actions more than a moment, I'm at the door, going out. As I get into the car, I realise I'm still in my glad rags, kitten heels and all. Logic suggests going back inside to change, but I always keep a fleece top and hiking boots in the back of my car and just now I'd sooner keep moving.

The roads are empty. I'd normally put my foot down, but bearing in mind where I'm going, I'm a good girl and stay within five or ten miles an hour of the speed limit. Up to Pontypridd. On to Treharris and Merthyr. Then the Heads of the Valleys road towards Ebbw Vale. Shapes and shades of coal mines. Their ghosts.

I make the turn to Llangynidr. National Park country now. Not mountainous exactly, but high moorland. No dead miners here, just sheep looming white in the tussocky grass. I stop at one point to check my position and can hear the wind sighing through the grasses. No cars. No buildings. No people. There were quarries up here somewhere once, but I don't know where and I don't think they still operate.

Turning down towards Llangattock, I have a sudden worry that I won't find the barn. No directions. Driving at night. My sat nav in the dark as much as me. But then I come to the turn in the hill. There's a little passing place and down a farm track, maybe four hundred yards away, there's a big white barn with a

249

light over its door. Just where Aled said it would be. I can see farm machinery and a large concrete yard and not much else, because of the feeble light.

The track is gated, but I think I'd feel safer walking than driving anyway. I change my cute little kitten heels for hiking boots, pull my fleece top over my dress. It's colder up here. Partly the height, partly being out of the city. The sky is half overcast. Some stars, amid long reaches of blackness. The pattern of lights reveals the landscape. Orange glow over towards Crickhowell and Abergavenny. Virtually nothing when it comes to the looming bulk of the Black Mountains beyond.

I'm scared, but it's a good fear. The sort that encourages action, not the sort that encourages me to kneel by my front door trying to retch up my supper. I feel clear and purposeful.

I walk towards the barn. I've left my knife and clutch bag in the car, because they seem silly out here. I find myself almost enjoying the feeling of exposure.

Once, I hear a sudden movement of feet. My adrenaline responds instantly, but it's only sheep — I can see their thick, stupid, lovable faces peering through the darkness — and I walk on.

I reach the concrete yard. There is no one here. No sound other than those belonging to a farm at night. I don't know what I expected to find or what I expected to do. There's a big metal sliding door, the sort they have in industrial sheds, but it's closed, and even if it's not locked, I wouldn't know how to pull it back. Beside it, though, there's a smaller door. Human size, not tractor size. I go up to it. Try it. Find it open.

250

I go on in.

It is a huge place. Barns are, obviously, but there's something about the huge roof, about the whole vast silent space that alters something in you, whether you like it or not. I move forwards, as though tiptoeing through a cathedral.

The place is lit — if that's the right term — by two incandescent bulbs hanging from long cords. They chuck out a hundred watts each, maybe, but in this space and this darkness the light seems to give up hope before it's travelled far. Underneath the near bulb, there are a few bales of straw, marking out a line across the barn. Further on down, beneath the other light, there's a row of paper targets. Human-shaped, not target-shaped. Picked out in black and white. Black to congratulate you for a chest shot, white to mark you down for a shot to the arm or head.

When I reach the straw bales, I find a handgun there. I don't know what sort. A cardboard box with bullets lies beside it.

I know that guns have a safety catch and I fiddle around, trying to work out if the safety catch is on or off. I've no idea. Only one way to find out.

I feel half like an idiot and half like I'm Cagney and Lacey. I adopt the pose. Feet apart. Arms out. Steady gaze. Fire.

Nothing.

I put the thing that I think has to be the safety catch into the only other position it can be in and do the same thing again.

This time it fires. The shot is astonishingly loud. Like when Penry hit me, only the audio equivalent of that. I don't know if my ears are sensitive, or if guns really are that loud, or if it's the sheer volume of silence in the barn that throws me.

As I put the gun down, trembling slightly in my arms, I notice that there are ear defenders there on the straw as well. I wouldn't even know what to call them if Aled Whatsisface hadn't mentioned the term. Good old Aled. One of Dad's boys. My ever reliable dad. The ultimate Mr Fix-It, the ne'er-do-well made good.

Since I'm here, I figure, I might as well use my time.

I learn how to load the gun, by sliding the magazine out of the handgrip. I practise doing it until it seems simple. I close my eyes and, in the dark, unload and reload the gun, then flip the safety to off with my thumb. I could probably be faster about it, but I can do it. On the straw, there are four boxes of bullets, all told.

I decide that one box can go on practice.

Fire. Fire. Fire.

Close eyes. Turn round. Then whip round to the targets and fire, fire, fire.

There are 250 bullets or so in the box. I fire about 150 of them. Some of my shots aren't hitting the target. Plenty of others are hitting white areas: head, hand, groin, leg. But there are plenty hitting black. The target I'm aiming at doesn't have much of a middle now. It's looking ragged.

My arms are aching from the effort of holding the gun out, and I put it down, sitting for a rest next to it. There was a posh girl in my year at Cambridge, also a philosopher, who gave names to every significant possession in her life. She had a teddy bear, of course, but her car had a name too. So did her phone. So did both of her laptops and her camera. For all I know, she gave names to her knives and forks as well — I don't know how far these things go with the English aristocracy. Me, I'm not the object-naming sort at all, but if I were, then I think this gun would be the first to get a name. A Huw, maybe. Stupid, but just possibly dangerous. Or a Brendan, dead as fishmeal but still terrifying prostitutes near you. Or maybe a Jane Alexander, neat, sleek and a little bit scary.

I decide to finish firing off this box of ammo, then leave with both the gun and one more box of bullets. If there are more than 250 people coming to get me, I'll just have to take my chances with the paring knife.

I get up again and start my routine. Arms together — ignore the ache — feet apart — both eyes open — breathing steady. Fire. Fire. Fire.

I do the turning-round stuff. I try shooting one-handed. My accuracy is definitely worse, but I still wouldn't like to be the target.

And then as I get ready for another "close my eyes, turn, fire" routine, I suddenly notice that the door I came in through is open. There's a man standing there. Flat cap. Checked shirt under thick farmer tweed. Ageless. Could be thirty. Could be sixty. He's looking straight at me. He inclines his head to acknowledge my presence, but otherwise says and does nothing. For the first time, I notice that up at the other end of the barn, the end that is unlit and in darkness, there are animals stirring. Cattle, I think. Sheep would be out in the fields. I can dimly see amber eyes gleaming in the darkness. I wonder what the cows make of my shooting. Whether this is something they hear often or almost never.

I wouldn't know. I pull my ear defenders off.

"Drop your shoulders," the man tells me. "And soft hands. Don't tense up. Ease the trigger. You don't want to jerk it."

"OK."

"Are you right-handed?"

I nod.

"Then left foot slightly forward. Just slightly. Shoulder's width apart. Select a new target."

I turn back to the gun. The shooting range has lost some of its dimness, now that my eyes are fully adjusted. Feeling the man's eyes on my back, I adopt my stance and shoot off a magazine of ten bullets in the space of three or four seconds. I try keeping my shoulders dropped and my hands soft. I've left my ear defenders off, but this time I'm expecting the noise and quite like it. It fills the space.

I turn back to the man, who only nods.

I interpret that as a "Go on" and shoot off another four magazines. I concentrate on my shoulders and hands, and my accuracy is better. I've got nothing to compare it with, but overall I'd say it was good.

I turn back to the man.

"Good enough. Keep your hands soft."

"Thank you."

Another nod. I turn back to the shooting, pull my ear defenders on this time and go on to finish the box. Soft hands, hard bullets. When I turn back again, the man is gone.

My arms are properly tired now, but I'm happy. I take the gun. (And just where, Monsoon design team, am I meant to stow this baby? Pretty frocks are all very well, but they're not made for carrying concealed weapons.) I also change my mind and take two boxes of bullets, not one. When Rattigan's army of the undead emerges from Cardiff Bay to snatch me, they'll need to number at least 501. Any fewer than that and I'm ready for them.

On my way out of the barn, I go over to the cows and promise that they can get some sleep now. Their breath steams, but they make no further comment. A hundred amber eyes follow me.

Out in the yard, nothing has changed. No one is present. Nothing moves. I walk up the track to my car and drive back the way I came. I'm thinking about Penry. About Huw Fletcher and Brendan Rattigan.

But mostly, I think about that kiss with Dave Brydon. Am I now his girlfriend? I don't think I've ever been that before with anyone. I probably came closest with Ed Saunders, but I don't think Ed thought me reliable, even then. A lover and a friend, yes. A *girlfriend*, though, I never quite managed.

Thinking about all this now, and for all my cactus-like charms, I realise I would like to be Dave Brydon's girlfriend. The sort who would remember his birthday, act appropriately in front of his parents and think to wear their most expensive knickers on St Valentine's Day. I don't know if that's an act I'll ever be able to pull off, but the idea is an appealing one. Something I feel ready to try. I feel giddy at the thought. Vertiginous.

And on the last stretch home, re-entering the city from the valleys above, I think about Dad. I've assumed he's on the straight and narrow now, because he tells me that he is and I generally believe what he tells me. But then again, if Dad procured the gun, he did so with remarkable speed and stage management. I could ask outright, of course, but that hasn't been the way we operate things. When I joined the police force, I made it pretty clear that at home we'd operate a "Don't ask, don't tell" policy. I've never asked. He's never told. As far as I'm concerned, I'm happy to let it stay that way.

I also wonder if my dad's unease around my joining the CID was because he still had things to hide. Things he wouldn't want my brothers and sisters on the force to know. It's not the first time I've wondered, but it's the first time I've had real doubt about the answer.

I get home sometime after two. I walk up to my front door with kitten heels and ammo boxes in one hand, gun in the other. For the first time in what feels like an eternity, I don't feel frightened at all.

CHAPTER
TWENTY-EIGHT

Bedtime. Easier now than it's been recently.

I leave the bed where it is and drag out a futon roll and spare duvet from beneath it. Theoretically, the futon is for guests, though I can't remember any guests ever actually using it. The futon goes on the floor where it can't be seen from the door. In the best traditions of these things, I heap pillows in the bed itself, so it looks like someone's sleeping there. Then I make myself at home on the futon, glass of water and alarm clock near my head, gun loaded and by my hand. I shove a chair up against the door, which won't stop anyone from getting in, but will make plenty of noise if they do.

All this is over the top. I know it is. But I feel safe and I sleep like a puppy, which is all that matters.

In the morning, my alarm goes off too early. I feel tired, because I'm a good three hours short of what I need. But who cares? At least I've mastered the art of sleeping in my own home. And I haven't even smoked since Saturday, which is good going for me, especially given the way things are with Lohan.

I get up and stare out at the place where I live. I'm right at the heart of Planet Normal. Its strangest resident maybe, but I don't care about that. I like a place where dads go to work in the mornings and people grumble when the post is late. If Rattigan's army of the undead is out there waiting for me, they're well disguised. There are some clouds dotting the sky. Those high stately ones that look like ships sailing in from the west. There aren't many of them, though, and the sun is already well into its stride. It's going to be hot.

Drift downstairs. Eat a nectarine straight from the fridge. Make tea. Eat something else, because we citizens of Planet Normal don't get by on a single nectarine. I unlock my garden shed and open a window in there, because if it's hot outside, the shed can get boiling. It'll be too hot even with the window open, but I lock up all the same. I always do.

I'd intended to shower and stuff, but I did all that last night and I've already let too much time drift by to do it all again now. Sharp means sharp, now, Griffiths. Apart from sniffing my wrists to make sure they don't smell of the firing range, I do as little as I can.

But I have to get dressed. That's easy, normally. Select a bland, appropriate outfit from the array of bland, appropriate outfits I have in my wardrobe. I used to own almost nothing that wasn't black, navy, tan, white, charcoal or a pink so muted that you might as well call it beige. I never thought those colours suited me particularly. I didn't have an opinion on the subject. It was just a question of following the golden rule: observe what others do, then follow suit. A palette of muted classic colours seemed like the safest way to achieve the right effect.

258

Since Kay turned fourteen or fifteen, however, she's campaigned to get me to liven up my wardrobe. It's still hardly vibrating with life. It still looks something like an exhibition of Next office wear, 2004-10. All the same, I have options now that I wouldn't have had a few years back. *And today I'll be seeing Dave Brydon.* He'll be seeing me. I want his eyes on me, and I want his eyes to be hungry ones, sexed up and passionate.

I dispense with my normal functional underwear and put on a bra and knickers from one of the posher M&S ranges. White lace. Summery and sexy. No one but me will see them, but it's a start. And then what? I'm indecisive to begin with, then opt for a floaty mint-green dress and a linen jacket. Brown strappy sandals. More make-up than I'd usually wear, which isn't saying a lot.

I stare at myself in the mirror. Mirrors tell you nothing you don't already know, huh? This one does. I see a young woman. Pretty. Tick the box, good solid passing grade, pretty. Also anxious. She looks a bit like she's off to see the man who might be on the point of becoming her new boyfriend. Good luck, sister, but I don't think you'll need it.

Sharp means sharp sends me running from the house. I've thrown my gun into my handbag, but the boxes of bullets stay in the house. Va-va-voom over to work, or as va-va-voomy as traffic allows. One camera almost catches me, but I'm fairly sure I braked in time. Gun from handbag to glovebox as I enter the car park.

I'm there in time to hear the huge overnight news. They've gone ahead and raided Sikorsky's place in

North London. Jackson is in London with DI Hughes. More people are going up now in support. No briefing today, because there's no one to give it and because no one wants to hear about yesterday when today is where the action is.

It's slightly weird news, and not just for me. The office is all at a bit of a loss. The poor guy — DC Jon Breakell — who's spent a week forlornly combing CCTV footage for anything that might be helpful now faces another day doing just that, well aware that there could be developments up in London that make the whole thing pointless.

And I'm at a loss too. Today was my "seeing Dave Brydon" day. My "floaty green dress" day. My day for make-up and girly sandals. Today wasn't like any other day of my life. It was going to be my first day practising to be Dave Brydon's girlfriend, and I was looking forward to it very much.

I find him at his desk, grabbing a few things before rushing off to London to join the boss.

"Hey, Fi," he greets me.

No touch. No kiss. Just a look in the eye that tells me I'm not imagining last night.

"Can I see you? I know you have to run. Two minutes."

He hesitates. We are seeing each other. We're about thirty-six inches apart in a well-lit office and neither of us has lost the power of sight. Brydon clearly doesn't want the kind of office relationship where we're both always sneaking off into the stationery cupboard for a snog, and nor do I. Still less does he want the kind of office relationship that inserts itself between him and duty.

But I force the issue.

"The stairs going down to the print room. Almost no one is going to be using them just now, and there are doors at the top and bottom which we'll hear if anyone uses them. I'll go there now. You follow as soon as you're done here."

"OK. Two minutes. See you there."

I run down to the print-room stairs, then hang around on the turn of the stair, where no one can see me. I'm fretting and anxious. Even this wait seems like too long.

Then the door at the top bangs and Brydon's tread starts to clatter down. He's both heavy and light. Heavy because he's a biggish lad, and light because he has a natural athleticism, a bounce that carries through into every movement he makes.

"Hey."

"Sorry to grab you. I just had to see you. Sorry."

Brydon is on the step above me and I'm talking somewhere in the region of his belly button. "First things first, Fiona," he tells me. He comes down a step, then hoists me up to where he'd been standing. We're still not eyeball to eyeball, but we're a lot closer.

"Do I see DC Griffiths in a dress?" he says. "Have all relevant authorities been notified?"

That's Brydon humour for you, like it or lump it.

"And heels," I say. "Look."

He smiles at me. A nice smile, but I know that half his mind is occupied by the clock. He needs to get off to London as soon as he can.

There are still no sounds on the stairs. There's a hum from the print room where one of Tomasz's machines is doing its thing, but nothing that needs to disturb us.

"I just wanted to tell you I might need to take things slow."

"OK."

"It's just . . . things can get a bit crazy in my head, and slow tends to be better than fast."

"OK."

"I don't want you to think that because I —"

I'm not sure what I'm trying to say, so I end up not saying anything.

"You don't want me to think that, although you almost walked out into a line of cars on Cathedral Road last night, you've got some kind of death wish."

"That's it," I say. "That's exactly what I was trying to say."

For a moment, I think he's going to kiss me again and I really want him to. I feel lust pulling at me like wind. But he doesn't. Fortunately for my composure, he bails out of the kiss and just chucks me under my nose with his index finger.

"Slow is fine," he says.

He's laughing at me again and I realise it's nice being laughed at. Did Ed ever laugh at me in this way? I don't think so.

Then he's off. Up the steps. Heavy and light. Thumping the door at the top open so hard that it

262

whacks against its doorstop. The stairwell echoes with the noise of his departure, a reverberation of wood against metal, then returns to silence.

I sit on the step, getting my head into shape again. My pulse rate is high, but it's steady. I count my breaths, trying to bring my breathing down to a more relaxed range. I move my legs and feet, to make sure that I can feel them as normal, which I largely can.

I'm feeling something, and I think I know what it is. But I do the exercise by the book, and the book says that I have to run through a range of feelings to find the best available match.

Fear. Anger. Jealousy. Love. Happiness. Disgust. Yearning. Curiosity.

Fear. Anger. Jealousy. *Love.*

Love.

This isn't love. Not yet. But it's heading off in that direction: love, plus a good old splash of happiness. This is the first time in my life that I've felt those twins prepare to take up residence. Please make yourself at home, my friends. *Mi casa es su casa.*

I go on with the exercise, though. Feel the feeling. Name it. Feel it. Put the two things together. Stay with the feeling. Don't forget to name it. Give it time. And don't let it take you over. Keep an eye on your heart rate. Watch your breathing. Check to see that you remain "in" your body. Feel those arms. Feel those legs. It can be useful to stamp your feet on the floor to make sure that you feel right down to your feet.

The door above me bangs open again. Two people. Neither of them Dave Brydon. I don't know either of them. I budge over on my step to make room for them. They peer at me, but don't say anything, just go into the print room.

This isn't love and this isn't happiness. But it's like I'm in the hallway and can hear their music spilling out of the living room. Their laughter and candlelight. I'm not there yet. I do know the difference. I've had just a single date with Dave Brydon. Nothing that remotely constitutes a relationship. These are early, early days and anything could happen from here. But for once in my life, for once in my hopeless crackpot life, I'm not just in the same timezone, I'm actually shouting-distance close to the love-'n'-happiness twins.

I feel the feelings, piece by miraculous piece. Bum on a concrete step. Heart thumping. A floaty green dress and sandals with two-and-a-half-inch heels. A man who hoisted me up a step because I was talking into his belly button. This is what humans feel like when they are getting ready to fall in love.

I get up from my step and walk slowly back upstairs to my desk. This is what humans feel like. This is what it's like to be normal. Fiona Griffiths, human being, is reporting for duty.

But what exactly that duty *is* today is not quite clear. There's a voicemail from Jane Alexander. Her boy is ill and she's been unable to arrange for alternative childcare, so she's stuck at home. She tells me to call her if I need to. In the meantime, though, my interviews for the day are probably off, unless I can find a DS who'll interview prostitutes with me, which, given the recent news, I probably can't. Jackson and Hughes and pretty much everyone else who counts is out of the office and won't want to be contacted.

I've got a stack of various tedious paperwork-type jobs to do, but few of them are urgent. Over the other side of the office, a couple of DCs are making piles of empty coffee cups and trying to knock them over by throwing a soft indoor rugby ball at them. There are yells of laughter when they succeed, more yells when they fail. I sometimes think it must be a lot easier to be a man.

I pull out the notes I made on all those Social Services files. April and Janet. Stacey Edwards.

There are a million points of comparison between their stories, but there were bound to be. It's not any old person who becomes a prostitute. It's the messed-up ones. Broken homes, muddled childhoods, some disastrously wrong steps in adolescence. Janet and Stacey both ended up in care because their parents were crazy, sick, violent or useless. In effect, they never knew their parents. The state took over. What kind of person could go through all that and not end up a bit crazed themselves?

That's part of what hooks me about *The Janet and April Show*. Janet had a crap life and she fought to give her kid a better one. She failed and yet it's not her failure that captures me but the depth of her trying.

Inevitably, I have the photos of April up onscreen as I review all this. The interesting dead ones, not the dull toffee-apple ones. It's not quite true that April is trying to tell me something. It would be more accurate to say that I already know it — whatever "it" is — and April's job is to remind me. I can't figure it out, though. I stare away from my desk out to the boys fooling around with the rugby ball.

I should be doing other things.

In London, they're searching Karol Sikorsky's house.

Last night Dave Brydon kissed me, and today he almost kissed me again.

In the glovebox of my car, I have a gun. At home, I have 490 bullets. The rest are already in the gun.

I'm thinking these thoughts when I get up to make tea. I'm on my way to the kitchenette when a phone starts ringing. It's not my desk — it's Mervyn Rogers's — but since there's no one else around, I pick it up.

It's Jackson. "Who's that? Fiona?"

"That's right. I don't think Merv's around. Do you want me to —"

"No, don't worry about that. Listen. We're in the house here in London and we've come across about a kilo of what we're pretty damn sure is heroin. It's going straight off to the lab, obviously."

"OK, so you want me to get on to the lab here —"

"Yeah. Let's see if we can make a connection between the stuff we've got here and the stuff at 86 Allison Street."

"And Tony Leonard? Kapuscinski? People like that. You want me to start seeing if we can connect them to the drugs?"

"Precisely. And listen, I want as many warrants as I can get. Leonard. Kapuscinski. Sikorsky's buddies, basically. Do you think there's any chance that your prostitute —"

266

"Ioana Balcescu —"

"Right, any chance that she'd broaden her evidence? Name some more names?"

"I don't know. I can try. But if we're right, then any number of prostitutes might be able to testify against these guys."

"Anything you can get on them. Minor stuff. That's fine. We just need enough to justify an arrest and a search warrant. I want to start interviewing with a charge sheet behind us."

"I'll get on to it right away."

"Take my name in vain if you need to. Don't let things get held up for lack of resources."

"I won't."

"OK, good. Any problems, shout. Any breakthroughs, tell me right away."

"Yes, sir."

Jackson has rung off before I've even finished my "sir". The office seems even quieter now. For a moment, I forget why I'm at Rogers's desk not my own, then I remember my tea, then decide against making any.

I call the lab straight away and let them know about the developments up in London. The London lab will liaise with our lab in any event, but it never hurts to let both groups know that we're breathing down their necks.

I call Jane Alexander and tell her that she might want to get herself into the office, childcare crisis or no. She thinks about it briefly, then says, "I'll see what I can do. I'll be with you as soon as I can."

I call Ioana Balcescu, but don't even get through to a voice-mail. I don't think she'll give us anything further anyway, though I'll keep trying.

Mervyn Rogers is back at his desk by this point and I drop by and give him a condensed summary of Jackson's comments.

"You were one of the guys who interviewed Tony Leonard, weren't you?"

"I was."

"Essentially, Jackson wants you to pull him back here and give him a third-degree-type interview. Tell him that we can connect him to a major drugs ring in London, plus the murder of the two Mancinis. And Stacey Edwards, come to think of it. Terrify him, basically."

Rogers grins. It's the sort of assignment that he'll relish. I'm aware that I've added a little salt to Jackson's instructions to me, but if there's a breach of procedure there, it's mine not Jackson's, and I'm ninety-nine per cent sure that he'd much prefer Rogers to hit Leonard hard and early. Leonard's career and character suggests that of a bit-part player, which means he's more likely than most to crack under pressure.

"I'll start making some calls," I add. "See if I can get anyone to name him as a dealer."

"Righty-ho."

Back to my desk. I call Bryony Williams at StreetSafe, but my call goes through to her voicemail and I don't leave a message. I call Gill Parker instead, and get her. I tell her where things stand and what I want from her.

She sounds doubtful. "I can ask around if you like. Let you know if any of our women respond to those names."

"That's no use to us, Gill, sorry. That's hearsay, and we're in a place where we need more than that. We need grounds to make arrests. That means reasonable suspicion, and that means specific, named women supplying on-the-record statements about crimes they have witnessed. We don't need to go public with anything. We just need material to put in front of a magistrate."

"Yes, but . . ."

Gill starts to tell me all the reasons why she can't do what I want. She speaks as though she's swallowed some social workers' dictionary of psychobabble. Every third word is something like "support", "facilitate" or "empowerment". It's the sort of thing that usually makes me come over all Tourette's on people. It's why I called Bryony first. But I persist.

I point out to Gill that it's hard to help sex workers challenge their negative self-imaging patterns when the sex worker in question is comatose with heroin, has duct tape over her mouth and is having her nostrils squeezed shut by some sex-trafficking arsehole.

I'm being good, so don't use the word "arsehole".

Gill tells me that she'll "forum the issue with colleagues" tonight. I remind her that so far two prostitutes have been killed and another one badly beaten up. I remind her that there may well be others that neither she nor we know about. "This comes from the very top here, Gill. We need maximum cooperation. There'll be a shitstorm if we don't get it."

I do use the word "shitstorm", but the word I had in mind was "fuckstorm", so I still count that as fairly professional. Gill tells me again that she'll do what she can and we hang up.

I call Jane Alexander again. She sounds stressy and says that she can be ready at three and work through into the evening, if that's OK with me. I tell her that's fine and I'll start lining up some interviews.

I do just that. Make some calls. Phone numbers that we have on our own database. Some further ones that I coaxed from other sources, including some of the girls I've already seen. Mostly I go through to voicemail, but I get one girl — Kyra — who seems to think that a police interview would be brilliant fun. She's probably off her head on smack, but she arranges for me to meet her and "the girls" in a house just off the Taff Embankment later that evening.

Result. I hope Kyra stays high, because she'll be more forthcoming that way. I text Jane to let her know the place and time, then grab the landline again ready to make further calls.

And don't do it.

I can't. I can't let go of the Huw Fletcher thing, and that means I can't persuade myself to do the things that Jackson would want me to do in the way he'd want me to do them. I do try though. I really do. I have the phone in my hand, trying to will myself to make those other calls, and can't quite do it. Instead, I call Rattigan's shipping division and ask to be put through

270

to Huw Fletcher. Same rigmarole as before, except that this time I ask to speak to a colleague — Andy Watson — and tell him who I am.

"Detective Constable Griffiths? Yes. How can I help?"

"I'm pursuing an inquiry that may involve Mr Fletcher, and I understand that he's been missing for some time now."

"That's correct. It would have been two, two and a half weeks since we've seen him."

"And you've reported him missing?"

"No, I . . . No, we haven't."

"You have tried to contact him on his usual contact numbers?"

"Um, yes." Watson checks briefly with a workmate, then more confidently, "Yes, landline and mobile. Also email. He's got the facility to check in from home."

"And no response?"

"No."

"So a man has been missing for two and a half weeks without explanation. You've not been getting any response to your attempts to communicate with him. And you haven't troubled to notify the authorities. Is that correct?"

Big gulp down the other end of the phone. That's what I love about being in the police force. The ability to intimidate. Being threatening without making threats. I love it.

Watson says, "Yes, that's correct," and I say, "If you want, you can make a formal report of his disappearance now. We need a report from a member of the public to start up a MisPer — missing persons — inquiry."

"Yes. Yes, OK. I'm happy to do that."

"Good. There's some paperwork I need to run through, then. I'll come over and see you. Be with you in about half an hour." Watson agrees and I hang up.

I add some notes to Groove. Good police procedure. Following a tip-off from Bryony Williams, a prostitution outreach worker, I make a call to investigate Huw Fletcher. I discover Fletcher is missing. I consider that fact relevant to Lohan. I determine to pursue enquiries on the ground. Jackson won't like it because I'm not making tea and taking notes, but he will like it when he understands I'm on to something. That's my reasoning anyway.

I'm about to click goodbye to my little dead Aprils onscreen, but instead of closing down, I bring up an image of Brendan Rattigan. The dead face of a dead man, or just possibly the living face of a living one. There'd have been a time in my life when I couldn't have handled that ambiguity at all, but right now it doesn't seem to bother me much. Indeed, I quite like it. There's something boring about people only ever being one thing or the other. Not Schrödinger's cat. Schrödinger's millionaire. Brendan Rattigan and his army of the undead, building castles on the floor of Cardiff Bay.

"I'm coming to get you, buddy," I tell him.

He sneers at me, but that's not going to stop me coming.

CHAPTER
TWENTY-NINE

Up close, Newport is ugly, but there's purpose to its ugliness. It's industrial. It makes stuff and moves it. A place of seagulls and docking cranes. Power lines, roundabouts, warehouses, trucks. Steel and seawater.

Rattigan's offices are in a low-rent estate on the edge of town, down below Usk Way on the western bank of the river. The grass around the car park is shorn so close that it's burned and brown. Car windscreens catch the sun and throw it at me over the tarmac. Over the other side of the road is a field, spiny with marsh grasses and a board offering land for sale.

Rattigan's building has corrugated-metal sides, painted a colour somewhere between grey and blue. A sign gives the company name, nothing else, no frills. Not many of Rattigan's millions were spent here. At reception, I'm whizzed straight through to a conference room. Do I want tea? Coffee? Sparkling water? Coke? A girl with the expression of a calf asks me these things, as though the provision of fluid was guaranteed to deflect the wrath of the CID. I unsettle her by saying no to everything. Before long, Andy Watson appears, two of his male colleagues and a secretary. They're all anxious. The men slide business cards at me, as though I care.

I start out hard-faced and tough, and information flows like sweet wine at a hen party.

Huw Fletcher was last seen on 21 May 2010, when he put in a full day at the office.

He did not appear for work on the 24th. Or the 25th. Or any day that week. His secretary — Joan, the one in the room with me now — called his mobile number and landline, and left messages. An email was also sent. I can have a copy of the email if I would like it. I would, and the email is promptly brought. I take a minute or so to read it, even though it's just two lines long and of no interest at all, but silence is frightening to the frightened, so I create plenty of it. I'm interested in the dates, though. The Mancinis were found dead on the Sunday night — the 23rd — but had been killed late on Friday or in the early hours of Saturday. The timing of Fletcher's disappearance could be just coincidental, but as far as I'm concerned, the coincidence is reassuring.

"The email you sent. Obviously, that means that Mr Fletcher has remote access to his emails."

Yes.

"Can you tell from here if they're being opened?"

Some discussion about that. The consensus is no, only maybe some IT person would say differently. I don't chase up. Instead, I say, "What date did you leave those messages?"

The secretary, Joan, says, "I sent the email on the twenty-seventh. That would be the Thursday. I think I called and left messages that day as well. Landline and mobile."

I record the date in my notebook. Slowly. Silently.

"Can you give me all the contact information you have for him, please?"

Yes, yes, of course. Joan rushes out of the room to oblige.

I turn to the men.

"Which one of you is Fletcher's manager?"

The middle man, Jim Hughes, says it's him. Hughes looks like a fat man who's lost weight. Either that or he was issued with skin that came two sizes too large. He's got dark hair and almost Mediterranean colouring.

"Is it normal for your employees to go AWOL in this way?"

"No. Not normal. No."

"I can understand that on the Monday, you weren't too concerned. One day is just one day. But by Wednesday or Thursday of that week, you must have had real concerns."

"Yes."

"Yes, but you didn't do anything or tell anyone?"

Hughes is less worried by my act than anyone else present, but he's careful to be helpful too.

"We sent someone round — Andy, it was you, in fact, wasn't it? — round to his house to see if he was there. No sign of anyone. No car. We assumed he'd just taken off."

"You didn't attempt to contact his family?"

"Family? He's unmarried. Lives alone."

275

That's news to me, but I hide it. "I meant parents. Other relations."

Hughes raises his hands. "We don't have any contact details for his family. I don't even know where they are."

Joan comes back into the room with a datasheet on Huw Fletcher. An address, among other things. I take it without saying thanks, but ask her to leave new messages on all Fletcher's lines, including his email. I tell her to say that a missing persons inquiry is being set up and could Mr Fletcher please make urgent contact with Fiona Griffiths. I leave the standard 0800 number.

I turn my attention back to Hughes.

"So weeks pass, you don't tell anyone. Why not?"

A short pause as he composes himself. He's a shrewd guy, is Mr Hughes.

"Why not? That's a fair question, and I'm slightly embarrassed now about the answer. But here it is. When Huw worked here, and when Mr Rattigan was still alive, the two of them had an unusually close relationship. They used to fish together. Deep-sea fishing, not standing on a riverbank. Huw used to come and go, keep his own hours, do his own thing, really. Back then, if he was away for a week, that was that. He wouldn't necessarily tell me in advance, but he always came back. To begin with, I used to try and keep him in line, but if he was off with Mr Rattigan or going about Mr Rattigan's business, then I was hardly going to have much luck doing that. So I suppose it just developed really."

"Deep-sea fishing? Overseas or . . .?"

"Don't know. I suppose I —"

"You suppose?"

"Well, I always assumed it must be local. He never looked like he'd seen the sun."

"And after Mr Rattigan's death?"

"The same. He went away a bit less. Maybe every month for several days, and we just counted it as holiday or sick leave. I imagined he was doing jobs or something for the family. Shouldn't be done on company time, in all honesty, but . . ."

"And on this occasion, 24 May, and since then, you thought it was just more of the same?"

"I suppose. Truth is, I don't like working that way. If he was gone, then so much the better. And if he'd come back, I'd have sacked him. Now that Mr Rattigan's not with us, I don't have to make the same allowances."

"You have no idea of what he might have been doing for Mr Rattigan or the family?"

"No."

"Did he have any special areas of expertise? Any special skills?"

"No."

"Was he good at his job? Or rather, precisely what was his job? What did he do for you?"

"Shipping management. Managing schedules. Sorting out bookings for shippers. Locating containers that have gone missing. Chasing up customs problems. Boring stuff really, unless you're in the business. Huw was fine at it, but nothing special."

"Did he look after any particular sector, or do you all do everything?"

Hughes looks at Watson and the other man, who's hardly spoken. "We all do everything, I suppose. Andy and Jason here deal more with Scandinavia, maybe. Huw handled most of the cargoes coming out of Kaliningrad, and some of the ones out of Petersburg. But any of us do what needs to be done."

"And you're always based here? Or you need to go out to the Baltic?"

"From time to time, yes. Mostly it's phone and email stuff, but it always helps to know the client. Andy was in Stockholm last week, and Jason, you'll be in Gdansk — what — the week after?"

"So Fletcher would have gone to Russia occasionally? St Petersburg and Kaliningrad?"

"Yes. And sometimes, maybe a bit longer ago now, he'd have spent as much time in Sweden as in Russia. That's what you get if you work for a Baltic shipping line."

I ask other questions and the answers aren't too illuminating. What goods do they transport? All sorts. Pulp and paper. Ores. Containers. Vehicles. Some petrochemicals. Anything.

Fletcher wasn't known to have a drink problem. Ditto drugs. No financial problems. No health issues. I fill out the pre-printed MisPer form. I ask for a photo and they say they'll see what they've got and email it over.

"Did you like him? Did you guys socialise with him?"

Everyone looks at everyone else, but it's Hughes who says, "Not much. We felt he was taking liberties. I was looking forward to him coming back here so I could fire him."

I leave the office. In the car park, I call through to the office with Fletcher's address and ask for a car registration. They come back with the details, and I ask them to put the registration plate on the wanted list. If Fletcher is in his car and driving around, then he'll be detected by the first camera or police car that he passes.

But I don't think he's driving around.

I head back to my car and call those prostitutes for whom I have phone numbers. Most don't answer. One does and doesn't want to talk. Another one does and says grudgingly that she doesn't mind seeing Jane and me later on this afternoon. There are other calls I could make, but I decide to leave them for later. At least I've tried.

I drive around till I find a place that sells me some food and I eat it.

It's been forty minutes since I left Rattigan Transport. Not quite enough, maybe. I drive around pointlessly for another fifteen minutes, then head up to Fletcher's house, the other side of the M4 in Bettws. A nice enough place, only it'd be even nicer if it weren't a skinny mile from the motorway and not much more from one of the ugliest towns in the world. Modern brick houses, double-glazed and comfortable. Speed bumps in the road and cars neat in their driveways.

Nothing remarkable about any of it, the house or the street, except that there's an unloved dark blue Toyota Yaris parked up in front of Fletcher's address, window wound down, and Brian Penry's darkly haired arm beating time to some inaudible music.

I'm not surprised to see him. I don't altogether know what the dark lines are that connect Rattigan, Fletcher and Penry — though I've got my ideas — but I do know that Penry has been good at protecting himself. Not the embezzlement stuff. He stole stupid amounts and in stupid ways because some part of him wanted to get caught and punished, but still — he's kept well clear of the bad stuff. I was pretty sure he'd have ways of watching Fletcher's emails or phone messages, or at the very least to keep himself informed if the police started to get on Fletcher's trail. That's why I was so explicit about getting Joan the secretary to leave messages for Fletcher on every phone and email address she had. Why I wanted her to give my name.

I wasn't sure that any of that would bring Penry, or what I'd do if it didn't. But I don't have to worry about that. Here he is.

Penry gets out of the Yaris and leans up against it, waiting for me.

"Well, well, Detective Constable."

"Good morning, Mr Penry."

"The home of the mysterious Mr Fletcher."

"The mysterious and missing Mr Fletcher."

Penry checks the road. No other cars. No other coppers. "No search warrant."

"Correct. We're making preliminary enquiries about a reported missing person. If you have any information that might be related to the matter, I'd ask that you disclose it in full."

280

"No. No information, Detective Constable." But he gets a key out of his pocket. A brass Yale key, which he holds up twinkling in the half-sunlight. "I want you to know that I have nothing to do with any of this. I made some money that I should not have made. I did not report some of the things that I should have reported. I fucked up. But I didn't fuck up the way he fucked up." *He* equals a jab of the index finger equals Huw Fletcher. "I'm not that sort of idiot. And I'm not that sort of bastard."

I reach for the key.

He holds it away from me, polishes it in a handkerchief to remove prints and sweat, then holds it out. I take it.

"Time to find out what kind of idiot you aren't," I say.

Penry nods. I'm expecting him to move, but he doesn't, just keeps leaning up against the Yaris and half smiling down at me.

"You're going in there alone?"

"To begin with, yes. Since I am alone."

"You know, when I was a young officer, a wet-behind-the-ears DC, that's what I'd have done too."

"Junior officers are required to use their initiative in confronting unforeseen situations," I agree. I don't know why I start speaking like a textbook to Penry, of all people. Maybe because it feels strange to be speaking to him like this. Last time I saw him, he practically knocked my head off, a thought that makes me step back a little.

"You're like me. You know that? You're like me and you'll end up like me."

"Maybe."

"Not maybe. Definitely."

"Can you even play the piano?"

"No. Not a single bloody note. Always thought I'd like to, but I get a brand-new piano in the house and I never touch it."

"That is like me," I nod. "That would be just like me."

His half-smile extends into a three-quarters one, held for about three-quarters of a second, then vanishes. He gives me a half-salute, slides back into the Yaris and drives off, slowly because of the speed bumps.

The street is empty and silent. The sunlight occupies the empty space like an invading army. There's just me, a house and a key. My gun is in the car, but it can stay right where it is. Whatever's in the house isn't about to start a fight, or at least I hope it isn't.

I approach the door, insert the key, turn the lock.

I feel a kind of amazement when the lock turns. It's like turning the page in a fairy story and finding that the story still continues exactly as before. At some point, this particular tale has to come to an end.

The house is . . . just a house. There are probably twenty other houses on the same street that are exactly like it, near as dammit. No corpses. No emaciated figures of runaway shipping managers chained to radiators. No weapons. No stashes of drugs. No heroin-injecting prostitutes or little girls with only half a head.

I tiptoe round the house, shrinking from its accumulated silence. I've taken my jacket off, and wrap it round my hand whenever I touch handles or shift objects.

I don't like being here. I think Brian Penry is right. I've got more of him in me than of, say, David Brydon. I wish that weren't true, but it is.

In the bedroom, there is a big double bed, neatly made with white sheets and a mauve duvet cover.

In the bathroom, just one toothbrush. All the toiletries are male.

In the living room, three fat black flies are buzzing against the windowpane. A dozen of their comrades lie dead beneath them.

In the kitchen, I open cupboards and drawers, and in the place where tea towels and placemats are kept, there is also cash. Fifty pound notes. Thick wodges of them. Held together with rubber bands. The drawer below holds bin liners and kitchen foil, and even more bundles of notes. These ones are stacked up against the back of the drawer, making multiple rows. A little paper wall of cash. With one finger, and still through my jacket, I riffle one of the bundles. Fifties all the way down.

I don't like being here at all now. I don't like being Brian Penry. I want to go back to plan A, which was to practise getting ready to be Dave Brydon's new girlfriend. To experiment with my putative new citizenship of Planet Normal.

I close the drawer and leave the house. The lock clicks shut behind me. I find an old terracotta flowerpot in the garden and stow Penry's key underneath it.

Back in my car, I find that I'm sweating and cold at the same time. I try to go back to that feeling I had on the print-room stairs. That feeling of being somewhere close to love and happiness. Living next door to the sunshine twins. I can't find them anywhere now. When I stamp my legs, I can hardly feel my feet when they hit the floor.

I call the Newport police station. It's all I can do, and I feel relieved when the silence is ended.

CHAPTER
THIRTY

The day goes crazy and the craziness keeps me sane.

Newport isn't our patch, it belongs to Gwent Police. As far as anyone else is concerned, there's no real connection between Huw Fletcher and Operation Lohan, so I shouldn't even be here. But since I am here, I stick around.

The first thing that happens — impressively fast, I have to say — is that a squad car turns up. Two officers, in uniform.

I identify myself and tell them that I was following up a minor lead from a CID case being led out of Cardiff. I report the essence of my conversation with Fletcher's workmates and show them the key that I've "found" under the flowerpot.

"Have you checked with the neighbours?"

"Yes," I tell them, having managed to remember to do that just a few minutes ago. "Most people are out. The one couple I could find to speak to haven't seen the individual for several weeks."

The officer I'm speaking to — an intelligent-looking sergeant who looks like he enjoys his pie and mash — radios the office. He needs approval to enter the property and soon secures it.

He takes the key and goes to the door, rings the doorbell and then knocks. A crashingly loud knock, from the lion's-head knocker that was probably Huw Fletcher's pride and joy.

For a moment, I've got this insane feeling that Huw Fletcher will just come to the door. I realise I don't know what he looks like. I imagine a slightly podgy forty-something with receding hair and ill-fitting jeans. I imagine him opening the door, bewildered by the police car on his driveway, the uniforms at his door. I imagine everyone turning slowly to look at me, the girl with a gun in her glovebox and a head full of make-believe.

A long drawn-out comedy moment. The end of my career.

But it doesn't happen. Nothing does. No one comes to the door. The sergeant and his colleague use the key to enter the house. I follow them because it seems silly not to. We peer into the living room, the kitchen, the bedroom, the spare room. Opening cupboards, looking under beds. No Huw Fletcher. No nothing.

The sergeant says, "Let's check the fridge. See if there's milk there."

God bless you, Sarge. You're an honour and ornament to your force. We troop into the kitchen. The sergeant opens the fridge, because fresh milk there would imply that the house has been recently used. His buddy opens a couple of kitchen cupboards. Because there's nothing else to do, I swing open the drawers.

286

The sergeant doesn't find any fresh milk. His buddy doesn't find anything he doesn't expect to find. But I come across all the cash, just where I last saw it.

"Bloody hell," I say, stepping rapidly backwards. "Look at that."

The sergeant looks and he says, "Bloody hell," too. The junior sidekick is more to the point and says, "Fuck."

The sergeant gets down, pulls stuff out of the drawers, takes a proper look at the cash. I'd guess that each bundle contains fifty notes. Fifty fifties, making £2,500 in each. And dozens of bundles, dozens of them. There's upwards of £100,000 here lying around with the kitchen foil and the spare tea towels.

We pull rapidly out of the house. The house isn't a crime scene exactly, but it's pretty clear that the forensics boys will want to have a look over it. The sergeant is on the radio back to base non-stop. A DI comes racing up from Newport.

And my role suddenly becomes rather more delicate. Everyone's staring at me. The Newport DI — a guy called Luke Axelsen — gets me into his car, offers me a cigarette and says, "OK. Shoot. What do you know?"

"Not much. Really not much."

"Good start."

But I tell him. About Bryony Williams and the stuff she was meant to have told me.

"That was yesterday? That doesn't seem like very urgent follow-up."

"No. It wasn't. Williams didn't really believe the rumours. She only mentioned them because I asked. It was a low-priority lead. When I called Rattigan Transport this morning and confirmed that the guy had gone missing, it became a little higher priority."

"Yes. I can see why."

He bites his lower lip. Thinking. He's thinking that he doesn't want to hand this case over to Cardiff and the South Wales Police. He wants to keep this as his case in Gwent.

"For what it's worth," I say helpfully, "I don't think that we've got enough to attach this case to Lohan. It's still only hearsay."

He's happy to hear that and then the craziness really gets going. Axelsen assembles a team to investigate Fletcher's disappearance. He briefs the team, then gets me to brief them on my angle. I keep it short and sweet, which is pretty much all I have to offer anyway. I'm asked where I think the money came from, and I tell them that I don't know. Drugs. Prostitutes. Drugs and prostitutes. Embezzlement. God only knows. "Just keep us in the loop on anything at all you come across. We'll do the same from our end."

All this eats a couple of hours and more. I'm hungry again, but can't find anything that looks edible. I text Brydon. I don't know what to say, so I just write, HOPE ALL'S GOING WELL. SEE YOU SOON. FI XX. I like those Xs. I like that, for once, they mean something.

I call Jackson, because I reckon I ought to let him know what's going on, but I go straight through to his voicemail and leave a raggedy kind of message for him. I'm not good with voicemails. They squeeze out all my natural charm and wit.

Then I don't know what to do. I want to get seconded to the Fletcher inquiry, but it'll take Jackson to sort that out, not me. Plus I'm meant to be in Cathays Park right now, on prozzie patrol with Jane Alexander.

Because I don't know what else to do, I start driving back into Cardiff. I've got as far as the M4, keeping my eyes left, as I always do, to see the sea as it appears and disappears between the trees and embankments. It bothers me somehow that something so large, so deep-bellied and dark, should be so good at hiding from view. The Atlantic Ocean, the world's biggest graveyard.

I think about Penry. Not so much how he intercepted those Fletcher messages, more why he came at all. Why help me out? Why give me a key? I think because the honourable Brian Penry wanted to do something to redeem the screw-up Brian Penry. I want to dislike the man, but can't quite bring myself to do it. Too much of me in him.

I'm thinking all this, driving in the slow lane with Radio Two shoving a Britpop retrospective at me, when I get a call on my mobile. I make a mess of the hands-free system and then I get it right, and when I do, Dennis Jackson's voice comes crashing out of the Peugeot's very capable sound system.

"Fiona, what the fuck is going on?"

Because of the almost surround-sound speakers, it sounds like the universe is asking me that question. God coming through in quadrophonic, bass booster set to full.

289

"I've no idea, sir," I say with a fair degree of truth, but I give him the bits and pieces I have. A conversation with Bryony Williams. A phone call this morning. "It all developed from there."

"Is this another solo effort by DC Griffiths?"

"Sort of, I suppose. It wasn't meant to be."

"Because I don't like officers flying solo on my inquiries. I especially don't like it — in fact, I bloody hate it — when I've given specific bloody instructions earlier in the day to get moving with the main line of enquiry into a murder investigation."

"Yes, sir." I tell Jackson what I've done on that front so far. The calls to the lab. To Bryony. To Gill Parker. To Jane Alexander. The chat with Mervyn Rogers. My first efforts to arrange further interviews with prostitutes.

I've managed quite a lot, in fact, and Jackson sounds somewhat mollified.

"And Rogers is on the case, is he?"

"I think he's beating the shit out of Tony Leonard right now, sir," I say, wondering if I'm being impertinent or simply in tune with the boss's mood.

"Yes, I hope he bloody is." The sound system goes quiet for a moment, which means either that God is thinking or that I've lost reception. But it's the former, because God comes back again. "Do you know how much money they've found in that house? So far, I mean. They're still pulling up floorboards."

"No, sir."

"Two hundred and twenty grand so far. One fifty in the kitchen. More in the bedroom. More in the bathroom. Axelsen just told me."

I don't know what to say to that, so I don't say anything.

Jackson doesn't know what to say either, so he's silent a moment or two longer, before saying, "Right. In the meantime, I want you doing what I asked you to do. That means chasing the frigging lab to make sure they don't forget about our bloody heroin matches. It means working with DS Alexander to get statements from sex workers in Cardiff. It means finding a way to get ourselves some search warrants for premises that may well have links to the Lohan killings."

"Yes, sir."

I don't say it out loud, because I don't think I need to, but I *have* just obtained police access to premises that contained evidence strongly suggestive of serious crime. Jackson's thoughts are running along the same lines because the next thing that booms out of the loudspeakers is, "You think it's a drugs connection? That's what you're saying?"

"Fletcher worked in shipping. Arranging cargoes out of the Baltic. Mostly Russia. He went away on numerous long trips. Plus the cash. Sikorsky has a pile of heroin in London. Fletcher has a pile of cash in Newport. If there are drugs around, there has to be money as well, and maybe we've just found it. Plus most heroin comes from Afghanistan, which means that the Russian transport route could make sense. It's all circumstantial, but the connections are there."

"And you managed to uncover the connection thanks to some community worker passing on some hearsay conspiracy bollocks from a prostitute, who's probably high as a fucking kite when she says it."

"Well, there *was* a missing person. And one who does connect, even if only remotely, to the Mancini house."

"Very bloody remotely." Another long pause. "Listen, are you driving?"

"Yes, sir. M4 back to Cathays Park."

"OK, pull off when you can and give me a call back."

God rings off without waiting for an acknowledgement.

I'm in Pentwyn near as dammit before I can make a legal stop, but I park as soon as I can and call back.

When I do, Jackson is brief and to the point.

"OK. Look. I told you not to fuck around with me. I told you to *do* what you were *told* to do, *when* you were told to do it and with no bollocksing around. And you can't do that, can you? You just can't bloody do it."

Part of me wants to pick a fight. Actually, sir, I *did* do everything you told me to do and I did it fast and I did it fine. I just did some other stuff as well. Oh, yes, and by the way, I obtained access to premises with 220 grand of almost certainly illegally procured cash and have launched a MisPer inquiry into the likeliest target.

But I don't say that. I just sit mute as Jackson lobs rockets at me.

"Fiona, what made you chase after Fletcher? Don't tell me it was hearsay conspiracy crap, because I won't believe you."

"It *was* a bit to do with that, sir, but there is another part that I can't tell you about. Sorry."

"It's not your father, is it?"

292

"No, nothing to do with him. I made a promise to someone and I have to keep it."

There's a pause. Crackle on the line. Microwave radiation from the formation of the universe.

"I would love to give you a formal warning. I really would. The police force is a structured organisation. There are reasons for the structures and we work better because they exist."

"Yes, sir."

"It's not like . . . It's not like the way your dad works. It's not like the way, I don't know, some Cambridge philosophy department works."

"No."

"And it pains me to say it, really pains me, but much as I would like to give you a bollocking for this, I can't quite do it. I've checked with Alexander and Rogers and the lab, and they tell me you've been on the case. And you did find two hundred grand in drugs money."

"Thank you." Yes, *thank you*. You noticed. Hallelujah.

"But you're not off the hook. I am not sure if you are the kind of detective we can use in South Wales. You're either very good or absolutely terrible, or a bit of both. And I can't use terrible. Do you understand?"

"Yes, sir."

"I've spoken to Gethin Matthews and Cerys Howells, and they agree with my assessment. You're not going to be able to play them off against me or the other way round. We're in the same place on this."

"I understand."

"OK. Now, if I asked you what you wanted to do next — interview with Jane Alexander in Cardiff or attach yourself to this Gwent inquiry — what would you tell me?"

"I'd like to do both. As much as I can. I think Jane and I are working well with our prostitutes, but I don't think we should lose sight of the Fletcher angle."

"You'll manage to do both, will you?"

"I'm not sure. Working with prostitutes is an afternoon or evening thing anyway. Maybe I could work in Newport in the morning, then come over to Cardiff for the afternoon."

"OK. Fine. Don't kill yourself, but a little bit of self-harm where you're concerned — that would do me fine. I'll call Axelsen and let him know to expect you. Don't get yourself into any trouble with him, because if you do, I will murder you. Literally murder you."

"Yes, sir."

"And no flying solo again with me, ever, under any circumstances. Is that clear?"

"Yes, sir."

"OK."

Jackson rings off. I'm in Pentwyn and I haven't been fired.

CHAPTER
THIRTY-ONE

Six days slide by almost unnoticed. Dark fish in an urban canal. Sleep and I aren't best of friends at the moment. I'm averaging four or five hours a night, and that only with the futon and gun arrangement. It's not the regular way to get some kip, I know that, but I gave up on being Little Miss Regular a long time back. I'm tired all the time and I'm not eating properly, but I'm surviving. I'm getting by. When I wake up at dawn, I go downstairs for a smoke, then come up again and read in bed, drinking tea and listening to music. It's not sleep, but it's not a bad substitute. It's all I've got anyway.

My mornings are spent down at Newport. Gwent Police has taken over a chunk of the Rattigan Transport building and our little team works out of a conference room there. It smells of warm laptops, copier paper and male sweat. Mine too, for all I know. The air con is another area where Rattigan seems to have saved his pennies.

And the stuff I learn. Stuff I never even knew existed. Like, for example, deep-sea fishing off British coastal waters. That image you have of it — all Hemingway, and bulging forearms, and Floridian sunshine, and ninety-pound marlins dangling from the scales — all that is bollocks. Maybe it's not bollocks in the Gulf of Mexico, but it's proper ocean-going bollocks if it's the Severn Estuary and the Irish Sea you're talking about.

In British waters, the sort that Brendan Rattigan and his best buddy Huw Fletcher used to fish in, you don't get marlin. You don't get tuna. You don't get fish that you want to hang from scales and show your buddies in the pub.

You get cod. You get whiting. You get herring, for God's sake. Turbot. Small cold fish swimming around in small cold seas. Grey waves and rain. It's a sport for blokes who bring tea with them in Thermoses and boast about how bad the weather was.

That first morning, I call Cefn Mawr and get Miss Titanium again. I tell her who I am. She's icy with me. Hostile. She doesn't say anything she shouldn't, but that's what you get from paying top dollar for your support staff. Even their hostility is classy.

"Look," I say, "I'm very sorry to have caused an upset last time. The inquiry was important and the questions did need addressing."

"Maybe so."

"I don't need to bother Mrs Rattigan this time, but perhaps I can ask you a number of simple questions. Just three. Literally."

"Very well."

"First, have you ever heard of a man called Huw Fletcher? A colleague or friend of Mr Rattigan's, perhaps?"

"No, never."

"Have you ever heard of a man called Brian Penry?"

"No."

"OK. Last question. A certain person currently under investigation claims to have been deep-sea fishing with Mr Rattigan. Not just once, but many times. Days on end sometimes. In the UK, probably. Or starting from here. So the Irish Sea, the North Atlantic. Perhaps the North Sea or the Baltic."

I haven't even finished before Titanium interrupts. "No. Your information is incorrect. I've never heard of the late Mr Rattigan showing any interest in fishing at all. He didn't even fish on the river outside the house here. I can't imagine anything he would have liked to do less. Will that be all?"

She's got a nasty edge of triumph in her voice. She wants me to believe that I've fucked up, that I've got it wrong, that we police are idiots. So I say, very warmly, "That's *exceptionally* helpful. No interest in fishing at all? *Excellent.* Thank you *very* much." I say that to offend and annoy her, and hang up satisfied at a job well done.

But that was a highlight. For the rest of the time, me and three junior officers from the Gwent force are simply sifting through heaps of tedious data. Vessels and routes handled by Rattigan Transport. Logistics issues. Client contacts. Bills of lading. Customs dues. Bonded warehouses. Emails. Phone logs. Bank statements.

No one knows what we're looking for. We all assume that we'll know it when we see it, except that I don't think we will. It's either under our noses already or it isn't here at all. We get Jim Hughes and his colleagues together and press them to supply any photos they have of nights out with clients or any other images they may have of Huw Fletcher's contacts. Most of them have nothing at all, but Andy Watson turns out to have a fair few on his phone, and we start collecting names and images. We can check the names against the criminal records system. The images we can start to show to prostitutes and the people from StreetSafe. It all feels like fishing in the dark. The cold, rainy dark.

Those are my mornings.

The afternoons are more or less the polar opposite of all that. Or not afternoons exactly, but early evenings. My routine is now this. By about two in the afternoon, I'm back at Cathays Park. I catch up on paperwork for an hour or so, then at three have a briefing with Jane Alexander. Not on Sunday, of course. I more or less take that day off, and Saturday is a half-day, though I'm too shattered to relax. But apart from those breaks that don't feel like breaks, we push on, talking to as many prostitutes as we can, trying to gain their trust, trying to find Jackson an angle that will break the case open.

To begin with, our technique was simple. We brought as many prostitutes as we could together in one place — their own homes or flats, of course; we avoided Cathays Park completely — and bribed them with cakes and chocolates, if need be. Then we showed them photos. Loads of them. Photos of the victims: Janet and April Mancini, Stacey Edwards, Ioana Balcescu. Photos of anyone associated with the crime scene or the primary suspect: Sikorsky, Kapuscinski, Leonard, Vaughan, Lloyd and anyone else we can connect to those names, Sikorsky's in particular. Any CCTV images we have that seem relevant for some reason. Photos from the Fletcher inquiry down in Newport: Russian shipping clients that just might have a drugs connection somewhere along the line. Piles and piles of photos.

It didn't work. The first couple of days we got exactly nowhere. Kyra, who had been so stupidly free on the phone with me, clammed up completely when she understood what we wanted. The other girls were sullen. As soon as we showed them photos that were really meaningful — Sikorsky, Kapuscinski, Stacey Edwards — they just stopped talking. They ate our cake, chain-smoked and squirmed under our questions like teenagers at a family do. Jane got tart and police-officerish with them, and the mood deteriorated completely.

After two days of that, at my suggestion, we tried another tack. We got Tomasz to print off bundles of celebrity photos from the Internet. Film stars, TV actors, singers. Cleverly, Tomasz added in photos of people who were only celebrities in Poland or the Balkans, photos that would get the East European girls chattering.

And chatter they did. The conversation flowed. We mixed up all the photos so there was no particular order to them, and the girls were vastly more talkative. When we showed them the Tony Leonard photo, two of the girls reported that he had dealt them drugs in the recent past. The pictures of Sikorsky and Kapuscinski made them clam up, but even then their clamming up was significant — a sign that they knew things they didn't want to say, not just a general protest against having police officers in their living room.

As we got out of the house that evening — a two-up, two-down a couple of hundred yards from the Taff Embankment — Jane Alexander was vertiginous with pleasure, doing a little dance of triumph down the pavement, a slim blonde Ginger Rogers waltzing to the river.

"That was brilliant," she said to me. "That was probably the best thing that's happened to me since being in the CID."

She phoned Jackson on his mobile, getting him at home. She told him that we had reasonable suspicion to arrest Tony Leonard for drugs offences, and enough grounds to apply for a warrant to search his house.

She listened a bit to whatever Jackson had to say. "Yes," she said. "Yes . . . Yes." With each new "yes", she tried to curl her hair back behind her listening ear, only to lean forward again, causing the hair to fall forwards. When she got off the phone, she did another side-shuffle, fist-pumpy thing of pleasure.

"Jackson's going to arrange a dawn raid. Apparently, the London lab has just confirmed that the London heroin matches the samples found at Allison Street. This could be it. It could be the thing that breaks the case open."

Because Jane was obviously so pleased I allowed myself to do a high five with her. I felt an idiot doing it — and didn't think that raiding Tony Leonard's house would give us what we needed — but I liked Jane in

Ginger Rogers mode, and I didn't want to be the party-pooper.

Sure enough, Jackson does organise a raid and starts to rip Leonard's house to shreds. Because I'm over in Newport a lot, I don't hear all the details, but I bet the lads involved loved it. Mervyn Rogers is assigned to do the interviewing and he'll love it. He does a good tough interview and Leonard will be a soft target. There's a decent chance that Leonard says something to implicate Sikorsky.

Meantime, Jane and I keep our noses to the grindstone. A grindstone that turns and brings us nothing further, beyond bloody faces.

Sikorsky is still out there. So is Fletcher. So is Kapuscinski. And so is Brian Penry, who probably knows how the whole thing stitches together. Keeping his mouth shut as people die.

I've stopped knowing who I am.

CHAPTER
THIRTY-TWO

By Thursday, I'm feeling ragged.

I've had my worst night yet. Three scant hours of sleep. Smoking in my dressing gown in the garden for the two hours from dawn onwards. Then back to bed for mint tea, energy bars and Amy Winehouse singing to me from downstairs.

I think about Brydon. On my weekend off — the one that didn't feel like a weekend and during which I never felt off duty — we tried to have a second date together. We met in the same wine bar as before. Cathedral Road. All very middle class. I dressed nicely and washed my hair just for him. I remembered about smiling and asking Brydon questions about himself. I remembered all about how I was meant to be girlish and supple and appreciative and not tough. But the date was still a flop. After I had asked Brydon the exact same question for the third time — "So, what do you like doing when it's hot? I can't see you as the sunbathing type" — he took control.

"Fi, are you sleeping properly?"

"No."

"Do you get bad dreams at all?"

"No."

"But it's this case, isn't it? It's getting to you."

"I suppose. Everyone's telling me that."

"But no bad dreams?"

I shook my head. None that I'd count.

Brydon nodded. This man was a soldier once and probably knows something about bad dreams. After our drink, Brydon took me next door to a pizza place. I asked for a salad, and he countermanded me, adding a pizza and dough balls and large orange juice to my order. He made sure I ate it too, bossing me into eating the bits I wanted to leave.

In the end, I just let him boss me. I probably forgot to smile lots and ask questions, but I'm fairly sure I didn't say anything offensive either. When I'd eaten as much as I could, Brydon called for the bill and drove me home.

"Don't worry, Fi. Whatever this is will soon be over. And there's no rush. With us, I mean. We'll just take it slow. OK? Get some sleep. Take each day as it comes. And we'll be OK."

I nodded. I believed him. We kissed. I couldn't really feel the kiss, but these days I'm not feeling anything much. Right now, I'm back in bed with mint tea on the bedside table, Amy Winehouse hollering underneath me, and my gun lying flat on my stomach. The gun is the only thing I can feel and I don't let go of it all the time I'm there.

At eight thirty, Amy Winehouse has fallen silent. Gone back to black. I call Axelsen over in Newport and tell him that I'm not feeling well and won't be coming over that morning. He's fine with that. I don't think he wants me on his team anyway.

Sikorsky still hasn't been found.

Under questioning from Rogers and gang, Tony Leonard has admitted to dealing drugs. Drugs that he bought from Sikorsky. He knows Kapuscinski by sight, but nothing more.

I feel increasingly detached from myself, from the inquiry, from Brydon, from everything. Because I know that I need human contact when I'm in this state, I play everything according to the book. Call my mum, chat with her. Call Bev, chat with her. Call Brydon, get his voicemail, don't leave a message but send a text instead.

I call Jane, who's in the office. I tell her I'm taking the morning off. She tells me not to worry. "You really need it." She tells me that she's got more prostitute interviews set up for tonight, but "only come in if you feel you can. You need some rest."

She and I never know what to call the prostitutes. They call themselves "girls", which seems patronising. We mostly call them "prostitutes", which seems derogatory. Gill Parker always refers to them as the "sex-worker community", which makes them sound like a cross between an important export industry and a bunch of special-needs kids. Which, come to think of it, at least has the virtue of accuracy.

At midday, I realise I haven't really eaten anything. I take the gun off my belly, put some clothes on and skedaddle out in search of something like food. I go to a sandwich shop up by the Aldi at the top end of the

Glyn Coed Road. It's a rubbish shop, but at least I know my way there, and I get the dozy shop assistant to put some gloopy tuna-sweetcorn mix into an ageing baguette. She completes the concoction with a lettuce leaf that's brown along the edges. But it's food.

I sit outside in the sunshine to eat it.

On a bit of grass opposite the Aldi, I check my phone. A message from Brydon. I'd forgotten that he was back up in London, and his text says, PROBABLY STILL BE HERE TOMORROW. SEE YOU AS SOON AS I CAN. DAVEX. These days, he texts me with a kiss at the end. He's found a macho way to do it, though, converting Dave into Davex. Or maybe he's just lazy about putting in the space. Or maybe I'm overanalysing. I think about texting back, but the worse my head is, the more tightly I cling to my Standard Operating Procedures. And Standard Date Girl Operating Procedure is to play it cool, so I do. I won't call or text again until this evening.

I can't quite put the phone away, though. I go on chewing my baguette, which isn't too bad in the mouth, but then turns to something like decorator's caulk in the belly. I was right to take the morning off, but I'm feeling a little lost. I like the banter of colleagues. I'd even like it if Jim Davis were on the case with me, sucking his yellow teeth and laughing his cynical "Hur-hur, hur-hur."

I make further progress with the baguette, but the blunt pointy end has an armour plating that I can't penetrate. I scoop out the last bit of tuna with my fingers, swallow that and chuck everything else away.

305

Then I hesitate no longer. I lick the tuna gloop off my fingers and send a text. To Lev. My contact, not Dad's contact. My own personal helper of the last resort. A wanderer on the dark side.

My text says, IF YOU'RE AROUND, I'D LIKE TO SEE YOU. FI.

Before I even get back to my house, I get one back. TONIGHT.

I feel relief. Lev's coming. Everything's going to be OK.

That evening with Jane, we're sitting with five prostitutes in a bedsit near Llanbradach Street. Photos. Chocolate cake. Cigarettes. Net curtains in the windows and carpet worn down to the warp. The battery pulled out of the smoke alarm, because it goes off otherwise. A pink lace top hung over the bedside lamp, because the whole place risked looking too classy without it.

Silly girls swapping clothes and comparing underwear and giggling at the photo of George Clooney and not telling us anything that would allow us to save them from whichever bastard is going around murdering their friends.

I lose it. Jane has shoved the photo of Wojciech Kapuscinski at them, and they're wanting to move quickly on to another image. And I lose it.

I shout. I really shout. These things aren't just a question of volume — though I give it all I've got — they're a question of energy too. Of really meaning it. And I really mean it.

"*Don't touch that!*" I shout at the girl, Luljeta, who's about to toss the Kapuscinski photo to one side. "Don't you dare fucking touch that! You know this man, don't you? Look at me. *Look* at me! You know this man, don't you? Yes or no? Give me a fucking yes or no. Don't lie."

Luljeta is terrified. The room — including Jane Alexander in her powder-blue linen dress next to me on the sofa — is utterly silent. And Luljeta nods.

"Yes."

"What's his name? Give me his name."

Luljeta pauses, trying to be tactical, but I'm too angry for tactics. I open my mouth ready to yell again, but Luljeta preempts me. Her voice is tiny but truthful.

"Wojtek. Polish guy."

"Surname?"

Luljeta shrugs, but that's probably real. She probably doesn't know.

"Kapuscinski, yes? Wojciech Kapuscisnki. Is that correct?"

"Yes, I think."

"And what do you know about him? I need to know everything. Not just you, Luljeta. All of you."

It takes time, and I have to yell twice more, but we get it. Kapuscinski is one of Sikorsky's thugs. Sikorsky is reputed to have organised and maybe committed the Mancini and Edwards killings. All that much is hearsay. No search warrants for hearsay. But then Jayney, one of the Welsh girls, pulls up her top. She's bruised and cut everywhere from her knicker line up to her shoulders. Old bruises now, yellow and purple, but still horrendous. Not just fists either. It looks like boots to me, and maybe a stick or iron bar or something as well.

"This was him," she says. She's crying as she says it and pointing to the photo of Kapuscinksi. "He's who Sikorsky mostly uses. He said that I'd been buying from someone else, but I hadn't. I just haven't been using as much recently. I had flu and wasn't working, but he didn't believe me. He just came in and —"

She continues.

Jane's perfect-policewoman mode is called for now. Her pencil is flicking across the pages of her notebook, prompting names and dates and times and places. Jayney's admission triggers something similar from Luljeta, and further confessions follow. Accusations, in fact, but they feel and sound like confessions. By the time it's over, we have material evidence not just on Sikorsky — where we already had it — but on Kapuscinski, a Russian called Yuri and someone else called Dimi.

Arrests to make. Warrants to obtain.

Jane takes about two hours to get through the evidence that comes tumbling out. I don't participate, or almost not at all. I feel drained and empty. I ought to be taking notes, to supplement Jane's, but I can't. I pretend to, but I don't really manage anything. Jayney has her top down now, but I see straight through it. All these girls look naked to me now. Little bodies, covered with bruises. Bruises that exist here and now, in Jayney's case. Bruises that exist only in the past or in the future — or in the past *and* the future — for the other girls here. Bruises that will go on existing, go on

308

multiplying, no matter what bunch of arseholes is controlling the drugs trade, because whenever young women sell their bodies for sex, there will be leather-jacketed men to make sure that the profits end up in other hands, other fists.

Twice, as Jane is doing her stuff, I put my hands up to my eyes. I want to see if I can feel any tears. I can't, but I don't know whether people can feel themselves crying or whether they have to make a physical check to be sure. Even if there aren't tears here right now, I've got a feeling inside that might be the sort of thing that normally goes with crying. I don't know, though. I'm not the best person to ask.

I would like to kill Sikorsky and Kapuscinski and Fletcher and Yuri Someone and Dimi Whoever.

And then, after I have done all that, I would like to resurrect the drowned and fish-eaten Brendan Rattigan from the waters of Cardiff Bay, so that I can kill him too.

I let Jane finish doing her stuff and sit next to her in a daze. I'm pleased she's here.

When we emerge onto the street, it is 9p.m. Jane has magicked a navy blue cardigan from somewhere and puts it on. I'm wearing trousers and a white top, but I'm not cold, or not cold in that way.

"Are you OK?" Jane asks.

"Yes."

Jane brandishes her notebook. "I'll deal with this, if you like. Jackson will want to know."

I nod. Yes. Jackson will want to know. He's got what he wanted.

"If you want to . . . I mean, if you want to tell Jackson with me, then you should."

I'm puzzled by that. I don't understand. I presumably say or do something to indicate my puzzlement, because Jane explains.

"I'll tell him anyway. That it was you who did that in there. I don't know how you knew to do that, but it worked all right. I'll make sure that Jackson knows that."

I shake my head. I didn't *know* to do anything. I just did it. "I lost it, Jane. That's all. I couldn't stand those girls keeping their mouths shut any more. I just lost it."

"You'll be OK?"

"Yes." Everyone is asking me that at the moment. "I think I'll go home. Is that OK? Sorry to leave you with all the follow-up."

"You go home."

The sky above is that mid-blue of summer evenings, neither light nor dark. The street lights are blinking on, but they're not needed, not yet. The house behind us is quiet. The little Edwardian street is mostly quiet too. At the bottom end of the road, the river files past, holding its silence. A river insect, confused by the lamplight, ends up fluttering around in my hair. Jane reaches for it and releases it.

"Thanks," I say.

She smiles at me, tidies my hair back into place where she and the insect ruffled it, then says, "Drive safely."

I nod and do just that. Sober and safe and under the speed limit. It's not what I want, though. Some part of

310

me wants the exact opposite. It would like a two-hour drive on empty roads and no speed cameras. A curving ride through the Brecon Beacons and Black Mountains. A sunset that never quite dies, just beckons onward into the next valley, up the next slope, round the next bend. No traffic, no direction, no destination.

I don't get that, but I do get home in one piece.

There's a ready meal in the freezer and I microwave it from frozen. It's icy in the middle when I eat it, but at least I eat it.

I think about a smoke and decide against.

I have a hot bath. I consider putting some music on, but can't think of anything that will alter anything, so I just leave the silence.

When I get out of the bath, I don't put on office clothes again. Lev's coming in a bit and he's not an office-clothes kind of guy. I wear jeans, gym shoes and a T-shirt. I'll add a fleece top if we go out.

Then Brydon calls. He's in London, but has just heard the news Jane brought in to Cathays Park. Huge excitement, apparently. He wants to talk all about it, but I close him off. We've spent enough time talking about work things in our lives, so instead we talk rubbish — nice, affectionate, directionless rubbish — for twenty minutes. Then he yawns and I tell him he should go to bed.

"See you soon, Fi."

"Yes, see you soon. I'm missing you."

"Likewise. Look after yourself."

I have an image of him making love to me on the living room floor. Urgent and intense. Not too many words. Not too gentle or too solicitous. A lovemaking that leaves bite marks. I wonder if that's how ordinary people have sex. It hasn't been that way for me, not even with Ed Saunders.

We say goodbye.

I'd snooze if I could, but my adrenaline is up and I don't know when Lev will be coming. I never do, except that it'll be far too late. Not a morning person, is our Lev.

I have the TV on. It's after *Newsnight* has closed down. There's a black-and-white film on BBC2. It involves violence against women, so I watch it with the sound turned off and even then all I can see is Jayney's bruises. I shouldn't even be watching it really. Sometime after midnight, I start to doze. And then I hear a car engine coming to a halt outside the house and catch a couple of headlamps shutting off.

I get my bag, check the gun, go to the door.

CHAPTER
THIRTY-THREE

Lev.

He looks like he always looks, which is to say like not much. Old jeans, a much-washed sweatshirt, trainers. Not a big guy, maybe five foot eight, something like that, and not particularly broad. Lean and muscled in his leanness, the way you might expect an ocean sailor or a mountain climber to be. Dark hair, always a bit too long and never very combed. Ambiguous skin that could place him anywhere in the arc that runs from Spain through to Kazakhstan and beyond, though I'm damn sure he's not Spanish. His age is similarly indeterminate. I used to think he was about my age when I first met him, a little older perhaps, but not much. Then I realised from one or two snippets he let slip about his past that he could be a fair bit older. He could be anywhere between thirty and almost fifty. I honestly couldn't narrow it any more than that. The one thing you really notice about Lev — or, more accurately, something you don't notice at all and only find yourself thinking about afterwards — is the way he moves. Catlike. That would be the normal term, but I imagine that whoever first developed that queen of clichés never spent much time looking at cats, who are always licking their bits or finding new ways to scratch themselves. That's not Lev at all. He's still mostly, but there's a poise in his stillness, a potential for sudden flowing action, which means that his stillness has more motion in it than anyone else's movement. More motion and more violence.

"Hey, Fi," he says, light pouring outward from the hall and his eyes already checking the space behind.

"Lev. Hi. Come on in."

We don't kiss or shake hands. I don't know why not. But it's hard to know what social rules to apply when you're in his presence. I don't think he knows.

I let him stalk around the house for a bit without saying anything. His normal procedure when he visits. Doors, windows, exits. Hiding places. Blind spots. Potential weapons. My kitchen morphs into a kind of conservatory at the back, which means a large area of glass opening onto the dark garden beyond. Lev fiddles around till he finds the switch for the security light, which bathes the back garden in 150 watts of halogen brightness. He leaves it on.

Then he's happy. He takes a chair and sits down. His inspection is of me now.

"What's up?"

"Nothing much. Just wanted to see you."

"Sure."

"Do you want something. Tea? Coffee? Alcohol?"

"Are you still growing?"

"Yes."

"Then I don't want tea, coffee or alcohol."

I laugh, stand up and get the keys. I unlock the French doors and we go outside. Lev steps out into the garden and instantly starts assessing the air and peering over fences. I fiddle around with the padlock on the shed and get it open.

There isn't much inside, because I don't like gardening. A lawnmower and a hoe, and I've never used the hoe. And there's the bench with the grow lamps and my marijuana plants. The poor dears have been much too hot recently, but they're doing all right. I brought the seeds home from India when I was there on holiday once as a student, and these plants are their daughters and granddaughters. I check the plants are watered, but otherwise leave them be. I've more or less given up smoking resin, but I dry the leaves in my oven and then keep bags of them under lock and key in the shed. I take one good-sized bag, then lock up again.

I roll a joint in my kitchen, but decide I want tea as well, so get Lev to put the kettle on. He does so, then wanders through to the living room to flick through my CDs, making clucking sounds of disapproval, before finding something by Shostakovich, which was a gift from a very temporary lover, I think, and before too long the air fills with dark-toned Russian pessimism, played out on the bassoon and a sea of violins.

"In 1948, did you know, Shostakovich used to sleep outside his apartment by the lift shaft?"

"No, Lev. Amazingly enough I didn't know that."

"His work had been denounced. Denounced for the second time. First time was in the 1930s."

"Well, I can see why that would drive anyone to sleep by the lift shaft."

"He thinks he is going to be arrested and he doesn't want the police to disturb his family."

"For fuck's sake, Lev, come and get stoned."

The joint is ready. It'll be my second of the day, but social smoking is excluded from my normal rules, which let me smoke a joint two or three times a week, in my garden usually. Four or five times if I feel my head is under pressure and needs the relief. I never smoke tobacco.

I make peppermint tea for me and dig out some chocolates. Lev, I don't even bother with, because I know that he'll sort himself out, and he does. He makes black tea, noxiously strong, finds a little jug of hot water and takes some Bonne Maman raspberry conserve from the cupboard. Slightly mouldy conserve, to judge from the way he scowls and dollops a few blobs down the sink before coming over to the table. Then I sit there, smoking, drinking tea and eating chocolate, while Lev smokes, mixes jam, tea and hot water in his cup and drinks that.

"So. What's up?"

I shake my head. Not because there isn't anything to say, but because I don't know what order to say anything in. Maybe it doesn't matter. I start randomly.

"I've got a gun."

"Here? In the house?"

I get my bag and give him the gun.

Lev gets all Lev-like with it, as I knew he would. He pulls back the slide to see if there's a bullet chambered, which there isn't. He pulls out the magazine to see if it's loaded, which it is. Checks the safety. Checks the sights. Checks the feel and heft of it. With the magazine out, and no bullet in the chamber, he takes aim and fires. First statically, still seated and at a fictive, motionless target. Then moving. Him, the gun, the imaginary target.

"It's a good gun. Have you fired it?"

"Yes. On a shooting range. I learned to keep my shoulders down and soft hands."

I show him.

"Good. The grip is OK? You've got small hands."

"It's fine, I think. It's a small gun, isn't it?"

"*Tak*."

Tak, I happen to know from my mate Tomasz Kowalczyk, the king of all things papery, is Polish for "yes". I'm also fairly sure that Lev isn't Polish. Then again, I'm not exactly sure what he is, and when he inserts foreign words into his English, I'm pretty certain that they come from half a dozen different languages, maybe more.

"You have done any real shooting?"

"No."

"That's why you called me?"

"I suppose. I don't know."

"You are under threat?"

"No. I don't know. Maybe."

"That's not very logical answer for a Cambridge girl."

"No one has threatened me. Not exactly. One guy hit me, but that was a whole different thing."

"Hit you? How? What happened?"

I tell him. Not the edited highlights, the full version. Lev needs us to act it out, so he can visualise where I was standing, where Penry was standing, where I landed, what happened next.

"You didn't strike him?"

"No."

"But you're on the steps, there, in that position?"

Lev has got me to adopt the exact position that I was in after Penry hit me. Arse on the bottom step. Legs out. Head and torso slumped against the wall. It's freaky being here. Frightening. Lev isn't Penry. Not as tall or powerful. But from down here on the floor any man looks two miles high.

"Yes. This position. I told you already."

"And the guy. What was his name?"

"Penry. Brian Penry. He's not such a bad person really. I might even like him."

"So Penry. I'm Penry. I'm in the right place?"

"Yes. No. A bit closer and nearer to the wall. Yes, there. About there."

I'm really uneasy now. Penry is dark. Lev is dark. Same place. Same posture. Because the hall light is behind Lev's head, he could almost be Penry.

"OK. I'm Penry. I've just hit you. You're wearing what?"

"What? A skirt. It was a fucking summer's day, Lev. I was wearing a skirt, OK?"

"No. I don't care about that. Your shoes. What kind of shoes?"

"Flats."

"I don't know what that is, flats. Did they have a sole, anything heavy?"

"No, Lev. I don't live in a war zone. I'm a girl. And it was a summer's day."

"OK, so no shoes. You can still strike the knee. Do it."

"Lev, I've got a gun now. Penry hit me once and buggered off. I didn't need to strike him. He just let himself out of the front door and drove away."

"So it was tactical, you are saying? You chose not to strike?"

"No, it wasn't like that."

"I'm Penry. I hit you once. I'm going to hit you again. Maybe I'm going to kill you. Maybe fuck you, then kill you. Probably that. Fuck you first."

He makes the tiniest movement towards me. There's something menacing in him, the light behind his head, the way his voice tightens, the way he's holding himself. I'm in terror now. Maybe that's the marijuana making itself felt, but I don't think so. I don't get paranoid on it. I get calmer. That's why I started smoking it in the first place. Why I still do. Self-medication. But the drug can't do anything for the terror I'm feeling now. I feel just like I did back on the step with Penry. A body memory, perhaps, but no less terrifying for that.

"Fuck you, then kill you."

Lev moves fractionally closer.

And then some instinct takes over in me. A fighting one. A killing one.

I lash out with my uppermost leg, my right one. I aim for Lev's kneecap and catch it cleanly. Lev spills

319

over backwards, and I follow through with a hard stamp down on his testicles, mashing down on them twice with my heel, then get poised to start kicking him in the windpipe until I've shattered his larynx and his windpipe and the poor fucker will be on his knees choking for breath and pleading for mercy and ready to feel the smash of my kneecap in his face.

"Good, good. Really good."

Lev never lets me really hurt him. He lifted his knee at the last possible second, so I caught him on the upper calf. As for the testicle stamp, he caught my leg with both hands and took the weight off it as it came down, shifting it sideways onto his thigh as he did so.

But I'm not there. I'm not in the world that Lev is in. Unarmed combat practice. Everything a series of moves and countermoves. I'm panting, partly from the exertion, but mostly because of a flood of feelings that I don't recognise. I don't even really feel them as feelings at all. I just feel spacey and out of my body and like I want to kick Lev's windpipe until he's breathing through the toe of my shoe.

I know he's talking to me and I have trouble focusing on his words. I do my best. He repeats himself.

"You were scared? At the time it happened, you were scared?"

"No. It was beyond that. Terrified. I felt helpless."

"But you weren't helpless. You could have disabled him. Like just now."

"I know. But I wasn't in that headspace then."

"No one ever is when it happens. You have to find a way to be there like this." Lev snaps his fingers. Then,

320

because Shostakovich is doing something that makes Lev happy, he raises a finger for a moment's silent appreciation and we listen to violins and oboes for a while.

We go back to the kitchen. I need to finish the joint and Lev needs tea with jam.

"The other situation you were in. Not recently. Last year or whenever. When you hurt the guy."

"We've been through that."

"So we go through it again. You've only been in two situations, right? We need to understand how you react."

"OK, in one situation, I beat the guy up. In the other situation, I let him knock me over and then I was so terrified I didn't know what to do next."

"Fine. So we go back to the first situation. We play it out again."

I draw down hard on the joint until I get to the little bit of cardboard I use as the filter and the very last of the weed has disappeared into my lungs. I don't know why I get Lev involved in things sometimes. He never lets go of them. Then again, that's exactly why I get him involved. I drop the stub of the joint into the remains of my tea and shift my chair, so it's in the right relation to the table.

"I'm here. TDC Griffiths, wet behind the ears, writing in her notebook. You're standing up, wandering around. I'm not feeling anything weird going on. Then you step behind me. Not that side. This side. You reach down and fondle my breast."

Lev reaches down and puts his hand on my breast. There's nothing tentative about his touch. There's no apology and nothing seedy. For Lev, it's just about realism.

"Ready?" I say.

Needlessly. Lev is always ready. He still has his hand on my breast.

"Ready," he says.

Then I move. As near as possible to the way it happened. Chair back. Slam my hand upwards to catch his jaw. I feel Lev jerk back in an imitation of pain and surprise. That pulls his fondling hand away from my breast, giving me room to grab his fingers and yank back against his line of motion. That's what broke the guy's fingers when it happened for real. I'm standing now and able to kick out at the kneecap. Lev is big on kneecaps, where I'm involved at least. If I'm in a fight with anyone, then I'm going to lose if it lasts more than a few seconds. Likewise, if anyone can get hold of me, they'll be far too powerful for me. Kneecaps and, to a lesser extent, testicles represent my principal means of immobilising my counterpart. For that reason, most of the instruction that I've done with Lev has focused on those fine body parts.

This time, once I've caught his kneecap in a nice clean blow, he stops.

"I fall now, right?"

"Yes. Kind of sideways and down. That way. Yes."

"But there was more, no?"

"The guy was rolling as he fell. I shoved him against the table. An instinct thing. But I pushed quite hard and the corner penetrated his cheek. There was a lot of blood."

"And then?"

"The fight was over. He had three broken fingers and a dislocated kneecap. Plus he was whimpering like a six-year-old and there was blood bubbling out through a hole in his cheek."

"OK, but then he's on the floor here. How had he fallen? This way? Like this?"

"Yes, like that. No, legs apart a bit more. Yes. Exactly like that."

"And then?"

"Lev, this was the very first time it had happened, OK? I wasn't in an ordinary state of mind."

"Of course you weren't. This was fight."

That's a big theme of Lev's. The reason why he teaches Krav Maga. The reason why the Israeli Special Forces developed the technique in the first place. Fights — real fights — don't happen on tatami mats. They don't start with people bowing to each other and sprinkling water from brass bowls. They start in pubs, in alleyways, in places you don't want to fight. They make use of whatever weapons come to hand. They don't have rules. They don't let you submit gracefully and make a respectful bow to the person who felled you.

Krav Maga is strictly real world. Functional. In Krav Maga, you don't get instructors saying things like, "And if your assailant comes at you with a sword . . ." It's all about making use of what you've got. Low-risk, efficient manoeuvres. Proceeding as rapidly as possible

323

from defence to attack. Maximum violence, maximum disablement. Fast, nasty, decisive.

At Hendon, when I was undergoing police training, we learned a set of techniques that were more jujitsu-based. Useful enough and quite pretty. But I was way ahead of them. I'd been working on Krav Maga with Lev since Cambridge, and my own aim in training at Hendon was to avoid revealing how much I really knew. I passed that course with the lowest grade possible. Petite, bookish, geeky Fiona. No one expected anything else.

"OK," I say, because I know Lev won't let go of this until I tell him. "I just stood over the guy and kicked between his legs until I could hardly feel my toes."

"He was disabled?"

"One burst testicle. Everything else was patched up OK."

"And your employers. You got into trouble for this?"

"Yes. Some. More than I wanted. But everyone believed me when I said that he'd started it. I told them that I was frightened. I said he went on trying to grab me and I used reasonable force in self-defence."

Lev, whose sense of humour is mostly buried as deep as an Iranian centrifuge, finds this funny and repeats it twice. "Reasonable force. Reasonable force." But that exhausts his supply of mirth and he turns to other things. He checks for tea, finds that everything has gone cold, that I've finished the joint and that Shostakovich has gone silent. He finds more music to put on and reboils the kettle.

"Not frightened, I think. Trauma."

He says "trauma" with one of his non-standard pronunciations. *Trow-ma. Trow-ma.*

"Good heavens. Why would that be? Someone slaps me across the hallway in my own house and I'm frightened. How strange."

"Not then. When the guy grabs your breast."

"That wasn't traumatic. I just overreacted."

"Exactly. And why did you?"

"Why did I? Lev, I'm not you. You've spent half your life training for these situations. I haven't."

He shakes his head. "OK. I know what inexperience looks like. I train people. I know. This not like inexperience. This is trauma. Sometimes it makes you too frightened to move. Other times it makes you go crazy. When we were there in the hallway, practising just now, and you decided not to be frightened, you were crazy inside. We were only practising, but you were crazy inside. I could feel it."

"You scared me. You did it deliberately. Penry didn't say the things you said."

"So? It was only words, and these were pretend words as well. You have the trauma inside you. That's why I find it so easily."

I'm angry with all this. I don't exactly know why I asked Lev to come. Or rather, I knew ever since getting the gun that I should get some instruction from Lev on how to use it. He'd have a contempt for firing ranges. That's not where pistols are fired for real. He'd want me to practise with a gun the way we practised Krav Maga. Tired. In bad light. With movement. Swinging lights. Running. Moving targets. Too much else going

325

on. Noise. The whole business about soft hands, lowered shoulders, left foot forwards is so much hooey. Something to worry about on a firing range and nowhere else on earth.

But, typical bloody Lev, he never operates to my agenda, only ever to his own. And right now his agenda is inventing some rubbish theory about my past.

"Lev, when I was a teenager, I had a breakdown. A really big, really bad, really serious breakdown. Stuff you wouldn't understand. If you want to call that a trauma, then fine. It was a trauma. But if you're trying to imply that there was anything else, then you're wrong. Just plain wrong. I've never been raped. Until that idiot, no one ever touched me inappropriately. I've got a sane, stable, loving family. I'd never even been in a fight until I started getting lessons from you."

"You have breakdown. When?"

"When I was sixteen. It lasted till I was eighteen."

"And at Cambridge, when I met you, you were how old?"

"Nineteen. I was still in recovery. I still am. I guess I always will be."

I met Lev at Cambridge. He was newly arrived in England and was making some money teaching combat techniques to students. I signed up with him. I didn't know why then. I don't know why now. I haven't tried to analyse it. I just feel safer knowing I can take care of myself if I have to.

"And you don't tell me about this breakdown until now?"

"I don't tell anyone, Lev. I never tell people."

326

"OK, so let me get this picture. You're happy little Fiona Griffith, wandering along through life, then in walks this great big breakdown for no reason at all. And when breakdown is gone, and you are in bad situation, you are either crazy woman or too frightened to move. So why would I think trauma?"

Silence. Or at least, silence between us. Violins from next door.

Lev realises that the kettle has boiled and makes more tea for himself. He raises his eyebrows to ask me if I want any. I say no, then change my mind and say yes. But I don't want tea. I don't want a joint. I want alcohol, which obliterates my mind much better than any joint ever does, and which I hardly touch because I've had some very bad experiences with it. Times when I've almost felt my illness back again, creeping into my bones and grinning at me like a gap-toothed skeleton. That's why I'm a dope-smoking teetotaller, or near as dammit.

"Maybe the breakdown *was* the trauma," I add. "For two years, I didn't know if I was alive or dead. You can't know what that's like. You couldn't do."

Wrong thing to say.

Wrong thing to say to Lev.

He sucks some more jam off his spoon and takes a swallow of tea. Then he crouches down opposite my chair. Makes me look into his eyes. Brown and fathomless. As deep as history. As empty as bones.

"For two years almost, I was in Grozny. Grozny, Chechnya. The Russians were there. Also rebels. Bandits. Jihadists. Mercenaries. Spies. Every fucker on

327

earth was there. Fuckers with guns. I was there because . . . doesn't matter. I stay because there is a lady and a little boy I care for very much. For two years almost. Because of who I was, everyone want me, nobody trust me, there is . . . shit, Fiona. There is shit. Every day. Friends are killed. Sometimes friends are killers. Every kind of bad thing that can happen is happening, and this is normal. This is how it is. Am I alive, or am I dead? I don't know. For two years, I don't know. Not me only, but everyone in Grozny. Everyone in Chechnya. I know what it's like, Fiona. I know."

I wave my hands in a gesture of pardon-seeking. "Sorry, Lev. Sorry. So maybe you do know. Maybe your thing was worse, even. But mine was different. I wasn't in Grozny. I was in Cardiff. And the shit wasn't happening outside, it was happening inside. It just came and took me over."

Lev nods. "Trauma."

"From nowhere. Trauma from outer space," I argue back.

"You sleep OK?"

"Yes. Like a baby. Better since I got the gun."

"And before?"

"Before that . . . sometimes OK, sometimes not OK."

"Dreams?"

"I never dream." And that's true. I never dream except sometimes when I wake up in blank terror and have no idea what I am terrified of. Nights with gaping horror in the middle of them and no reason why. A

328

skull grinning in the dark. Nights when I have all too little difficulty in identifying my emotions.

"Fear? You get frightened sometimes for no reason?"

I'm about to tell him about those nights of terror, but then I desist. I remember that prickling feeling I could never quite place. It's been worse recently, but I've had it, or something like it, as long as I can remember. Maybe fear is the right name for it. Maybe that feeling is fear.

I tell Lev, "Maybe," and instantly know that my "maybe" is wrong. That feeling is fear. And I've had it all my life. So I correct myself: "Yes. Not maybe. Yes."

Lev nods. "Trauma. You have trauma. What do the Americans call it? All their soldiers come home with it."

"PTSD. Post-traumatic stress disorder."

"*Da*. That. PTSD. You have that."

We leave it there.

I can't argue any more. I've never been attacked. I've never been raped. My family home is as safe and protected as you could ever ask for. I wasn't even bullied at school, for heaven's sake. I don't have dodgy uncles. I've never been felt up at a bus-stop or groped in the cinema. Little Miss Sheltered. That's me.

Except that Lev's right. I know it. I have trauma in my bones and I'll never be at peace until I deal with it.

I stand up. I'm far too tired. Lev is sitting and I rub the back of his neck and massage the strong muscles running down to his shoulder blades. For a minute, just that, nothing else. Me massaging. Him leaning into it. Violins.

I wonder how old he is. I wonder what else he's seen. We know nothing about each other, not really.

"Thanks, Lev. Are you staying? I'm off to bed. The keys are there if you want them."

I show him the keys to the garden shed. There's a fifty per cent chance that Lev will stay all night, smoking dope and listening to Shostakovich. There's a fifty per cent chance that he'll be gone in the morning. I used to pay him for Krav Maga tuition back in the early days, but stopped a long time ago. I don't know why. He just stopped asking for money. These days, I don't know what our relationship is. It's not like friendship. Not in any normal way. But then we're both freaks. Me because of my head, him because of his history. Maybe what we have is friendship. The freaks' version.

"Goodnight, Fiona." The gun is still on the kitchen table and he pushes it towards me. He knows that I'll be sleeping with it. "If you get into a situation, remember you have trauma. Your instinct will tell you to do too much or too little. Both are bad. Use your head, not this."

He points to his heart.

I nod. I know what he means. I've got a slogan for it.

"Fuck feelings, trust reason," I say.

He grins and repeats. He likes that.

"Fuck feelings, trust reason."

CHAPTER
THIRTY-FOUR

I'm too tired. Much too tired.

I slept decently, because of Lev, but even so I was late to bed and my alarm blitzes me awake at seven fifteen. Five hours sleep, not even, and that's been my best night for a while.

I blink myself into wakefulness. I'm still on the futon, not the bed. My hand found the gun before it found the alarm clock.

I take a shower. Lev is sleeping on the upstairs landing. I don't know why he chose there, but there'd have been some reason. He wakes up as I go past, or at least opens his eyes. With Lev, you can never really tell what's awake and what's asleep. I go back to my bedroom for a pillow and give him that, though there was an entire bed in the spare room if he'd wanted it, then I go ahead and shower. Even after the shower, my face looks tired. I choose soft, comfortable clothes and go downstairs. Lev has left bags of grass all over the kitchen table. I roll him a joint for when he gets up, then lock the rest of it away. I eat something.

I go into work. Not because I want to, or because I care about any of it. Just because it's what I know to do.

I know I've been a bit odd recently — odder than usual, I mean — but I can feel that something has intensified overnight. It's because of Lev. Him and his theories about trauma.

Trow-ma. Mine or his? Maybe he's no longer able to tell the difference. I wonder what he was doing in Chechnya. A bad place to be. Trow-ma.

As I drive into Cathays Park, I bang my palms on the steering wheel, press down into my toes. I can feel my body, but only dimly. Through anaesthetic. Layers of padding. Bev Rowland says a cheery hi to me as we meet on the way in and it takes me half a second to remember who she is.

Eight thirty. Jackson gives the morning briefing. He's in a crumpled shirt, no tie, no jacket. He's been up all night and he's looking tired but happy.

"We'll keep this short," he says. "Most of you know the important stuff anyway. Last night, two officers, DS Alexander and DC Griffiths, obtained evidence that three men — current identifications Wojciech Kapuscinski, Yuri Petrov and a third man known to us for the moment only as Dmitri — have committed serious assaults on local sex workers. One local woman, Jayne Armitage, exhibited signs of an extremely serious beating, which would constitute a grave offence in its own right, but as you all know, we believe these men are connected to Karol Sikorsky and quite likely also to the Operation Lohan murders, which still represent our prime focus.

"Overnight, we've succeeded in arresting Kapuscinski and Petrov. They are being interrogated now. They shared a flat down in Butetown, less than half a mile from Allison Street, and needless to say, we've got our forensics guys crawling all over the flat right now. The flat is a proper mess, which is a good thing, because it increases the likelihood that we find something of value. No definite news yet, but we're right on top of it.

"I also want to say publicly that this inquiry owes a lot to Alexander and Griffiths. It's not easy getting these street workers to talk. They achieved it. Many officers would have failed. Well done."

He's going to continue, except that he's interrupted by a round of clapping. Jane isn't even here. She had a late night last night and she's got a family to manage. I don't know what to do or feel, so just sit there looking like an idiot. A task I perform with considerable ease.

Jackson continues.

When Petrov was arrested, he had a little black address book with a Cardiff address against the letters "KS" in Cyrillic. The initials are assumed to refer to Karol Sikorsky and the house in question is currently under surveillance. If there's no movement at the house within twenty-four hours, a warrant will be applied for and the house searched.

Meantime, DC Jon Breakell gets his moment of glory. CCTV from a month back on Corporation Road places Sikorsky and Mancini together. He gets a round of clapping too.

Mobile-phone records have already established that Sikorsky was in the relevant areas for all three incidents under investigation: the Mancinis, Edwards and Balcescu.

Officers, including Jim Davis, have been sent back to Ioana Balcescu to see if she'll be willing to give us a formal statement.

I feel a bit weird about all this. The inquiry is moving rapidly towards a close. Perhaps Sikorsky is already back in Poland or Russia or wherever he comes from, but if he isn't, then it's becoming increasingly likely that we'll get him and arrest him. Ports and airports have been watched since we got the DNA sample from Allison Street. Interpol has his details.

In any case, Kapuscinski, Petrov and Leonard are all now under arrest for provable offences. Once we have completed all the forensic work on the properties associated with them, it's highly likely we'll be able to put together a case for murder too. The mood around the room is jubilant. Good old Jackson. Old Reliable. All we need now is Sikorsky and everyone's joy will be complete.

I know why Davis has been sent to re-interview Balcescu. Jane Alexander isn't available. I'm around, but knackered. When inquiries reach this stage, everyone has to be willing to do everything, even if they're not the ideal person for the job.

I know all that, but I can't help thinking of Jim Davis talking to Ioana. "We're asking you to confirm for us statements you made at your previous interview, with officers Alexander and Griffiths, on Monday 31 May. We're asking you recklessly to endanger your own life. We're asking you to overlook my yellow teeth and DS Alexander's unfeasibly blonde hair. Any questions, Ms Balcescu, hur-hur-hur?"

I think of Ioana's battered body. Of Jayney's bruises. Of Stacey Edwards's corpse. April's blind little head. Images I should avoid. I'm not feeling well.

Trow-ma.

Jackson ends the briefing with a request for questions or any further points worth communicating.

I want to stick my hand up. I want to say that down in Newport, a man went missing leaving over £200,000 in cash. I want to say that I looked into Charlotte Rattigan's eyes. That her husband — her late husband? — liked to fuck street girls. I want to say all sorts of things, but I can't, because although I've just garnered a round of applause for being Detective of the Day, no one except me cares about any of these things. If I tried to say anything now, I'd be like the cartoons on the back page of the newspaper. The funnies at the end of the news bulletin. "And in other news . . ." That'd be me. The pet rabbit who got stuck up a tree. The cat who does a YouTube dance with the dog.

I keep schtum.

The briefing breaks up. Everyone feels that success is imminent. About to get the killer. Job done. Beers all round. *All* round? No, not quite, because the office comedy act here, Miss Fiona Griffiths, doesn't drink beer. Not a real police officer, see, but we're proud of our efforts to increase diversity. Look! Watch her drink some fizzy water. See her rip into her wholegrain energy bar. We hire all sorts these days and we *still* catch the bad guys.

Bev Rowland seeks me out, worrying that I'm looking ill. She has a face as round as the moon, only kinder and more talkative. She starts to fuss and cluck me into well-being, but I'm not fussable today. I tell her that I'm going to catch up on a few emails, then take off. I don't tell her that I'm planning to take off for Newport, and she accepts my answer.

We agree to rendezvous for tea once we've checked our emails, and I wander upstairs.

A mistake. Hughes catches me at my desk. A trap. A Hughesian trap.

He says something about timesheets and interview notes. I don't really listen. It's not his case anyway. Lohan belongs to Jackson. Penry belongs to Matthews. Fletcher belongs to Axelsen. When I tune in again, Hughes is saying something about the Stacey Edwards autopsy. He's telling me that because I did a good job with the last one, I can do this one too. Go along on Monday afternoon, to take notes as Hughes and Dr Aidan Price seek to bore the pants off each other in what will surely be a world-class boring match. It'll be a tense affair, but my money's on Price.

I'd forgotten that there would be an autopsy for Edwards. There has to be, of course, I just hadn't thought about it. I say, "Yes, fine. That's fine," but I can't work out what I feel about seeing Edwards again, because I can't figure out much about anything. I go on saying, "Yes, sir," whenever there's a gap and eventually even Hughes has had enough and he goes away again. I look at my emails for twenty minutes. Can't work out what I'm doing with them. Text Brydon. Get a call back. Chat for ten minutes, which is all he can spare. Drink some peppermint tea and manage a half-sensible

336

conversation with Bev before heading back over to Newport.

The team at Rattigan Transport has shrunk to just two, and neither of them is on the case full time. We have a house full of money, a missing person, but no actual honest-to-God crime. There'd be more urgency about this if there were a proper crime. I should have stuck a dead body in Fletcher's bathroom before calling in the uniforms.

I get myself to the conference room and the computer that's been allocated to me. The girl who has the expression of a calf gets me some undrinkable tea in a plastic cup that buckles when I try to pick it up.

Once settled at my desk, fog claims me again.

I once went on a walk in the Black Mountains with my aunt Gwyn. It started out misty but pleasant, the collies racing ahead of us through the bracken, a little frost, a nice day. Then the mist thickened, as though the light had hardened, or grown more dense. And then the world was gone. Vanished into the silence and the cold. The collies still came and went. I don't think they had a problem. But Gwyn and I were suddenly wanderers on the void, a Vladimir and Estragon of the mountains. Gwyn had known these hills all her life and even so we were forced to descend until a hedge stopped us, and then we skirted the rest of the way, the hedge always on our right, until at last we came across the gate and the lane by which we had entered. Had we somehow missed that gate, I think we could have been wandering there for ever.

It's like that today, only without the collies, without Gwyn and without that blessed gate. Axelsen is around more often today than he has been. He's in and out, keeping an eye on things. I listen to him assigning me a task — listing overseas clients visited by Fletcher in the last two years, for example — and I nod my agreement, and two hours later, I have a sheet of doodles and I'm trying to remember what it was I'm meant to be doing. Axelsen thinks I'm taking the piss. So do the others on the team. I tell them sorry and I'll do better.

As soon as I tell them and they get off my case, the fog immediately descends again. I can't remember what I said five minutes before.

Cod, whiting, herring, turbot.

What about halibut? What's a halibut? Some kind of flatfish, I think. Google tells me that you can catch halibut in the North Atlantic. It tells me that for six months, the halibut has eyes on both sides of its body and swims in the normal fishy way. Then, after six months, one eye migrates to the opposite side, the fish rotates 90 degrees in the water, and it spends the rest of its life with both eyes staring up at the roof of the sea, and no way at all of looking down. A fish with vertigo.

I can't see Rattigan wanting to catch halibut.

Every time Fletcher went off on a "fishing trip", there was a Rattigan ship coming in from the Baltic. Usually Kaliningrad, sometimes Petersburg. That would be a more impressive fact if Rattigan didn't operate a fleet of such ships.

Kaliningrad. Major exports: Russian gangsterism, Afghan heroin, criminality that combines capitalist organisation with Soviet murderousness. Best of both worlds.

I forget what Axelsen has told me to do, so instead I call all the fishing vessels available for charter on the South Wales coast. I ask them if it would be possible to inspect their log to see who chartered them, when, for how long and where they were going. Most of them say yes, if I want. A couple say that should be fine but that they'll need to refer it elsewhere in their, no doubt colossal, corporate structures. One skipper from West Wales hangs up when I tell him who I am. A little further truffling tells me that the hanger-upper is Martyn Roberts, based out of Milford Haven, and he has a criminal conviction for armed robbery and another for GBH.

I tell all this to Axelsen the next time he visits.

"Do you think Rattigan went fishing with Fletcher?"

"No."

"So why would either of them want to charter a fishing boat?"

"I don't know."

"You're remembering that Rattigan owns an entire fleet of ships? That if he wanted a boat, he could buy one? That Fletcher's day job was arranging charters for Rattigan's fleet?"

"Yes."

"And that Rattigan has been dead for almost a year?"

"Yes."

"So do you think maybe this all is a red herring?"

"A red halibut maybe."

I laugh. I think it's funny, so I laugh quite a lot. Axelsen doesn't think it's at all funny, so I shut up.

"Have you got that list I asked for?" he says.

I scrunch my eyes up and start to give that question some serious thought, but then the fog creeps in again and no answers seem to arrive. I can't remember what list he wanted.

I wonder if he'd be interested in hearing about halibut instead, but there's a look on his face that suggests not, so I say nothing, which is a pity, because they're interesting fish. Halibut have white bellies, so from below they look like the sky, and dark upper bodies, so that from above they look like the ocean floor. A light side and a dark side. And the light side travels blind.

"Are you feeling OK? You don't look well."

"I don't feel well."

"You weren't in an accident or something?"

I shake my head. I don't remember the day terribly well, but I'd have remembered that, surely.

"You look like someone in shock. Why don't you go home, get some rest, take it easy over the weekend. You're no bloody use to me at all the way you are now."

I nod. I try to look wise, as though we're making a tough judgement call together and after due consideration I've come down in favour of his assessment.

"I'll go home. Yes. Good idea. Sorry." I'm not sure why I'm saying sorry, except that "no bloody use" is a phrase I've heard before, and not in a good way. I say, "Sorry," again and sit at my desk to clear my things.

Axelsen goes off to catch criminals and make the world a better place.

Before I go, though, I type "shock" into Google and get up a Wikipedia page. It offers me three alternatives:

- Shock (circulatory), a circulatory medical emergency
- Acute stress reaction, often termed "shock" by laypersons, a psychological condition in response to terrifying events
- Post-traumatic stress disorder, a long-term complication of acute stress reaction.

It takes me some time to understand this. It took me some time to discover all those interesting things about halibut too. But I don't have circulatory shock. That's something you get in hospitals and has nothing to do with me.

PTSD. That's what Lev told me I had, but that's a long-term thing. A continuing response to something that happened way back.

Acute stress reaction is more interesting, though. "Often termed 'shock' by laypersons." It's a bit harsh to call DI Axelsen a layperson. He's a detective inspector with the Gwent Police, for heaven's sake, but layperson or not, maybe he is on to something. Here's what Wikipedia says about it:

Acute stress reaction (also called **acute stress disorder, psychological shock**, **mental shock** or,

simply, **shock**) is a <u>psychological</u> condition arising
in response to a terrifying or traumatic event.

A bit further on, I learn what my symptoms are
meant to be:

> Common symptoms sufferers of acute stress
> disorder experience are: numbing; detachment;
> derealisation; depersonalisation or dissociative
> amnesia; continued re-experiencing of the event by
> such ways as thoughts, dreams and flashbacks.

Numbing? Tick. Yes, got that. Detachment? Yep, that
too. Derealisation? Not too sure what that is, but if it's
what it sounds like, then I've got it. Depersonalisation
or dissociative amnesia? Yes, got that big time and, back
in the day, used to have it mega big time. World-class
depersonaliser, I was. Never beaten, seldom matched.
But then there's that last bit. Continued re-experiencing
of the event by such ways as thoughts, dreams and
flashbacks. No. What event? I try to find something on
Wikipedia that will tell me what event I'm meant to be
experiencing, but can't find anything. But what about
my night-time terrors? The gaping horror at midnight?
The skull grinning in the dark? Do those things count
as dreams or flashbacks?

If they do, then I tick every box. Tick 'em big. Tick
'em good.

But what's the event? There isn't any event. Lev
thinks there is and layperson Axelsen thinks there is,
but there isn't. There's no event.

It's odd this. Even in my dazed state, I know it's odd. When I first got ill, there was this big investigation into why. What made it happen? My condition was something that safely brought-up teenagers weren't meant to get. It made no sense. Psychiatrists pushed and prodded and Social Services tried to foist their crappy little theories onto my poor old mam and dad. No one got anywhere. There was no explanation that made sense, so the whole question — certainly in my mind and I think in everyone else's too — got shoved aside. My illness was just one of those things. No more logic than an earthquake. Wrong place, wrong time, tough luck.

And now, when I least expect it, Lev and Axelsen are telling me to think again. Continued re-experiencing of the event. There isn't an event, but Lev and Axelsen and Wikipedia all beg to differ.

Next to me, the phone goes. One of my teammates picks it up. There's a muttered conversation, which I don't follow, because I'm hot on the pursuit of knowledge and can't concern myself with trifles. The phone conversation ends. The teammate approaches.

"That was Axelsen calling to check you'd gone."

"Ah, yes." I remember that now.

"I'll take you to your car, shall I? You'll be all right driving?"

I nod. Very meek. Very submissive. I'm led out to the car park and drive home so carefully that I'm honked at on the M4 for doing forty in the slow lane.

CHAPTER
THIRTY-FIVE

I reach the house vaguely expectant, but there's nothing there. Lev's gone, as anticipated. No messages on the machine, no texts.

The kitchen is all tidied up. Not my doing. Lev's. He's left a note for me on the counter, though: *FF, TR.* Fuck feelings, trust reason. A very good slogan indeed, though I say so myself.

I start to apply it. Think, Griffiths, think.

First, this whole issue about shock. Clearly, I tick most of the boxes for PTSD. Pretty clearly, I am looking and acting like someone in the grip of major-league shock right now, this minute.

At the same time, however, I'm missing the single most crucial ingredient in the formula, a "terrifying or traumatic event". That's a puzzle, but not one that needs to be solved right now. I decide to leave it.

Next, I need to find some way to lessen these symptoms. I'm not managing them well at the moment, and I know how dark they can get. I make a list of my standard techniques for dealing with head-craziness. My list runs: 1) smoke a joint, 2) bury myself in work, 3) go to stay with Mam and Dad, 4) breathing exercises, etc.

I immediately cross out item one. I smoked too much yesterday and dope only goes so far. It's excellent self-medication, but it only helps when my problems are mild to moderate. Right now, they're moderate to bad, with the course set for hard to severe.

Item two is likewise forced to bite the dust. I've just been sent home by the Gwent Police. Everyone on Lohan is looking at me strangely and telling me to go home. I've got no work to bury myself in. And the work wasn't helping.

Item three is more interesting. It would probably work. Not straight away, but give it a few days and I'd be right as rain. But it feels like a backward step. A palliative, not a cure. I decide to leave that one aside and come back to it if there's an emergency.

Number four is like a pair of sensible shoes or a high-fibre cereal. Good for you, but sinfully dull. All the same, four is a good 'un. I'll come back to it shortly.

Floating around, though, is a possible number five. Making love. I've never had many lovers. A few women early on. Then two or three spottily awkward male students at Cambridge, ickily overeager to get into bed with anything in a skirt, and I was ickily overwilling to let them. Then one sort-of but not-quite boyfriend after Cambridge. A nice chap. Runs a bookshop now. And Ed Saunders. Ed was the only one I felt right around. In bed and out of it. With Ed, I think I used to use sex as a way of coming into being. A trick akin to smoking dope or running home to Mam and Dad.

And now Brydon. Part of me wants to go rushing off to Brydon. Get him into bed. Make love urgently enough that I could use it as a way to feel myself again. *Use* him.

I only have to understand that to decide against it. With Brydon, I want to do things right. I want to learn the art of being a girlfriend. A proper one. A permanent, stable one, for whom lovemaking is about nothing more than making love. Simply that. Not a fucked-up sort of self-medication.

I make a cup of tea and spend forty minutes doing exercises. Breathing first. *In*, two, three, four, five. *Out*, two, three, four, five. When I've done fifteen minutes of that, I start my bodywork. Move my arms. Move my legs. Feel them as I move them. Stamp on the floor to see if I can feel down to my feet. Ed Saunders would be proud of me, though he might be a bit concerned to learn my thoughts on the topic of lovemaking. Or perhaps he already knows.

I think he already knows.

One day, I will apologise.

But for now I need to focus on things closer to home. I've done the immediate essentials, but what next? What should I do next? What do I want? Nothing comes to me, so I get out my paper again and write, *What do I care about?*

Almost immediately, I write in strong capitals, *APRIL MANCINI*. I move my pen, ready to add further names to the list. Janet Mancini. Stacey Edwards. Ioana Balcescu. The names of the victims. And maybe there are other things, other people I want to find out about. Rattigan. Fletcher. Penry. Sikorsky. But my pen doesn't move. *APRIL MANCINI*. That's who I care about. She's all I care about. The toffee-apple kid.

With a sudden awful rush, I realise that I've forgotten her funeral. I promised to go to it. I even promised to tell the nice lady — Amanda, I think it was — who phoned the helpline early on and started crying when I told her how Janet and April died. She was going to come to the funeral too.

I phone the office. I can't find anyone there who knows or cares. I phone the hospital. Ditto. But I'm not on maximum power, so I'm probably asking the wrong people in the wrong way. Instead, I phone Bev Rowland. She doesn't know, but promises to find out, and sure enough calls me back in ten minutes. The funeral is going to be on Tuesday, the day after the autopsy. Unless something unexpected crops up at the mortuary on Monday, Stacey Edwards and Janet and April Mancini will all be cremated the following day.

I thank Bev and put the phone down.

I feel instantly more human. I know what I'm doing now. I need to arrange a proper funeral for April. I don't know why, but I do. April needs me to.

I phone her school. Insist on being put through to the head teacher. I encounter a bit of resistance from a pointlessly obstructive receptionist, but my juices are rising now and I'm getting harder to resist. I bulldoze my way through to the head teacher and tell her that April's entire class needs to come to the funeral. She tells me that their lessons have already been planned. I tell her that someone dropped a sink on April Mancini's head and she isn't lucky enough to have any lessons. The head teacher tells me, tartly, that the crematorium is too far from the school and it's too late to organise transport. I tell her that that's absolutely fair enough, so when does she want transport and how many kids are there in April's class? Ten minutes later, I call back, having hired a coach to come and pick up the children. The head teacher says fine. She even thanks me.

Zoom, zoom. My speed is picking up. Next stop, neighbours. Not neighbours at the squat, because they barely knew Janet, but at the estate in Llanrumney where she used to live. I get a local print shop to print 500 flyers. Nothing much. Just typed details about the funeral arrangements and at the bottom a request for information: JANET AND APRIL MANCINI WERE MURDERED. CALL IN CONFIDENCE. That and my phone number.

I drive round to the estate and find a couple of kids mooning around on BMX bikes. I offer them fifty quid to distribute my flyers to every house and flat on the estate. Twenty upfront. Thirty when they've done it. I tell them I'll check three random doors to ensure that the flyers have been delivered. They have a brief discussion, then agree. I stick around for just long enough to check that the flyers are entering some letterboxes, then off I zoom.

There's a drug users' drop-in centre that Janet used to use. I go there and get them to put up a notice. A helpful woman serving teas says that she'll email a few people who might be interested. Good on her. I ask her if she knows any women's centres that might be interested in knowing about the funeral. She says yes and she'll get straight on to it. I tell her she's an angel.

I call Amanda, the lady who cried. I tell her when the funeral is. She cries again, promises to come and says she'll phone some of the other mothers.

Back to Llanrumney. The kids are still shoving flyers through letterboxes. Good enough for me. I give them the thirty quid.

I ask them if they want another fifty quid for doing the same further up the road, around Stacey Edwards's old stomping ground. They look at me as though I'm mad, and I take that as a yes. I phone the print shop again and get them to run off more flyers, only with Stacey Edwards's name in place of Janet and April's. I tell the kids where they can pick up the flyers and tell them to call me when they're done.

The kids pedal off, delighted at my inability to drive a decent bargain.

Zoom, zoom.

What else? Flowers. Music.

I call the Thornill crematorium. What do they do for music? They've got tapes. I don't want tapes. I want an organist. I want a choir. I want a parade of trumpeters, for fuck's sake. After a bit of discussion, it seems that I can get a string quartet and a solo vocalist for 400 quid. That seems steep to me, but I say yes. I do ask about a trumpeter, but they're out of stock, alas.

I have this conversation as I'm driving to Cardiff Market. Not on the hands-free, just juggling the phone, the steering wheel and the gearstick as I drive. I know that sounds bad, but it helps build concentration and does wonders for the coordination. Like rubbing your tummy and patting your head, only harder.

I arrive at the market as it's closing. A clutter of stalls housed in a palace. Like some entrepreneurial refugees got stuck in a Victorian railway terminus and set up shop there. Stallholders are taking down their sports shirts, their ethnic jewellery. Pulling shutters down over veg boxes and bookstands. A pleasant end-of-day mood. A box of red apples being flogged off for £2 the lot.

I run round looking for a flower stall, find one and ask the bloke in green wellies how much for his flowers. He looks at me like I'm barking. He points to the buckets of flowers. Each one has its own little blackboard on a spike, with prices chalked on each board. I look at him like he's barking. I don't want one stupid bouquet, I want his flowers. I want the shop.

Once I manage to explain this, he asks me if I'm serious, then quotes a price of 500 quid. I've a feeling I could get them for a lot less, but I don't want April to think that I'm tight, so I say yes, but can he help get the flowers into my car and can I have the black buckets as well?

He agrees, which proves to be a bad move on his part, because my lovely Peugeot isn't really the acres-of-boot-space sort of car and it takes half an hour of careful wiggling to get everything inside.

I get a call from the BMX kids and go to pay them. Then home.

Eat. Drink. Make some more calls. The church in whose parish Janet Mancini was found dead. Ditto the one in the part of town where she used to live. Ditto Stacey Edwards's old parish. I speak to the vicars. One of them agrees to say a blessing. He's nice about it actually. A good soul. I say to him, "You don't happen to know a trumpeter, do you?" and, Lord bless the man, he does. He gives me a phone number, and two minutes later, I have my trumpeter. He asks me what kind of music I want played. I say I don't know, but I want it to be upbeat. Not funereal. Triumphant, if he can think of something. He says he can. He says his rates are sixty quid for up to two hours, but given the circs he won't charge anything. I tell him that he's my new favourite trumpeter.

I call a couple of newspapers and place funeral notices there. I pay extra for all the bits and bobs. Extra words, bold type, boxes.

I'm just wondering what to do next when I get a call. It's Brydon, back at Cathays Park. He says that the office is going full pelt on Lohan and the forensics on the Kapuscinski house look positive. I don't care about that and say so.

"Listen, I've got the day off tomorrow," he says. "I thought maybe we could —"

"Yes."

"You don't know what I was going to say."

"What were you going to say?"

"I was going to say maybe we could spend some time together."

"Yes."

"I'll call you tomorrow morning, then? We could go somewhere."

That sounds like a man-plan to me. *We could go somewhere.* Gosh, the imagination! But I don't argue. A man-plan is good enough for me. We ring off.

I'm slowing down now. Tired but in a good way. I need to get an early night tonight, so I can catch up on some sleep, but there are things to do first.

I make up some bouquets. I'm not the world's best bouquet-maker, but I don't need to be. I make about twenty, tie them with kitchen string and drop them on the passenger seat of the car. In each bouquet, I've put a handwritten note: *Most of all, I would like it if you came to the funeral. But I am also a police officer. If you want to tell me anything at all about Brendan Rattigan, Huw Fletcher, Wojtek Kapuscinksi, Yuri Petrov or Karol Sikorsky, then please call me, in total confidence, on the number below. Very many thanks, Fiona Griffiths.*

I drive down to the Taff Embankment. Blaenclydach Place. It's a bit early for things to be really busy, but Friday night is crazy night, and the girls are already out, hunting for custom. I know a lot of them now. Some of them even like me.

One bouquet at a time, one prostitute at a time, I approach.

With each girl, I explain who I am and why I'm here. I'm a friend of Janet Mancini's. Also of Stacey Edwards. It's their funeral on Tuesday. I wanted people to know. I also wanted to give out flowers.

I meet Kyra, the stupid cow who gave Jane and me nothing at all that first time we met her. She's wearing platform shoes with a five inch heel. She's absurdly happy to see me, which means nothing about me, everything about how recently she's taken smack.

"Flowers? For me?" she asks.

"For you. Or for you to bring along to the funeral to place on the coffins. I don't mind. Either way, the flowers are to commemorate the women who died. And Janet had a little girl, so the flowers are for her too. She was six years old and her name was April."

Kyra looks at me as though I'm crazy, but she takes the flowers. Same with the other girls I meet. They think I'm nuts, but I tell them that I'll see them at the crematorium on Tuesday.

It takes me four hours to hand out most of my bouquets. I'm beginning to sway with tiredness when I hear a familiar voice from behind. Bryony Williams. Equipped with her ciggy, her canvas jacket and her messy hair. And a bouquet-wielding prostitute who I vaguely recognise. Altea, she might be called.

"I heard someone was doling these out," says Bryony, indicating the flowers. "Thought it might be you."

I grin. "Three more to go and I'm done for the evening."

Bryony says she'll do them. I tell her about the notes I've put inside and she nods approvingly.

"Where did you get the flowers?" she asks.

I bought the shop, I tell her. I explain that I want people to come to the funeral. I don't know why it feels important, but I think it's because Janet and April and Stacey had such unnoticed lives. I want them to go out

353

in a blaze of glory. I tell Bryony about my trumpeter and the coachload of school-children.

She gives me a hug, hard and long. When she comes away, her cheeks are wet.

I envy her her tears. I wonder what they feel like. I wonder if they hurt.

CHAPTER
THIRTY-SIX

Saturday.

Dave Brydon calls me at eleven. I'm ready for him, give or take. It's another proper summer's day, a hot one. I've tried on four different outfits and ended up with the pistachio-and-coffee striped top that I was wearing the day Penry hit me, a long skirt and flat shoes. I look nice. I look all right.

When he calls, I'm amazingly nervous. I think he is too. We start out very awkward and only start to shake free of it when we decide that rather than him coming to collect me, or vice versa, we should meet out of town somewhere. The beaches are going to be absolutely heaving today, but I don't mind that. I'd quite like it. We agree to meet at Parkmill on the Gower Peninsula. He tells me to bring my swimming cossie. I tell him that I bet he's got white legs and that he burns after ten minutes in the sun.

We hang up. I don't have a swimming cossie. I can't even swim very well, but I do have a couple of bikinis, and after trying them both on, I choose the one that gives me a tiny bit more cleavage and wear it under my clothes.

I drive to Parkmill. The traffic is ridiculously slow because we've chosen the worst day of the year to make the trip, but I don't care. Brydon and I talk to each other on the hands-free, comparing notes on how rubbish the traffic is. We agree not to talk about work. The awkwardness is evaporating in the heat.

He gets there first and tells me which café he's in. He says we can pretend this is a blind date, that we've never met before.

I get to Parkmill, park and go to find Brydon. I'm so nervous that, fifty yards away from the café, I have to stop and collect myself. But it's a natural sort of nerves. No depersonalisation. No losing touch with my feelings. I'm nervous but OK.

I spend a moment texting Bryony. I think I need to stay away from the streets tonight, and I tell her that I'm on a date and won't be able to break off. I tell her to spend as much money on flowers as she wants, give them out to whoever she wants, and that I'll pay. That leaves me with a stackload of flowers to deal with, but I'll just take them to the funeral with me.

Then, as I move closer to the café, I see Brydon at table. White parasol flapping in the sea breeze. Shadows jumping to avoid the sunshine. He's nervous too, and I realise that he's nervous because he cares. Cares about me. I feel a wave of pleasure at that thought. What have I done to be so lucky?

I come up close and he sees me only at the last minute. We play our blind-date game for a bit, which definitely helps to deal with the nerves. I'm awkward and klutzy, but Brydon accepts it in a way that makes it seem endearing, not edge-of-breakdown weird.

Brydon does have white legs and I bet he will burn before the day is out. In this light, his hair looks properly blond, not just sandy.

We eat lunch. Brydon has a glass of beer. We walk along the beach. He swims. I sort of swim. We splash water at each other. I try to duck him under and fail totally, until he laughs at me and does this huge pretend drowning act. Then he picks me up and drops me in. I shriek, but I like the way my body feels in his arms. When I'm duly ducked, we stand up, and he kisses me. I feel Comrade Lust tugging at me again, but I send the good comrade packing. Me and DS Brydon are taking things slow. I'm going to be his girlfriend, you know.

When we're tired — which comes fairly early in my case — we drive back to my house. I cook spaghetti bolognese and we eat it with a bottle of extremely cheap red wine that I have knocking around for such contingencies. I have only a token sip, but Brydon manfully disposes of half the bottle.

When the bolognese is done, Brydon washes up. I'm meant to dry, or do something, but I don't. I just watch him. The way his hair is speckled with ginger and has tiny salt crystals glittering close to the scalp.

I kiss his neck and ask if he's all right to go off home. I'm trying to be sensible. I know that I need to take all this slowly and I am just trying to say, in a nice Date Girl way, that I'm not ready for sex quite yet.

He doesn't take it that way.

"Not exactly," he says, with exaggerated patience. "No. Not unless you've got me a special licence to drive with raised blood alcohol levels."

I stare at him. Is he serious? He's had half a bottle of wine and won't drive the ten minutes it'll take him to get home?

For a second — maybe ten seconds — I'm genuinely panicked. I think this is some kind of ruse on his part to get into my knickers. *Oh, no, Fi, I can't possibly drive home. I'll have to spend the night here. No, I can't use the spare room. Come here, my beauty.* My panic is temporary, but immediate and all-consuming. Comrade Lust is nowhere to be seen. Shuddering, knock-kneed, in the understairs cupboard. It's as though my reason has been taken over by a troop of Methodist grandmams, wagging their fingers at me and declaiming, "They only want one thing, you know."

I don't know what look I have on my face, or what I say or do. What I do know is that Brydon reacts like the sane me would expect him to react.

"Hey, hey, hey, it's OK. I can't drive, but I can order a taxi."

He phones for one, ostentatiously, calming me down. When the cab firm asks what time he wants to be picked up, he says to me, "We've got time for coffee, haven't we?" The Methodist grandmams go into overdrive, chorusing about the double entendre in the word "coffee", but I am already calming down and tell the grandmams to shut up. I tell Brydon of course he's staying for coffee.

He orders a cab for half an hour's time.

I make coffee for him, peppermint tea for me.

"Sorry," I say. "I'm not very good at this."

There's a question on his face, which I answer. "I'm not a virgin, but . . . I'm not very experienced." I think about that answer and realise that it's the truth but not the whole truth. "Also, I'm an idiot."

"Duly noted."

"You do know that I'm not quite like you, don't you? That I'm a bit strange?"

He makes a joke. Deflects. Is a man.

I persist. "No, really. It matters. I'm not like you. If that's a problem, then . . . I don't know. But you need to understand that. Sometimes I'll go to places that you've never been. I might need your help."

He looks at me. I can't interpret the look on his face. He says, "Well, if you do, just ask," which sounds like the right thing to say, but somehow isn't.

I don't quite know what the best thing to say is, so I say what is almost certainly the wrong thing.

"And I'm not a big one for rules. I don't get on with them very well."

"I'm a police officer, Fi. So are you."

"Yes, but . . ."

"Rules are our business."

"I know . . ." But the gun. The marijuana. The thing I'm planning for Monday. The thing I'm planning for later in the week. The list of possible buts is long and getting longer. I don't finish my sentence. Nor do I push the point. Another rule of mine: always, always put off till tomorrow anything that doesn't have to be

359

done today. I don't apply that to work, but I do to pretty much anything in my personal life.

For our last twenty minutes, we cuddle together on the sofa. Brydon is a good kisser. A broader repertoire than you'd guess. He's good on the passionate knee-wobblers, but he's got a good range of nibbly, nuzzly, intimate, flirty kisses too. I wonder again what I have done to be so lucky. As I'm wondering, my phone bleeps the arrival of a text. It's Bryony. She tells me she's giving out flowers and notes like crazy, and finishes, HAVE A GOOD TIME. YOU DESERVE IT.

"Anything important?" says Brydon.

"No."

We go on cuddling till the taxi comes and it's time to see him off at the door. I feel like a true citizen of Planet Normal. I am going to be a girlfriend. This is going to be my boyfriend. We're police officers, you know. CID. My boyfriend is law-abiding, so this is him leaving in a taxi. And here am I seeing him off at the front door. Watch us kiss goodbye. Watch me smile and wave. Just look how normal I am.

Once the taxi leaves, I don't close the front door right away. I hold on to it, this feeling. I am a citizen of Planet Normal. This is my boyfriend. I am his girlfriend. Look how happy I am.

CHAPTER
THIRTY-SEVEN

Sunday is a nothing day. Pretend to clean my flat. Fail to go to the gym. Forget to eat anything much. Go to my mam and dad's for tea and end up staying till ten. I talk to Brydon twice on the phone, but we don't see each other. Slowly does it.

The next morning, Monday, is another one of those weird ones. I come into work — bang on time, no fogginess, no shock — and find that life has once again moved on. Over the weekend, they kept an eye on what they believed to be Sikorsky's Cardiff address. After no sign of any movement there, they launched a dawn raid this morning and searched the place. A massive SOCO-type operation, the biggest yet by all accounts. Office rumour says that forensics have taken some clothes and think they have a blood splash on a trouser leg. If the blood is April Mancini's, then Sikorsky is inching ever closer to a life sentence. Better still — and unbelievably — the address has yielded a roll of duct tape and some cable ties from a DIY shop. Both used, though still in the original shopping bag with the receipt. Rumour has it that the cut end of the duct tape in Edwards's flat matches the roll in Sikorsky's bag. It's unbelievable how stupid most criminals are. Unbelievable and lucky. We'd have a hell of a job convicting them otherwise.

All we need now is Sikorsky himself. The prosecution case feels largely complete. But a case isn't much use without a criminal to convict. To get as far as we have without getting our hands on the probable killer feels frustrating, to say the least. The betting around the coffee machine is that Sikorsky is already in Poland or Russia. If the former, then we've a twenty or thirty per cent chance of getting him, because the Poles aren't too corrupt and because they're EU members who try to behave themselves. If Sikorsky is in Russia, then we're pretty much fucked.

Most officers reckon he's in Russia.

If I had to guess, I'd say he was there too.

Meantime, Axelsen's effort seems to be winding down. Traces of cocaine have been found in both Fletcher's home and in a desk drawer. We already know, from my interview with Charlotte Rattigan, that the big man used to take the odd bit of coke when he was still alive, so the ruling assumption is that Fletcher was dealing. That's where his cash came from. Some drug-world problem made him do a runner. He might be in another country or dead. Whatever it was, it must have been a pretty urgent problem to make him leave 200 grand in cash lying around. As for the whole Rattigan fishing-trip thing, it's being assumed that Rattigan and Fletcher were coke-buddies. Fletcher got to hang out with — and sell drugs to — rich people.

Rattigan got a kick out of hanging out with criminals. Stranger things have happened.

Because it's all go on Lohan, because Axelsen isn't exactly desperate to have me back in Newport, and because Jackson and Hughes both have other things on their minds, no one really cares what I do today.

Just as well. I'm busy with funeral stuff and I want to save my energies. Yesterday afternoon, I called a journalist at the *Western Mail* and told him about this people-power demonstration of solidarity that was expected at the crematorium. Because bugger all happens on a Sunday, which means they're always desperate for material to fill the paper on a Monday, we've got the whole front page of the newspaper: "Hundreds Expected at Dead Girl's Funeral." Gill Parker of StreetSafe is quoted as saying that the funeral is expected to show Cardiff's opposition to violence against women. A rent-a-quote local pop star is reported as saying much the same thing, and implies that she's intending to be there herself, although if you look carefully at the way she says it, she's left herself plenty of wiggle room.

I spend some time on Facebook groups and other Cardiff women's-group things, getting the word out. I call the coach company and ask them if they can provide more transport if need be. They say yes. Then I call eight head teachers of schools close to April's. I tell them that there's a big kids' movement wanting to protest against violence. I tell them that transport is arranged and paid for. They just need to call the coach company to arrange pick-up times. Six of the eight head teachers sounded really interested. I think the newspaper headline helped. Maybe the pop star too. I call the crematorium and tell them to expect 800. I call another flower place and tell them to send £1,000 worth of flowers to the event. They say what sort of flowers and I tell them the sort with petals.

When I give them my card to pay, they tell me it's declined. I tell them to try £800, then £700. That seems to work, so I tell them that I'll pay them £300 later in the month when my pay comes in. They say OK. I haven't yet paid the coach company either, so they'll have to show some patience too. Payday is the middle of the month, so I'll only have to get through a week without money. Should be a doddle. The only thing that bothers me is the state of my fuel tank, but my Peugeot, bless her, is pretty much full. She needs to be.

All the time I'm making calls, I've got April's little dead face up on my screen. "We're doing good, kid," I say to her. She smiles at me. She's never had a funeral before, so she's looking forward to this one, and quite right too.

I'm doing all this when I spot Brydon drifting over. He smiles at me and sits on the corner of my desk. Nothing unusual. We haven't talked about it much, but neither of us want the office to know about our relationship, so we play it cool. Only a lift of his eyebrow as he sits indicates that he quite liked the way he spent Saturday. I wrinkle my eyes back at him, to indicate the same thing. If truth be told, I feel a little odd about the way we finished. That thing about rules.

364

Was that really Brydon telling me that he was going to have a problem with little things like the odd speeding ticket or unlicensed handgun? I was hoping for more give and take than that. But still, no need to worry about that now. Always put off till tomorrow . . .

"What was it again?" he says. "Bastard, Thieving, Wish-He'd-Go-and-Top-Himself Penry? That was your phrase, I think."

"Drown," I say. "It was drown himself."

"He's just come in downstairs. Wants to plead guilty apparently."

"Does he? Ha!" Some noise like that anyway. Not a real word. I'm trying to work out what this means, and I get up to go, grabbing my bag and a book from my desk drawer.

"I'll see you again soon, will I?" says Brydon, who doesn't want me to rush off.

"Yes. Not this evening. I can't do this evening, I've got family coming round for dinner. The day after tomorrow? Are you free?"

"I am, yes. Subject to operational requirements."

"Then, subject to operational requirements, you've got yourself a date, Sarge."

I rush off downstairs.

If you want to plead guilty, you notify the court, not the police station. If Penry came here, it was to send me a message. I waste a minute or two trying to find out where he is, or was, and discover that he came in, spoke briefly to the duty officer, then walked out again.

I go outside. Which way? The office occupies one of the best addresses in central Cardiff. We're a stone's

365

throw from City Hall, the Welsh Assembly, Cardiff Uni, the National Museum, the Crown Court and loads else. But if Penry wanted to see me, he'd make himself easy to find. That probably means one of the two parks. Either Bute Park the other side of the tennis courts or the various different bits of green space that make up Cathays. I choose Cathays. Alexandra Gardens, the one with the war memorials and the roses. Ghosts enumerated in bland official stone. I can see that appealing to Penry's sense of humour. Either that or I just like the ghosts.

I walk over there, then walk up the park from the south end. It's a warm day, though overcast, and with a firm wind pulling inland from the sea. Not comfortable weather. Weather that hasn't made peace with itself. There are a few picnickers, but Penry isn't one of them.

I find him at the top end, on a bench. Drinking takeout coffee from a paper cup. He has a brown paper bag next to him, with another coffee cup in it.

"For you," he says, passing it over. "I forgot you don't drink coffee."

"That's OK. Thank you." I take it.

Now we're here, I don't know what to say, so I say nothing. It seems to me the ball is in his court anyway.

"I saw the thing in the *Mail* this morning," he says.

"That's people power for you."

"Yeah. And a little birdie tells me that the good folks of Gwent have got Fletcher nailed as a coke dealer."

"That's very naughty. Dealing coke."

"What are you going to do?"

I shrug. I'm not very focused on Fletcher at the moment. April has most of my attention. Still, a civil question deserves a civil answer, as my granny used to say.

"Don't know. Find him. Catch him. Arrest him. Prosecute him. You might be cellmates, you never know."

"I doubt it. I've got a lawyer who's very sympathetic. Police hero wounded in the line of duty. Lots of flashbacks. Difficult stuff psychologically. Poor lad needs a bit of support, but doesn't get it. Goes off the rails. Feels awful. I'm going to try to cry on the witness stand, but I don't know how that'll come off."

"You'll be wonderful, I'm sure."

"What do you reckon? A year? Maybe out in six months. Worst-case scenario. An open prison too, probably."

I don't say anything to that and for a while we just sit in silence, letting the wind comb through the park, looking for answers. It's Penry who breaks the silence.

"He might be dead already. Hard to arrest a dead man."

"Oh, I don't know. At least they don't run." I pause. Penry knows more about this than I do, and most of what I "know" is supposition. "Can I just check a couple of things with you? First, has Fletcher really been as stupid as I think he has?"

"Oh, yes."

"And he's as dangerous as I think he is? Dangerous on his own, I mean."

"On his own, he's about as dangerous as my old nan. Not even. My nan had more balls than he does. Or did. Whichever."

I nod. Good. It's nice to have those things confirmed.

Penry asks, "Do you know where he is?"

"No. Not exactly. But out west somewhere. Beyond Milford Haven. Why? Do you know?"

"No, not exactly, but you've got it about right. I know it's right on the coast, like not even a minute's walk away. That's all I know."

"You've never been?"

"Not my cup of tea, any of that. I didn't want to see it."

"You had his key. His phone number. You could check his emails."

"Listen, *he* wanted me involved. I totally refused. He gave me cash, his phone details, his email passwords, his bloody door key. He begged."

"You kept the cash, though."

"That bloody conservatory. I don't even like the bugger."

The bugger that was purchased fifteen weeks after Rattigan's death. Money that had come from Fletcher, not Rattigan.

"It wouldn't look good in court."

"Fuck, Fiona, *none* of it would look good in court. But I didn't help them. Either of them."

I raise my eyebrows at that. I don't believe him.

"Listen, forget courts. Just you and me."

I nod. "OK."

"It started — pure chance. I was in Butetown. Saw some idiot drive his Aston there. Interested to see what kind of idiot stepped out. It was Rattigan. I recognised him. Talked to one or two of the girls. I found out everything and he knew I'd found out. I think it could even have been Mancini who told him."

"So you started to blackmail him? It wasn't operational advice, it was just blackmail?" Somehow that feels worse.

"Not really. That's the stupid thing. It was hardly even that. Rich bastard knows I know and starts giving me money. Invites me to the racecourse. We find we actually like each other. Rich bastard, corrupt copper."

"But you weren't corrupt. Or hadn't been."

Up till now, we haven't really been looking at each other. We've been staring out at the park, letting the world spin on its axis, doing what it does. But now Penry wants my gaze as well as my attention. He touches me on the shoulder and gets me to look at him. I do that, investigating his features more carefully than I ever have done before. The tough-cop act is only half of Penry, maybe less. The bigger chunk of him is more solemn, more thoughtful.

"You're right. I'd been a good cop. That thing about crying on the stand, it's not all bollocks. I *did* feel cut off from the police service, as it happens. One moment, I was the bee's knees, the kipper's knickers. Medals from Her Maj and letters of commendation from the home secretary. Next thing, it's just a monthly pension and invites to the annual police dinner. I was disoriented for a while. Rattigan felt like a way out."

369

"A way out —" I begin, but Penry stops me.

"I know. People died. Don't think I don't know. That's why I started ripping off the school. A cry for help. Isn't that pathetic? I've turned into the sort of person I used to hate."

I don't answer or push the point. Penry's immortal soul is not my concern.

The wind travels inland from the sea. Hurrying up from the south. Rushing about, confused by the city, peering in every nook and cranny, rustling leaves, moving picnic blankets, blowing up skirts and dresses. A wicked wind, a restless wind.

"Then Rattigan dies."

"Yes. I thought that was it, and so it was really. Fletcher, well, he was just as much of an arsehole, but he wasn't fun to hang around with."

"But?"

"But nothing. He wanted me in. He thought I'd jump at the chance. But I didn't. I've only been into his house once and that was to tell him he was a fuckwit."

"Did you hit him?"

"No. Wish I had, though."

"Me too."

There's more I want to ask, but Penry touches my arm and points.

"See that man there?"

It's a man in a suit. Forty-something. Pleased with himself.

I clock the man, then look back at Penry.

"Ivor Harris," he tells me. "Ivor Harris, MP. North Glamorgan. A Tory."

I shrug. "The Conservative Party is legal, you know. Even in Wales."

"You want to know his first name? It's Piers. Posh Piers. He changed to his middle name because he thought it would attract more votes."

"So? That's allowed too."

"Best buddies with Brendan Rattigan. Coke snorters. And he knew. Not the whole thing, maybe, but he knew enough."

"You don't know that."

I wonder for a second how Penry knew that posh Piers would come a-wandering by, then realise that he didn't. We've got our backs to the National Assembly. This park belongs to the ranks of the powerful. You probably couldn't spend an hour or two here and not find someone who used to hang out with Brendan Rattigan.

"I *do* know that. Rattigan couldn't get high without boasting about it. And Ivor bloody Harris is an MP. Brian bloody Penry is a criminal."

"Same difference."

He laughs. "Yeah, fair enough." He lets that comment die away, then adds another. "Do you want to know how much personal income tax Rattigan paid?"

"I didn't, but I do now."

"Nineteen per cent in the UK. Nothing at all overseas. And most of his income came from overseas. He probably averaged under ten per cent in taxes. Because he's rich and has clever lawyers. Brendan Rattigan, Ivor Harris's buddy."

"Yeah, but it's better, isn't it? Being like us, I mean. Ordinary work, ordinary money, ordinary tax."

Penry laughs. "Ordinary criminal, ordinary jail time."

"Yes, that too. Even that."

He's done with his coffee. He scrunches up the cup. He can have mine, if he wants more, but he doesn't.

"Weird thing is, I'm a bit scared of prison. I didn't think I would be."

"You'll be OK."

"I know."

"I'll visit you, if you like."

"Would you? Really?"

I nod. "If you like."

"I would like. Yes, I would."

The more I know Penry, the more I like him, despite all that he's done and not done. We sit on the bench and stare out into the park. Harris has gone from view now. No more MPs to despise.

"Here. I've got something for you."

I give him the book that I took from my desk drawer before coming out. It's *My First Book of Piano Classics*.

"I didn't know if you were into classics more or pop stuff. I thought maybe the classics."

He's touched. Genuinely moved. I only got the book on the off chance. I'd intended to post it, but hadn't got round to it.

"Thanks, Fiona."

"Fi."

"Fi? Thanks, Fi. I'll let you know how I get on."

"I'll want a recital."

He nods. We're in silence for a moment, but he knows what I'm about to ask and he's here to tell me.

"Fletcher. That place, where he is now."

I nod. "Yes?"

"It's a white house or shack or something. A little tower or something. I only saw a photo once, and I didn't look for long. But I know it's white. And beyond Milford Haven. And right close to the beach."

"Mooring?"

"I don't know. I just don't know."

"You had a sailing-club T-shirt on the time I came to your house."

"Did I? Never been sailing, though. I haven't been there."

"OK." I believe him.

"I'll come with you, if you like. I'm not much use for most things, but I know how to hit people."

I laugh out loud at that. I don't tell him that I've practised stamping his testicles to pulp.

"I'll be OK. A girl's gotta do what a girl's gotta do. And it's only one man, isn't it? One that your old nan could take out."

"You hope."

I stand up. I chuck my still full coffee cup into a bin.

Penry nods farewell. "Good luck, sweetheart. You might be like me, but don't become me."

I grin at him, looking braver than I feel. "I'll be OK. And good luck yourself."

When I leave him, he's still on the bench, the book open in front of him, his fingers practising movements on an invisible keyboard.

CHAPTER
THIRTY-EIGHT

The mortuary visit with DI Hughes isn't as fun as the one with DCI Jackson. Hughes and Price do have a boring contest, and Hughes comes out of it much better than I'd expected. Price scores heavily with his torrents of uninteresting detail, but Hughes counters with that depressive hostile thing he does, an adaptable technique and one that really works for him. In the end, I can't call a winner. There's no knockout, and the judges will have to make a decision on points.

By the time they're done, I've filled twenty-one pages of my notebook. I'm rustling like taffeta, just like the first time.

The room we're in contains Stacey Edwards on a proper autopsy bench, and the two Mancinis on gurneys. They were only wheeled in here so Price could make one or two points of comparison between the corpses. They're all going to be burned tomorrow. Released up through a chimney into the sky. The weather tomorrow is forecast to be like today. Windy, dry, hot, overcast. A good day to be burned, I reckon. The wind will give little April her freedom at last. Freedom and light.

Finally, finally, neither Price nor Hughes can think of anything else that's worth saying. We cover the bodies and leave the room.

I look down at my watch.

"Gosh, is that the time?" There's a big hospital clock on the wall that says that it is. Six o'clock, near as dammit. "I'm meeting someone for a drink. Thank you so much, Dr Price." He gets a handshake, then to Hughes, "If it's OK, sir, I'll touch base with you tomorrow. I'll have my notes typed up first thing."

"That's fine . . . Fiona." It took him a moment to remember my name, but he got there soon enough. He's forgiven. "See you tomorrow."

I rush off to the women's changing area, gown flapping, boots galumphing. Behind me, the men stroll through to their section, still talking.

My heart is doing a thousand beats a minute, and it's welcome to them all. I yank off my gown. My fingers are trembling so much it's actually hard for me to undo it properly and I end up just ripping it off. Kick my boots off, slip my shoes on and edge back towards reception, listening. The men are in their changing area, doing whatever they're doing.

"Goodnight, then!" I yell, getting an answering murmur from the boys.

There's a security button by the main exit. I press it, the door clicks, and I open it, then let it slam shut. The sound echoes for a moment off bare walls and the polished hospital floor.

For just a second, my heart switches off and I have a moment of something that passes for clarity. Fiona

Griffiths, this is not what you do. Not now. Not ever. Just say no.

I don't listen.

Apart from anything else, there's a certainty in my bones that says the opposite. It says, Fiona Griffiths, this is your opportunity. Use it. Use it now. Use it well. It's never coming back.

Quietly now, I slip off my shoes and walk back to the Ladies' in my stockinged feet. I turn off the light, making sure that the switch doesn't click. The room is bare and empty. Nothing to see.

It's not too late to reverse course. I know that. Free will is offering me escape routes with every second that passes and I don't take any of them. Heart still beating too fast, but feeling strangely calm, I open the cleaning-cupboard door, walk inside and pull the door gently shut.

There's a bucket there and I sit on it. I'm in the dark. Hidden. Invisible. Forgotten.

I wait.

Noises from outside. Mostly hospital ones. The ventilation system. A window cord tapping in a draught. An electronic beeping from some machine somewhere. The little clicks and creaks of any large building.

And then I hear Hughes and Price walk back out into the reception area. A short pause. Keys. Some muttered conversation, then the click of the front door. The slam of it closing. The turn of a lock. Two pairs of footsteps walking away.

Now it really is too late. Escape routes well and truly sealed off. I'm incredulous at what I've just done, but I'm partly incredulous because I don't regret it at all. My decision feels entirely right. I feel intoxicated by the simplicity of it all.

For about an hour, I don't move. Bum on a cleaning bucket in a cupboard outside a silent changing room. I don't even allow myself to shift my weight around or stretch out my legs.

Then I do. Jackson and Price aren't coming back. I very much doubt if hospital security patrols here at night. The dead aren't known for their rowdiness, and presumably the point of those lock-down security procedures is to make sure that what I've just done can't possibly happen.

I'm all alone in the mortuary. Alone with the dead.

I assume that Price has locked the exit and that I'm stuck here for the night. I don't think I've ever been so excited — so happily excited — in my life. I let some more time pass, take things slow. No need to rush.

Then finally, I wander out into the reception area. I poke the rubbery-looking plant with my finger to check that it's real, and it is. There are a few odds and ends on the reception desk and I shift them around just to feel my own presence here a little more. There are no security cameras in the ceiling, no nothing. There's a card on the desk addressed to somebody called Gina. I read the card — nothing interesting — and put it back.

I'm suddenly aware of being a bit cold. I'm wearing a dark skirt, tights, white shirt and a jacket. For obvious reasons, mortuaries are kept on the cool side and it's

377

not going to get any warmer overnight. I put on the low-heeled office shoes that I was wearing earlier, to keep my feet off the floor. There's something weird about being so formally dressed, given the circumstances.

I wander about a little more. I try a couple of the internal doors. They all open easily. Why wouldn't they? The entrance is locked and the place is empty.

In the women's toilets, I put the lights back on and stare at myself in the mirror. Short dark hair. Low-key make-up. Dutiful, efficient little face. I can never work out if I look like me or if I look nothing at all like me. I don't know. I run hot water over my hands, then wet my hair, spiking it up, the punk look. More me, or less me? I don't know, but leave it spiked.

I'm nervous now, really nervous, but I know exactly what happens next.

I dry my hands, turn off the lights and walk calmly over to Autopsy Suite 2, where the bodies of Stacey Edwards and the two Mancinis are lying. The door is closed, but I know it's not locked from having tested it earlier. I pause for just a moment. Not gathering strength, but, well, pausing. If I were the praying kind, which I'm totally not, then this would be a praying moment. I don't rush it. I'm about to put my hand to the door when I find myself checking that my shirt is tucked in and not rumpled. That's right, Griffiths! Got to look smart now.

I go inside. Outside, it's starting to get dark and the room is full of shadows. An evening room. I don't put the light on. I don't uncover the corpses. Just move slowly around, orienting myself.

There are two workbenches, a "dry" area for papers and such-like, and a "wet" area for organs, innards and other delights. The anglepoise lamp. Some wall charts. Nothing much. The room has its share of hospital noises, but it's the quietest place I've ever been. The most peaceful.

I say hello to Stacey Edwards first.

She looks much the same as she did the first time I saw her. No duct tape. No cable ties. But equally dead. I hold her hand for a while and stroke her hair. No reason really. She's not why I'm here. But it would feel wrong to leave her out just because I don't feel a connection to her. This is the last night of her stay on earth. She'll be joining April and Janet in the winds tomorrow, racing northwards to the valleys and the hills. Aunt Gwyn's farm and the mountains and the plovers.

"You'll be all right, love," I tell her. "I'll tell Gwyn to give you a wave."

She doesn't react to that. She doesn't know Gwyn, so I can't blame her.

"You were brave. Did you know that? It was because of you that this whole thing came out. You did a good job. You did your bit."

She likes that. We still don't really have a connection, but I stick around a bit longer so she doesn't think I'm running away.

Then I shift across the room, to the side of Janet Mancini's gurney. Not a good word, that. *Gurney.* Clumpy and undignified like orthopaedic shoes. They're only on gurneys because they've already been sliced and diced. They were moved in here as accessories to the Price-Hughes bore-fest. No point in moving them back anywhere. Not tonight, their last on earth.

I decide that for me, for tonight, for Janet and April, those gurneys will be their biers. They can lie in state like a medieval queen and her young princess.

I unshroud Janet. Top to toe. I fold the cloth up and leave it on the dry workbench, which probably, I think after I've done it, breaches hygiene rules.

The room is dark enough now that most colour has gone. Janet's hair still looks coppery, but so dark that it's hard to tell any more. It's wonderfully soft and long. I've never had long hair, or at least not since I was eight or nine, and I envy Janet's more-than-shoulder-length tresses.

There's a circular wound at the back of her head where Aidan Price would have sawn through the skull so he could remove the brain for analysis. He's a tidy worker is the good Dr Pedant and the join is a neat one. Feeling naughty now, I lift away the trapdoor of bone and feel inside. Emptiness. There's something wonderfully liberating about the feeling. To be so dead that your skull is actually void, now there's a trick most corpses don't manage to pull off. I allow my fingers to roam the cavity.

I don't cut myself off from myself, the way I normally would. I've got all night, so I allow myself time to explore. The skull feels like the largest thing in the universe, containing galaxies. I let my fingers drift among the stars, enjoying the space and the silence. I think of that Llangattock barn. That space, that silence and all those amber eyes.

When finally I fit the skull back together again, it closes with a hollow *clop*.

Janet's expression hasn't changed at all. It's hard to say what her face is communicating. Release, I suppose. That would be the normal thing to say, but then again I'm aware that my citizenship of Planet Normal is on temporary hold while certain irregularities with my papers are investigated — and in any case, I don't think "release" is correct. She doesn't look like she's been released from anything. Whatever it is, it's more than that, purer. It's as though death has perfected Janet, brought her to the best possible version of herself, untouched by life's misfortunes and untouchable now, untouchable for ever.

I run my hand right down her body to her feet. All her internal organs will have been removed, weighed, measured, analysed. Sometimes they're returned to the body. Other times they're disposed of and the body is packed with cheap fillers. They use pipe insulation for bones, for example. But her skin feels wonderful. It's partly the cold, I suppose. Cold skin always feels smoother, but the truth is that Janet Mancini is a pretty woman with good skin, and she isn't all that far from being a real beauty.

I push gently down on her feet, so they're pointing like a dancer's, not stuck out at ninety degrees like a policeman's. My fingers can almost completely close round her ankle, whereas I'm an inch away from being able to the same with my own. I wonder what Mancini

381

could have been with a better start in life. A nursery-school worker. A secretary. A sales rep. Strange things to think about when she's lying cold and naked in front of me, and when I know the commercial uses to which that nakedness was once put, but still. She wasn't a prostitute. Not really. Not properly even in life, and certainly not now.

"Who killed you, Janet Mancini? Was it Karol Sikorsky?" I ask her softly.

She doesn't answer.

"We're going to get him. We're going to get everyone who ever hurt you."

She still says nothing.

"You did your best, I know that. You always did your best."

I have an impulse to cover her again, but I realise that the dead don't care. Their nudity is as neutral to them as pale blue hospital cloth and white gauze. Bier or gurney, they don't care about that either.

I unwrap April.

Her little body ends at the nose. No eyes. No forehead. No empty cavity in the skull. But she has her lovely little smiling mouth, her skinny little kid's frame, and a hand that happens to lie outstretched towards me. I hold it. I hold it for long enough so that my skin cools down and hers warms up. We're the same temperature now. I feel like we already know each other. We're old friends.

"And who killed you, little April?"

She doesn't reply.

"I was born in April too, you know. Perhaps we have the same birthday."

She smiles at me. She likes that.

"You worried about your mam, didn't you? It wasn't easy being you. But you know, she did her best. You did your best. And there's absolutely nothing in the world to worry about now."

Nor there is. Not for them and not for me. I'm not sure how long I stay with the pair of them, but the room is totally dark now, just a little violet light coming from the lamps in the car parks outside.

I've got stiff, so I pace briskly around a bit. I explore the rest of the mortuary. There are three other cadavers that I can find. One old man, a real character, I'll bet. Good-Time Charlie I call him, and he flirts outrageously back at me. Then an obese fifty-something guy. I don't get on with him at all. I don't even give him a name, and he's not sorry to see me go. Last up is a lovely silver-haired woman, naked as the moon and grinning upwards at the ceiling as we sit and chat. I like her best of all, as it happens — Edith, she is — but it was Janet and April who brought me here and so it's back to them I go.

I pull April's bier over to Janet's, so I can sit with the mother and hold the daughter's hand. I start telling April a bedtime story about Gwyn's farm and what it'll look like from above. We enjoy the story to begin with, but then we prefer silence and we just sit, the three of us, not talking but feeling happy together.

April is Janet's daughter.

That's what April was trying to tell me all the time and I've only just twigged. April is Janet's daughter. Janet herself never really knew her mother, because she was taken into care from an early age. Same thing with Stacey Edwards. The same thing with so many of these prostitutes.

But Janet stayed close. She did what she could. She wanted to be April's mam and did all she could to be the best one she could possibly be. And April appreciated her mother's efforts. April was Janet's daughter. Same genes, same blood.

That's what April was trying to tell me.

I would laugh at the simplicity of it all, only this is a night for silence, so my laughter is silent too. One more thing for my to-do list this week.

I'm as happy now as I've ever been. Everything is going to be all right.

After some time, I feel tired, so I butt the two biers against each other and lie down in the middle to sleep. I sleep holding April's hand and with my face up against Janet's enviable copper hair. We sleep the sleep of the dead.

CHAPTER
THIRTY-NINE

It's somewhere after dawn. I'm as stiff as a board and as cold as last night's tea. Janet and April are doing just fine. They're probably laughing at me. Yeah, right, sisters. Not one brain between the pair of you.

I shove the two gurneys back into their proper positions and re-cover the corpses. I give each of them a kiss before I go. Janet on her forehead, April on what there is left of her cheek. Stacey gets a smacker too.

"Goodnight, ladies. Goodnight, sweet ladies. Goodnight. Goodnight."

I give them a blast from *Hamlet*, just so they know they've spent the night with a girl who knows her Shakespeare, then pull my attention back to escaping the train wreck that threatens to undo not just my career but everything I've sought to build over the last few years. If the good Dr Pedant and gang come back in the morning and find me here, then I'm going to be properly kippered, and quite right too.

This problem has only just occurred to me. It didn't once enter my thoughts when I pulled my disappearing stunt in the Ladies' last night. It didn't really occur to me when I was planning this particular escapade.

385

I wonder if I have a misplaced degree of confidence in the way this week is going to turn out.

I try the main exit door, but it's locked, as expected. There's a fire exit, but it's got a big green sign telling me that the handle is alarmed and I decide not to risk it.

Oh crap. I'm really not the climbing-out-of-windows sort, but there's not much else available. Janet and April's window is small, high, and I can't see anything to help me on the outside. Then I remember the viewing room, and thank God, thank God, thank God, it has a decent-sized window and the inestimable blessing of the catering-facility roof. I chuck my bag outside, which sort of commits me to following it. I wonder what to do about my shoes, which aren't wildly impractical as office shoes go, but which aren't made for climbing out of second-floor windows either. I take them off and they follow the handbag outside. Then my jacket. It's not in the way, but I don't want to ruin it. I wonder if there's anyone in the catering building and whether they've noticed that someone is chucking their wardrobe down on top of it.

I stand on the chair that I've pulled over to the window and try to clamber out. My skirt is not designed for vigorous athletic activity, but I decide that climbing naked out of a mortuary is worse than climbing out clothed, no matter how undignified. So I tuck my skirt into my tights and bundle myself out. I hurt my thigh on the window catch as I climb out, then my upper arms on the lip of the window as I drop down. My left ankle hurts too. I am really, really not cut out for this kind of thing.

Skirt out from tights. Jacket on. Shoes on. Handbag gathered tidily under an arm. I paste my hair down, but know it's not going to look right without a shower. Still, though, except for the fact that I'm standing on the roof of the University Hospital of Wales's catering facility at five in the morning, I look thoroughly respectable, though I say so myself. There are a few people floating around the hospital campus, but mostly the kind of support-staff types who don't really care whether there's a madwoman on top of the catering facility or not. I probe around for a while, looking for a way down. Alas, nobody thought that a ladder would be a good idea, so I end up hanging off a drainpipe, dropping a few feet to the ground and hurting my ankle for a second time, only worse.

I sit among a pile of bin bags for a few minutes swearing until I feel better.

I hobble over to my car and blip it open. Where to now? My first instinct is home to Mam and Dad. They're only a few minutes away and Mam's always up ridiculously early anyway. I start driving that way, through Cathays Cemetery, up Roath Park to the Lake and the world of big houses and easy living. Then literally no more than thirty seconds from their front door, I change my mind. I pull the car around in a too-fast U-turn and head for home, my home, not theirs.

I'm wildly happy. Huge ocean waves of happiness come crashing down around me and I run yelling and laughing through their surf. Last night was great, but it was peaceful. This morning is great and it's anything but. I want to honk my horn, kiss strangers, drive at a hundred miles an hour, swim in Cardiff Bay and shower the whole world with roses. I put the soft top down, drive too fast and play Take That at maximum volume.

I can't stop smiling and I don't even try.

CHAPTER
FORTY

The funeral is a hundred million times better than I expected. There are so many people here that the crematorium at Thornhill can't accommodate them. Most of the service is held outside and amplified on loudspeakers so that people can hear everything, despite the growl of the M4 just beyond the trees. Probably eighty per cent of those present are schoolkids, here only because their schools decided to make a statement, but I don't care. Schoolkids are the perfect audience anyway. The ones April would care most about. My trumpeter is fantastic. The string quartet is a bit too polite and quiet to make much of an impact, but quite frankly April and Janet and Stacey are flabbergasted to find themselves with a string quartet at all. The solo vocalist is much better. Apart from mine, there's not a dry eye in the house, and my eyes hardly count. The rent-a-quote pop star does turn up. She reads a sentimental poem badly and everyone cries. There are heaps of flowers too. I don't know if they're all mine, but I don't care. They've all got petals, and that's the way April and I like 'em.

A conveyor belt takes the coffins out of the room where the service takes place and off to the furnace.

Red curtains divide one side from the other. When April's tiny coffin goes sailing down the conveyor belt to the curtains, everyone in the entire building starts clapping. I think some of the schoolkids started it, because they didn't know what they were meant to do but felt they had to do something. Anyway, whoever started it, it was the right thing to do and it only takes a moment for everyone, inside and outside, to be clapping and clapping hard. The trumpeter — my favourite trumpeter — seizes the moment and goes straight into a riff that's happy and sad and final and sweet and triumphant all at the same time. The Mayor of Cardiff pops up from somewhere to make a speech, which is very short and perfectly judged.

I think it's possible that I'm the only one not to have tears in my eyes. Most people present actually have tears running down their cheeks.

I wonder what that would be like. I wonder how it feels.

But not mostly that. Mostly, I'm with April on her last journey. Into the fire. Up the chimney. Into the wind and out across Cardiff and all the hills of Wales. She's happy now. Her and Janet. Her and her mam. Stacey Edwards too, I expect. They're all happy now. Happy ever after.

CHAPTER
FORTY-ONE

After the funeral, a couple of things.

Brydon was there. I don't know how he knew I cared, because I didn't make a song and dance about it in the office, but anyway, there he is. He doesn't come close to me at the service itself, because he wants to give me space. But as everyone spills out of the crematorium itself into the municipal, flower-beddy bit outside, he comes up and squeezes my arm.

"You OK?"

"Yes."

"That was quite a send-off."

"Yes."

"Must have taken a fair bit of organisation on someone's part."

I smile at him. "Yes."

We chat a bit longer, and I notice that Brydon is taut about something. Is he angry? Angry with me? I don't know. If he is, I don't know why. But this isn't the place to ask him, so we say a few more things to each other, feeling strained, then say we have to rush off to something else. Which in his case is probably true. We've still got a date for tomorrow night, theoretically. Whatever it is will come out when it's ready.

More important, though — more important for now, anyway — is something that Bryony Williams has for me. She's here, of course. No black for her. Rainbow top and big chunky beads. The kind of thing I'd look awful in. She gives me a huge hug and tells me I'm fantastic.

"Good trumpeter," I say. "He wouldn't even charge me."

"I should bloody well hope not."

She goes on to say how much she liked the poem and how well she thought the pop star read it. I agree because I don't want to spoil the mood. She says something about it looking good on television, and I'm confused because I didn't know anything about TV, but sure enough there was a camera and a sound man up in a gallery at the back. I see them packing up their stuff and leaving.

"And I brought you this," she says.

She holds it up. A sheet of paper. One of my notes. Nothing on it, other than my own handwriting.

As I start to look puzzled, Bryony switches the paper round. On the back, someone has written, *Try the old lighthouse. Kill the bastards*.

"You know that bag I carry around with me when I'm on patrol? Soup, condoms and health leaflets. That's what it's full of normally. When I was unpacking it on Sunday night, I found this inside. I don't know who put it there or when. I don't know what it means."

The old lighthouse.

I do know what it means. I'll need to spend some time with Google Earth and Postcode Finder to get a location, but that's just a question of time. *Try the old lighthouse.* You bet I will, sister. *Kill the bastards.* I wasn't planning to, but what the heck, you never know.

I realise I'm grinning like an idiot.

"You look like you've got what you were looking for," says Bryony.

"The last twenty-four hours," I say, "have been the best of my entire life."

CHAPTER
FORTY-TWO

Morning.

Just a week or two away from the longest day of the year. The merry old sun noses above the rooftops just after four, but the sky is full of light and emptiness long before that. I'm awake by about three thirty, having only got to sleep sometime after midnight, but I wasn't expecting to sleep, so I'm not worried when I don't.

I put some music on downstairs, find some food and roll myself a joint. I lie in bed listening to music, eating and smoking. I handle my gun with my eyes shut. Safety on, safety off. Magazine in, magazine out. I reload the magazine with my eyes shut. I like the way the bullets clip in. It's neat, precise and metallic. Reliable and with a purpose. I like my joint too, but in an entirely different way. If the gun represents the daddy, then the joint is the mummy. Embracing, comforting, soothing. It's not about purposes, but about simply being. Or adding kindness to whatever already exists. And it too has a welcome reliability. It too is something I depend on.

I think about April's funeral yesterday. Little April, blind and dead, now free to take the next steps on her journey, whatever they may be. Already her connection with me is looser. Looser in a good way. She told me the thing she needed to tell me. A thing so laughable in its simplicity that I can't believe it took me so long to notice it. Fiona Griffiths, prize-winning philosophy graduate, can be a total idiot at times. I quite like that. I prefer people who aren't too simple.

By four thirty, I'm restless. There's no need to wait for anything. So I get up, shower and dress. Boots, trousers, top, denim jacket. An impulse takes me to the mirror and I rub styling gel through my hair, spiking it up. Then make-up. Red lips, killer eyes. The rock-chick look. Tooled up and ready to motor.

I'm in the car and driving by a quarter past five. There's rain coming in later, so the weatherman promised last night, but the day opens fine and bright. The world feels like it's on parade for a morning inspection. Shadows ruled out on roads and pavements with stencil-edged accuracy. Lawns mown. Cars all present and correct. Nothing moving except me.

I'm out of Cardiff in no time at all, then flying west, the sun at my back, Amy Winehouse on the CD player, energy bar, handcuffs, gun, ammo and phone on the passenger seat. My Peugeot's shadow flies along the road in front of me and I fly after it, trying to race the turning world.

Cardiff. Bridgend. Porthcawl. Port Talbot. Swansea.

It was about here Brydon and I turned off for our day out on the Gower Peninsula. The sea lies somnolent and glittering on my left, watching me as I drive. It's not impressed.

Then beyond Swansea, to where the motorway runs out.

Pontardulais. Llanddarog. Carmarthen.

This is real Wales. Deep Wales. Old Wales. This isn't the Wales created by the Victorians, all coal and iron and ports and factories. This is the Wales of the Celts. Of opposition. Opposition to the Normans, the Vikings, the Saxons, the Romans. Opposition to the invader. An F-off sign, lasting centuries. Out here, people speak Welsh because they've never spoken anything else. Using English marks you out as a foreigner.

St Clears. Llanddewi. Haverfordwest.

I'm driving more slowly now. Picking my way out of Haverfordwest towards Walwyn's Castle. Unfamiliar lanes. Cows on the road. Just been milked and on their way to pasture. A farm worker with a hazel switch and a collie walks behind the cows, nudges them into their field, then raises a hand at me as I pass. I wave back and drive on.

Through Walwyn's Castle to Hasguard Cross. Beyond that to the edge of the peninsula. Sea on every side now, except my back, and I'm not going back anytime soon. St Brides on my right. St Ishmael on my left. And straight ahead, my target. A nowhere place in a nowhere land. An old lighthouse that lights nothing and protects no one.

Not just an old lighthouse but, according to the Postcode Finder, the Old Lighthouse. And it's white. I know that from photos of the Pembroke Coast Path I managed to find on Flickr. White and close to the beach. West of Milford Haven. Martyn Roberts's boat was based in Milford Haven, and this western outcrop is remote and hard to access, unlike the more crowded east. Until I get there, I can't be entirely certain, but every possible indication is pointing to the same location.

I'm further from Cardiff now than Cardiff is from the western edge of London. This is the tip of infinity, the edge of oblivion.

It's seven fifteen and I'm ready.

CHAPTER
FORTY-THREE

A mile or so away from my destination, I park up. The verge is so thick with tall stalks of cow parsley that I have to mow a swathe through them to get off the road. All their pretty white decapitated heads. The air above the car engine shimmers with the rising heat. Gulls wheel above me, and the sea chuckles at my presumption.

Gun. Phone. Handcuffs. A pocketful of ammo. I don't need anything else. With a bit of luck, I'll only need the cuffs and the phone. I check it for signal and am relieved to see that it's running at full strength.

I walk slowly towards the lighthouse, cutting through the fields and navigating by feel. It's not hard. I'm aiming for the sea, and the sea is all around me. A couple of wheat fields first, the crop just starting to show the first hints of gold. Sea breeze. Gorse and broom blazing yellow in the hedges. Then a field of sheep and my first view of the lighthouse.

It's a smaller building than I'd constructed in my head. A stubby little tower, disused and doing nothing. A low building beneath it, almost barrel-shaped against the slope. A door, with half a dozen stone steps running up to it. Two windows that I can see. Maybe more that I can't. A dirt parking area with a Land Rover, nothing else. There's a barbed-wire fence round the property and a locked gate, but nothing impenetrable. More of a warning to tourists to keep their distance than anything else.

I'm relieved to see just the one car. Two would have scared me.

But then I see something that I don't like at all.

Along the coast, maybe four hundred yards along, there's a boat moored offshore. A blue boat with a dirty white stripe along the side. Martyn Roberts's boat, if the image on his website is to be trusted.

Martyn Roberts, the only charter-boat captain in South Wales who didn't want me to check his sailing log. Martyn Roberts, who hung up on me when I was at Rattigan Transport, making enquiries. Martyn Roberts, the ex-con.

As I watch, a rubber dinghy chugs out from the shore. It's hard to tell from this distance, but it looks like there are three figures on board. Hard to tell, but I'd say that two of them are male, one female.

I feel unprepared. An amateur.

I feel the way I feel when I've seen Lev fight for real. Still practice fights — I've never seen him try to hurt anyone — but fights where he's up against someone with almost his own level of training and ability. I realise when I watch those things that I'm a million miles from being ready for serious conflict. I realise how vulnerable I truly am.

I should have brought binoculars. I should have been here two or three hours ago. I should have come with Penry, or Lev, or Brydon, or all three of them.

I should have forced a meeting with DCI Jackson and insisted on him sending a full armed response unit to the scene and threatened to resign if he refused.

I could even do that now. Call Jackson, tell him where I am, tell him what I think is going on. Tell him that I need helicopters and divers and marksmen and vehicles here in an instant. But those things can't be here in an instant. All that's here is me and no time to lose.

I take the gun out of my pocket and start running.

Running fast through the sheep field. Then there's another field — a long slope of cropped grass and lichened limestone, nothing else — running down to the sea's edge and the lighthouse. The windows are angled away from my direction of approach. The door opens right onto it. I need to hope the door doesn't open. I need to hope no one walks round the side of the building.

Fifty yards from the lighthouse, I stop. Heart yammering, blood racing.

This is it. What Lev prepared me for.

You never get a fight where or when you want it. You never get the fight you prepared for. You only ever get the fight when it reaches out for you. And that moment is now. Battle music.

I let my pulse rate slow, then scale the locked gate and walk purposefully towards the lighthouse door. I keep my eyes on the door. Every five paces, I sweep my gaze round everything else. The little dinghy has reached the boat. There is nothing stirring in the car park. There's a little shack housing a woodpile and some basic tools. There is no one moving to either side or behind me. The sun and the sea are my only audience. Seagulls yell their disapproval.

I get to the base of the stone steps.

I can't tell if the door is locked.

There is no sound from anywhere, except sea, sky and gulls.

If the door is locked, I'll shoot the lock out. If the door is unlocked, I'll sweep it open with my left hand and have my gun up and ready in my right. I visualise both motions, then ascend the steps.

I'm there in an instant. Time seems to be moving in jerks. Quantum jumps from one state to another, no smooth passage in between. I'm at the door. Ready. Go.

My left hand tries the catch. It's free. Sweep the door open. Gun up and ready to fire. Heart in my mouth doesn't say it. Heart somewhere through the top of my head and thumping around in the ceiling joists.

But there's no threat inside the room.

Just horror.

Huw Fletcher is there all right. The man I wanted to catch. Alive and catchable.

He's not going to offer much resistance either. Not the way he is now. Poor old Fletcher is in a state of disassembly. He lies against the wall, mute, unmoving, eyes staring through me and beyond into the ruins of his future. On the floor next to him lie the fingers of his right hand. His ears. His tongue. And, grotesquely, his scrotum, looking like the bits that butchers feed their dogs. Blood leaks from between his legs, from his mouth, arm and the side of his head. He's alive, but the loss of blood may yet collect his soul.

I don't feel sorry for him. I feel a fierce rage, made fiercer by coming face to face with its target. These are strong feelings, but they are mine and they are human. They belong to me and I am not afraid.

I say nothing to Fletcher. I do nothing to help him. I care about him not at all.

Treading round the pools and splashes of his blood, careful not to make a footprint, I make for the flight of steps heading down to the cellar.

I have my gun in a double grip now, but it has become part of me. An instinct. A single being. I am Lev and my name is vengeance. What lies below me is worse, I know it, than anything that lies bleeding above. I kick open the cellar door and sweep the room through the sight of my gun.

I have found what I came for.

CHAPTER
FORTY-FOUR

And what I find is horror. A horror beyond description. A horror that I know, even before my gun sight has finished sweeping the room, will last the rest of my days. Time's ruinous fingers may one day muddle and obscure this moment, but what has been done here can never be set to rights, can never be undone.

What I see is four women. They are naked, except for long T-shirts, white once but grubby now. Each of the women is chained by her ankle to one of a number of iron hoops set into the wall. The floor is covered in straw. Lots of it, like a freshly prepared cow barn. A bucket full of shit and piss steams in the corner under a single tiny window. The women are dirty. Their hair is rank and uncombed. They're all too thin. All bruised, some nastily. They've got the staring eyes of people who are shocked beyond shock, and steaming high on heroin to boot. There are ten iron hoops altogether. Six of them lie empty.

I take all this in and, in a movement as natural and spontaneous as drawing breath, I vomit. A single reflexive gag that splatters into the straw at my feet. Just one. Time is moving ahead again with its jerky quantum beat and the reflex that made me retch is already jerking away from me into the past.

So it's to be like this, is it? I've to deal not just with Fletcher but with all Sikorsky's ugly buddies too. So be it. Fuck 'em all, every one. It is what it is and I am ready. I just hope Roberts's shitty little trawler isn't yet full. If it is, then I'll for ever hate myself for arriving too late.

It's one of those situations, one of those blessed situations, where for once my instincts move faster and more wisely than my brain.

Before I know it, I'm signalling "shush" to the women — I doubt if any of them speak much English — and ripping my clothes off as fast as I can, hurling them into the angle of the cellar door where they can't be seen from the stairs. There's a stack of more dirty white T-shirts in the corner of the room, piled on top of some army-surplus grey blankets. I take one of the T-shirts and put it on. I hate the feel of it, the way it makes a slave of me, but in this place slaves are invisible, and invisibility is my friend.

I frisk my own clothes to grab ammo from my jacket pocket, then decide I need my boots and put them on again. There are only ten bullets in my gun. If it comes to unarmed combat, I'll be more effective if I can kick. Kneecaps, testicles, windpipes.

I make for the far corner of the room. There's a single bulb in the centre of the ceiling, but it doesn't cast much light in my corner. I lie down, covering my booted feet with a blanket.

I make the "shush" signal hard and aggressively to the women, two of whom have started talking rapidly in what I think might be Romanian. They don't stop talking, but then I aim my gun at their heads and they do. They are still all staring at me and I try to gesture at them to look away. I'm only half successful, but half is better than not at all.

I lie there, in the straw, in the fuck-pit created by Brendan Rattigan.

A place for him to bring girls from Eastern Europe. A place to get them high on heroin, to rape them, abuse them, half starve them, knock them around, until they dropped dead or until he decided he wanted a fresh supply. Rattigan and whichever of his buddies happened to amuse themselves the same way. Rattigan and his rich little fuck-buddies. Fuck-buddies who pay ten per cent income tax, because they've got the same lawyers as he had.

I don't know if Fletcher shared the same tastes, or if he was just happy to be Rattigan's fixer, the guy who made it all happen. I'm guessing a bit of both, but Fletcher was only ever really the ops man. The guy who got the girls onto the ships, then off again. A shipping guy. The logistics man.

Then Rattigan drops into the sea. Properly dead. No messing around. A common-or-garden plane crash. Stupid sod probably too vain to put on a lifejacket, too arrogant to take orders from his pilot. And, with the boss's body still bouncing around the floor of the Severn Estuary, the idiot Fletcher, a pygmy who mistook himself for a giant, decided to go it alone.

Presumably there were clients who Rattigan chose to bill. Perhaps they chose to pay. Perhaps Fletcher thought this was a business venture he could expand.

A mistake. The worst of his life — a mistake that has currently cost him his ears, tongue, testicles and fingers, not to mention the blood blackening the floorboards upstairs. Did Fletcher decide to keep the boss's name? Rattigan's name? Quite possibly. Balcescu reacted to Rattigan as though he were alive. Perhaps Fletcher pretended that the boss had faked his own death, was still alive and still operating. Or maybe Balcescu was just behind the times. Either way, her reaction was one of the clues that led me to this place.

Anyway, for a while, Fletcher made some money. The business worked. But if you want to play hardball with the gangsters of Kaliningrad, you've got to be as tough and as hard and as ruthless as them. Rattigan was. He had the cash. More than that, he had the ability, the charisma, the swaggering drive, the aggression. Fletcher was a pygmy waddling around in the clothes of a giant. Before too long, he tripped over his own hem and his nice Kaliningrad friends took advantage. Probably they didn't like someone making a fool of them. More than likely they thought that if Fletcher had an operation that was making money for him, it would make even more money for them. They decided to march in, take over Fletcher's turf, tighten up.

Janet Mancini was the first victim. That debit card of Rattigan's. Once upon a time, he screwed her, told her more than he should have done, but let her live. Janet, foolish girl, said more than she should have done — to her friend Stacey Edwards, I'd guess — and word got back to the lads from Kaliningrad. She got to hear that she was in danger. Escaped to her squat, but she needed to be in a different continent. A different street wouldn't do. The people hunting her tracked her down and killed her. April too, for no reason beyond ensuring that her little six-year-old mouth held its silence. No doubt Sikorsky was the killer, but he was just a hired man, the small fry. The Mancini case, for me, was never about Sikorsky.

The same thing with Stacey Edwards. She spoke too much. Threw accusations around. Made a noise. Sikorsky visited her too. Killed her in a way that sent a signal. The sort of signal that the Kaliningrad boys are so good at sending. Silence or else.

All this I'd pretty much worked out. Speculation most of it, as DCI Jackson would certainly have told me, but you can't always reach the truth — certainly no interesting truth — without a little wild surmise along the way. Perhaps the exact story will prove to be slightly different in minor respects, but I'd bet my life that I've got the gist right. More than likely, the full details will never emerge. They usually don't.

But I hadn't reckoned on this particular endgame. It hadn't occurred to me that the Kaliningrad clean-up would extend out here. I hadn't guessed they might be this effective and this ruthless. I hadn't thought laterally enough, because I thought the pygmy Fletcher would represent my only opposition.

More fool me. But you live and learn, as my granny would say. Of course, it might be "die and learn" in this particular instance, but there are worse things than being dead, as I know better than most.

I wriggle down into the straw. I feel the prickle of its cut ends through my T-shirt. Straw against my breasts and thighs and belly. You couldn't live for long like this and not become half beast. Kept alive so a bunch of rich guys could fuck you, then beat you, then dump your body out at sea when they were done. It would be hard to stay human, living like that, dying like that.

The room is silent now. The two Romanians have ceased their chatter.

The gulls outside are inaudible here. There's just the tick of straw settling down and possibly, unless it's my imagination, the drip of Fletcher's blood from upstairs.

I remember the targets at the firing range. Black and white. Black to congratulate you for a chest shot. White to mark you down for a shot anywhere else. I imagine my targets. Imagine their black centres. Bring to mind all the bull's eyes I scored, at longer range and in worse light conditions, that night in Llangattock.

Once again, I am ready. I am perfectly still and perfectly ready.

CHAPTER
FORTY-FIVE

It takes longer than I think. Longer than I want. Perhaps my perceptions of time are altered. Perhaps the Russians are taking their boat out into the Irish Sea before coming back here. Or perhaps something else. Maybe something obvious, like stopping for tea, or having a bite to eat. Must take it out of you, after all, slicing off Fletcher's body parts, hauling women onto Roberts's handy little motorboat. A comrade must want a bite to eat after all that work. Black tea and jam.

I don't know how long it is, but I'd guess an hour, before I hear boots on the steps outside, the door opening and voices.

Voices and laughter. I don't recognise the words, but I guess from the tone that they're talking to Fletcher. Laughing at him.

I hope so. I hope Fletcher is still alive. I want him alive, and mute, and crippled, and behind bars for the rest of a very long life. He deserves no mercy.

Then the boots and the voices come downstairs.

My heart rate doesn't change. There is no separation between me and my feelings. For once in my life, I have no difficulty at all in feeling alive, in feeling the way a human is meant to feel. It sounds crazy to say it, but I feel at peace. Integrated.

They are still talking as they come down the steps. Stone steps, with stone walls on either side, and a cellar all of stone as well. The sound of these voices is tubular, echoey. Hard to gauge how distant they are.

I have my face pressed down into the straw. To these men, one more slave-woman is just a counting error. But my rock-chick make-up will give me away and I want that moment to be as late as possible, so I deliberately deprive myself of a full view.

These are excuses perhaps. Excuses for getting my timing a second or so out. But I don't blame myself. I'm not Lev. This is my first time with this kind of thing, and the first time is bound to be a learning experience.

I assume that there are two men. The two I saw taking the girl onto Roberts's boat, now come back to collect the next one.

I wait for both men fully to enter the cellar. If they've noticed that there are the wrong number of women here, they haven't yet shown any sign of it. The man in front has a leather jacket on over a white T-shirt. The one behind is shorter and I don't see him properly. They are killers. Russian killers. Sikorsky's chums here to complete their business.

I move. Still lying prone, I sweep my gun out in front of me. Aim up, at the first man's chest. Not black on white the way it was at the firing range. Here, the man's white T-shirt is the target and at this range I cannot possibly miss.

I fire.

I can't even hear the shot. My senses are leaping way ahead of my brain. They're telling me what I need to know and what I don't. The concussion of the shot is irrelevant. All that matters is that it's a perfect bull's eye. A chest shot. Lethal.

The man goes down, and I'm leaping up, firing as I move.

The second man is moving too, jumping back to the cellar steps. My first shot misses altogether. My second shot hits him in the hip. My third in the leg.

If I had wanted to loose that third shot into the chest, I could have done. But I didn't. I want there to be nothing swift about the way that justice claims these men. The first man had to die. There was no other practical solution. The second one has his hip smashed and his thigh pulverised. He's not going anywhere.

And, fool that I am, I think I'm done. This is where Lev would be still moving. Reloading. Keeping the initiative. This is where I'm thinking, Thank fuck I'm finished.

And I almost am.

Mr Kaliningrad the Third comes plunging down the stairs, a gun in his hand, aiming to kill me. He only doesn't because he's temporarily confused. He must have come down expecting a man, or at the very least someone with proper clothes on. All he finds are five half-naked women, and it takes him a second too long to work out which of them has been shooting up his buddies.

He shoots. I shoot.

The air is ablaze with sound. So loud that I register the concussion more than the noise itself. As if some natural disaster — a flood, a hurricane, an earthquake — were translated into sound and compressed into this narrow gap of time and space.

I don't even know what is happening.

Don't know until the hammer of my gun clicks and clicks and clicks on emptiness.

Don't know until I notice that the man I was shooting at has a smashed hand, a smashed shoulder and a pair of bullet wounds that straddle the gap between his lung and his kidney. He's not shooting. He's not standing. He's not even moving much, unless you count his good hand, which keeps touching different parts of his body and coming away crimson and horrified.

All the time I was shooting, I thought he was shooting back at me. I have to check my own body, by eye and by hand, to convince myself I haven't been hit. I realise that, thanks to my tiny advantage, my having enjoyed a clear target and him being confused by a choice of five, he never even got a shot away. I'm standing over him as I work all this out, watching blood jet from his belly, pulsing in time with his heart.

But my brain is starting to engage properly now. My moment of triumph is over and there were steps up above me just now, running hard out of the lighthouse.

I snap handcuffs over the two wounded men, cuffing them to each other. I try to reload my gun, but my hands are shaking so much I can't do anything right. Instead, I grab the Russian's gun, which lies useless on

412

the floor, and then I'm up and out of the lighthouse. Running past Fletcher. Down the steps and out of the house. Through the gate, which has been unlocked and is swinging open.

It's the cliff path I'm after.

I don't run hard. I'm not sprinting. I'm not in good enough shape to run at maximum pelt and then be useful for anything afterwards. A couple of times, when the view widens, I see a man running ahead of me. Jeans and a T-shirt. He can't have a gun, I think, or he wouldn't be running.

The ground underfoot is OK. It's dry enough and there's a proper path. But it's not even. Rocks protrude. There's churned ground where puddles once lay. Gorse roots and sudden twists. I need to keep my eyes on the path in front of me, so I'm able to look ahead less than I'd prefer.

Then I come round a bend and come face to face with the man.

Waiting for me.

He has no gun, but he has an axe. Snatched from the woodpile at the lighthouse, I guess.

I raise my gun and fire.

Nothing happens. There's no bullet in the chamber. I pull the trigger again and still nothing happens. Apart from pulling the trigger, I have no idea what I'm meant to do.

If I had more time, I'd sit down with the gun on my lap. Figure it out. It can't be a very complicated device, this gun. I must be able to manage it.

But I have no time. I know it and the man knows it. I chuck the gun far back into the field behind me, depriving my opponent of a weapon that he presumably does know how to use, but that's not much of a victory at this stage.

The man grins. He's not even swift or oblique in his triumph. He's thinking, I've got the bitch and I can take my time. Take my time and enjoy it.

He draws the axe back. It's a long-handled thing, not a hatchet. Its head and shaft are grey-brown, a tone equidistant between wood and rust. The sun lies behind the man and the axe, so he's just silhouette and his shadow etches its double on the grass.

I suddenly realise, this is Sikorsky. He hasn't escaped. He's not in Poland or Russia. He's here in Pembrokeshire, completing his assignment.

I think, I'm stupid, but you're stupider.

Something Lev taught me. A distrust of long-handled weapons. They feel good in the hand, but they take too long to swing. You expose yourself as you swing them. Too easy to evade, and especially for me. Small fighters lack power, but we move faster. Right now, I'd sooner have speed than power.

I give Sikorsky his moment. The axehead up in the sun. The semi-naked woman in front of him. A lovely day for murder.

"Zdravstvuite, Karol," I say pleasantly.

He swings. His movement is over-signalled. Too big and too slow. I move to one side, deflecting the axe shaft with an arm. At the same time, I kick hard at his shin. As hard as I can. As hard as I've ever kicked.

414

It's not the best move in the world. A good kick at a kneecap has more scope to disable. But you can't really miss a shin, and right now I'm in risk minimisation mode. The boots I'm wearing today were ones adapted for me by Lev himself. Steel-tipped. Nasty.

The Russian discovers the meaning of pain and for a second or two is out of action with it.

All the time in the world.

Another hard kick to his other shin brings him to his knees. Then I get a clear shot at his testicles and take it. As he comes down, his chin comes towards me and that gets a hammering as well. He's on the ground moaning now, so I kick him once more on the side of his head. A really hard one. Steel toecap connecting with bone. His head jerking back and a spray of blood droplets making patterns in the sunlight.

I can imagine Lev congratulating that kick.

Sikorsky jerks spasmodically and lies still. Not dead, because he's still breathing, but there are blood bubbles on the corner of his mouth.

I'm not sure what to do now. I don't have my handcuffs with me. My phone is back at the lighthouse. The guy is hurt, but he'll recover. I can't afford to let him get to the boat.

I peer over the edge of the cliff. I'm not brilliant with heights, but I'm not awful, and in any case these are special circumstances. The cliff's not all that high, maybe fifty feet, and it rolls down at seventy degrees or so to the vertical.

Good enough.

I give Sikorsky another good kick in the head. No point in taking chances. Then bundle him over the edge. All a bit improvised, but improvisation is my strong suit. He rolls down like a sack of potatoes wrapped in a carpet. He bounces lifelessly, like a punctured football. I can't see the base of the cliff, so I don't know what happens at the bottom. I can't even hear anything. Half deaf from the gunfire earlier, I can't even hear the waves.

I'm tired now. Unbelievably thirsty.

I trudge into the field behind me and find the gun. There's a slide on the barrel. You pull the slide back to chamber a bullet. See. I knew it wouldn't take long to figure out.

The journey back to the lighthouse seems like a hundred miles and I feel every inch of it. Despite my T-shirt, I feel completely naked.

I don't like violence. I know I've learned it. Studied its dark and unpredictable arts. But I don't like it. What I've just done revolts me. What has happened here is revolting.

When I get back to the lighthouse, I can't go in straight away. To the house of horror. Fletcher's mute, repulsive eyes.

For a minute, maybe two, I sit on the stone steps and just let myself be. I'm not consciously practising my breathing, but these things have become part of me now, and I do it without noticing sometimes. *In*, two, three, four, five. *Out*, two, three, four, five. My pulse rate slows. I feel calmer. I notice what an extraordinarily beautiful day it is. What an extraordinarily beautiful place. Cropped grass, lichened limestone and the endless cerulean sea.

Since parking my car on the verge above the lighthouse, there has been no barrier between me and my feelings. None at all. I've never been myself as much as this for as long as this.

In, two, three, four, five. *Out*, two, three, four, five.

Then I drag myself inside. That dark interior, home to so much cruelty.

Fletcher is alive but unconscious. The bleeding seems to have stopped, so I decide not to move him. I don't trust myself to make good decisions now. Get the professionals to look after things.

I go downstairs, picking my way over the two semiconscious men and avoiding the one very dead one.

The women stare at me. They don't know they've been saved. Maybe they don't know they were about to be killed. In any case, given what they've been through, their salvation lies a good way off. They may never find it. Janet Mancini never did. Stacey Edwards never did. It's no good living in a world at peace if your own head is at war with itself.

I can't find the keys to unlock the women, and in any case that's not a priority. I check the two handcuffed men. They're not in good shape, but they're alive and I don't feel like giving them first aid. I find my clothes and my phone. There's no signal in the cellar, so I walk back outside to the steps. I call Jackson.

He starts to give me a bollocking for going AWOL and I interrupt. I tell him where I am and what I've found.

I tell him that there's one man dead, and four others who might or might not be dead by the time help arrives.

I tell him about the boat.

"There's at least one woman on it. I'd guess more. Maybe as many as six. I'm pretty certain they were going to be taken out into the Irish Sea and thrown overboard. You need coastguard vessels to approach from the sea. Ideally a helicopter from above, and divers ready for an instantaneous rescue job if whoever is on board tries to dump the evidence. And if you can find some snipers from anywhere, you might want to take them."

Jackson, bless the man, takes me at face value. He believes me. He tells me to stay on the line — I called his mobile — then I can hear him yelling orders, using his landline, getting the clean-up operation mobilised. Every now and then he checks in with me. Precise location of the vessel. Identifying marks. Number of men guessed to be on board — not that I have an answer to that one, but it can't be many. Probably just Martyn Roberts.

It's easy for me now. Someone else is making the decisions, getting the job done. I unzip my boots and take them off. These little stone steps make something of a suntrap. A nice place to lie around. But I get dressed properly. Trousers. Top. Boots. I remember about the ammo in my jacket pocket and take it out. I pop back inside and leave it on the table in the upstairs room. I give it a quick polish in the lining of my jacket to remove some of my prints and sweat, but if there's some left, then so be it.

I leave the Russian's gun next to the ammo.

I'm gunless now. Fully clothed, I feel naked.

Too naked. Bracing myself one last time against the horror, I go back inside and retrieve the gun. I smell it. It hasn't been fired today. Chances are, it hasn't been fired in any place that would give our ballistics people the opportunity to get the measure of it. These days, guns are one-use-only affairs. Used once, then ditched. The throwaway society.

The Russian gun is bigger than mine, but not too big. Not unusably big. I quite like the heft of it, the greater weight, the absence of compromise. A gun for grown-ups.

I wonder what to do with it.

Hand it over to the good folk who are about to arrive. That's the answer that every good copper would come to without much need for thought.

Keep it for myself. The answer my instinct prefers. I liked having a gun. I slept better for it. I felt more complete owning a weapon and knowing how to shoot it.

But it's been a big day and these questions feel bigger than I want to address right now, so I don't try. In the field above the lighthouse, there's a little stone sheepfold. An old one, from the look of it, set down and into the hill. I go to the shed with the woodpile, root around for a moment or two and find an old fertiliser sack. I take it and wrap the gun in it, then jog up the hill to the sheepfold and stow the gun in its fertiliser sack somewhere down in the rocks at the back. You can just about see where I've hidden it, but it looks like an old bit of dirty plastic. A good place for a gun to be.

I'm just walking down the hill from the sheepfold when I hear a helicopter coming over the hill and spy two boats skimming fast over the waves from St Ishmael. The helicopter has its side door open and two rifle-toting snipers looking out.

Good work, Jackson. Fast work too. I remember that there's an RAF base not far up the coast. No doubt this is their chopper and their gunmen. Jackson's call probably made their year.

Behind me, I hear sirens. Police cars. Ambulances. Big men who know how to deal with the mess I've helped create. I welcome their arrival.

By the time they come, I'm sitting on the stone steps, shaking and shaking and shaking.

CHAPTER
FORTY-SIX

One of the very best things about Wales, the whole of Britain really, is the quality of its coppers. You get the odd rogue, of course, and more than a few idiots, but for solid-gold common sense, good hearts and incorruptibility, then you can give me a British copper any day of the week.

Dennis Jackson is making me drink milky, sweet hot chocolate at a café in Haverfordwest. He's ordered me beans on toast because he thinks I need to eat. I do my best.

"Four women on board," he tells me, then pauses. "I don't know if you want to hear this now, but given what you've already seen today, I suppose you may as well know."

I nod.

"Four women. None of them English speakers. Duct tape over their mouths. Hands cable-tied behind them and breeze blocks chained to their ankles. They were just going to take them out to sea —"

"I know."

"Take them out to sea and —"

"I know."

"Can you imagine it?"

Detective Chief Inspector Jackson, he of the bushy eyebrows and the growly demeanour, can't complete his sentence. He doesn't need to. I know what he was going to say and I know how he feels.

I think I feel the same. Almost. I don't have tears at my disposal, of course, and I don't have that easy familiarity with my own feelings that Jackson has. But still. The glass wall between me and my feelings has got thinner these last few weeks. At times it hasn't even been there at all. I haven't been normal, but I've been closer to normal than I've been since before I got ill. I can tell how DCI Jackson feels and I think I feel something almost similar. The feeling is a sad one, but nothing is as bad as not feeling anything at all.

I feel so proud of myself for being here, sharing the same emotional space as Dennis Jackson, that part of me wants to laugh for happiness. I make sure I don't, though. It'd be a mood-spoiler.

"It wouldn't have been the first time," I say. "I think Martyn Roberts was doing the same old work for new customers."

"Yes. I agree. I'm sure you're right."

I make a face and try to eat some beans. They seem like heavy going, so I drink some hot chocolate instead. Jackson asks the waitress to bring another. I would object, except that I know he'll override me.

I only stopped shaking about ten minutes ago.

"I expect one day you'll want to tell me how you knew to go looking in a remote Pembrokeshire lighthouse. You'll probably also want to tell me how come you decided it would be a good idea to storm in there yourself instead of asking me to supply the required resources."

"First question: I had a tip-off," I say. "Conspiracy hearsay bollocks from a prostitute. As for why I didn't tell you, well, you'd have told me it was conspiracy hearsay bollocks. Unwarranted speculation. And I don't blame you. Would you even have got a search warrant?"

"Fiona. You're one of my officers. I won't say you're the easiest person I've ever managed, but you're still one of my officers. You could have got yourself killed today and it's my responsibility to make sure that doesn't happen."

There's a pause there and I leave it be. Maybe I drop a little shrug in there, but mostly I just leave it. Anyway, Jackson is on a different train of thought now.

"Though, bloody hell, Fiona, you seem to have looked after yourself all right."

He shakes his head instead of continuing, but I get the gist. How come a little will-o'-the-wisp thing like me ends up wreaking so much destruction? When the cavalry did come charging over the hill to rescue me, I was so grateful for their arrival and in such a state of shock that it took me about forty minutes to remember that I'd found Sikorsky, the guy that everyone had been looking for. When I remembered, and started trying to tell people about it, and how I'd tipped him over a cliff, they assumed that I was blathering nonsense and kept telling me that everything was fine now, everything was being taken care of. Eventually, I had to grab a couple of people and lead them down the cliff path to the spot. Since there was an axe sticking out of the gorse just where I told them it would be, and a spray of blood on the path where I'd kicked the guy's head in, they had to take me seriously. It took them fifty minutes to reach the base of the cliff, because they had to get the RAF chopper to fly out some ropes and tackle, and when they did, they found Sikorsky, battered but alive, on the rocks at the bottom.

"I guess I must have learned something at Hendon after all," I suggest.

"You know there's going to be an inquiry here? A massive one. Blow-by-blow forensics, the whole works. Don't get me wrong. I think you did a good job today. If you'd killed all of those fuckers, it wouldn't bother me personally. But when a police officer discharges a firearm —"

"I know."

"There has to be an inquiry. And when there's a dead man and three others seriously injured —"

"I know."

"Sikorsky is in intensive care. Injuries to the skull as well as half the bones in his body. I don't know if —"

If he'll live or die. I shrug and Jackson echoes me. We don't care.

"You fired in self-defence."

Half-statement, half-question, but not one I disagree with. "Yes, sir."

"That first shot, the man you killed, was fired from a distance. There are no powder marks, and the entry wound was very clean. There's no sign that any of those coming at you discharged a firearm."

424

"They'd have killed me, sir. They'd have killed me the same way they were about to kill all those women."

"Fiona, this isn't a bollocking. You won't get one from me about this. For a change. But you're going to be asked a lot of questions. You'll need to have some answers."

"To be honest, sir, I've no idea what happened. I'm more of a logic type than an action type. The whole thing's one big blur really."

The waitress comes with hot chocolate and gives it to me. There's something maternal in the way she hands it over. Or rather, it's as though I'm special needs and she's looking at Jackson to check that she's doing the right thing.

He nods her brusquely away. He's not done with me yet.

"One big blur. That's cute, but —"

"I think there must have been a gun on the table when I came in. I picked it up. I knew I was in a dangerous situation."

"OK. And you wanted to deny firearms to the suspects you were there to apprehend. Good. Then you went downstairs to pursue your investigations further."

I stare at Jackson. My brain isn't working too well, and it has to turn over a couple of times, like a car starting in the cold, before I get what he's doing. He's giving me my lines. Rehearsing me.

"Yes, sir. I went downstairs to" — a blurry moment when no words come to me, then it passes and I continue — "to pursue my investigations further. I

425

sought to liberate the women I found, but they were secured with chains."

Jackson nods. I'm doing well. "And you weren't able to call for help, because . . ."

"Because of the women on the boat. If Sikorsky's men had heard police sirens, the women could have been tossed overboard immediately. I had to let those men come to me, so I could . . . um . . ."

Shoot the fuckers.

"Arrest them," says Jackson.

"Exactly. So I could arrest them."

"When they entered the cellar, I expect you identified yourself and gave them an opportunity to surrender their weapons."

I stare at him. He really means this? Hello, you must be the Kaliningrad Gangsters. I'm Detective Constable Griffiths, just about the most junior member of the South Wales CID. Following budgetary cutbacks, I'm all that's left of our armed response unit and, in the spirit of community togetherness, I'd very much appreciate it if you could lay down your weapons and turn yourself in. Maybe we could all tidy the place up afterwards.

Jackson holds my gaze without a flicker.

"I expect you shouted, 'Police,' or, 'Drop your weapons,' or something like that."

"Police. I probably shouted, 'Police.'"

"Good. You shouted, 'Police,'" says Jackson, neatly excising my "probably". He continues, "They raised their weapons, clearly intending to fire."

"Yes." That bit is true.

426

"And in the subsequent firefight, you — fuck it, Fiona. You killed one, disabled two and all without any of them getting a shot away."

"That's the blurry bit."

"Then you beat Sikorsky to a pulp and throw him off a cliff?"

"Not throw. It was more of a roly-poly thing."

"OK. You rolled him off a cliff, because of a continuing desire to protect the women on the boat. Correct?"

"Correct."

"As soon as the threats were secured, you made contact with me, and we came in to apprehend Roberts and secure the vessel."

I nod.

"At least you left something for us to do." Jackson laughs into his coffee. "And by the way, I think you're right. I think if you'd come to me with hearsay and speculation and no grounds for a search warrant, I'd have told you to go away."

"I thought I'd find Fletcher. Maybe some women. I had no idea the Russians would be there. If I had, I wouldn't have gone. And I was confident that I'd be able to handle Fletcher on my own."

"I'll say so. Bloody carnage it was in there. Carnage." He chuckles for a while, then changes the subject. "Janet Mancini. Do you reckon she was taken there and got away? Or found out some other way?"

"I'm totally guessing now," I say, "but I'm pretty sure the lighthouse was only used for imported goods. I think Rattigan must have had sex with Mancini at some point — perhaps several points — but in Cardiff, in whatever place she normally serviced clients. He'd have been high. Talked too much. Maybe he even liked her. The honest truth is, I think he liked her. He wouldn't have told her otherwise. He must have dropped that debit card in her flat and she kept it as a souvenir. Her client, the millionaire."

"Or kept it for its blackmail potential."

"Or thought about buying stuff on it, before losing her nerve. Could have been anything."

"Pity he's not alive," says Jackson. "It would be nice to send him to jail, wouldn't it?"

"Yes. Yes, it really would."

I try another forkful of beans, but they're not going anywhere and Jackson moves my plate so I stop annoying him by pretending to eat things that are never going to end up eaten.

"Fiona, if anything like this happens again, tell me first. If you've got some conspiracy hearsay bollocks that you believe in, tell me and I'll believe it too. No more solo flights on my watch, ever, for any reason, ever. Do you understand?"

"Yes, sir."

"But well done. I don't know how many rules you broke today, and I hope to God I never find out, but you saved some lives. You won't get any crap from me about that. Well done."

I ought to say something in response, but I can't think of anything straight away. Then Jackson's mobile chirps and he answers it. He's giving someone directions to the café. I tune out. I'm not feeling quite myself. I think I need to go home and lie down. I probably shouldn't drive too fast on the way back. I'm feeling a bit too sleepy to go fast.

A moment later, Jackson straightens.

"Well, well. Look who it is. Your ride home."

I look. It's Dave Brydon, bouncing into the café with that step of his, heavy and light, always heavy and light. He is looking for me and his face is full of emotion. Jackson takes my car keys off me, promises to get my car back to the house and slots me into Brydon's car for the trip home.

"Are you OK, love?" asks Brydon as he buckles me in.

"Did you just call me 'love'?"

"Yes."

"Then I'm OK. I'm really fine."

The rain that the weatherman promised us has ridden in from the west. It's one of those rainstorms where huge raindrops whack down on the windscreen, where the road is sheeted in water and where even with the wipers on full, it's hard to see more than a dozen or so yards ahead. But I don't care. I'm half asleep. Safe and sound. And David Brydon called me "love".

CHAPTER
FORTY-SEVEN

It's a day and a half later. I'm on leave, as much leave as I want. My only jobs are to eat and sleep and get myself in shape again. Jackson's orders.

Every now and then, someone from the investigation team comes along and wants to ask me something about something, and I answer as best I can. There are things I can tell them and things that I can't or don't want to, so I tell them the first set of things and withhold the second. Strictly speaking, in fact, there are two investigations. One is the culmination of Lohan, the second is the IPCC inquiry — Independent Police Complaints Commission — which has to take place whenever a police officer discharges a firearm so as to cause death or serious injury. I'm not in trouble, exactly, but Jackson did well to rehearse me. These things are taken seriously.

I stumble my way through without making a hash of anything. Shock is my excuse, and it's more than an excuse anyway. I've got it. Proper shock. "Traumatic or terrifying event" and all. It's nice to have a textbook case of the syndrome for a change. I recognise that Lev was right and Axelsen was right and Wikipedia was right. I have lived with something like shock for as long as I can remember. I can't remember ever having lived without it. So to have it now, in a proper setting and with as much support as I could ask for, is something of a relief. It feels like another part of my descent to Planet Normal. At least this time I have a reason for feeling weird.

At five o'clock, Dave Brydon comes round. The two weeks of warm weather that we've had seem to have been dispelled by that Pembrokeshire rainstorm. The weather outside is cold and windy. I haven't glimpsed sun since Haverfordwest and I've got the central heating running all the time, thermostat set to twenty-four degrees.

Brydon has a couple of grocery bags — chocolate for me, beer for him, ready meals for us both — and bounces over. I'm on the sofa, under a duvet, watching kids' TV and enjoying it. There's a story on about a podgy hedgehog who's too fat to curl up into a ball, and I find I genuinely want to know what happens.

But I'm a grown-up, and I've been doing almost nothing all day. I switch off and we kiss.

His range of kisses goes on impressing me. Right now, he's scoring high in the tender-kiss department: 5.8s and 5.9s every one of them.

We chat a while. He tells me how Lohan is going. Not really an investigation now. More like a massive clean-up operation. Given what we came across, no magistrate is going to refuse Jackson warrants to search whatever the heck he wants to. There's a huge forensics operation at the lighthouse. The emphasis is on identifying any punters who may have used it and left a genetic trace of themselves there. Cefn Mawr is being turned over too. There's almost certainly nothing there, but it amuses me to think how little Miss Titanium is going to like it. I hope she knows I'm responsible. Charlotte Rattigan I feel sorry for, though. She's not my sort of woman, but she's just another injured party. A long list.

As for the women from the lighthouse, they're being given one-to-one rehab care. Bryony Williams is one of those involved. The women are being shown photos and asked to identify any men who may have raped them. It's going to be a lengthy process. Lots of photos, lots of questions.

I've told the team that I know for a fact that Piers Ivor Harris, MP, was one of the men involved. That's a lie. I believe Penry when he says that Harris would have known about Rattigan's little hobby. Knew about it, and kept silent. But neither Penry nor I have any way to know whether Harris was more personally involved, and I only hand over Harris's name because I want to frighten him and mess up his life as much as possible. If they can find a connection between Harris and the lighthouse, then so much the better. Ditto any connection between any of Rattigan's other friends and the lighthouse. Everyone who ever set foot in that place without reporting it to the police should do time in jail for the rest of their lives.

Nor do I absolve Penry. His silence was as lethal as everyone else's. Sins of omission look prettier, but they still meant duct tape and breeze blocks out in the Irish Sea. Only two things make Penry any better than the

432

rest. First was, he swears to me that he knew nothing about the murders. He knew about the sex trafficking. The violent sex. The slapping around and worse. He says he didn't know the rest. I believe him. And second, at least he nudged me, in his own Penryish way, to the right answers. Of all those involved, he was the only one who tried to do something.

If the current investigation uncovers Penry's role and jails him for it — jails him over and above what he gets for the embezzlement, I mean — then I'll be pleased. That would be the right outcome. Deserved.

But I won't work to make it happen. Penry helped me, and I won't repay that help by grassing on him. *He that is without sin among you, let him first cast a stone.* We're both sinners, him and me.

Brydon and I chat and sometimes just fall silent. We haven't yet made love, though we're getting closer. I don't want to make love from a state of shock. We don't. Me and Brydon. My boyfriend.

So we kiss and we cuddle and we chat, but as time goes on, I notice that he's starting to get a little taut. Like he was after the funeral.

I ask him what's bothering him. He says nothing and I say that I can tell there is something. Whatever it is, it's better to get it off his chest.

Deep breath. Sigh. He gets up and paces around.

He's a restless sort, is Mr Brydon. A Labrador retriever. If he hasn't been exercised properly, he just can't sit still. Maybe I need to get him a rubber bone to play with. And something to keep his coat glossy.

We both start speaking at the same time.

"Look, Fi, I didn't want to —"

"Did you have any dogs when you were a kid?"

I'm the girl, so my question trumps his.

"We always had Labs. Black Labs."

"Did you have any favourites?"

"Oh God, now you're asking. Loved them all really, but I suppose Buzz. He was the one we got when I was eight or nine. He was my best buddy back then."

"Buzz? Buzz." I try it out. It fits. "I'm going to call you Buzz. I don't like Dave, sorry."

"Buzz? All right. He was a cracker, he was."

"So, Buzz, you have something to ask me."

"Look, it's a stupid thing, but it's been bothering me. That night, Monday, before the funeral. We were going to see each other, but you said you couldn't because you had family over. I thought I'd give you a ring, see if you felt like me popping round afterwards. Just for a quick drink or whatever. No answer from your landline. I was in the area, because I was a having a drink with a mate round the corner in Pentwyn Drive. I probably shouldn't have but I came past your house. Lights off, no car. No people. No nothing.

"Now I was worried. I don't know why. I'm not — damn it, Fi, I'm not normally the jealous type. Not paranoid. But I felt worried. I know you'd been at the mortuary with Hughes, and I just went over there. I don't know why really. Like I say, it's not like me. But there was your car. In the middle of the bloody car park. A long way away from any damn family party. And a long time after you'd finished with Ken Hughes."

434

He winds up. He's embarrassed at having pried, but he also needs an answer. Deserves one.

My first instinct is to fob him off. Create a story. Make something up. I'm supple and inventive. I could do that easily. But Brydon — Buzz — is now my boyfriend, and boyfriends deserve better. It's time for explanations.

I don't know where to start.

I am scared of saying anything at all.

I find myself alone with the truth and unsure what to do with it. I could just try speaking it, the naked truth, and trusting that Buzz, my new boyfriend, will not be freaked. I could do that. I could do it now.

Unsure of myself, I start out gently.

"As a teenager, I was ill. You know that?"

He nods. He does. Everyone does.

"Do you know . . .? I don't know if anyone knows what I was ill with. I don't know what the office gossip is."

"There's no gossip, Fi. I've always assumed it was some kind of breakdown. It's not my business and it's in the past now anyway."

I smile at that. "In the past". That's what healthy people say about things and there's no one in the world healthier than DS David "Buzz" Brydon.

"Do you want to sit?" I say. "It's hard to talk to someone marching around like this."

He sits down opposite me. Old face, serious face.

"Thanks. Yes. Some kind of breakdown, that's correct. The breakdown was a special sort of breakdown. Special enough that it gets its own name.

Cotard's. Dr Jules Cotard. *Le délire de négation.* Cotard's syndrome."

Brydon stares at me, sombre and without judgement. I know that he doesn't know what I'm talking about, but I'm getting there.

This is very hard.

"It's a syndrome that sounds funny to outsiders, not funny at all to those who have it. It's a delusional state. It's much more than a breakdown. I was properly, *properly* delusional. A crazy."

Brydon nods. Not scared. Not judgemental. I know that if I nudge him, he'll repeat that thing about it all being in the past, but I want to keep talking before I lose my nerve.

"And the reason why Dr Jules Cotard got to put his name to this particular syndrome was its oddity. In a mild form, patients suffer from despair and self-loathing, but my form wasn't mild. Not mild at all. I had the full monty. In a severe state, patients hold the delusional belief that they don't exist, that their body is empty or putrefying."

I want to stop there, but when I check Brydon's face, I can tell he hasn't got it. No normal person would get it from what I've just said.

Deep breath.

Say it, Griffiths, say it out loud. Say it to the good man sitting opposite you. Tell him everything and trust that things will be all right.

And I do.

"Buzz, for two years, I thought I was dead."

A pause.

436

A long, long pause.

Time enough for me to worry that I now have an ex-boyfriend. That I'm being marched to the nearest rocket station on Planet Normal and am about to be blasted back into the orbit from whence I came. It feels like neither he nor I have blinked for an eternity.

"And that's what you're telling me? That that's where you were that night? In the mortuary."

I nod. "With Janet and April mostly. The Mancinis. And Stacey Edwards actually. In the autopsy suite."

He reaches over to me. We're both on the sofa now, me leaning against one arm, him leaning against the other, feet and legs intermingled in the middle. He takes hold of my hand and starts talking to me in the voice that people reserve for the genuinely nuts. It's OK. There are people who can help. It won't be the same as it was before.

I interrupt him. His mistake is inevitable, of course. Anyone would make it, but the wrongness of it makes me laugh.

"No, no. I'm not feeling crazy. I know what craziness is like and this wasn't like it at all. I've seldom felt so alive."

That's my logic. To me, it makes sense, but my skills at regular human logic are never that brilliant and this evening my compass is all askew.

"You spent the night with three corpses, all murdered, and —"

I put up a hand. Time to stop this. "Buzz, I'm going to need to ask you for some understanding. Sorry, but hear me out. Ever since I made my recovery — well, it's

437

not even like that. Cotard's is something that recedes, it never really goes away. Not that I'd admit that to my shrink, mind you. But it's there. I always know that I could one day go into it again. I've been afraid of it every hour of every day since getting better."

"Your shrink. You still . . .?"

"Not really. With a case like mine, there's a consultant assigned to me, in case stuff happens. I'm meant to go in for a chat every now and then, but I don't. Haven't been for years."

"And that night. In the morgue . . .?"

"That night wasn't really a thought-out thing, it was more of an impulse thing. I just felt I needed to be with some dead people. It wasn't just the Mancinis, it was —" I'm about to talk about Stacey and Edith and Good-Time Charlie, when I realise that's probably going too far, so I check myself. "It was the others there as well. You know, to you, they're dead. They're alien. It actually bothers you that their hearts aren't beating and that their organs are mostly missing.

"To me, they're just people. They're dead people, but I've been dead myself. I find them pleasant company. Easy, contented, pleasant. If I'm being honest, I find them easier to get on with than the living. I know that sounds strange to you, but you're not like me. No one is."

"There's nothing . . .? Jesus, Fi, whether it's true or not, please tell me that there's nothing funny in all this, is there?"

I gawp at him. I don't know what he means, so I try to guess what an ordinary decent human would ask in a

438

moment like this. Then I get it. "Anything sexual? Is that what you were going to say?"

He nods, pleased that I didn't make him come out with the words.

"Nothing even a tiny, weeny, remotest bit like sexual. Dead people aren't interested in sex. That's not a joke. We're not. I mean, I wasn't when I was ill as a teenager and they're not now. They're just . . . they're just dead."

"OK. Let me get this straight. Stop me if I get it wrong."

I agree. The mood is getting lighter now. I'm not thinking very clearly, but I know I've said the worst thing — the big thing, the Cotard's thing — and Brydon hasn't leaped up off the sofa. He's still here. He hasn't given up. That doesn't mean I'm in the clear, I know that, but the worst thing that could have happened hasn't happened yet.

I listen to Brydon's attempt to summarise my summary.

"Once upon a time, there was a doctor. Dr Cotard," he begins.

"Correct."

"He gave his name to Cotard's syndrome."

"Bang on."

"For two years, you were unfortunate enough to suffer from the aforementioned syndrome."

"Two-ish. Dead people aren't all that concerned about time."

"OK, so about two. Then you got better. Or better-ish."

"I did."

"A few — I don't know what, panic attacks maybe? — but nothing you couldn't handle."

"Correct." Not quite correct actually. The first three years or so after "recovery" were awful. Those years at Cambridge were the worst, with the ghost of my own death peering at me through every gloomy window. I don't even like thinking about them. They feel worse, in a weird way, than the two years of Cotard's itself.

"Then you find yourself on police business in a mortuary."

"With DI Kenneth Hughes engaged on Operation Lohan."

"Quite so. And . . . I don't know. Help me out on this bit. You needed to be with some dead people. Why?"

"I don't know. If I knew, I'd tell you. I think it's because I felt safe enough. I felt sufficiently alive that I could dare to be with the dead. Does that make sense? I was alive, they were dead, we spent some time together. And I felt fine. For the first time since I was fourteen or fifteen, my Cotard's wasn't anywhere to be seen. It was gone."

I suddenly notice that Brydon's face is full of emotion. There's more emotion there than I'm feeling myself.

"That's amazing, Fi. If that's true, that's bloody brilliant."

"I don't know if it's true. Like I say, it hasn't *gone* gone. I don't think it ever will."

"Well, don't bloody spoil it now. You had me going there."

440

"It was a good night. It really was."

He nods. How many in the world could hear all this and be as accepting of it? Outside my family and mental health workers, Brydon is the first person I've ever talked to about my illness.

"What was it like, Fi? How can anyone think they're dead?"

"I can't really tell you. I suppose I had thoughts. My brain was still able to function. But I don't think I had any feelings. No emotions. I couldn't really feel pain. Human touch was a bit funny for me. Numb or something. It never really felt like anything. So what was I meant to think? In a weird way, believing myself to be dead wasn't so far wrong. I mean, I *wasn't* alive. Not really. Not the way you are now."

Brydon takes all this in.

"Well, bugger me," he says at last.

I take his forearm and bite it, hard enough to leave a mark. "Dying is when you can't feel that."

"Uh-huh. And how dead are you feeling today?"

He bites my arm, but gently.

Something that has been between us slides away so completely that it's hard to remember what it ever felt like. Brydon's face looks two shades brighter. I'm feeling myself differently, like gravity has just altered, lessened.

It doesn't happen straight away. It doesn't happen in a bad, rushed or inappropriate way, but before too long we are cuddling, and the cuddles turn into foreplay, and the foreplay turns into lovemaking. *Making. Love.*

441

We don't make love on the floor, we use the sofa. And it's not bitey-passionate and wordless as I'd imagined it, but it's tender, committed and heartfelt. It's perfect for the moment.

I spoke the truth and we are making love.

I spoke the truth about my illness and we are lying on my sofa making love.

I cannot believe my good fortune.

When we're done, we laugh and eat ready meals. Brydon drinks beer and I sip minuscule amounts from his can. "Buzz," I say, rubbing my head on his bare chest. "Buzz, Buzz, Buzz."

He strokes my head and neck with his free hand. When he belches, he smothers it and says, "Pardon."

We cuddle, mostly without words, for half an hour or more. Brydon is lovely, but I can also see that he's taken aback by my Cotard's. I don't blame him. Anyone would be. It's not a small deal for anyone. It probably doesn't help him to remember that two days ago, his new girlfriend killed one person and made a real mess of three others. That's not your classic feminine love-gambit.

"Buzz," I say, "I think maybe you need an evening off. Time to yourself. Think about everything. It's a lot to take in. I know that and it's OK."

He starts to protest, but I'm not having it and he pretty soon sees that what I'm saying makes sense. Brydon's nice about the way he does it, but he's happy enough to leave.

I see him to the door.

There's one more thing that I had thought about saying. I almost say it to him on the front doorstep. But I don't. Only when he's in his car, and waving at me, and off down the road and out of sight, do I let myself say it.

"And, my dear Buzz, there is one other thing. I think it's possible that I'm falling in love with you."

That sounds so good I say it again.

"I'm falling in love with you." The nicest words on Planet Normal.

CHAPTER
FORTY-EIGHT

My to do-list is not quite done. Almost but not quite. One more call to make.

I make a call. Mam and Dad are both at home. I tell Mam three times that I've already eaten, then drive on round.

A strange feeling, this. There have been so many varieties of strange over the last few weeks, but this is a whole new one. *Anticipation.* That's what the shrinks would call it when working their way through their lists of feelings. *Anticipation, Fiona. You are thinking forward to an event in your future. You aren't yet sure how that event will turn out. There is a range of possible outcomes. Some good, some bad, some mixed. The feeling associated with that state is called "anticipation".*

Anticipation, Doctor. I think I understand. But may I check my understanding with you, to be sure I've got it right?

Of course, Fiona. We're here to help. Glances enthusiastically at nurse.

Very well then, Doctor, let me review things. For the last three weeks, give or take, I've been working on a case where a little six-year-old girl had her head

444

smashed in by one of those monster Belfast sinks. You know the sort I mean. You probably have one in your own kitchen. The rustic look. Expensive. Anyway, this girl had the top of her head obliterated by a large chunk of kitchen ceramics, leaving just her little mouth to smile at me. And smile she did. For most of the last three weeks, I've had that little girl's picture up on my wall or on my screensaver, or both. Haunted me, you could say, only it was a very nice haunting. I liked it. Invited it, in fact. And just to be clear, it was the dead girl who haunted me. I'm afraid to say it, but the live one never interested me all that much. Are you with me so far?

Tightly. Through gritted teeth, *Yes. Yes. We were talking about anticipation, Fiona. A present-tense feeling about some future event.*

I'm getting there, Doc. You can't rush these things. Now, I felt like the little dead girl had something to teach me and I just wasn't getting it, so I decided to spend a night with her in the mortuary. The big one, down at the University Hospital.

Overnight? In the mortuary? Tone of extreme shock. Nurse edges closer to door and fat red panic button. *Please try to focus on the subject. We were talking about anticipation. You wanted to check your understanding of the term.*

The mortuary, Doc. Where they keep dead people. Why? Are you bothered by the dead? Do you have uncomfortable feelings around them that you find hard to deal with? Perhaps you should find someone to talk to. Anyway, I spent the night with her and her mother

445

— her mother is dead as well. Did I mention that? Lovely hair. Coppery. And skin like you wouldn't believe — and I learned something very interesting. Something that I need to discuss with my parents. In a funny way, I think that conversation may alter the entire way I view my own personal history. Possibly in a good way. Possibly not. There may well be — what did you just call it? — a mixed outcome. So I've got a feeling inside me now — tingly, excited, nervous, agitated — and I think I want to call that anticipation. Do you think that's the right word? It feels like it is.

Yes, Fiona. I think you've got that right. Anticipation. The feeling of looking forward to an event in your future. We'll move on, shall we?

That's roughly how those conversations used to go. To begin with, I managed to freak the doctors out without having any idea of what I was doing to make it happen. I didn't know what I was saying that made them do the whole "she's a freak" exchange of glances with the nurse. I often used to end those sessions with the doctor telling me that my medication needed to be "adjusted" in order to "make me more comfortable", which, roughly translated, meant they were going to increase the dosage of whatever I was on in order to make themselves feel more comfortable. At least once, and maybe more than once, I ended one of those sessions being "restrained" by two burly psychiatric nurses as the doc administered a sedative by injection. The funny thing is, you'd think that someone would go into mental health because they enjoyed working with the mentally ill, but I realised that that wasn't it at all.

Maybe it was for a few people. The saints, like Ed Saunders. But most of them seemed to have entered the profession because they hated mental illness. Hated it and wanted to punish it. Drug it into acquiescence. Obedience. Yes, Doc. No, Doc. Is that what you advise? Then of course! I'll open my mouth. Take the pills. Pretty little pink things on their white paper tray. Swallow. Smile. Thank you, Doc. I feel more comfortable already.

Once I figured all this out — and this was probably around the time that my condition started to ease anyway — I used to go into those sessions and deliberately mess with the doctors' heads. Yank their chains. I'd say outrageous stuff that would upset them, but at the same time be careful to say or do nothing that would allow them to get out their needles or their frigging prescription pads. I started to get legalistic on them as well. Researched my rights under the law and started to challenge them about whether something they wanted to do was legitimate under paragraph whatever of the Mental Health Act. I was clever, well-read, inventive, obstreperous — and a moody-cow teenager, of course. Bolshie and argumentative. My dad's never had a brilliant relationship with authority figures either, so if I started to get antsy and legalistic, he couldn't help himself. He'd come weighing in with his lawyers on my side, writing letters, demanding judicial review, making complaints to the General Medical Council. Making a pest of himself. I don't know if we achieved anything, but in a weird kind of way it was fun. I bonded even more closely with my dad because of it.

Yet, years on from all of that now, I have to say that those doctors gave me something. Concepts and techniques I still use today.

Anticipation. The feeling of looking forward to an event in your future.

That's what I have now. Tingly. Excited. Nervous. Agitated. A feeling that somehow combines all those things and mixes them up into a confection that's greater than the sum of its parts. *Anticipation.* What I'm feeling right now.

I drive up outside my parents' house and brake to a halt. Select neutral. Engage handbrake. Ignition off. Listen to the engine die. *In*, two, three, four, five. *Out*, two, three, four, five. Hold and repeat.

Anticipation.

CHAPTER
FORTY-NINE

Mam says, "I didn't cook, because I know you said you'd eaten, so I just thought I'd put out a few bits, in case you wanted to pick."

Sausages. Potato salad. Tomato salad. Lettuce. Coleslaw. Salamis. Cold ham. French rolls. Caerphilly and Welsh goat's cheese. Pickles. Bottled beer, including zero-alcohol beer for me. A few bits.

Dad looks at the spread and his eyes widen. On the way through into the kitchen, we had to stop to admire the "World's Best Mam" trophy, which now looms over the kitchen door like something about to collapse. I told Dad how wonderful it looked and made eyes at Mam to say how frightful it was. I give it about six weeks. Three months, tops.

Kay and Ant arrive to share the feast as well. Everyone present has already eaten, but Mam is the only one not to pick her way through a whole lot more. Before too long, Kay gets half a chocolate cake from the fridge, and she and Ant start to mine into its defences and soon leave it pretty much ruined. Everyone talks about their own thing, and nobody cares much that no one else is listening too closely.

The clock ticks to nine o'clock. Ant's bedtime, and the signal for Mam to settle down with her box set of DVDs.

I say, "Mam, Dad, do you think I can have a chat with you?"

Kay's eyes widen. Whatever it is, she wants to be a part of this, but I tell her that it's private, if she doesn't mind. She does mind, but not so much that she can't be persuaded to go up to her bedroom and spend the next two hours talking to her friends by phone, text and IM.

That leaves me, Mam and Dad alone in the kitchen. We've clearly moved into some new social-emotional territory and Mam's instincts are slightly confused. For her, any new territory of this sort needs to be marked by the production of something edible, but we've all just gorged ourselves on a second supper and even Mam can't quite bring herself to do the same all over again. So she compromises by making tea. Dad rushes off to get port, whisky, brandy, Cointreau and some noxious-looking Italian liqueur the name of which he can't pronounce but which was given to him by one of his Italian contractors with some highly coloured promises about its alcoholic potency and which he can't wait to try out on someone. Since he knows I'm all but teetotal, that person is unlikely to be me, but he likes creating a show anyway. And the glasses look nice.

Eventually, the clatter is over. Mam and I are sharing herbal tea. Dad has a mug of builder's tea alongside a tiny glass of the Italian liqueur. Truth is, even Dad doesn't drink much these days. Ant's in bed. The sound of Kay talking upstairs is just about audible down here. The kitchen clock ticks.

"Mam. Dad."

I start out, then stop. In a way, I don't want to make them tell me, I just want them to disclose everything of their own volition. But I know I have to prompt it, and I'm not sure how. I get a photo from the hallway next door. Silver-framed. A recent one of the five of us. Mam, Dad, me, Kay, Ant. I hold it face out, so that my parents can see it and I can't.

"I think it's time we came clean with each other. Time you came clean with me. It's OK. I'm ready for it. Really. I'd prefer it."

Mam and Dad look at each other. They're worried, but I'm pretty sure they know what I'm talking about.

I see that I need to nudge a bit more, and so I do.

"I've been spending some time with this little girl I came across because of work. The cutest little six-year-old, a real smasher. Anyway, I came to realise that this little girl had something. She was her mother's daughter. That sounds so stupid, doesn't it? Her mother's daughter. But the mother had this unbelievably troubled life. I won't go into it all, but it wasn't easy. And she made these huge efforts to keep her daughter with her. The authorities wanted to take the little girl into care, but the mother always fought back. She wanted her daughter to have a better life than she did. In the end, she wasn't entirely successful, but she tried. She gave it her all.

"Anyway, as time went by, I felt increasingly sure that this little girl had something to teach me. Something

451

really obvious, as it turned out. I felt the little girl was telling me that I wasn't my mother's daughter. Nor my father's. That little girl had a terribly difficult life, but all the same she had one thing that I didn't."

I hold up the photo.

Dad is tall. Mam is tall. Kay is tall and slim and gorgeous. Ant is racing upwards. And that leaves Fiona, the over-intellectual, fish-out-of-water, runt of the litter.

"It's so obvious really. I'm not like you at all. Not physically. Not . . . not in other ways too. And don't get me wrong. I love you both so much. You and Kay and Ant. This family is by far the best thing that ever happened to me. But I need to know where I came from. Maybe I wasn't ready before. But I am now. I'd like to know."

I don't say it, and I won't say it, but there's more to my intuition than April's insistent hints. It was the thing that Lev said as well. And Axelsen. And Wikipedia.

I've been in shock for most of my life. I've ticked almost every box. Indeed, if you think of my Cotard's as being simply the most extreme, the most extravagant form of depersonalisation going, then you could argue that I've also suffered from the most extreme, the most extravagant form of shock going. When it comes to my mental life, I've seldom done things by halves.

The only problem with the Lev-Axelsen-Wikipedia hypothesis was the single box left unticked. The one box that absolutely had to have been ticked. The event. The traumatic or terrifying event. The event that never happened.

What I said to Lev was true. I know that my family was safe. No physical or sexual abuse. No alcoholism. No hint of divorce. Very few marital arguments. No threat from outside. No dodgy uncles. No assaults on me from strangers. No family in Wales could have been safer. Dad's money, his energy, his reputation were walls thicker than concrete. Any hypothetical evil-doers would have preferred to mess with any family in Cardiff sooner than make enemies of my dad. All my life, I've been as safe as anyone can wish to be.

All my life, for as long as I can remember.

But traumatic events can reach far back into the past. Further than childhood. Further than memory. What happened in the first year or two of my life? Why can I recall my childhood only through a fog of forgetting? Why did my Cotard's stalk out of nowhere to ruin my teenage years? Why do I sometimes wake with night terrors so vivid that I am drenched in sweat and lie, lights on, awake and staring, through the rest of the night, sooner than risk going back to whatever it was that visited me in my dreams?

I don't say these things out loud, and I will never say them to these two people who have loved me so dearly, but it is time for answers and they know it.

They look across the table at each other. Dad puts his hand on Mam's and rubs it briefly. Then he gets up, says, "One moment, love," and leaves the room.

Mam and I are left alone with the ticking clock.

A ticking clock in a silent room.

She smiles at me. A brave, uncertain smile. I smile back at her. I feel OK. The anticipation I felt before has quietened down. I'm not quite sure what I feel now. Or to be precise, I'm in touch with the feeling, I just don't have a word for it. It's like a melting inside. A liquefying of something solid. It's not a bad feeling. I don't mind it. I just don't know what it is. I don't think that even my doctors could give this one a name.

Dad returns to the room.

He's carrying some things. A photo and an old plastic shopping bag.

He sits at the table. Smiles at me, at Mam, back at me.

The clock ticks too loudly in the silence.

We're all nervous. It's as though the room itself, the empty space, the entire house is in a state of anticipation. The doctors would probably tell me off for saying that. They'd say that empty space can't have feelings. But they've never sat here as I am doing now. They've never known what it's like for the whole of your life to sit trembling on the cusp.

Dad shows me the photo, passes it over.

It's a photo of me aged about two and a half. Pink dress. White bow. Tidy hair. Shy smile. A small white teddy bear. I've never seen this photo before, but I recognise the car I'm sitting in. It's Dad's old Jaguar XJ-S convertible. The roof is down. The day looks reasonably sunny. I can't see enough of the street to tell where it is. I've got no reason to think there is anything odd about the photo at all.

I look at Dad.

"Fiona, love. That photo was taken on 15 June 1986. It was taken by this camera here."

454

He takes it from the bag and passes it across the table. A small brown camera in a leather case, with a leather neck strap attached. The camera looks older than 1986. Maybe a lot older.

"And we found the camera the same day as we found you. We'd just gone to chapel — your mam still had me going in those days — and when we came out, there was the car, just as we'd left it, only with a little miracle inside. You. We came out and there you were. Sitting in our car with this camera round your neck. When we had the film inside the camera developed, there was just this one photo. A photo of you. There was no note, no nothing. Just this amazing little girl in the back of our car."

I hear all this. It makes no sense at all and it makes perfect sense at one and the same time. It's like that moment in a theatre where one stage set is revolving in from the left as the last one is disappearing on the right. You see both things at the same time. See them in their entirety. Understand them. But you also know that one thing is replacing the other. That the thing you thought was your world is about to disappear, never to show itself again.

"You found me?" I say. "You just came out and you found me?"

"Yes. Your mam and I had wanted children. We love the little bleeders, don't we, Kath? But we'd had troubles conceiving. I don't know why. The two girls upstairs both arrived in the ordinary manner. But anyway. We came out of chapel. We'd have been praying about it. We always did. And there you were. Thank you, Jesus. The answer to our prayers. Honestly. Our own little miracle. And not even the crying, puking sort. The Good Lord had got you through all that, sent you to us clean and sweet and nice to meet. Even your own little teddy bear."

"Of course . . ." Mam says, uncomfortable with Dad's implication that they just drove off with me.

"Yes. Your mam's right. We had to tell someone, so we did. If your real mam and dad had shown up, we'd have handed you over. We wouldn't have liked it. Wouldn't have wanted to. We fell in love with you straight away. I mean, the very instant. But we'd have done right by you. If your mam and dad had come looking for you, we'd have handed you straight back."

Mam then starts to tell more. The adoption process. How it was "you know, a bit complicated, what with your father and all". An understatement, I should think. The late 1980s were, as far as I can tell, Dad's reprehensible heyday. I remember, when I was five or six, sitting at table and Dad roaring with laughter to his friends about how he was the most innocent man in South Wales. Five prosecutions and no convictions. I should think that the adoption authorities were loath to hand a child over to someone who seemed certain to end up in jail, and any police reports they required would hardly have been flattering, but then again when my dad wants something, he generally manages to get it. By hook or by crook.

I listen to Mam talking, but I'm not interested in the adoption process. I'm interested in me.

"How old was I?"

Dad shrugs. "No one knows. At the time, we guessed two, maybe two and a half. Just going by height, we were. But you've never been the tallest lass, have you, love, so maybe we were a bit out. Perhaps you were older."

"Didn't you ask me?"

"Oh, love. We asked you everything. Where your mam and dad were. Where you lived. What your name was. How old you were. Everything."

"And?"

"Nothing. You wouldn't speak. For — what was it, Kath? — maybe eighteen months you wouldn't speak. You understood things all right. You were a sharp little thing even then. And we had you tested and poked at and all. They couldn't find anything wrong with you. Not a sausage. And then one day, you just started speaking. You said, 'Mam, can I have some more cheese, please?' Isn't that right, Kath?"

Mam says yes and she echoes him. "'Mam, can I have some more cheese, please?'"

I echo her echo. *Mam, can I have some more cheese, please?*

Something inside me has changed. The scene shift is complete. I can't see or feel the old world any more. This new world is now mine. It makes no sense. It raises a million questions. About who I was, where I came from, how I came to be in Dad's car, why I couldn't speak or wouldn't. About those missing two or three years. About what happened in that time that stored up such trouble for my future life.

And yet all of that doesn't matter, or not this minute it doesn't.

Dad has the last few things out of his bag. The pink dress with the white bow. The teddy bear. A hair grip. A pair of shiny black shoes with some white knee socks tucked into them. He passes them over the table to me.

My past. My mysterious past. The only clues I have.

And even as I bury my head to smell the dress, I know that these things don't matter either. What matters now is what is happening inside me. The thing that was liquefying before has melted completely. An old barrier has gone. Vanished. It's been extinguished.

I feel strange and something strange is happening.

I pull my head up and away from the dress. I put my hands to my face and they come away wet. Something very strange is happening. A feeling I don't recognise. I am leaking from somewhere.

And then I do know. I know what is happening.

These are tears and I am crying.

It is not a painful sensation, as I always thought it must be. It feels like the purest expression of feeling that it is possible to have. And the feeling mixes everything up together. Happiness. Sadness. Relief. Sorrow. Love. A mixture of things no psychiatrist ever felt. It is the most wonderful mixture in the world.

I put my hands to my face again and again. Tears are coursing down my cheeks, splashing off my chin, tickling the side of my nose, running off my hands.

These are tears and I am crying. I am Fiona Griffiths. Paid-up citizen of Planet Normal.

Cotard's Syndrome

Cotard's syndrome is a rare but perfectly genuine condition. Jules Cotard, a late-Victorian French psychiatrist, gave his name to it and also came up with the phrase "*le délire de négation*", a pithier and more accurate description of the illness than anything in use today.

The condition is an exceptionally serious one. Its core ingredients are depression and psychosis. Modern psychiatrists would probably argue that it isn't a disease in its own right, more an extreme manifestation of depersonalisation, the most extreme form of it, in fact. Some patients report "seeing" their flesh decompose and crawl with maggots. Early childhood trauma is implicated in pretty much every well-documented case of the syndrome.

Full recovery is uncommon. Suicides by patients with the condition are, alas, all too frequent. Indeed, my wife, who is a neuro-feedback practitioner, has worked with a Cotard's patient who ended up taking her own life. *Talking to the Dead* is written, in part, to honour that patient's courage.

Fiona Griffiths's own state of mind is, of course, a fictional rendering of a complex illness. I have not aimed to achieve clinical precision. Nevertheless, the broad strokes of Fiona's account of her condition would be largely familiar to anyone acquainted with it.

Also available in ISIS Large Print:

The Blind Goddess

Anne Holt

A drug dealer is battered to death on the outskirts of Oslo. A young Dutch student, covered in blood, walks aimlessly through the streets of the city. He is taken into custody, but refuses to speak. Five days later a shady criminal lawyer called Hansa Larsen is murdered. The two deaths don't seem related, but Detective Inspector Hanne Wilhelmsen is unconvinced. Soon, she uncovers a link between the bodies: Larsen defended the drug dealer.

But there are powerful forces working against Hanne; a conspiracy that reaches far beyond a crooked lawyer and a small-time dealer. The investigation will take her into the offices of the most powerful men in Norway — and even put her own life at risk . . .

ISBN 978-0-7531-9114-9 (hb)
ISBN 978-0-7531-9115-6 (pb)

The Dead Won't Sleep

Anna Smith

A decomposed body washes up on a beach near Glasgow. The victim, Tracy Eadie. A junkie, prostitute and only 14-years-old. Rosie Gilmour, tabloid journalist and crusader for justice, receives evidence linking police officials with Tracy's disappearance. It seems Tracy, and the secret that was supposed to die with her, are not content to rest. Digging deeper, Rosie uncovers a sickening network of corruption and abuse, tracing back to the top of the establishment. And to powerful figures who want their secrets kept hidden. Rosie has found the story of a lifetime. Yet living to tell it will be her greatest challenge.

ISBN 978-0-7531-9024-1 (hb)
ISBN 978-0-7531-9025-8 (pb)

As Darkness Falls

Bronwyn Parry

Haunted by her failures, Detective Sergeant Isabelle O'Connell is recalled to duty by DCI Alec Goddard to investigate the abduction of yet another child from her old home town. With the killer playing a game of cat and mouse they have only days in which to find the girl alive — but they have very few clues, a whole town of suspects and a vast wilderness to search. For Isabelle, this case is already personal; for Alec, his best intentions to keep it purely professional soon dissolve. Their mutual attraction leaves them both vulnerable to their private nightmares — nightmares that the killer ruthlessly exploits . . .

ISBN 978-0-7531-8968-9 (hb)
ISBN 978-0-7531-8969-6 (pb)

The Lieutenant's Lover

Harry Bingham

Misha is an aristocratic young officer in the army when the Russian revolution sweeps away all his certainties. Tonya is a nurse from an impoverished family. They should have been bitter enemies, yet they fall passionately in love. It cannot last and, as the political situation grows ever worse, Misha is forced to flee the country.

Thirty years later, Misha seeks to rebuild his life in the destroyed city of Berlin. Then, one snowy winter's day, he glimpses a woman who resembles Tonya. Can this be his lost love? Drawn into a dangerous double game of espionage and betrayal, the two lovers struggle to find each other, as the divide deepens between East and West.

ISBN 978-0-7531-7712-9 (hb)
ISBN 978-0-7531-7713-6 (pb)

The Sons of Adam

Harry Bingham

On 23 August 1893, two boys are born. Alan is the son of Sir Adam Montague, Tom is the son of his under-gardener. They are raised together and it seems that nothing can come between their friendship.

A tragic misunderstanding in the trenches of WWI turns them to the bitterest of rivals, struggling in the most cut-throat business of them all — oil. Only one thing remains more important than making their fortune . . .

Across three continents and two world wars, their conflict continues. Until, on the eve of the D-day landings, with world history hanging in the balance, the two men meet again . . .

ISBN 978-0-7531-7253-7 (hb)
ISBN 978-0-7531-7254-4 (pb)

ISIS publish a wide range of books in large print, from fiction to biography. Any suggestions for books you would like to see in large print or audio are always welcome. Please send to the Editorial Department at:

ISIS Publishing Limited
7 Centremead
Osney Mead
Oxford OX2 0ES

A full list of titles is available free of charge from:

Ulverscroft Large Print Books Limited

(UK)
The Green
Bradgate Road, Anstey
Leicester LE7 7FU
Tel: (0116) 236 4325

(Australia)
P.O. Box 314
St Leonards
NSW 1590
Tel: (02) 9436 2622

(USA)
P.O. Box 1230
West Seneca
N.Y. 14224-1230
Tel: (716) 674 4270

(Canada)
P.O. Box 80038
Burlington
Ontario L7L 6B1
Tel: (905) 637 8734

(New Zealand)
P.O. Box 456
Feilding
Tel: (06) 323 6828

Details of **ISIS** complete and unabridged audio books are also available from these offices. Alternatively, contact your local library for details of their collection of **ISIS** large print and unabridged audio books.

Tort

346.03 G

BPP Professional Education
32-34 Colmore Circus
Birmingham B4 6BN
Phone: 0121 345 9843